RESISTANCE

DIVIDED ELEMENTS - BOOK I

RESISTANCE

DIVIDED ELEMENTS - BOOK I

MIKHAEYLA KOPIEVSKY

KYRÍJA

3 5 7 9 10 8 6 4 2

KYRIJA
North Arm Cove, NSW, Australia
www.kyrija.com.au

A CIP catalogue record for this book is available from the National Library of Australia

ebook ISBN 978-0-9954218-2-0
paperback ISBN13 978-0-9954218-5-1
paperback ISBN10 0-9954218-5-5

Cover Illustration by Ethan Scott

For Elijah

ONE

Usually, she feels nothing. Not the impact of her feet on the fractured bitumen surface; not the tingling of sweat at her nape; not the heavy thudding of her heart. Usually it all disappears into a kind of weightlessness – a nothingness that comes only with pure focus. With *flow*.

But tonight it's different.

Anaiya's concentration fractures, thoughts of the Peacekeeper time trials pricking along the edges of her consciousness. Her times had been good, but her ranking had not shifted. Instead, the gap between second and first had seemed to lengthen. Solidify.

And with that had come an unfamiliar emotion: a hard, spiky insistence she could not shake. Even now, she feels it – an itch she cannot scratch, a cut that threatens to fester.

Distracted, she stumbles against the uneven road. Pain, sharp and insistent, blooms in her ankle and races up her calf. She winces, but does not cry out – Fire Elementals are bred to be hard.

Correcting her stride, she accelerates to make up for the error, frowning as tonight's patrol partner pulls ahead. Niamh moves effortlessly, his speed a natural extension of the power within him. He is faster than her.

The pain in her ankle ratchets higher, growing in synchronicity with the spiky feeling at her core. Ignoring them, she pounds her feet against the crumbling bitumen, pushing herself harder to pick up the pace. To catch him.

Focus, Anaiya.

Regulating her breathing, she strips her mind of pain and memories, forces herself to surrender to the free-run. Slowly, her muscle memory takes over. Aerials segue into wall spins; vaults and backflips stretch her body into long, languid curves. The movements consume her, until the pain recedes and details blur and there is nothing but the white noise of being in motion. As it should be.

And then she enters Precinct 20. Sensations crash into her consciousness, splintering her focus and pulling her out of flow. Tall apartment buildings, ten and twelve storeys high, line up along the edges of the street like sentinels. They amplify the noise that spews out of open windows from the identical units – sounds generated by wallscreens on full volume, by rough sex and drunken parties.

The Fifth night is always the worst, its twilight hours providing an easy junction between the two great loves of all Earth Elementals – hard work and easy living. Anaiya has witnessed it on countless patrols before, the migration en masse from factories, construction sites and retail counters triggered by the setting of Otpor's brown sun.

She assesses the scene before her. Earth Elementals of all generations sprawl in narrow laneways – engaging in idle gossip, drinking cheap synthetic alcohol, and erupting into raucous parties that will inevitably descend into drunken orgies. Or violence.

Or both.

Frowning, she shakes her head and pulls her gaze away from the debauchery to locate her partner. Niamh stands a few metres away, silhouetted under a lone fluorescent street light. Head bent and fingers pushed to his ear, he is speaking into his wristplate, but the words are lost against the dense wall of noise that surrounds her. She could walk over to him, hear what he is saying, but she knows Niamh. Knows he likes doing things his own way. In his own time.

The spiky feeling threatens to resurface. It sings to her, calls for her attention. Instead, she returns her gaze to the Earth Elementals and waits for Niamh to finish his call.

Seconds later he joins her. "Suspect is likely intoxicated but unarmed. We have approval to subdue with necessary force."

Anaiya nods and strides towards the main entrance of the target apartment building, but Niamh grabs her by the arm before she can get too far. Shaking his head, he points towards a service door on the side wall.

"We don't have clearance to enter via alternate access points," she says.

He doesn't respond, heading towards the door regardless. The spiky feeling returns, tingling in her core – a slight bristle, a flare of frustration. She shakes her head to clear the emotion and follows him.

"We don't need clearance," he says, reaching the door and testing its strength.

With one sharp kick, the door shudders away from its hinges, coming to rest awkwardly against the stained wall inside. Anaiya hesitates, uncomfortable at breaching even minor protocol. Niamh, as always, has no such reservations, entering the stairwell with a calm confidence. Sighing, she clenches her fists and reluctantly follows him.

In the cavernous space, the random mashup of high-decibel noises seems to grow, bouncing and reverberating against the polymer walls. Ignoring the distraction, the two Peacekeepers ascend the stairs at pace. It is only when they reach the fourth floor of the building that the sound of screaming becomes discernible.

Sprinting up the final level, they arrive at the unit of interest. Niamh, his lifeline already unravelled, jams it into the small access terminal fixed to the wall, unlocking the door with a loud click.

As the heavy steel slides away, the sound of screaming snaps to silence.

Anaiya and Niamh enter the unit wordlessly and are confronted with harsh light and sharp smells. A large male, two generations older than Anaiya and Niamh, stands over a diminutive female. The female lies prostrate on the floor, the left side of her skull bleeding profusely. At the sound of their entry, the male spins around clumsily, his eyes wild with hydroxyphen.

Anaiya grabs one of the syringes secured at her belt, her mind future-searching – rapidly identifying and exploring the possible outcomes of her available actions. In a moment she has risk assessed them all, weighing up the potential dangers and evaluating their range of success.

She charges at him – her feet light on the tarnished floor, her grip on the syringe secure. The dull roar of her target assaults her ears, but she ignores it.

He crouches, wobbles, throws his arms out defensively. The incoherent roar switches to profanities, something about "crushing your skull". It skims the surface of her focus, never taking hold.

The reek of alcohol is stronger.

Eyes twitching, he pushes an unsteady leg forwards. He thinks he can get to her. A smile flickers across her face. She feels it pull at her lips.

Feinting left at the final moment, she catches him off-balance. It is the opening she anticipated. He stumbles. She leaps. Swivelling mid-air, she lands behind him. Stabs the needle into the bulging vein in his neck.

He slumps to the floor immediately, the restraint serum rendering him unconscious.

"Clear," she yells, glancing down at the incapacitated male before shifting her focus to Niamh.

Niamh looks up from his place kneeling beside the motionless victim, her shattered skull still leaking blood onto the grey linoleum floor. He shakes his head, plugging his lifeline into his ear. Anaiya takes in the blood spatter patterns, the globs of grey matter and fragments of bone, while Niamh calls it in.

"Peacekeeper 2021949 calling in a Code 25. Victim, Earth Elemental, Female, seventh lustrum, deceased. Perpetrator, Earth Elemental, Male, seventh lustrum, restrained. Requesting Forensics and Detainers."

Pulling the cable from his ear, he stands up and looks around the unit. His eyes are bright, betraying the thrill that mirrors her own. Like all Peacekeepers, they thrive in moments like these – as if their bodies are naturally attuned to the energy of the situation.

Anaiya turns her attention back to the perpetrator. Plugging her lifeline into the Elemental's wristplate, she records the incident to his file, looking down at her own as she finishes.

It is 2230 hours. The Forensics and Detainers will not arrive for at least another half an hour. Thirty long and uninterrupted minutes stuck within four cheap polymer walls. Thirty minutes with nothing to do but keep vigil over two lifeless bodies.

Anaiya's feet shift and she paces a tight circle around the scene. Peacekeepers are not meant to stay still.

"Sit down, Anaiya."

The command is issued with Niamh's trademark exasperation, raising Anaiya's hackles. Her first instinct is to retort, but instead she forces her feet to still. The tension in her tonight, in her reaction to Niamh, is distracting and unsettling. And unwanted. She pauses, lets it fade a little, and finds a seat on one of the tattered vinyl dining chairs.

"Do you think he's attacked her before?" she asks.

"Maybe. Check him."

She scoots the chair closer to the unconscious male and leans down to access his wristplate. Downloading his incident file, she scrolls through the list. "Three prior assaults in the last twelve months." She looks over to Niamh, who is ejecting his lifeline from the deceased's wristplate.

He reads out a list of dates. "Sixteen eleven, seventeen eight, twenty-three four?"

Anaiya checks the dates of the assaults, the same numbers appearing in the log of incidents. "Yeah." She looks over at the dead body at Niamh's feet. "Why do they stick around?"

The question is directed more to the female than to Niamh. She has seen it too often before – female Earth Elementals who stay in unnecessary domestic relationships, enduring months and years of abuse and violence until it ends in permanent detention, disability or death. It is not unfamiliar to Anaiya, only unfathomable.

"Why do Air Elementals pray? Why are Water Elementals so boring?" Niamh replies. "It's who they are. It's what they do."

Anaiya regards the dead victim bled out on the grimy floor. She feels no pity for the pathetic creature: she feels nothing but the boredom of waiting and a slight curiosity bubbling to the surface of her mind. "But, surely it isn't *conditioned* in them – It's not like it's part of their Elemental alignment."

"Obviously it's not conditioned," Niamh says, rolling his eyes. "Just like Unorthodoxy is not conditioned. Some Elementals just make bad decisions. Their alignment only determines the type of bad decision."

Thirty-seven minutes later, the Detainers and Forensics arrive. Anaiya lets Niamh take care of protocol as the unconscious male is pulled from the ground and hauled down the stairs into a waiting vehicle. The female is similarly removed from the apartment, the Forensics gleaning no more evidence from her broken body.

Anaiya and Niamh leave the building a few minutes later. Outside, the haphazard congregation of Earth Elementals has swelled. The two Peacekeepers move silently through it, scanning the crowd for any signs of disturbance or unrest. The lights from the retreating detention vehicle cast a red glow over everything.

A twin beeping pierces the noise. Anaiya looks down at her wristplate.

Code 545. Precinct 3. Two Air suspects. Aggressive. Unarmed.

"Let's run."

Niamh doesn't need to say anything else. Her body wants to run and his words launch her into a full sprint without question or hesitation. A lightness seeps into her psyche as she free-runs through the dilapidated streets of Precinct 20, its details blurring as her heart rate spikes with anticipation and exertion. She doesn't look behind her for Niamh; she knows he is following.

Moments later, she senses him next to her, but still she keeps her eyes ahead – trained on the wall nine, eight, seven metres in front of her. Just when it seems momentum will carry her into the solid mass, she launches herself at it – fingers reaching out and gaining traction on the uneven surface. Her boots push against the wall, propelling her upwards until she balances on its narrow ledge.

Anaiya's centre of gravity is perfectly aligned – her right foot grounded; her left untethered but stable. Momentum wants to carry her forwards; her arched back holds her steady.

She steals a glance at Niamh, who balances beside her. He

flashes a familiar wicked grin back and they leap together from the tangible mass of the wall. Anaiya's body curls, turning a full revolution and sending the world into a kaleidoscope of fractured, off-centred images. Her feet hit the roof of the adjoining building half a second before Niamh's, launching her into a dive towards the next obstacle.

And so it continues. She and Niamh free-running with flair and speed across the Eastern Cardinal Area of the city.

As their destination nears, Anaiya feels herself pushing harder. A vague sense of urgency – a subtle electric shock – shivers along her nervous system, and her body responds in turn. Her legs stretch farther and her hands grasp higher, her tic tacs becoming more difficult, her passements more dangerous.

If she can just win this time…prove that she can be better.

Can be the best.

She had been the best. Once.

Niamh is matching her efforts, threatening to pull ahead. She pushes harder, delves deeper – dredging the rapidly depleting reserves of energy in her core. The effort burns, a physical pain that threatens to pull her out of flow. She ignores it, refines her focus, channels the pain into something useful.

The Precinct 3 marker, a thin column of composite steel, pierces the street not twenty metres away. The need in her flares, her desperation sharpens. A final burst of speed pushes her forwards. The metal marker brushes her shoulder as she clears it, its surface cool and unyielding.

But not before Niamh.

Niamh is first.

Niamh is always first.

He has come to a stop ten metres or so ahead of her. Anaiya slows to a jog in response, eventually shifting to a slow, deliberate walk before crouching down in a squat. It takes her longer than it should to shake off the disappointment and frustration that threatens to grow in her rib cage.

Anaiya has never liked losing, but losing to Niamh has lately grown a sharper edge.

She battles it, focussing instead on her breathing. Her

wristplate flashes as her vital readings count down from her accelerated state to normal. She glances up, a small sense of tainted satisfaction blooming at seeing Niamh still in a recovery position. He looks over at her and grins. Her satisfaction evaporates.

Looking down at her wristplate, she scrolls to the alert. Without waiting for Niamh, she starts off in a jog towards their ultimate destination. Behind her, Niamh's low-pitched chuckle grows and bounces off the nearby walls. The spiky feeling erupts again, harder this time to ignore. She shakes her head forcefully to clear her mind, careful to maintain her pace.

He catches up to her moments later. The tension in Anaiya's mind and body is smaller now, less threatening. The two of them stay silent, easing into a familiar synchronicity, matching pace as they work their way towards Le Marais.

Anaiya hears the street party before she sees it. Loud, dense beats pulsate among bright notes and trance-inducing melodies. Squeals of delight and peals of laughter fill the gaps: a hundred Air Elementals crowd a small laneway. Tattered polyester lounges are scattered about the space, occupied by Elementals sipping basic cocktails, engaging in deep conversation and various levels of personal intimacy. Around them, other Elementals dance and skip and twirl – vibrant swathes of multi-coloured material transformed into a moving visual feast.

Anaiya sees the same emotional abandon in the whirling of Air Elementals as in the debauchery of Earth Elementals. As a Fire Elemental, she can understand the thirst and demand for action that characterises the Earth Element, but she has never understood the cerebral ways of the Air Element – their obsession with thoughts and ideas and emotions is entirely alien to her.

"Time to shut it down," she says to Niamh.

"Time to shut it down," he confirms.

The nearby power sub-station is easily identifiable amongst the flamboyant infrastructure of the laneway. Accessing the control panel with a swipe of his wristplate, Niamh connects his lifeline and flicks the heavy white switch. Immediately, the sound and lights of the laneway, and the surrounding three blocks of streets, are killed.

The two Peacekeepers waste no time advancing on the gathering.

Anaiya free-runs to the back end of the laneway, repelling off walls and launching off lounges and tables, to reach the exit before too many Air Elementals can disperse.

"This is a Code 545 violation," she begins, her voice loud and authoritative. She can hear it echo as Niamh, at the opposite end of the laneway, calls out the same edict. "Organised Public Gatherings of more than ten Elementals in non-residential spaces, unless duly authorised, are strictly forbidden. Cease and desist all activities and await processing. Attendees will be Cautioned. Organisers will be Detained."

She stands lightly on the balls of her feet, ready for the inevitable runner. She's not disappointed – there are flashes of movement to her left as two Trainee Elementals rush forwards. Anaiya smiles. The fire that had burned after losing to Niamh has found a new target.

The first Trainee, a straggly looking male Anaiya has pegged as a Music Composer, practically trips over his own feet as he tries to evade Anaiya's counter-advance. With a clean hit, she sends him buckling to the laneway stones, turning smoothly to land a roundhouse kick on the chest of the second runner. The female grunts at the impact, her olive skin turning pale, her eyes widening in surprise. She collapses, clutching at her fractured collarbone. Anaiya will tag them later.

An older female strides forwards, scowling at Anaiya and the disabled Trainees. Her stance is combative and her eyes give Anaiya no doubt that she wants to claw shreds of skin off her.

Anaiya smiles and shakes her head – a simple sweep of her head left to right.

The small action has the desired effect. The older female hurls a gob of spit at Anaiya, the harmless projectile hitting Anaiya's shoulder. Anaiya steps in, one hand wiping the spit from her shoulder, the other grabbing her assailant's wrist at heart point six, disabling her arm and triggering a loud cry of pain.

"Uh-uh," Anaiya says, reaching for a syringe at her belt.

The female grunts – a deep guttural sound that widens Anaiya's smile.

"Fucking fascist Fire –"

The Air Elemental doesn't get a chance to finish. Anaiya's syringe enters her neck without resistance, sliding down into the trapezius and ejecting the restraint serum in one fluid movement.

The rest of the gathering is processed over the course of an hour. After the last Air Elemental has been cautioned and the Detainers have removed restrained Elementals for further processing, the site is turned over to Earth Elementals for waste and debris removal.

"Drink?" Niamh asks.

Anaiya checks her wristplate. It is close to midnight – their shift ended over an hour ago. The thought of burying tired limbs and erratic thoughts underneath a flood of synthetic alcohol is tempting, but an adrenalin surge is still tearing along her veins. And there's a tension with Niamh she can't quite shake.

All she wants to do is run. "Pass."

Niamh shrugs. "OK, Ani. Control the fire."

She appreciates the sentiment in the familiar Fire Elemental farewell, but the reminder is unnecessary. Anaiya is nothing if not disciplined.

The thought is less comforting than it used to be.

She doesn't watch as Niamh departs the scene, turning in the opposite direction and setting off in a slow jog. The sound of her footfalls strips away her thoughts. With each step, she increases her rhythm until the streets and buildings of Precinct 3 are a blur beneath her feet and hands. Obstacles and inconvenient infrastructure become ideal props for her kash vaults and cat jumps, her body pulling as much joy from the Eastern Area precincts as it can before it reaches the kilometre-wide perimeter that separates the city from its Border Wall and the Wasteland beyond.

Eventually, the sparse buildings of the outer precincts give way to the fat cylindrical air recyclers that signal the beginning of the Edges. Massive concrete behemoths whose depths extend for hundreds of metres below the ground, they groan constantly with the tedium of inhaling and digesting the polluted air of Otpor. The hum of their turbines mixes with the blood and footfalls in her ears, mimicking the sound of a thousand synthflies beating triple wings against rotund bodies.

Anaiya shifts her trajectory early to circumnavigate them without losing speed. With the squat structures at her back, the Border Wall finally settles into focus. She reaches the base of the wall within minutes, glancing up just once to search for the silent, invisible Watchers before commencing a meditative zigzag jog through the nearby cluster of industrial structures. Seconds stretch into minutes, the rhythmic beat of her footfalls and heavy shadows working to empty her mind of all thought.

For a long time all she is aware of is the constant sound, the comforting jolt, of one foot after the other slamming against the densely packed gravel.

And then she hears it. A discordant sound catching in her ears – a plaintive mewling that sets itself apart from the noise of her feet, that distinguishes itself from the sounds of the river and air recyclers.

Deviating from her normal course, she lets her ears guide her, following the sound through the maze of maintenance infrastructure that dominates the landscape. Her eyes dart around the unfamiliar space, seeking out unexpected movement. With each step, she grows more confident of what she will find, the strange noise growing in volume and clarity.

Turning a sharp corner ahead, Anaiya's eyes fix on a low-lying mass of heaving fur, easily found beneath the flickering lights of the water sub-station. She approaches cautiously.

The bitch is in labour. Her dark, patchy fur is slick with sweat and her emaciated frame swells and shrinks with each choked gasp. Black eyes are punctuated with the erratic light from above. Feral dogs, like most mammals, are not common in the city. Most find their way through gaps in the Border Wall to suffer their fate in the Wasteland. But occasionally, out here in the Edges, a few still stalk for meagre meals of rats and scraps.

Anaiya watches as the dog suffers through its delivery – a small litter of four pups expelled over the course of twenty minutes.

The first quickly attaches itself to the bitch's underbelly, desperate to sustain what little life still beats beneath sticky fur. The next two stumble wearily and collapse to the dark bitumen with barely a whimper. The runt emerges lifeless.

The chaos, so typical of the animal kingdom, disgusts Anaiya. It is so inefficient, so vastly inferior to the structured order of Elemental life. In Otpor, all Pre-forms are anonymously hatched in the state's Nursery. There are no families, no dependents – no gene lottery that is natural procreation, and no social constructs tethering adults to Premies. The eradication of familial bias leaves only pure loyalty – to Otpor, to the Orthodoxy, and to one's Element.

But dogs are not Elementals.

Anaiya turns and walks away. The bitch would die within the hour and the surviving pup, cut off from its life source, would die with her, from starvation or at the jaws of a hundred merciless rats frenzied at the promise of a decent meal.

A mother was all a pup had. There were no Fire Elementals in a dog's world that would guarantee peace, no Water Elementals to find solutions, no Earth Elementals to keep the wheels of progress turning, no Air Elementals to inspire and teach Orthodoxy. Dogs were not conditioned to their natural element – they ran scattered and haphazard. And died alone in deserted streets.

Heading west towards her apartment in Precinct 5, Anaiya shuns her usual free-running speed for a slower pace, debating whether to join Niamh after all. The lights of the Edges cast long shadows on the road and Anaiya moves between them, the shifting from light to dark reminiscent of the flickering sub-station light. So close to the air recyclers, she can trail her hand against their concrete form and feel their vibrations. Their shells are cold and rough to her touch, abrasive and indifferent. She unlatches her lifeline and patches a call to Niamh.

"Talk to me," he says. In the background she can hear other voices.

"You still up for that dri–"

The texture beneath her left hand has changed, the feel now wet and slick. She pulls it away from the recycler's frame.

"Ani?"

She presses a button on her wristplate to activate the diode; a bright white light hitting the recycler and shining in the glossy swathe of paint that covers it. She walks backwards, her light growing to encompass the entire surface area.

"Niamh?" Her voice pitches high on the first syllable, wavers on the last.

"Ani, what is it?" The background noises recede.

"I'm sending you my coordinates, I need you to get here as fast as you can. Alone."

A brief chime signals that he has disconnected his lifeline and severed the communication. Anaiya flashes her light across the road to the nearest recycler. The beam wavers as small tremors attack her hands.

Schooling her trembling hands to still, she shines the light again at the recycler. At its base, she finds its coordinates etched in the concrete and messages them to Niamh.

Bracing herself, she turns back around. The harsh light picks up the thick covering of paint. The smell is foreign to her, the Co-op having ceased the manufacture of paint after the introduction of coloured polyenamaline more than four generations before her conception. It has a sharp and slightly sweet scent, hinting at its synthetic origins, but more bitter and pungent than those she has previously encountered.

The mural rises the full ten metres of the recycler and spreads across the facing half of its circumference. The image is vivid – a crumbling set of black flames, rendered with streaks of grey and white to appear as fragile structures of charcoal and ash. Dead fire. She forces her attention to the large red lettering that dominates the bottom metre of the mural. Her heart rate spikes momentarily, but she does not flinch.

RESISTANCE.

The word burns as if a hot brand has taken to her pupils.

She can't look away. She knows, instinctively, that if she closes her eyes, the word will appear like a negative imprint in the darkness.

A forbidden word. One of the few that shall not be spoken. It thickens her tongue and tightens her throat just thinking about it.

Anaiya wants to retch.

Where are you, Niamh?

She exhales slowly and turns her light off. Unwilling to stand in the deep shadow, she moves to where the light of the city touches the road. She scans the area for the perpetrator, but there are no tracks and no signs of anyone else still lurking. She returns to the recycler.

Five minutes, ten minutes. Her eyes move constantly to her wristplate, gauging the time, waiting for Niamh's call. Old memories, sharp and sticky, are making their way up through her mind. She bats them away.

Fifteen minutes.

And then she hears the footfalls of someone running at pace. Coming into view, Niamh pulls up short, looking around but finding no conflict. He settles into a slow jog, his eyes on Anaiya, the confusion clear on his face.

Before he speaks, Anaiya turns back to the recycler and lets her diode light it up.

Niamh falls still beside her. "Any intel?" he finally asks.

Anaiya shakes her head. "I was on my return and just found it. No presence or movement. The Edges were clear." Her voice is steadier now.

"It will have to be handled discreetly," Niamh says, eyes still trained on the image. "You can't be here when the Forensics come, Ani."

The memories return. It's almost ten years since the first, and last, case of Heterodoxy. Since the Public Execution of Kane 148.

His name skitters through her mind. A name she will not speak aloud, that is still reviled even if it is not forbidden.

She nods absently, her feet still rooted to the spot, her mind circling with thoughts of Resistance and Heterodoxy and Execution.

"Ani!"

She snaps out of the mind loop.

"You have to leave now, Anaiya. You can't be connected to this at all."

TWO

Over the next few weeks, rumours of Heterodoxy filter through the Fire Element like embers, flashing bright and dying quickly to leave a thin veil of ash that rises and stirs with every prompt. Despite direct sightings being limited and a need-to-know protocol strictly enforced, the mere suggestion that Heterodoxy has resurfaced brings a new energy – a strange anticipation and aggression – to the Peacekeeper Corp.

The mood among Anaiya's peers is tense and excited and *thirsty*.

It puts her on edge.

She checks her wristplate again, scrolling past the numerous sent messages and unanswered calls to Niamh, frustrated at the lack of communication.

From their most recent discussion, she knows another three murals have since surfaced, spread out across disparate precincts that transcend Elemental and geographic divides. But that was a week ago. Since then, Niamh has been hard to find. Like rumours of Heterodoxy, Peacekeepers whisper about a promotion in recognition of his finding the first case.

Nothing comes between Niamh and his ambition. Not even the truth.

She grimaces at the unfair assessment. After all, she had readily agreed that they should delete her involvement in the discovery. It was a win–win situation: Anaiya avoided unwanted and inevitable scrutiny; Niamh gained a promotion.

A loud *whoop* of excitement pulls her out of her heavy thoughts, her eyes focussing on the lithe figure ahead bouncing off crumbling Otpor walls.

"Less torque on the vault," she calls out, but her voice is flat and the instruction goes unheeded.

Tonight, she is paired with a Trainee Peacekeeper. At eighteen, the Trainee has already completed her orientation and the first two years of her induction. Less than a year away from graduating into the Peacekeeper ranks, an excited anticipation radiates from her every movement.

A memory of Anaiya's first night patrol as an orienteer threatens to surface, but she pushes it down with force. Despite her best efforts, the face of Kane 148 flashes in her memory.

She watches the Trainee skip ahead, turning handsprings and repelling off the ten- metre-high walls of Water laboratories in Precinct 11. Something in her high-frequency energy, the easy paradox of inexperience and confidence, murmurs in the depths of Anaiya's mind. Only weeks ago, she was full of the same energy and abandon, but tonight her free-running is tame, basic. Patrols have a different feel about them now. There is a tension that follows Anaiya, that settles on her shoulders and clouds her periphery. Speed eludes her and anticipation and dread anchor her feet.

The story of Kane 148 runs like a jagged razor along her neural pathways. It mixes with fractured memories to create a tale that is part legend, part myth. Even Anaiya doesn't truly know where the facts end and superstition begins. She isn't sure that anyone does. The standard narrative comes to her unbidden, delivered in the clipped tones of the Fire Trainer who had repeated them every day for the entirety of her first year of induction.

Orthodoxy is right belief and right action. Unorthodoxy is wrong action. Heterodoxy is wrong belief.

Unorthodoxy is negligence and recklessness. Heterodoxy is an illness, an unnatural mutation.

Unorthodoxy can be rectified. Heterodoxy can only be terminated.

In the two hundred years since Emancipation and the Establishment of the Cooperative of Otpor, there has been only one case of Heterodoxy.

A flash of colour draws her eyes to the road ahead. The Trainee is like a synthfly, darting ahead before returning just as fast. A whir of limbs, her hair streaming behind her.

Kane 148, a Fire Elemental of the thirty-sixth generation, suffered a brain injury during a common Air aggression. The injury impaired his cerebral apex, mutating his Fire alignment. Kane 148, damaged, developed Earth Elemental tendencies. And became Heterodox.

The Trainee is impatient, frustrated by Anaiya's stubborn refusal to free-run. Every few minutes, she halts her aerial acrobatics to stare pointedly back at her. Anaiya ignores her, but nonetheless lengthens her stride.

Kane 148's Heterodoxy deepened. His internal disalignment threatened to disalign the Otpor Cooperative. For his safety, and the safety of Otpor, his Heterodoxy was terminated.

Kane's Heterodoxy wasn't confined to him. It was like a virus, spreading to other predisposed Elementals, infecting them. Unlike the viruses borne of synthfly mutations, which transmit linearly and are easily contained and treated, the 'virus' of Heterodoxy spread exponentially, gaining mass as it travelled along the networks of those exposed to it, and those exposed to the infected.

Kane 148 was Executed.

The event had been a public spectacle, hosted in the Trocadero and broadcast on all communication channels.

The memory of his face floods her synapses.

Anaiya was, of course, at the Execution; she watched it all from a front-row position. Effortlessly, she recalls how his dark eyes rolled back, filled with a whiteness that saw nothing; how the veins at his temples tensed, engorged with synthetic liquid designed to cure the Heterodoxy and arrest his heart. Silence his mind.

Just as the rise of Heterodoxy had been exponential, so too was its decay. The outbreak reached its half-life in two days and was eradicated within the week. Cut off from the source, the infected were cured.

The Heterodoxy was defeated.

The event had been burned into Otpor's collective psyche, spawning scores of movies, high-vis wall stories and docutainments that saturate communication channels. Reminding citizens of the horror. Conditioning Elementals back to obedience.

And balance was restored.

Anaiya's peripheral vision picks up movement as the Trainee approaches the intersection ahead, gaining speed. Running at the wall on the far side, she leaps up and pushes herself off, twisting and repelling to gain access to the high ledge on the wall opposite. Anaiya watches closely, envious of the Trainee and her ignorance of the new Heterodoxy.

The Trainee unexpectedly turns left, following a group of Water Elementals scurrying down a side street. The road veers on an acute angle, hiding them as soon as they pass the intersection. Anaiya picks up her pace and follows the severe line down towards the cluster.

She sees it before she realises its significance.

The Trainee stands immobile at the front of the throng, captivated by the image. Before her, paint drips down the alleletrite wall. The image of the ashen flame is familiar, but here it is isolated, as though cast adrift among the currents of the River Syn. It sits above the other three Elements, raining blackened shards of debris on Earth, Water and Air.

Disunity. Imbalance.

Resistance.

The forbidden word explodes in her mind, spurring her into action.

She moves as a shadow between the bodies, her ears straining to hear the hushed conversations of cowed Elementals. Some have seen other examples tonight in various precincts – the same image tainting walls throughout the Eastern Area. Some speculate quietly about its meaning, attempting to translate the image as a threat or challenge.

"…hubris of the Fire Element…"

The words are muttered with an unexpected aggression, the tone low and sharp. The sting causes Anaiya's head to whip around, seeking out the speaker.

A mix of Elementals surrounds her – low-level Water Elementals in cheap polyester suits, trainee Air Elementals in gaudy colours and lithe postures, older Earth Elemental labourers coated in dust, and off-duty Fire Infrastructure Protectors with straight backs and folded arms. Despite their differences, most stand with their eyes cast down, some daring to occasionally glance up at the mural but never at Anaiya.

Their reluctance to meet her gaze is not the usual deference to a Peacekeeper. This is avoidance – from fear or anger or…

Resistance.

She needs to take control of the situation quickly. Capturing an electronic copy of the image with her wristplate, she strides to the Trainee. Shaking her from her stupor, Anaiya orders her back to headquarters with a message for the Head Peacekeeper. Watching the Trainee disappear into the distance, she turns back to the scene, finding what she needs with a middle-aged Water Elemental standing at the back of the crowd.

"I need your jacket."

He nods quickly and shrugs out of it. Keeping his eyes trained on the mural ahead, he extends his wristplate towards Anaiya. She connects to it with her lifeline and uploads the formal compensation note.

With the heavy polyester jacket in her grip, she strides through the crowd, pushing aside the mass of Elementals. She reaches up as high as she can and brings down the thick material across the wet paint. The mural streaks into a dark mess of mangled colours. She turns to the crowd and raises her voice. "Time to move along."

No longer entranced by the image, the crowd disperses. A few of the younger Elementals throw dark glances over their shoulders. Others huddle together, talking in hushed tones as they retreat. Anaiya returns to destroying the image.

By the time the Forensics arrive, the street is quiet and the Heterodoxy unrecognisable. Anaiya downloads her copy of the image, throws them the paint-sodden jacket and sets off at a sprint without looking back.

Her journey is directed towards her apartment, but she takes an indirect route, weaving through the precincts. She doesn't free-run, instead preferring the simple rhythm of her feet hitting the hard ground below. With each crash of her foot, each jolt of her body, comes a steady stream of endorphins that should allow her to control the fire and assess the situation rationally.

Her mind is a tangled web of incomplete thoughts and dangerous images. She pushes herself harder, demanding her legs move faster. A single conclusion is forming in her mind, clawing its way to the surface, threatening to throw her off-balance.

Blood beats loudly in her ears and pain blooms behind her eyes. It all fades in comparison to the incessant cry of her frantic mind.

Heterodoxy is taking hold.

In the days of Kane 148, Heterodoxy had quickly shifted from strikes and protests to riots and anarchy. Stores were looted, buildings torched, Elementals murdered. There had been a rabid thirst back then, as well. An unleashing of some pent-up aggression that had been so carefully contained by the Orthodoxy.

She feels that same aggression leaching from the new cracks in Otpor's shared consciousness. Feels the weight of its insistence.

A dam ready to break.

Anaiya enters her apartment an hour later. Her wristplate glows and reflects off the dark walls. Midnight.

Her pulse is still dominant and her body tense. She focusses on the physical sensations, pushing all other thoughts from her mind. With heavy steps, she makes her way through the apartment, shedding her clothes to leave a trail behind her from the entryway to the bathroom. She doesn't bother to turn lights on, making her way to the shower by the glow of her wristplate, habit and feel.

She runs a cold shower, stepping in and letting the hard jets of water pelt her skin. Her hair falls like a dead weight down her back, picking up mass as it saturates with the stream of water. Her skin tingles with the cold hail of droplets. Turning her face up, she submits to the oncoming rush of water and closes her eyes.

Within the boundaries of her mind, the mural expands to take up all available room. The forbidden word dominant and menacing. She shivers.

Minutes later, the white noise of the shower is interrupted by the sound of her apartment door sliding open. It bangs back into place with a loud crash. She keeps her eyes closed. Only Fire Elementals can gain entry via any access point, regardless of what Element it is coded to. There are a number of Peacekeepers who feel comfortable enough to enter her unit uninvited, but there is only one who would do so after midnight.

When the footfalls sound on the acrylate tiles of the bathroom, Anaiya turns her head and opens her eyes. As she expects, Niamh stands there, a feral light of energy and abandon shining in his eyes. Without speaking, he undresses.

Anaiya turns back to the water. His body, for a few brief seconds, is warm when it connects with hers. Their sex is intense, but passionless. They don't speak, focussed entirely within their own heads and bodies, using the act as a way to expel the memories of the night.

This is the way of Fire Elementals. Promiscuous and competitive by nature and nurture, sex is a sport, and a release – the satisfying of higher energies that push and pull them every day. Tonight, Anaiya uses it to empty her brain of all thought and images, centring her consciousness in the act and the tactile sensations that demand attention.

When it is over, Niamh touches the space below her breasts, above her navel. It is where, they are taught, the Fire Element originates in them.

"Control the fire, Ani."

After he leaves, Anaiya turns off the shower and steps out. She doesn't bother to dress after towelling herself dry. Instead, she lies on top of her neatly made bed and stares at the ceiling until the dawn light appears.

Her wristplate flashes 0437 against the nascent illumination. Pulling herself out of bed, she steps into the main room of the apartment. Sinking into a worn polyester lounge, she plugs her lifeline into the remote control and presses the top button.

The lounge room wallscreen flashes to life. Out of habit, she pushes the scan button to let the screen run through all the channels. But this morning, all one hundred of them are broadcasting the same thing.

Joshu 820's face flickers frame by frame as the wallscreen moves through the channels at three-second intervals. The star of the quintessential Kane 148 movie, Joshu has always been synonymous with the 'Orthodoxy Resistor', but Anaiya has never found the likeness believable. Joshu's face is round and full, whereas Kane's was sharp angles and deep shadows. Joshu is slender and graceful, but Kane was muscular and restrained. Joshu's eyes carry the same ambivalence and lack of depth Anaiya has seen in countless Air Elementals, but Kane's eyes – they always burned bright; with intelligence and passion and righteousness. Right up to the moment of his Execution.

Projected on the wall, Joshu slumps against the narrow black polyenamaline pillar, kept erect only by way of the heavy restraints that shackle his neck, wrists and ankles. It is the seminal scene of the movie. Anaiya arrests the scan and the wallscreen shifts from its staccato tempo into the natural flow of the movie.

Joshu, as Kane 148, is lit by scores of floodlights – his face clearly illuminated, his long hair stirring in the breeze that rushes across the city as the sky darkens. Anaiya remembers that breeze, remembers it unexpectedly raising the tiny hairs at the back of her neck as nightfall arrived. Her memories merge with the story unfolding on her wallscreen.

Behind Kane 148, the symbols of the four Elements are projected on the massive concrete plinths. An anonymous voice begins its monologue as three Pathology Technicians stride across the reflective stone floor towards the defeated Elemental.

"In the beginning, there was sickness, violence, hunger, poverty and inequality. Before the Singularity, before Emancipation, there were no Elements and people wandered lost and unaligned. In the Wasteland of humanity, however, there emerged a group of people who saw potential. Potential for humanity to rise above. The Principals discovered and built the path of prosperity, stability and integrity. They created the Cooperative of Otpor and strengthened it with the Orthodoxy."

The three Water Elementals have reached the screen, where Kane 148 remains silent and unmoving. Simultaneously they reveal their large syringes to the crowd.

The moment is melodramatic, a carnival retelling of the truth, and yet it causes Anaiya's throat to constrict. She remembers the three Technicians, and, while the syringes were smaller, she recalls how the floodlights had picked up their metallic sheen, causing them to flash like tiny daggers.

Together the Technicians inject the contents of their syringes into Kane 148's skull. The shot zooms in to show an extreme close-up of his eyes. Pupils dilate – attempting to suck in the vibrant light that engulfs him, even as his life force escapes from them.

"Orthodoxy – the right belief and true knowledge that all humans, born or created, have an innate dominant Element that defines them. An Element that determines their attitudes, perspectives and abilities. An Element that, when properly aligned and strengthened through conditioning, produces maximum productivity and optimal functioning of the individual, the Element and the Cooperative."

Anaiya tears her lifeline jack from the remote control. The wallscreen blinks to black and plunges her into a darkness that is broken only by the hint of sunlight and the ever-present green tint of her wristplate. She closes her eyes to it and leans back into the lounge.

Kane's face swells to dominate the darkness. The face of the mentor she had idolised and the traitor she had reviled.

THREE

The Kane 148 movie replays on an endless loop across all one hundred channels for the next week. Curfews are introduced and additional Peacekeeper patrols are scheduled and implemented. Cardinal Area Commands coordinate among themselves to ensure full Peacekeeper coverage across the North, East, South and West Areas, and by the end of the week, another three instances of Heterodoxy are discovered. Anaiya falls into her bed at the end of each shift exhausted, only to lie there with thoughts of Orthodoxy and Heterodoxy cutting her off from sleep.

This morning, she is patrolling alone. With Peacekeeper resources stretched too thin, the normal protocol of patrolling in pairs has been suspended. She plods through the streets of Precinct 20 with a heavy heart, her eyes scanning the uneven surfaces of building facades tinged brown under the haze-covered sky.

Being the Third Day, the streets are heavily populated with Water and Earth Elementals keeping to their standard working schedule. They stream from the underground caverns that house subterranean public transport stations and meld briefly, forming a heaving mass of diversity and difference.

As usual, the Earth Elementals are rowdier than the staid Water Elementals. They bustle and push, in deep contrast to the orderly ambling of the others. It is not unusual, except…it is sharper, somehow. The weight is heavier.

Weight. She thinks of it now in the context of the Fire Elemental slang. Every crowd, emotion, and situation has a weight – a frequency that relates to its potential for Unorthodoxy. Gatherings of drunken Earth Elementals are heavy; Gatherings of Air Elementals in supplication to the Ultimate Muse are light.

This random, moving collection of Elementals has a weight. A growing charge that threatens to release its energy.

Her eyes scan the crowd, searching for likely triggers: small disturbances that, under weight, can quickly get out of control. Her heart races with anticipation and something else – a quickening, an unsettled tension.

The scuffle seems to erupt spontaneously; a push gone too far, an unsteady foothold. To Anaiya's left, a cluster of Elementals crashes to the pavement.

Immediately, the weight shifts, ratcheting higher. Anaiya sees the Elementals blink away their contentment and habitual apathy, can see their eyes fill with the base emotions that lie at the core of their Elemental nature – aggression, fear, suspicion, doubt.

It shifts her internal alignment and stokes the frustration and rage within her.

Control the fire, Anaiya.

She moves towards the disturbance, trying to keep her emotions in check, reminding herself this is not a normal situation. She knows that this is just the way of Heterodoxy – taking the primal emotions that motivate Elementals and untethering them, pulling them into a directionless chaos bereft of the discipline that raises them to a higher purpose. Curiosity becomes suspicion, physical strength becomes violence, creativity becomes rebellion, and righteousness becomes rage.

Within herself, she feels that pull to the fight – a rage simmering in the depths of her belly, yellow bile churning in her gut. The fire threatening to bloom.

Striding closer, she ignores the suspicion and anxiety in the faces of the Water Elementals. They move aside for her readily, keen to distance themselves from the impending melee.

In the centre, limbs flail wildly as a small group of Earth Elementals trade blows. The grunts and sharp cracks of breaking bones carry in the otherwise still morning air. Earth Elemental onlookers regard her with cold stares, inconvenienced by her mission and tense with the decision to join the fray or comply with the Orthodoxy.

Anaiya's rage notches higher, flickering at the edges of her mind and presenting her own alternative, Unorthodox options. She imagines breaking the nose of the nearest Elemental with a swift palm heel strike, removing the male in front of her with a sharp leg sweep. The images flare bright and brief in her mind's eye; it takes her a second to clear them. It is one thing to respond with appropriate force, another to lose control of the Fire and vent her aggression.

"Clear it out," she yells, plucking a syringe from her belt and zoning in on the core group of rumbling Elementals.

The crowd pauses around her and, for a brief moment, Anaiya has the uneasy expectation that the weight will shift against her – that they will not only ignore her directive but actively target her.

She sucks in a deep breath and lets her eyes sweep the crowd for signs of rebellion. The range of human emotion present in animated eyes, drawn faces and set stances sends synthflies to her stomach. A slight sweat pricks at her forehead and palms, her feet tingling with the need to urgently do something.

And then the weight evaporates. One by one, the spectators look away, dropping their eyes and relaxing their stances.

Needing no further invitation, Anaiya rushes to the four at the centre of the mass, restraining the closest with a quick injection to her straining neck. A smaller male, with deep scars peeking between new gashes, turns to face her, but she arrests him quickly with the flourish of another syringe, its needle finding its target high in the arm that reaches for her neck. He drops heavily, falling into the third offender, sending him toppling into his opponent. The two crash to the pavement awkwardly, presenting Anaiya with easy access for restraint.

A little breathless, she looks around again at the crowd. Few Water Elementals have stayed to witness the event, but a large group of Earth Elementals stand stubbornly at the periphery of the circle she has created.

"I said, clear out," she yells again. Her voice is louder this time, but still unsteady.

One by one they disperse, but not before muttering curses and obscenities in her direction. She watches them warily. Ignoring the temptation to cite them for a Code 8 offence, she connects her lifeline and patches a call for backup.

A movement at her feet draws her eyes down. One of the offenders is murmuring, the product of a misplaced syringe or resistant biology. Images of a sharp heel strike to his offensive skull tease at the edges of her mind and, for a moment, the raging fire within her pushes her to engage.

It lasts only a second, the temptation of Unorthodoxy winking out as quickly as it emerged. She exhales a shaky breath and reaches down with a new syringe, watching as the restraint serum silences the Elemental beneath her.

It is late by the time she returns to her apartment. Twice she was called out to assist other Peacekeepers, twice confronted with the same struggle for restraint and Orthodoxy.

In the older Fire Elementals it had appeared as impatience – a crankiness that drew deep lines in their foreheads and tension at their fists. But, in the younger Peacekeepers, it had been more visible – freshly fed, it rose quickly to the surface as an adrenalin-fuelled rage, an ego-led aggression.

Rubbing at bruised skin and tired muscles, she glances at her tattered lounge. Normally, she would zone out after a hard patrol in front of the wallscreen, but the face of Joshu 820/Kane 148 already stalks her in her lucid and dreaming states. Instead, she changes into a pair of dark kevlar jeans and a simple cottonex shirt and steps out into the city under a darkening sky.

Her agitation sets her feet at a quickened pace and for the first time in what seems like forever, she unleashes her fire in the free-run.

Arriving at Precinct 13, Anaiya walks up to the unmarked Wild Rover door, passes her wristplate over the handle and pushes. Inside, the izakaya is brightly lit with lines of fluorescent globes streaking across the high ceiling. Anaiya pivots away from the entry and heads straight to the bar.

It is still early and only a handful of Fire Elementals fill the space, drinking synth alcohols and sitting at tall tables, watching avatar sports on sectioned wallscreens. She stands next to a small group of Infrastructure Protectors, who speculate loudly about whether their factories of responsibility are next to be targeted for the theft of viscous synthetic dyes dripping Heterodoxy on Otpor walls.

"What can I get you?"

Anaiya turns back to the bar. A tall Earth Elemental, a generation older than her, addresses her with a scowl. Anaiya frowns, but quickly shakes it off.

"A dodeca," she replies, plugging her lifeline into the bar terminal to pay.

The bartender returns with a large glass tumbler. The blue liquid fizzes as the enhancer crystal hits its surface and sinks. Anaiya nods her thanks and takes the glass to a small corner table against the far wall. The drink, a favourite among Peacekeepers, combines a mild alcoholic sedative with a crystal edrazine enhancer – the cocktail triggering rapid-fire hits of dopamine and oxytocin in the brain. Anaiya takes a few sips and then sits back to let the chemicals do their work.

With each passing minute, she can feel the agitation and anger leach from her body. The fire in her belly cools from a white-hot rage to a single flickering flame. With her glass now half empty, the dodeca has lost its bitter taste – her tongue now numbed to the harsh chemical residue.

Around her, the cavernous space fills with Fire Elementals as various corp shifts come to an end. A young male Peacekeeper, still in his kevlar uniform and standing alone, catches her eye. Tall, angular, good muscle tone.

Finding Anaiya's gaze, he flashes a confident smile and, minutes later, he saunters towards her. Reaching the table, he towers over her, blocking the harsh light and sending her into shadow.

Anaiya doesn't react, watching calmly as he extends his left hand, proffering another glass of dodecahedrazine. She takes it from him as he raises his own drink. Without breaking their gaze, he clinks the glass softly against Anaiya's and raises it to his lips, draining half of it.

Anaiya pauses, appraising him. Two years out of training, he is confident and cocky. His eyes glitter with the edrazine and a hint of a smile plays on his lips. He is attractive enough.

Anaiya finishes what is left in her glass and stands. He puts his empty glass on the table and looks at Anaiya. She nods. He opens his mouth to speak, but she cuts him off. "Your place."

Without waiting for his reaction, she strides towards the door – but before she reaches it a figure steps in front of her.

"Sorry, Ani, no playtime tonight."

Niamh looms before them, no fun and all business. The young Peacekeeper attempts to step forwards, but Anaiya places her hand against his chest, keeping her eyes on Niamh.

Niamh shakes his head at him and Anaiya feels the young Peacekeeper hesitate before he finally retreats.

"So, you've deigned to be seen among the plebs," she says, eyeing the golden circle around his flame insignia, the mark of his promotion.

Niamh turns his bemused glance from Anaiya to the retreating Peacekeeper. "And I find them wanting."

"Jealous?" Anaiya quips, her voice soft with the dodeca.

Niamh ignores her poor attempt at a joke. Fire Elementals are competitive, but basic emotions like jealousy are reserved for Air and Earth Elementals.

"How many have you had?" he asks.

"Two," she replies. "Both in the last hour."

He reaches into his pocket and pulls out a small atomiser. "Here," he says, handing it to her.

Anaiya takes it from him and sprays two sharp bursts of liquid adrenalin under her tongue. She feels the fog of the dodecahedrazine begin to lift as she works her mouth to get rid of the metallic taste the adrenalin has left behind.

"Good?"

She nods. Niamh opens the door for her and she walks

through without looking back.

Where have you been? What else have you learned? Why haven't you made contact?

The questions hammer through her sobering mind, but she doesn't speak them aloud. If Niamh wanted her to know the answers, he would have already offered them.

"Keep up," he throws over his shoulder as he breaks into a sprint.

The haze of the Wild Rover dissipates as the adrenalin hit pushes Anaiya to run faster. Despite Niamh's early lead, she catches up to him easily and settles into a synchronised rhythm, matching him stride for stride. They are not competing tonight.

Niamh takes a westerly direction, away from the Command headquarters, and she briefly wonders where they are headed. When they pass the Eastern Area boundary, Anaiya frowns in his direction but maintains her silence and her pace.

The tall administrative buildings of Precinct 8 rise before them like emblazoned spears, their glass structures lit with hundreds of strontium aluminate pods. The streets are quiet, with only a handful of Water Elemental Technicians and officers still working; it's only two hours before curfew commences.

In front of her, Niamh leaps and pivots off a low-rise wall. Anaiya follows instinctively. When she lands, she finds him waiting for her at the entrance of a nearby building.

"This is a Sec Level 5 briefing, Ani," he says quietly before plugging his lifeline into the wall terminal.

The glass double doors slide apart with a sharp hiss. Her adrenalin levels spike again, despite the synthetic residue from her previous dose having long expired. Level 5 is the highest level of secrecy for classified missions and operations. She nods her understanding and passes through the doors in front of him.

The inside of Water Elemental buildings are unfamiliar. With the Eastern Area made up primarily of industrial and cheap residential precincts, the sterile and orderly interiors of the administration building provide stark contrast. Their boots hit the polished floor with dull thuds. He doesn't speak and Anaiya again resists questioning him.

They continue like this, striding along the empty corridor in silence, until they reach a small, unmarked door. Anaiya scans the wall for the terminal, but none is to be seen. She watches Niamh approach the door, expecting him to swipe his wristplate over the handle. Instead, he knocks three times in rapid succession. He pauses and looks back at Anaiya. Then, with a sly grin and a wink, he knocks twice more.

Incredibly, the door clicks open to reveal an empty stairwell. Following Niamh through the doorway, she closes the door shut behind her. Inside, she notices a small electronic gauge, its display screen running an erratic line across its width.

"Ani, what –?"

Anaiya blinks as the gauge registers Niamh's voice, sending a series of spikes in the display line. Surprised by the new technology, she taps the wall next to it three times, seeing the sounds as medium-peaked spikes on the display, then another two times. The door behind her clicks open.

"Ani, what are you doing?" Niamh asks, exasperated. "Let's go."

Anaiya sighs in frustration, but pushes the door shut and meets him on the stairs.

"Try to keep the noise down until we're up two flights. After that it's sound proof and we can run."

Moments later they enter a dark, narrow hallway punctuated only by a small pool of fluorescent light that spills from under a closed door. Anaiya follows Niamh silently as he strides down the hallway and enters the floodlit room.

It takes her eyes a while to adjust to the brightness and she blinks rapidly until, slowly, details emerge.

The room is windowless and sparsely decorated. Wallscreens blink off at their entry, leaving faint memories of maps and faces and rows of text. An older Elemental sits behind a large desk, its surface glowing as she scrolls through and taps away. The light illuminates the embroidered insignia on her jacket collar – three spheres connected in a broken triangle. The molecular structure of water.

A Commander.

"Sit," the Commander says, not looking up.

Anaiya and Niamh take a seat on the opposite side of the desk.

"This is a Sec Level Five briefing," she continues. "Please present your lifelines to the terminals in front of you to disable recording functions."

Anaiya and Niamh plug their cables into the row of terminals in front of them. A quick beep and a small green indicator light tell them the operation has been processed. They disengage from the terminal and wait.

After a few moments, the Commander looks up. Her eyes flicker from Anaiya to Niamh and then back.

"Anaiya 234." Her voice is strong and commanding.

Anaiya is unsure of whether the address is a statement or a question, so she nods.

"Peacekeepers and Neural Technicians are initiating a joint Task Force to combat the recent episodes of Heterodoxy."

Anaiya blinks, caught off-guard by the unusual pairing. Fire and Water partnerships are not uncommon – both Peacekeepers and Border Watchers have always worked with Water Elementals to gain access to technology, complex data analysis and target profiling. But never have these partnerships involved Neural Technicians, the Water Elementals responsible for testing new generations and conditioning Premies.

The Commander continues, oblivious to Anaiya's confusion. "Despite current surveillance and profiling attempts, we have been unable to narrow down our search to a specific group of Elementals. We have, however, achieved ninety-five per cent certainty on which Element, precinct and competency the perpetrators belong to. Despite this success, we do not have enough to identify and detain the core of the Resistance."

She pauses and fixes her stare on Anaiya. "And so we must take additional and radical steps to succeed in our endeavours. Deputy Commander Niamh assures me that you are a Peacekeeper of the highest calibre – obedient, adaptive, dedicated, et cetera. He had no hesitation in recommending you for this mission."

"What mi–?"

The Commander glares at Anaiya, stopping her mid-question and continuing as if there had been no interruption. "Recent technological advances in neural testing and conditioning present us with an opportunity to identify the perpetrators by infiltrating their environment. As one of them."

Anaiya's mind stutters over the words, struggling to understand what they mean. Neural testing and conditioning are for Premies entering the last year of their first lustrum. With the four year-old mind exhibiting maximum plasticity and cognitive potential, it is the perfect age for determining elemental alignment.

Anaiya finally grasps what the Commander is proposing. "You want to change my alignment."

FOUR

Time is no longer the fluid, dynamic thing that Anaiya knows it to be. It slows and stretches, even as her mind races.

Changing one's alignment is impossible. Is anathema. *Heterodox.*

Tiny beads of sweat set her skin itching and a dense nausea drags at her stomach – that same feeling of abject misery she had felt at finding the first mural rushes over her.

The Commander betrays no recognition of Anaiya's discomfort. "I want to have you tested to see if you are compatible for realignment. And then, if you *are* compatible, I want to temporarily realign your limbic brain to provide a neural disguise that will allow you to infiltrate the Air Element under investigation."

Anaiya glances at Niamh, but he continues to stare resolutely ahead.

"I don't understand," she says.

The Commander's right eyelid twitches and a hint of a sigh escapes her lips. "As a highly confidential and risky operation, I can't tell you more until you are confirmed on the Task Force."

"How can you be sure it will be temporary?" Anaiya persists.

Niamh kicks her under the desk, but she ignores him.

The sigh is clear and unmistakable this time. "The realignment will only target your limbic brain – the primal part of your brain responsible for reactions and habits, the part of you that responds instinctively. Your neocortex, the higher part of the brain that is conditioned during Premie training, will remain untouched. At the end of the operation, your limbic brain will be reassigned to your true Element."

"Why me? Why not Niamh?"

It comes out sounding desperate, but at this point she is no longer able to maintain the cool facade she cultivates every day as a Peacekeeper. A dull panic, like a hand over her mouth, is rising in her mind. The same feeling that assaulted her as a Trainee, watching as her mentor was Executed – the feeling of being in a situation with no clear exit, of being given an impossible task, of standing on a precipice. Of being out of her depth.

"The mind of Deputy Commander Niamh was deemed too rigid to attempt realignment. And his particular mix of skills are better utilised behind the scenes." Her voice is colder. Harder. She regards Anaiya with a fierce stare as if silently forbidding her to ask another question. When Anaiya falls quiet, she nods to herself and leans back in her chair. "Now, are you prepared to be tested?"

Anaiya's mind races with her choices and their implications. If she says no, she will look weak and unfit to be a Peacekeeper. If she says yes, she will lose part of her that makes her a Fire Elemental. She will lose herself.

Niamh's voice interrupts her thoughts. "Ani, we can beat the Heterodoxy with this. You can erase his legacy with this."

His words steal all the oxygen from the room.

Kane 148's legacy.

The legacy that has haunted Anaiya and the Peacekeeper Corp for almost a decade. The legacy of being intimately associated with the original Resistor.

Pressure, like an invisible cage, closes in on her. Her brain grinds through the rational considerations, holding out against the confusion and a rising sense of panic.

This is what she was trained for. What all Elementals are conditioned for. Beyond whatever responsibilities their position demands, the first duty of all Elementals is to maintain the Orthodoxy. Anaiya has diligently defended and enforced it for years. Detaining offenders and punishing breaches. Protecting it from even the slightest threat of Unorthodoxy. Safeguarding it.

As a Fire Elemental.

Anaiya sits stiffly in her chair, not daring to move. She feels the weight of Niamh's gaze on her. She nods her head. Defeated.

The Commander peers at her. "If you *are* compatible, you *will* be realigned."

Anaiya's skin tingles and her throat feels as if it has shrunk in on itself. But her decision was made for her the moment Niamh collected her from the Wild Rover.

She nods again, mute.

The Commander permits herself a small smile, tapping on her desk screen and standing up. "Excellent. We will commence the testing immediately."

The high-pitched beeps and loud click announce the visitor before he is seen. He steps over the threshold and walks straight to the Commander's side, gripping a small glass screen and ignoring Anaiya and Niamh in true Water Elemental style.

"I want to know as soon as you get results," she says, passing him a mobile storage unit, which he promptly connects to his screen.

The male, nondescript in his blue suit, nods obediently.

"Anaiya 234, you are dismissed," the Commander says, taking her seat again behind the desk.

Anaiya looks to Niamh, who this time has the decency to look back at her. He gives her a smile that fades at the edges and never reaches his eyes. Anaiya's stomach leaps with a thousand synthflies.

"Control the fire, Ani," he murmurs, the words magnifying in the cavernous room to be heard easily.

Her heart stings with the same feeling she gets when looking at the Heterodoxy, when remembering Kane 148. A sharp, fine-pointed blade piercing its depths.

Betrayal.

But there is nothing for it – her path has been set – so she controls the fire and follows the anonymous Technician out of the room and down the hallway.

The neural laboratory is small, white and brightly lit, like so many of the pathology rooms in which she has deposited overdosing Air Elementals or wounded Earth Elementals. A light cottonex slip hangs on a small hook next to the gurney: the only soft thing in the room.

"Please put the slip on and lie face up with your feet closest to the door," the Technician says before leaving her alone.

Anaiya undresses quickly, hampered only by small tremors that shake her hands. The slip is thin and provides no warmth in the sterile environment. She ignores the protests of her mind and body and clambers onto the gurney as per her instructions.

Minutes stretch together, amplifying the silence and providing too much space for her mind to twist and tumble. The torrent of potential outcomes, borne of one future-search after another, gives rise to a growing panic. Desperate to escape the mind loop and distract herself from ominous thoughts, Anaiya eventually resorts to accessing the basic entertainment features of her wristplate.

The default time screen clicks over and presents Anaiya with an ascending row of cards. Her fingers flick across them rapidly, the game honing the Fire skill of snap decision making. She doesn't think, just reacts – swiping, tapping in quick staccato movements, watching as the cards flip and move and stack. A smile plays at the corners of her mouth, triggered by the memory of a Water Elemental playing the same game before a Peacekeeper briefing years ago, his games spanning large expanses of time as he deliberated his every move, fingers hovering over cards for eternities before they tentatively descended.

Eventually, the Technician returns, ending her petty distraction. He is followed by three other lab-coat-wearing Water Elementals. The first takes Anaiya's lifeline and plugs it into a small machine beside the gurney. A wallscreen flashes to life, revealing a dashboard of her vitals. Her heartbeat becomes a soundwave of peaks and troughs; her pupils, black circles on a micro-measured target. Graphs and three-dimensional brain maps flicker as they receive updated information from her lifeline.

Another Technician steps forwards to blindfold her. She doesn't need to see the wallscreen graphics to know her heart rate is spiking. She forces herself to regulate her breathing, drawing deeper breaths and exhaling slowly. Warm hands fit her ears with a dense material. At once she is both blind and deaf, completely isolated in the cold and sterile room.

Her heightened senses of touch and smell sing with the pinch of skin on the inside of her elbow and the sharp smell of too-sweet chemicals as a needle burrows deep into her basilic vein. A rush of warmth runs up her arm and calmness floods her body. Anaiya wraps herself in it, sinking deeper and deeper into overwhelming contentment and peacefulness.

It doesn't last long.

The blackness is punctuated with a vivid image of the dead female from her last patrol with Niamh. The vision is breathtaking in its details – the head has collapsed in on itself, opening up a large part of the cranium. Blood, red and sticky, clings to the exposed bone and coats short brown hair. Globs of blood spill onto the floor, mingling with the crushed brain matter.

Anaiya vaguely remembers the fire that erupted in her when she first saw the image, standing in a run-down apartment in Precinct 20. But there is no fire this time. There is nothing. Just the image in all its detail.

Screams and shrieks fill her ears. The sounds are primal and full of pain and despair. Anaiya's brain ticks over with the thought of citizens in danger, but the fire is absent.

Confusion pushes its way to the forefront of her mind. Should she be worried about this? Is something wrong? Where has the fire gone?

The questions trip over one another on their way to her consciousness, urgent and insistent. She doesn't flinch, letting them wash over her.

The darkness and silence eventually return to her. On the edge of her thoughts, she registers her skin being prepped for another injection. Unlike the first, this one is an icy cold torrent raging along her nerves.

Anaiya gasps as her limbic brain switches back on and the memories of the vision and sounds replay in her mind. Her back arches, threatening to throw her up into a sitting position, but her arms catch in tightly fastened restraints. She doesn't remember them.

Panic and rage are now fully blooming in her and she thrashes on the gurney, trying to escape her confinement. Trying to escape the darkness and silence that are now thick and oppressive.

She barely feels the pinprick of the next injection. Her body ceases its death throes and falls heavy and immovable. Her mind becomes fuzzy before shutting down into a sedated and dreamless sleep.

When she wakes, it is in a large, dimly lit room. An unfamiliar Water Elemental walks over to her and checks the recovery history flashing up on the small terminal screen beside the bed.

"Your recovery period has concluded," he says matter-of-factly. "You can take the lift down to the ground floor exit."

Anaiya looks around, taking in the empty room. "Is the other Fire Elemental still here?" Her voice scratches along her dry throat.

The Water Elemental frowns. "I'm not sure what you mean. You were the only admission to recovery we had all night."

Anaiya looks down at her wristplate to check for any missed messages. A single encrypted note sits in her inbox. Waiting until the Nurse leaves, Anaiya opens it using her inbuilt decoder and waits a few seconds as the garbled text rearranges itself into a message.

Sec Level 5. Results are positive. Present to Room 35.1. 48.8917° N, 2.2408° E at 0900 hours on 18 Capricornia 205 AE

She sits up slowly, struggling to make sense of what has happened.

Results are positive.

Her brain buzzes with flashes of half-formed memories of the testing. She regulates her breathing in the hope it will clear her mind, but panic is a rabid mutt, tearing around her brain, gouging scratches with every twitch.

Positive.

She struggles to make sense of her rising panic. With each shallow breath, scattered thoughts coalesce into one fundamental conclusion.

I will be realigned.

FIVE

The morning is unusually warm when she exits the Administration Building. Ducking her head, she avoids the glances of Water Elementals who seem to swarm the streets around her, intent on getting as far away from Precinct 8 as she can.

Ignoring the steady trickle of sweat that itches between her shoulder blades and pools in the small of her back, she slams her feet along unfamiliar roads and boulevards until she reaches Precinct 3. Noises, smells and colours call to her, pulling her along the satellite streets that shoot off from the Starboard Road and into a large crowd of Elementals.

The Samedi Markets stretch lazily along the full stretch of the road, backing onto the northern river ramparts and spilling into the tributary laneways and arcades. Earth Elementals browse ugly plastic jewellery and second-hand polyester shirts. Water Elementals rifle through broken technology for salvageable parts and even Air Elementals wander around soaking up the atmosphere and gliding their fingers over digital sketchbook pages. She weaves in and out through them, slowing down and speeding up to twist and pivot into gaps and take advantage of the invariable lulls in the swell.

The scent of cola-roasted pigeon wafts in the stale air. It is a Samedi Markets speciality and a welcome respite from the synthetic nutrition pressed into pills and swallowed daily by all Elementals.

The smell of the pigeon mixes with the guano smoke, evoking for Anaiya memories of childhood dares along the riverfront. Her stomach growls in anticipation and she realises that she has not eaten since yesterday's shift. Unable to resist, she makes her way to the hawker's stall, finding a small group of Peacekeepers standing casually around the fire pit.

Lumen, one of the Fire Elementals, nods in greeting as Anaiya approaches. Both assigned to the Eastern Area Command upon graduation and only a generation apart, they have patrolled together numerous times before.

Anaiya nods back. "Hey, Lumen," she says, reaching the group.

Lumen finishes the last of her pigeon, tossing the bones into the pit and wiping her stained fingers on dark kevlar jeans. "Want some?" she asks, indicating new pieces of marinated pigeon roasting on the grillplate.

Anaiya nods as Lumen reaches back to grab a piece. She wraps it in one of the polyester scraps poking out of a plastic dispenser and hands it to Anaiya. "We bought fifty pieces," she explains, laughing.

"Thanks," Anaiya says, before biting into the hot flesh.

Meat juices coat her lips and fingers, crunchy skin gives way to a thick layer of rendered fat, flavour explodes on her taste buds. It has never tasted so rich, so sweet.

The other Fire Elementals continue to talk around her. Their tone is casual, but Anaiya notices how they position themselves to form a collective watching post that eliminates any singular blind spot. Even the Trainee is on alert, his laugh absent-minded as his eyes flicker across the crowd.

A flash of movement at her feet catches Anaiya's eye and her foot slams down immediately in response. The rat's ripened body collapses and splatters underfoot, leaving a mangled mess that Anaiya wipes off the bottom of her boot and on to the rough stones of the market floor. She thinks back to the dog in the Edges.

That's what happens when you don't belong to an Element.

The thought is bitter and sharp. She turns away from it and lets her eyes wander across the crowd. Tension pulls at the festivity, a taint to the sun-filled streets. A weight.

"Getting heavier," she notes to Lumen.

The older Peacekeeper nods, breaking away from the conversation to stand next to Anaiya. The Trainee fills the space between them, keeping the circle's vision complete.

"There's a few of us scattered along the ramparts, but I'm not sure whether we're keeping an eye on the situation or increasing the weight," Lumen confides.

Anaiya scans the crowd. Lumen is right, the presence of the Fire Elementals is affecting the crowd's behaviour. Nearby, a group of Air Elementals catches her attention. Like the Peacekeepers, they are an odd collection comprising males and females of different generations. Some of them scowl openly at the Peacekeepers. Others refuse to look, keeping their heads down and fidgeting. One, a male the same generation as Anaiya, stares straight at her. He doesn't scowl or shift his feet; he just stands there, arms folded against his chest, unblinking. She senses his weight, his defiance.

Her fire flares bright and hot and she finds herself staring back. He doesn't flinch under the scrutiny. Doesn't cower as he should. The fire builds. Lumen stirs beside her: her hand on Anaiya's shoulder breaks the standoff. She doesn't speak the words, but Anaiya hears them anyway.

Control the fire.

But she no longer *wants* to control the fire. She wants to feed it. To sear it to her insides. To bring it to a white heat that can never be extinguished.

She stares back at the Air Elemental, relishing the slow build of heat in her core. It is easy for her as to build animosity with him, their two Elements diametrically opposed in the Elemental design. There has always been tension between opposing Elements, but never has it escalated into direct conflict – the strict order of Otpor and conditioning to Orthodoxy setting an upper limit to natural animosities.

But the world is changing and Anaiya's mind swims with visions of Heterodoxy, with Air-created blasphemy and Resistance. The weight of the crowd around her grows heavier, feeding her latent rage.

And then it erupts.

A loud crash shatters the ambient noise of the market, followed by loud shouts and high-pitched screaming. It is not the fight she wanted, but she turns from the Air Elemental and towards the commotion.

Beside her, the other Peacekeepers break into pairs and advance on the melee with speed and precision. Not to be left behind, Anaiya breaks into a sprint and reaches the edge of the intensifying chaos as Lumen breaks through the first layer of offenders.

Anaiya shoves her way past her immediate obstruction, sending a young onlooker stumbling to the ground. From her left, a hand reaches across her chest to prevent her from moving forwards. She brings her forearm up quickly in a counter-strike, ignoring the sudden give as the opposing ulna breaks, unmoved by the scream of pain that follows. Across the crowd she sees one of the male Peacekeepers bring low a heavy Air Elemental with a strong blow to the face and quick injection to the neck.

A sharp jostling to her right is diffused quickly with a leg sweep. A heavyset Earth Elemental turns around, arms flexed and biceps tense, her eyes lit with excitement. Anaiya pushes out at the Elementals to her side, giving herself enough room to time a well-placed roundhouse kick to the female's kidney, dropping her to her knees where she can offer no resistance to the restraint serum.

Stepping over the motionless body, Anaiya pushes her way into a better position, the remaining crowd thinned out by the relentless advance of the other Peacekeepers. This close, she can see the core of the skirmish – three dominant Air Elementals raging against a Compliance Enforcer. A light-footed female brandishes a large broken shard of glass at the Fire Elemental, her screams of 'Corruption!' and 'Oppression!' reaching above the wall of noise to either side of Anaiya. The other two Air Elementals overturn nearby stall carts, throwing random projectiles at the Enforcer as he ducks and moves – prevented from escaping by the insistent push of the crowd.

At the other edge of the conflict, Anaiya spies Lumen approaching the final circle of onlookers, the two of them making eye contact and silently communicating their plan. Lumen nods and Anaiya strikes out with a swift push kick to the kneepit of the Elemental in front of her. He falls to the ground, providing the prop she needs to launch up and over the final circle of spectators.

She reaches the inner core at the same time as Lumen and two of the other Peacekeepers, her fingers already cradling a syringe down by her side. Without needing to communicate with each other, the four Peacekeepers rush to restrain their targets while covering the Enforcer.

The glass-wielding Air Elemental screams at her, pulling her arm back to hurl the jagged blue weapon. With a quick flick of her wrist, Anaiya shoots the perfectly weighted syringe across the space between them and into the Air Elemental's thigh. Advancing rapidly on the offender, she registers the sight of the shard falling and shattering on the ground. Easily deflecting the amateur attempts to fend her away, Anaiya pushes the Elemental into a submissive position before properly restraining her with an injection to the neck.

"Clear," she yells, spinning around to appraise the rest of the situation.

The other two Air Elementals lie in crumpled heaps, rendered unconscious by the restraint serum or their fall. The two male Peacekeepers have been joined by four others – spread along the circumference of the inner circle, their focus is outwards, supervising the gradually dispersing crowd. Lumen kneels by the injured Compliance Enforcer, hand pressed to her ear where her lifeline patches her in to headquarter communications.

The heat of the day and Anaiya's exertion registers faintly at the edge of her consciousness, but it is a cold sweat that breaks out over her skin. Her fingers tingle, leaching out the adrenalin that had rushed through her body seconds before. The tremors do not lessen; instead they grow, spreading out along her limbs until her arms, torso and legs tremble in unfamiliar spasms.

She tries to still her mind, to focus on her breathing and calm her body. The threat of the shocks becoming more violent spurs her to move her feet, one shaky leg in front of the other. She passes through the gaps in the crowd silently, the faces of Elementals around her failing to coalesce in her vision.

Her mind is quiet, reset to its survival factory setting, shut down and getting her only as far as the cold, hard floor of her apartment, where she falls asleep without so much as taking off her boots.

She wakes from her stupor to a frigid morning – the cool air a fitting backdrop for a colder truth. The day of her realignment procedure has arrived quickly and without ceremony. Her mind shivers with the realisation that the rest of Otpor will continue on its familiar trajectory, oblivious to her turmoil and to impending sacrifice.

She leaves her apartment without a second glance back. Unlike Earth and Air Elementals, Fire Elementals have never been sentimental about inanimate objects.

Or animate ones.

There is no one for her to say goodbye to, no one to mourn her disappearance or offer words of encouragement. There is just the hot Otpor sun, the dusty brown sky and the crumbling pavement leading to her destination.

The journey to Last Defence will take her to the westernmost edge of the city. She could take a more scenic route, along the Syn River or through the Southern Area precincts, but there is no point. Her future has been decided, and delaying it will bring no comfort. She runs without pause along the seven kilometres that separate her from her new life.

The Avenue of the Elysian Fields is wide and unobstructed, allowing her an easy path. Occasionally, she swerves around clusters of Elementals moving slowly on foot or bicycle, but her speed does not falter. Her gaze is glued to the forty-storey hollowed cube that is Last Defence – the indomitable structure growing more immense with every kilometre that flies under her thundering feet.

Drawing closer, her gaze scales the sleek lines of its bevelled facade, inlaid with white tiles and large windows. Beyond the thick squared arch, the dark skin of the Border Wall and the red-tinged brown of the Wasteland sky create a perfect contrast. The colours are vivid, the image striking.

She has viewed Last Defence a hundred times before, yet, in this moment, it is as if she is seeing it with new eyes.

Entering the left tower of the arch, she brushes past Elementals milling about in the lobby. Snatches of conversation rise above the general cacophony and slam into her ears.

"...curfews aren't working..."

"...another one in Precinct Twelve..."

"...Air Elementals are being persecuted..."

The weight of the gathering swirls around her, the heavy anticipation of the crowd sending her gut cramping. She ignores it all, setting up barriers in her mind and focussing solely on reaching her destination.

Arriving at the room on the thirty-fifth floor, she blinks against the harsh white light. An older Technician in her eighth lustrum is there to collect her.

"Anaiya 234?"

Anaiya nods.

The Technician pauses, a small frown furrowing her brow. "I know you."

It takes Anaiya a moment before the recognition becomes mutual. It has been almost ten years since they last saw each other.

"You were his protege," the Technician continues. "They thought you were infected."

She had been a Psychoanalyst, one of the many who had tested and watched and assessed Anaiya in the lead-up to Kane's Execution. In those early days Anaiya had been assessed as a primary candidate for infection. They had thought she was more vulnerable, that her conditioning was still too raw, her Premie mind still plastic after only one year of orientation.

They had seen her worship him, emulate him in all his celebrated Peacekeeper ways. They had seen him favour her, seen him spend more time on her training and advocate more fiercely for recognition of her potential.

Under Kane 148's tutelage, she had been better than Niamh. She had been the best.

"I wasn't infected."

The Technician steps forwards to appraise Anaiya more

closely. "No. You weren't infected. But you were certainly *affected*."

Anaiya feels herself shrink away from the scrutiny, then bristles at her display of weakness. It immediately reminds her of the days after Kane's Execution. The never-ending examinations, the constant judgement, the certainty that she had been tainted. That she was Heterodox.

The Technician steps back. "But no longer, it seems."

Anaiya smiles through tight lips. Convincing Water Elementals she hadn't been infected by the Heterodoxy had proven much easier than erasing the contamination from her connection to the Resistor. She had learned to push harder, be better. Had forced others to see past Kane's legacy. To only see her and her dedication and skill and obedience. But, somewhere in that darkened past, she had become weaker. Less. As if Kane had taken some part of her with him to the grave.

"Your procedure is scheduled in Room 35.1," the Technician says, opening a door to a wide corridor. "You can go in now."

SIX

Anaiya's world no longer looks the same, no longer feels the same.

The days following her initial realignment procedure have been much like the realignment itself – brief, painless, yet entirely disorienting.

Relocated to Last Defence, Anaiya finds herself severed from her former life. Forbidden to access her former precinct, Area or Peacekeeper colleagues, her days are spent in the isolation of her new room – a small and bare box containing only a bed, a side table and compact washroom.

Most of the time, she stares out of the window, her eyes drawn to everyday contrasts – the interplay of light and shadow, the subtle tones of grey and brown on buildings and infrastructure, the contrast of bright polyesters and neutral kevlars on the Elementals below.

Her ears, once only attuned to sounds of distress and unrest, now pick up the hidden beats and melodies of Otpor's streets and precincts. And with these sights and sounds come strange reactions. Her gut tightens, her throat constricts, her eyes tingle.

The city is affecting her, changing her. She can taste it when she breathes, feel its heartbeat when watching the life pulsate on the streets below. She is constantly feeling, but no longer feels like herself.

The numbness of her first days has worn off. The schism in her mind brings with it constant migraines, symptoms of the war it endlessly wages with itself – one minute delighting in new sensations, the next, admonishing its lack of focus. Each attempt to resolve the conflict only leaves her tense and tired, sending her into a deeper malaise.

Even now she rubs at her temples, shielding her eyes from the relentless fluorescent lights in the corridors that stretch between her room and Laboratory 16.1. A deep heaviness pulls at her heart as she enters the lab, eclipsing even the migraine building in her skull. This will be her fifth realignment procedure.

She is halfway through undressing when a familiar Technician from her earlier sessions walks in.

"Don't bother changing. We'll be working on conscious limbic response monitoring today."

His voice is deep and flat, thudding into the dense walls that surround them.

Anaiya pulls her kevlar jeans back up and shrugs back into the long-sleeved black shirt she'd left crumpled on the floor. Pulling on her boots, she takes the time to look at the Technician. He is a generation older than her, the five years showing in his leaner frame and a depth to his eyes. His stance is casual, his weight centred on his right leg, hips pushed out to form a languid, obtuse angle from his head to his feet.

He is not attractive, but he is assured and intelligent and something indefinable that nevertheless intrigues her. All of it – the Technician, her appraisal of him, her reaction to him – it all happens in the space of a glance. Before her realignment, he would have been just another Water Elemental in a white coat. Now, he is a complex collection of parts, each hinting at an untold story.

He looks up from his wristplate and over to Anaiya.

"Ready?"

Nodding, she zips up her left boot, absent-mindedly trailing her finger along the interlocked teeth, eyes still trained on the Technician. In the large, circular room next door, a second Technician greets them in the perfunctory way of all Water Elementals. She holds a small black box, into which she plugs Anaiya's lifeline before fastening it to the belt loop of Anaiya's jeans.

She stands too close, fumbling with the clasp. Anaiya can smell the sweet traces of shampoo still lingering in her hair, can feel the tremor of energy trapped between their two bodies in tight proximity. The levity of these sensations is in sharp contrast to the heavy, insistent beating in Anaiya's chest and rapid throbbing at her temples.

Finished with attaching the device, the Technician moves to Anaiya's side – her steps light, her eyes empty. Her touch on Anaiya's forearm is warm, but the pierce of the needle and fluid injection leaves a chill.

"The procedure will begin in a few minutes," she says, completing the final checks of Anaiya's vitals.

The Technician lets go of Anaiya's arm, letting it fall heavy to her side, before leaving her alone in the cold, windowless room.

Anaiya waits for the medication to kick in, but moments pass and she feels no different. Her eyes trace alternating patterns in the tile work of the curved walls, grouping them in different combinations, picking up the slight differences in how they reflect the dim fluorescent lighting. A soft hum of electricity ripples through the air, resonating gently in her ear.

And then it begins.

The white tiles disappear. Anaiya blinks, her eyes clouding for a brief second. When they clear, she finds that she isn't in the room any more: she is in Precinct 5.

Smells and sounds come rushing to her as she steps into the dappled sunlight of Purlunge Van Square. The braided section of the River Syn is less than five hundred metres to the north and it tugs at Anaiya as a current to flotsam. She yields to her instinct and pivots on her heel towards the water.

Part of her wants to move slowly to take in every sensation of being where she *belongs*. The concept comes to her unbidden, clear yet unfamiliar. She doesn't challenge it, just lets it wash over her.

Part of her wants to free-run, to encourage the breeze against her face, feel the smooth, cold steel under her palms.

After a few halting steps mired in hesitation, she pushes at the barrier in her mind – feels it snap – and propels herself forwards into the smooth motion of a sprint.

She weaves between the sparse collection of Elementals, repelling off the walls of buildings and launching into aerials to clear minor obstacles. Buildings, like broad-shouldered Border Watchers, stretch either side along the narrow Rue Dayburn. The effect forces Anaiya's eyes to focus in on the small section of river wall framed at the end of the road. With each leap, aerial and vault it zooms larger and sharper.

Accelerating until only a few buildings remain between her and the wall, she falls into the free-run. Her right foot flexes under a deep lunge, giving her the kinetic energy needed to launch at the final facade; her left finds traction, pushing her higher. Arms extend to grasp the slim horizontal beam that straddles the gap between the opposing buildings. The motion carries her into a backwards somersault – the wall, sky and road streaking in a blur of colours that pulls her eyes shut.

The impact of the river wall under her feet pulls her down into a low crouch, perfectly balanced and steady. She straightens slowly, her eyelids unfurling to reveal the sight before her.

She has seen it before, passed it countless times on her patrols of the Eastern Area. But the sight of it now arrests her.

She is still. More still than she had ever thought was possible in a body full of blood and adrenalin.

The eastern facade of En Dahm fills her vision, presenting four of the fourteen stone arms that buttress its elongated rotunda. It stands offset to her left, its form dissonant with the flat matrix of rectangular prisms flanking it either side. Like Last Defence, the structure predates the Singularity and is devoid of the synthetic rationality of post-Emancipation architecture. It is beautiful.

Tiny details flood her senses, her brain both struggling and delighting in shapes and lines and scales she has never given consideration to.

Absorbed as she is, it takes a while before the echo of an unformed sound filters through her consciousness. There is a delay, a pause in her mind as it transitions from its appreciation of En Dahm.

She swivels, pivoting with precision on the river wall.

A body lies face down on the uneven surface of the road.

Blood flows like miniature rivers along the contours. It mixes with the sand and dirt and debris, forming pools in some areas, thickening to congealed ribbons in others.

Anaiya's mind groans as her consciousness switches gears. Belatedly she remembers to scan the area for the perpetrator, her eyes fixing upon a figure two blocks away, running west.

Confusion settles upon her like a wet rayweave blanket, her mind caught in an impossible conflict. She needs to run after the perpetrator. She needs to protect the victim.

The urgency to do something is stifling, but her body refuses to move. She stands there, heart contorting in her chest, unable to do anything.

SEVEN

Blackness.

Anaiya only becomes aware of it, the deep comforting nothingness, when she is pulled from it.

She is in another lab, lying on a low bed. Her cheeks are damp and cool. The room is too bright and her head hurts. She reaches up to contain the throbbing in her temples, but her left arm jolts as the length of her lifeline stretches taut between her wrist and a large panel inlaid in the nearest wall.

A move to her right shifts her attention – the male Technician from the round room looms large beside her bed.

The round room.

Precinct 5.

Fragmented memories, like razors, slash at the soft, vulnerable parts of her mind.

Her body trembles, then shakes, then pitches in violent convulsions. Her lungs push out loud, incoherent cries of injury. She hears them as a stranger would, their sound intimate yet distant. Her chest heaves as though she has free-run at full speed for an hour and her eyes flood with tears as if surrounded by synth toxin smoke. Her tears fall, unimpeded, in long streams down her temples.

She shuts her eyes tight, struggling to shut out the memories and the sight of her body in tumult, but a smooth, cool touch against her cheek sends them flying open. The Technician stands over her, grasping a small narrow-necked bottle, collecting the liquid evidence of her weakness – of her shame, confusion and despair.

Anaiya's right arm lashes out at him, but he evades the feeble effort easily. A sharp prick at her neck elicits a wail from her lips, but the acute sensation brings with it the welcomed blackness and so she relents and is subdued.

Blackness.

She knows it now. Realises, in the deepest folds of her mind, that it is her ally.

She clings to it. Welcomes the way it wraps around and consumes her.

She embraces it, lets her mind linger in the deep kiss of nothingness and submits entirely to it.

Blackness.

She feels it shift in the tremors of her subconscious. It trembles like a dog in labour. Skittles like Wasteland sand grains over the empty roads of the Edges.

She fights to keep it, to make it stay still, to remain with her in the nothingness.

But it pays her no heed. Her consciousness is slowly stripped of it, her mind an inky midnight sky losing its hue at dawn.

The numbness slakes off her like dead skin, revealing a raw and vulnerable mind.

The light invades her awareness, allowing no quarter for retreat. Meeting the light is difficult. Her eyes resist opening, their lashes sticky with the dense residue of old tears. She will not endure another failure. With more effort, they pull apart – slowly, with resistance.

The room is darker than she had anticipated. Her fingers claw clumsily at her neck, scratching at the point of skin irritated by so many injections. She doesn't stop, letting her nails scrape away the dermis until the blood paints her fingers black. Still she digs, fingertips reaching for the synth concoction that is responsible for her weakness and that courses through her veins.

A vague shadow falls across her face. Anaiya doesn't recognise the Nurse, her eyes drawn to the syringe in his right hand, flashing gold as he moves. Her throat burns with the hoarse roar that she pulls up through her chest and from her lips.

Rage, a fire – her fire – wells inside her, building in intensity.

"Stay away from me," she rasps.

Her eyes never stray from the syringe and the golden liquid that steals her fire.

The Nurse lays his cold hand on her, the syringe inching closer.

"No…"

The single syllable pulls all but final reserves of energy from her.

"Please," she whispers, disgusted at her own vulnerability and desperation.

Blackness.

No longer deep and all-consuming. Its hold on Anaiya is weakened.

Nonetheless she remains in it, using it to help centre her thoughts, deepen her resolve. She has lain awake, floating in the tepid shadows, for a few hours. The passing of time is marked simply in her mind by the succession of small noises and faint smells drifting into the room.

She lies there quiet and still as the chill of reality sobers her mind. In the calm of the blackness she can rationalise her situation, can see that the injections have been sedatives and not enhancers, can recognise that the cause of her altered state is not the synth-medication numbing the pain in her neck and tightness in her muscles.

Can accept that she has been realigned.

The concept floats in her mind, a razor wrapped in so many layers of soft polysilk. She notes it, but otherwise ignores it, careful not to unwrap the buffer that her subconscious has woven. Instead, she concentrates on her breathing. It is a simple Fire Element technique taught to Trainees to help them to make rational, coherent decisions in spite of the significant amounts of adrenalin generated by their typical activities.

The air tastes sweeter than before, free of the astringent synth chemicals that dominate the Last Defence laboratories. She inhales deeply, drawing the long breath down into her diaphragm and holding it there, feeling it swell within her. And then she exhales slowly, pushing her belly against her spine and squeezing the air from her lungs.

Footfalls sound in the corridor outside the room, but she keeps her eyes closed and continues her breathing regimen.

Inhale, hold, exhale.

The footfalls grow louder.

Inhale, hold, exhale. Inhale, hold, exhale.

Slowly she opens her eyes. Details flood her senses. She doesn't fight them, just lets them wash over her. It is easier this way.

Less painful.

She is in her room. Muted afternoon sunlight slants through the west-facing window. The male Technician from the round room stands a metre from her bed, casting long shadows over the bedsheets and Anaiya. He approaches her silently. She takes in his trademark gait, the way his short hair is combed into ordered peaks at the front, the familiar creases at the corner of his violet-tinged eyes.

With each observation comes the rush of involuntary responses triggered by limbic associations now programmed in her mind. Her chest swells, her heart rate quickens, her skin tingles.

She doesn't yet have the words to describe all of the unfamiliar emotions raging through her body, threatening to take her breath away.

Inhale. Exhale. Hold.

She rides out their initial assault – pushing them away, building barriers in her mind – until she is a distant observer, assessing them with cold indifference.

Each transition between her irrational limbic response and her measured neocortex assessment is a victory – a vindication of her innate authenticity as a Fire Elemental, an encouragement that she will survive the realignment intact and be victorious in her ultimate mission.

The Technician's touch is gentle as he unwraps her lifeline and plugs it into his screen. She watches his face intently as it fades from the typical studious intent to something more personal. A small smile breaks at his lips, softening his features. Anaiya feels a smile appear on her own lips in immediate response. And then it passes.

"It worked," he says in a voice soft and clear.

She hears the pride in it, the relief.

"I know," she says.

His brow furrows and he appraises Anaiya more deeply. "What does it feel like?"

He asks it out of professional curiosity, to sate the Water Element's unyielding quest for knowledge. He asks with the presumption of rational, incisive, clear-headed analysis that he has come to expect from Fire Elementals.

But how can she articulate the chaos of her mind? Before the realignment, she had known satisfaction and ambition and adrenalin and determination. Clear, sharp emotions that left no residue. The new emotions are different, messier...some heavier and denser, others lighter, more fragile, more brittle. Happiness, sadness, fear – names she has heard from a thousand perpetrators, but never felt herself.

"It feels different," she concludes limply.

The Technician blinks, his smile fading and the distant professionalism reappearing.

Anaiya feels the warmth drain from her, feels her chest tighten. A split second later, her Fire neocortex steps in to soften the blow. But deep in her subconscious she can feel the sadness still lingering, adding to a collection of things she has wrapped and buried.

"Your vitals are much better," the Technician states, reaching down to release her from the restraints. "We weren't sure whether your mind would recover."

Anaiya doesn't immediately register the admission, her focus taken with her liberated wrists. A heartbeat later it catches in her chest. "You weren't sure?" She pushes herself up into a sitting position.

The Technician is once again absorbed in the data flashing on his screen.

"We obviously knew it would be more complex than the Premie alignment," he says distractedly. "Premie minds are completely elastic. Their alignment is a natural progression. It conditions the mind, strengthens it." He looks over at Anaiya. "Alignment does to the mind what physical training does to undeveloped muscles," he explains. "Juvenile muscles respond readily to alignment and conditioning because it promotes them to an advanced state."

Anaiya nods slowly, understanding the truth of what he is saying, but unsure how it relates to her situation.

Satisfied she is comprehending, the Technician turns back to his screen. "But, obviously, you aren't a Premie," he continues. "Your mind has already been conditioned to its optimal state. Realignment takes a mind perfectly conditioned for one function, rapidly undoes that conditioning, and reconditions it to perform optimally in another function. Realignment is like…" He pauses, searching for the right analogy.

"Training for a marathon, rushing through a recovery and then performing a sprint," Anaiya finishes for him.

The Technician nods, accepting her contribution. "Yes. If the predisposition for marathon running is too strong, or the recovery period not sufficient…"

Anaiya doesn't hear him finish. She is remembering her third week as a career Peacekeeper. She was so keen to impress, to continue the trajectory she had established as a Trainee, to cement her reputation as a Peacekeeper worthy of note and escape Kane's legacy.

An Earth Elemental Trainee, high on dex and still young and fast enough to gather speed, led a pursuit through the Eastern Area after hitting an enhancer supply warehouse. Anaiya had been the first to see evidence of the break-in, to identify the perpetrator more than half a kilometre away and to set chase.

Moments later Niamh caught up to her and was matching her pace for pace. She pushed harder, but it wasn't enough, and he started to pull ahead. She had pushed harder still, ignoring the strain in her calves, which built to a groan and then to a scream. She had pushed until she caught up to Niamh, both of them fighting as much to beat the other as to catch the perpetrator.

The pain was sudden, as if an invisible baton had slammed point down into her right calf, rupturing an internal sac and releasing liquid fire up and down her leg. It pulled her up and sent her crashing into the hard pavement of the road; the pain in her damaged arms paled in comparison to the white-hot explosion in her leg. In that instant, she had forgotten about the perpetrator, about Niamh streaking ahead.

The pain had surrounded her. Consumed her. It took the air from her lungs, speech from her lips, thoughts from her mind. Pain – endless, excruciating pain.

She had spent four weeks in the Curei Infirmary after Biomechanic Specialists had stitched back the grade three tear and inoculated the calf with repair cells. Four weeks of incapacitation and immobilisation. She had often woken to the sound of Nurses debating whether she would ever run again.

Could that have happened to her brain? Could Neural Technicians even fix a broken mind?

"But, it has recovered, hasn't it?" Anaiya asks, returning to the beginning of their conversation.

The Technician nods, absorbed by the screen shifting under the incessant flickering of his fingers.

"As far as we can tell," he confirms vaguely. "We'll run a few more tests and conduct some more conditioning over the next few days to increase our degree of confidence."

Anaiya lowers herself back onto the bed, sinking her head down into the deep softness of her pillow. The Technician finishes his analysis and exits the room.

Leaving Anaiya to walk the edges of her mind, testing for cracks.

EIGHT

A fuzzy sense of anxiety follows Anaiya around for the next week as she is subjected to more procedures, tests, evaluations and simulations – all designed to maintain and strengthen her new limbic brain.

There is no break in the routine and Anaiya wonders whether her feet are wearing grooves into the polyenameline floors as she traipses back and forth between her room and the 35th floor laboratories.

Opening the door of Laboratory 35.1, she takes a deep breath and prepares herself for the injections and electrodes and analysis machines.

"Hello, Anaiya 234."

The Water Commander from the Code Five briefing in Precinct 8, from another lifetime, stands in the centre of the lab. Flanked by two Technicians, she betrays no interest in Anaiya's arrival, entirely focussed on the mobile screens flashing before her. Anaiya's anxiety sharpens, sending synthflies to her belly.

"Your results show good progress," the Commander says, not looking up from the screens. "You are ready for the next stage of your realignment."

With a flick of her hand, she dismisses the Technicians, before beckoning Anaiya to follow her through to the control room – a small annexure located off the laboratory where the Technicians undertake their observations and analysis.

"Sit," she commands, lowering herself into a large, cushioned chair.

Anaiya takes a seat on one of the nylon office chairs, the situation faintly reminiscent of their last encounter.

"You're scheduled for deployment in a few weeks. You will continue realignment strengthening and conditioning, but as of tomorrow you will also commence training for your new competency."

It is the moment she has been dreading. As inevitable as it is, the assignment of a new competency will mark the end of her time as a Peacekeeper.

Temporarily.

The clarification isn't as comforting as it should be; 'temporarily' has no clear end date.

"You've been assigned as a Sound Creator."

The pronouncement catches her off-guard. "Excuse me?"

The Commander raises a single eyebrow at the interruption. Anaiya's face flushes with heat. She hadn't meant to speak up. But she hadn't expected to be assigned as a Sound Creator, either.

It was supposed to be Dancer.

Dancer made more sense – her body and mind were already attuned to the physicality, flexibility and coordination required. It was an easy cover to maintain. It was an easier transition to make.

"I know nothing about Sound Creation."

The familiar sigh is unmistakable. "Hence the training. Which you will commence tomorrow."

She waits, narrowing her eyes at Anaiya, clearly communicating she will not tolerate another interruption. Anaiya remains silent, unwilling to give voice to her growing confusion.

"You will report to the Nursery at 0800 hours, where you will be oriented with hypoxia-affected Air Elementals. That is your backstory. You are not to engage with the other Elementals – you will not be expected to, nor put in a position to. Do you understand?"

Anaiya nods. Hypoxia is the perfect alibi. Passionate outbursts are typical for Air Elementals – triage rooms consistently fill with dazed Musicians and Graphic Artists who stumble in broken and bloody after intense fights. Head injuries are commonplace and, when they escalate to genuine trauma and oxygen deprivation, brain damage inevitably results in demotion to a lesser competency. Unable to interact in their original environment or derive inspiration from it, affected Elementals are often transferred to new competencies in new Areas.

"Good. You are dismissed."

Anaiya's feet fly over the well-worn streets of Precinct 1. The early morning air is cool and still and the path she takes is marked by its absence of Elementals. Warehouses sit idle; their windows dark and flumes silent. Minutes pass and the smell of the river grows stronger. She had never noticed it before her realignment, but now she picks up the individual scents that make up its distinctive smell. The sour tang, the musty undertones.

Ahead, the walls of the Nursery loom into view and, this close, she can hear the sounds of hundreds of Elemental Pre-forms; laughing, crying, yelling, playing. Next year they will be tested and aligned. A year later they will spend their final year at the Nursery, the final year of their first lustrum, being conditioned to their Element. And then another generation will be created, and the cycle will begin again.

Anaiya's memories as a Pre-form in the Nursery are fractured and cast in the surreal light of a four-year-old's memory. She remembers long days confined within the Nursery walls and an overwhelming curiosity about the outside world. More vivid are her memories as a Premie – the ten years she spent with her Fire cohort. There had been fifty of them – fifty Premies to make up one of six Fire cohorts. In the beginning she had thought she would spend the rest of her life with them, that they were connected somehow.

She laughs now at the sentimentality, even as it dredges something raw up from her centre. In the end, only three Premies from her cohort graduated as Peacekeeper Trainees. Only two are still alive to remember it.

And here she is again, the same trepidation she felt almost

twenty years ago rushing over her as she enters the Nursery grounds. She expects the feeling to lighten as she makes her way to the designated training room, but it only grows heavier, weighing down her steps and slowing her arrival. She pulls at the loose sleeves of her Air attire, irrationally wishing for the tight familiarity of her Peacekeeper uniform.

"And that is everyone," an older Water Elemental intones, nodding at Anaiya as she enters the room. "You may commence the training."

While the room is small, it easily accommodates the Sound Creator Trainer, Water Observer and the two hypoxic Air Elementals already seated at individual desks.

Anaiya takes a seat at the remaining desk towards the back of the room. Its surface is inlaid with an expansive sheet of leibler polymer that reflects a softer version of Anaiya back to her. She reaches out to touch it. At the slightest pressure of her fingertips, the entire table flashes to life. A vibrant green streak appears as evidence of her contact, accompanied by a bright shimmering noise that gains in pitch as it fades in volume.

The rest of the room immediately turn to regard her, the Water Observer scowling at the unexpected interruption.

"Well, then," the Trainer says, a broad smile settling on his face. "Let's start Sound Creating."

"Plug your lifelines into the desk jack," the Water Observer instructs. "I will be monitoring your vitals throughout the training. I've overseen the alignment of hundreds of Premies over the years, of course, but have also worked with Elementals suffering irreversible hypoxia, teratogenesis and neurocognitive injury. Some anxiety, headaches or distress is normal for these sessions; anything more serious will be immediately addressed."

She looks around the room at each of the students, watching them plug in their lifelines before nodding to herself and taking a seat at the terminal at the front of the room.

"Excellent," the Air Trainer says. "Welcome to Module One."

A tap on his glass screen and the room fills with sound. Anaiya's desk screen shifts into a complex dashboard that flashes different colours at different intensities as the music itself shifts, rising to crescendos and fading to whispers.

"To begin with, I just want you to observe the music. Find its shape, watch its movement."

The complex melody condenses into a simple piece. Anaiya locates its pattern on the desk screen, watching dense beats appear as pixelated squares that grow in height with increased volume and deepen in colour with depth of register. Hollow sounds send yellow waves across the lower part of the dashboard; metallic sounds translate as spikes that peak narrower for higher pitches.

With each swipe of the Trainer's hand, a new piece of music emerges. The room is filled with the fast and dense pieces Anaiya listened to as a Peacekeeper and then with the intricate melodies of her realignment. Another swipe and the room is filled with a bright, pacy tune that bounces as it builds. He swipes again and strong, consistent beats vibrate with clear, metallic chimes. Again and again, the Trainer swipes his hand across his glass screen, allowing the music to fill the room before condensing it into distinct structural parts for the students to learn.

Anaiya becomes absorbed with the dashboard. Her eyes dart between the various displays until she no longer merely hears the music, but genuinely sees it. With each change of colour, wavelength, peak and column, she anticipates the accompanying change in the music.

Her earlier trepidation fades as the music takes control, her mind ejecting unnecessary thoughts and complicated memories, completely absorbed by the visualisation in front of her.

Almost instinctively, her fingers reach out to touch the abstract images on the screen. The sounds amplify.

Intrigued, she delays her next touches, smiling when the expected echo ripples along the melody. The music patterns grow in complexity, but in them she sees the opportunity for new tangents, mirror images and echoes.

Her fingers swipe and tap and flicker over the screen in intricate patterns, sometimes complementing the dominant music pattern, sometimes competing.

The push and pull of the melody's path – sometimes submission, sometimes transcendence – is a free-run in miniature;

its fluctuating pace, its saut du fronds, kash vaults, demitours – all echoes against a set landscape, all flourishes of various frivolity.

And then there is no landscape, no dominant melody, just the music that emerges from under Anaiya's fingers. It is bold, and soft, and spiky and tentative, and all the things that she is. It peaks and lulls, and finally it stops.

The silence rushes into the room and she looks up.

The other two students stare at her, and the Observer is scowling again, but the Trainer is beaming.

"Well," he says. "It seems we have a Symbiotic."

Symbiotic.

It is a word that she hasn't heard since her graduation. All Elementals have a strong compatibility with their designated competencies, but as with most things, there are degrees of difference. For Premies, the stronger the affinity to a competency, the higher the rank they graduate in to.

Symbiotics were Elementals who had *complete* affinity with their competency. They weren't rare, but they weren't common. When graduating as a Peacekeeper, Anaiya had hoped she would be graded Symbiotic, but no Peacekeepers of her generation had earned that honour.

The Water Observer barks out a short laugh.

"I don't think *Symbiotic* is an appropriate assessment," she says, shooting a disapproving look at the Air Trainer. "There is no precedent for hypoxic Elementals to be Symbiotic. The likelihood is *negligible.* And in any case, that would be an assessment for a Neural Interpreter."

"Of course," the Trainer responds, hands held up in submission.

The Observer nods, placated, and the two other students smile, returning their gaze to the front. Anaiya slowly exhales.

Not Symbiotic.

Perhaps. But there had been an ease to her Sound Creation, a thing born of intuition and not focus. It had taken years to reach that state of flow with her Peacekeeping. The thought is unsettling.

"Let's continue," the Trainer says, flashing Anaiya a wink before pulling up the next module.

NINE

The weeks pass by in a haze of limited awareness. The tests are easier – simpler to navigate, simpler to leave behind as she transitions back into reality. The Sound Creation modules continue to provide more interest and less challenge.

But the nights are harder to navigate. In the darkness, the muscle memory of her Fire identity calls on Anaiya to escape the walls of Last Defence and free-run through the glittering streets below. It fights against the subconscious of her Air identity, the part of her mind that sings sweetly, begging her to give voice to the music that builds and cascades within.

The conflict between her two desires renders her immobilised – leaving her consumed by the need to do both and disabled from doing either.

Normally, the nurozav dulls the pain, but tonight the pills offer no relief. She swallows another two, then four – their bitter coating flashing with hints of salt ash. With her heart fluttering, she glances again at the decrypted message on her wristplate.

Deployment Briefing commences tomorrow. Attend to R4.16 - 48.870622°N, 2.316869°E at 0600. Confirm acknowledgement immediately.

It is her first reminder of life as a Peacekeeper since the realignment. It is supposed to bring her relief from the confusion, to plug her back in to her old life and provide an escape from this limbo. Instead, she finds herself lying on the cold, hard floor of her apartment letting the nurozav steal away her thoughts and fears.

Hours later, an insistent beeping vibrates up through her arm and pricks at her consciousness, waking her an hour before the briefing is to commence. As she sits, her stomach roils violently and she lurches forwards, choking on the acrid bile that comes up with the meagre contents of her stomach.

With shaking hands she grabs a discarded shirt lying nearby and rubs it vigorously over the floor to erase the evidence. She showers and dresses quickly and it is only when she has finished pulling her boots on that she opens the map application on her wristplate to check for her destination. A small red circle appears centred on the screen, positioned in an administrative quarter of Precinct 8.

Anaiya's right hand hesitates over the wristplate before she taps on the circle to confirm the location. Even before the details come up, she knows she has been there before.

Outside Last Defence the morning sky is still dark, the Precincts still quiet. Running brings her no relief, her leaden feet thudding along the streets of Otpor to Precinct 8's Peacekeeper headquarters.

It is only a short distance from Last Defence, but the avenues seem longer, time stickier. Her mind prickles with the hint of an imminent threat.

As a Peacekeeper, she had relied on her body's subtle appreciation of danger to rapidly assess situations, diffuse weight and pre-empt attacks. Now, it acts like an opposing magnet, resisting every step she takes towards her destination, pulling her back towards Last Defence.

The thought of deployment teases at her mind's edges, but it is the thought of seeing and of being seen by Fire Elementals that causes her throat to tighten and stomach to shrink. She wonders if they will recognise her as an imposter, as damaged, as some sick joke.

Minutes later, the shadow of the familiar ten-storey building pulls Anaiya up short. She stands there, shallow breath catching in her chest while her eyes scale the facade to take in details of the reflected city. Peacekeepers sprint past her, flowing around her at speed while she stands motionless. She avoids looking too closely at them, her gaze never straying from the building before her.

Her first step towards the building's entrance is an echo of her first step as a Premie leaving the Nursery. And of her first step as a Peacekeeper graduate entering the Eastern Area on assignment. But where those first steps were full of hope and excited anticipation, this one is full of confusion and anxiety.

She pushes against the inertia holding her tethered to the courtyard and continues forwards. Her instincts keep her head low, her feet dragging her to the building's entrance. Through the entryway and lobby and up the eastern staircase, she doesn't pause until she has swiped her wristplate across the panel outside room 4.16 and entered the space.

Inside, a small gathering of four Peacekeepers stand around in their characteristic inwards-facing circle, all angles of the room observed by at least one pair of eyes. The two facing Anaiya look up casually as she enters. The female on the left is of Anaiya's generation. Her stance is relaxed, but the readiness flashing in her eyes is reflected in the way she centres her weight forwards and keeps her arms hanging loose and unobstructed by her side.

Anaiya was once like this.

Her eyes drop to the Peacekeeper's solar plexus. In her mind, Anaiya sees herself reach out to steal the Fire from this stranger and use it to replace the flame that has been extinguished inside her.

Consumed by her thoughts, she doesn't notice when the other two Peacekeepers turn to regard her. It is only when a deep, familiar voice calls her name that she tears her gaze away from the female.

"Hello, Ani."

Anaiya breathes in the melodic syllable, the diminutive catching in her throat. It has been a lifetime since she last saw Niamh, yet she sees him clearly as she did then – sitting unmoved in Last Defence as she agreed to sacrifice her Fire. The pang at her centre deepens in intensity and sharpness. While many emotions are still unknown and unfamiliar to her, betrayal is not one of them.

Anaiya nods her greeting, unable to speak with her throat still constricted. The other three Peacekeepers appraise her silently.

"All right, let's begin," he announces, gesturing towards the row of bench seats that sit against the wall to his left.

As Anaiya takes her seat with the other three, Niamh activates the wallscreen at the front of the room. A large map of Otpor appears on the wall, each precinct coloured to represent the Element dominant there and dotted presumably with the locations of Heterodoxy events.

"All of you have been summoned here today as recruits for Operation Inferno. As of now, all substantive Peacekeeping duties will cease until the successful conclusion of the Operation. Your Area Commanders have been informed that you have been appropriated for Special Ops but do not know the target or mission. You are not to tell them. As of today, all of you, except Anaiya, will be transferred to this Precinct for the remainder of the Operation. You will answer to me, and only me, as Task Force Commander."

Anaiya glances down to the insignia embroidered just below his left collar. The golden insignia is now encircled by a thick red line. *Peace Protector.* Niamh has been promoted. Again. How much has her realignment contributed to his new standing?

"I don't need to tell you how dire the situation is," he continues. "As of today, we have thirty confirmed cases of Heterodoxy, all presented in the same format."

The screen switches from the map of Otpor to a graphic run of all thirty murals. The first two are instantly familiar, representing the first case she discovered in the Edges and the one she removed in Precinct 11. She watches transfixed as the remaining twenty-eight cases are presented. Isolated in her Last Defence room, with no wallscreen or information terminal, she has been protected from the increasing spate of attacks.

"Water Elementals have crunched the data and have developed a target profile at a ninety-five per cent confidence interval."

The screen shifts again, zooming in to Precinct 18 within the Northern Area Command.

"Based on their intel, we are looking at an Air Elemental inhabiting or extremely active in Precinct 18, likely within their fifth or sixth lustrum and assigned to a Graphics-related corp –

Advertising, Gaming Development, Propaganda.

"Water Analysts will continue to feed us intel from the Northern Area Command and we'll target surveillance in rotating hubs across the various divisions of the Precinct. Jenna, Tristan, Che – you'll be following up leads, gathering additional intel on the ground and cultivating informants."

The other three Peacekeepers nod their assent. Their task is a familiar one. They have not been selected on their ability to perform the task, but because of a demonstrated excellence in one of the core Peacekeeping attributes – speed, rapid response or ability to sense weight. Anaiya sizes up each of the Peacekeepers, trying to assess which attribute they excel in. The two male Peacekeepers, Tristan and Che, ignore her pointed gaze. Jenna, however, returns it evenly.

"And what does she do?" Jenna asks, never taking her eyes from Anaiya's.

"Anaiya will be doing close surveillance."

Anaiya surrenders her gaze from the confrontation with Jenna to look at Niamh. She notices for the first time the way his eyes crease slightly when that half-grin, half-smirk plays at the corners of his mouth, notices how his T-shirt pulls when he reaches up to brush strands of hair from his face. His gaze again locks on Anaiya, but this confrontation elicits an entirely different response.

She recalls in rapid succession all the times they have been intimate, sensations and images flashing like a channel scan through her memories. His hand trailing on bare flesh, teeth sinking into the soft part where neck meets shoulder, the sweet musk of sex, the wildfire of abandonment in his eyes. They come to her heavier, laden with meaning not there before. Their sex is no longer categorised with the other practical and physical acts. It holds a deeper attachment, contains a previously hidden music.

Caught off-guard by her thoughts, she hurriedly breaks her gaze with Niamh, fixing her gaze to the map on the wallscreen.

"And how is she going to do that without compromising the Operation?"

Anaiya waits for Niamh's rebuke of Jenna's interruption, but it never comes. She surreptitiously observes the body language engagement between the two. Jenna does not share the straight-backed posture or folded arms of the other two Peacekeepers and she holds Niamh's gaze easily. Niamh has shifted his wide stance, his torso now angled towards Jenna. Anaiya takes in the way his left hand rests on his hip, fingers tangled in his jean belt loops, while his right scratches the stubble at his chin, fingers dragging along his angular jawline. The recognition of familiarity between them slams into Anaiya.

"We have our ways."

She concentrates on Niamh's eyes, looking for hints of disgust or embarrassment. Instead they glitter, accentuating the smile that broadens across his face. It is a smile she knows, though not the smile of his betrayal. It is the smile of pursuit – of adrenalin and anticipation. Memories of free-running with him – patrolling the city and going toe-to-toe with offenders – bounce off each other in her mind. They should be good memories, but instead her stomach tightens and a familiar anxiety tickles along her nerves.

"…in Precinct 18."

Niamh's voice breaks Anaiya out of her reverie. He is facing the wallscreen, swiping his hand across its surface to bring up a larger-scale map at street level of the precinct.

"Our job is to feed her the right intel to give her access to the right spaces and the opportunities to come into contact with our Elementals of interest."

He swipes his hand again to reveal a communication hierarchy.

"Jenna, Tristan and Che, you will feed your surveillance and informant data directly through to me, which will be passed on to Water Intel Analysts along with any other data coming in from the Northern Area Command and other Area Commands where Heterodox murals continue to appear. This intel will continue to shape our investigation strategy – we will meet every week here at headquarters to discuss our plan going forward.

"Anaiya, I will contact you remotely to give you your instructions. You will receive an encrypted message with the codeword 'inferno' within the first three lines of content. Once you are in a secured location, you are to call the number that will appear in the second last line of text."

Anaiya nods her understanding of the standard Peacekeeper protocol.

"Under no circumstances are any of you to have direct contact with Anaiya. All comms are to come directly from me or directly to me. You will see her in the streets, you will see her in contact with Air Elementals of interest. You will not approach her. You will come to me with your surveillance intel and I will direct your next course of action. Is that clear?"

The other Peacekeepers nod silently. It is a point that doesn't need emphasis; Peacekeepers are obedient to their superiors by nature and conditioning. They will not be briefed on her realignment procedure. It will remain as Niamh's secret to keep.

The next four hours are spent going through intelligence supplied by Water Intel Analysts. Anaiya drifts in and out of attention – one minute, absorbed by the information that flashes on the wallscreen and streams from Niamh's lips, the next, distracted by the shadows along Niamh's jawline or fixated on the patterns that the street grid of Precinct 18 trails across the wall.

Once again, it is Niamh who breaks her out of the maze inside her mind. He triple taps on the wallscreen and it shuts off in a quick burst of light. The briefing has concluded. Anaiya hesitates before she moves, letting the other Peacekeepers head towards the room's exit before she stands up.

She watches uncomfortably as Jenna lingers when passing Niamh, pushing up on her toes to whisper something into his ear. She watches for Niamh's reaction and looks hurriedly away at the broad grin that grows on his face.

One…Two…Three…

Anaiya looks up. Jenna is exiting the room and Niamh stands, arms folded, staring at her. His grin has faded into an easy smile. Anaiya's heart rate spikes and heat threatens to travel up from her belly to her cheeks.

It is just Niamh.

The same Niamh she raced through the Nursery grounds. The same Niamh who matched her jump for jump, vault for vault, aerial for aerial as they free-ran across the Eastern Area. The same Niamh who touched her and took her in the shower.

The heat is threatening to return.

"How do you know Jenna?" she asks quickly, without thinking – her unfiltered limbic brain coming to the fore.

"We worked on a task force a few years back," he says, looking briefly over his shoulder at the empty doorway before returning to face Anaiya. "We've been intimate a few times."

It is nothing unexpected, yet she cannot respond. The pause grows pregnant and suffocating.

"Why, Ani? Are you jealous?"

She can hear the teasing in his voice, see it in the way he cocks his head to the side and quirks his lips up into a faint smile. A hazy memory of the last time they were together, when she asked the same flippant question, tickles in the back of her mind.

It floats in the background, utterly dominated by a more urgent and intense reaction: she's overwhelmed by her realisation that this complex tapestry of emotions that have plagued her since she walked into the room have a name – a name she knows and is ashamed of.

Anaiya *is* jealous. Jealous of Niamh and Jenna and their intimacy. Jealous of their pure Peacekeeper status and untouched Fire Elemental minds. Jealous of the Anaiya she used to be.

It hits her like a well-weighted blow to her stomach, knocking the wind from her lungs and all coherent thought from her mind. She closes her eyes tightly, grabbing at her stomach.

Through the fuzziness she can hear Niamh asking if she is OK, feel the weight of his hand at the small of her back.

A faint voice in the depths of her mind is screaming to her through the layers of panic, confusion, shame and jealousy. She clings to it, letting it become clearer until it pierces her neocortex.

Clear it, Anaiya. CLEAR IT.

Beat.

Blink.

Snap.

Her eyes clear and the weight at her core lifts. Anaiya feels the familiar sloughing of her brain as it pulls back the messy layer of limbic thoughts to reveal a clear neocortex. She looks into Niamh's eyes, no longer pools to drown in, just brown-tinted orbs fixed in his face like any other pair on any other Elemental.

"Sorry," she says in a tight, clear voice. "The realignment medication."

The quasi-lie rolls easily off her tongue, her Air brain gifting her an advantage at last. Niamh's frown fades and he nods, accepting her explanation.

"How has it been?" he asks, a Peacekeeper inspecting his weapon for faults.

Anaiya pauses, giving herself time to word her reply, to frame it as a proper Peacekeeper would.

"It is what it is. I just want to complete the mission and return the Orthodoxy."

TEN

The subterranean worm is quiet when Anaiya boards it pre-dawn.

So it has come to this.

Traversing the city by public transport was for the disabled or the lazy. For stationary Elementals. Peacekeepers were meant to fly along streets, not shuttle along tunnels.

I am not a Peacekeeper.

The admission is a difficult one. One that has not grown easier over the weeks leading up to this day – the day of her deployment.

She sits in the last seat of the last segment with her back against the wall. Resting her head against the window, she rubs her right hand along the raised pattern of skin that runs up her left arm. A shiver of sensitivity hinting at pain blooms along her forearm, the ink still raw.

The skin ink was the final orientation into her Air identity before her deployment. The Designer had been instructed to embellish her with a typical pattern, authentic but not conspicuous. The Air Elemental had rolled her eyes at Anaiya, grumbling about sterile Water Technicians with no understanding of art, and then she had asked Anaiya what it was that she wanted to be marked with.

Like her limbic realignment, the mark would be temporary, the superficial decoration removed and her body healed upon completion of her mission. So when the Skin Designer had asked her for her preference, she had not properly considered it. She had toyed with the idea of something to remind her of her Fire, but in the end, had submitted to her Air identity.

The Skin Designer had worked without pause, hand flashing over the mobile screen in direct response to the music transmitted from Anaiya's wristplate to her ears. Once finished, she had uploaded the design into the skin printer and positioned Anaiya's arm in the small gap between it and the steel bench. At the last moment, she had offered her earphones to Anaiya.

Music from Anaiya's time at Last Defence, the music she had created in transition from Fire to Air, played over and over on repeat, while the prick of twenty fine needles stitched their way along her forearm.

Even now, despite the angriness of tortured skin, the talent in the design is remarkable. As it was that afternoon in the Nursery, her music is perfectly visualised.

She sighs and pulls the sleeve down over her forearm. The mechanical worm passes through three precincts before anyone else boards her segment. Two Air Elementals sit in the seats closest to the door. Their voices carry to Anaiya, drunken squeals about the night's adventures in Air izakayas. Anaiya plugs in the earphones connected to her wristplate, closes her eyes and lets the sound of the music and the motion of the worm wash over her. Precinct 18 is still forty minutes and a changeover away.

Fifteen minutes later, Anaiya changes at Riverside Station, pushing through the throng of other Elementals trying to board. Turning the sound down on her wristplate, she listens for announcements on platform departures and worm disruptions and begins to weave her way through the crowds towards Platform B. Lower-caste Water Elementals, with their kydex satchels and polyester suits, scurry with their heads down, jostling each other as they race to make the express service from the affordable residential precincts in the South East to the main administrative precincts of 1 and 2. Anaiya bristles at the invasion of her personal space, but does not react, forcing her head down and her feet to keep moving.

The crowd eases as she makes her way down the connecting tunnel; the sparsely populated space of Platform B a welcome relief to her fraying nerves. Finding a spot in the middle of the platform, she allows herself to lean against a structural post connecting the bitumen floor to the tiled ceiling.

She closes her eyes, and the sounds of the platform crystallise into an undulating melody – the staccato of footsteps, the fading in and out of voices as they near and then pass her, the steady hum of aluminate lights kept charged by the friction of the city's worms against their tracks.

It is an interesting symphony, full of both familiar and unfamiliar sounds, but with a cohesive rhythm that pulls all the noises together as a single piece. Anaiya gives her mind over to the music, letting it wash over her without analysing or deconstructing it. Just enjoying it.

Without warning, a discordant, high-pitched squeal breaks the easy rhythm of the platform, echoing in the mouth of the tunnel. Anaiya turns towards its origin as the noise bounces against the enamalite tiles and builds in timbre.

Peacekeepers in dark kevlar uniforms are already free-running towards the sound, vaulting off the tunnel walls and turning aerials to evade the messy throng of mixed Elementals. Anaiya watches their precise choreography, the sight catching her breath and culminating in a familiar longing. There is something beautiful and complex underlying the natural simplicity of their movements. She twists to follow their dance, watching transfixed as they close in on the disruption.

An older Earth Elemental, stumbling and cursing, is swinging wild punches at a cowering Water Elemental. Younger Air Elementals stand to the side, wristplates in a mock salute, recording the spectacle for uploading and rapid distribution to the masses.

Her eyes glaze past them, her focus consumed by the rough tears in the Earth Elemental's skin, the scars along his forearm and the emptiness in his eyes. He is an outcast in a microcosm of Air and Water Elementals, staring down the wrath of Fire Elementals alone and disoriented. His stance falters and his attempts at violence present as harmless swings.

Anaiya's heart beats faster and heavier with every disconnected attempt, every metre gained by the approaching Peacekeepers. She watches as a younger Peacekeeper in virgin kevlars lands a flawless aerial just metres from the stumbling Elemental.

Anaiya sees the outcome before it happens – her mind future-searching in a hybrid mix that is neither the short-term, clinical approach of a Peacekeeper, nor the vague and imprecise wanderings of her Air limbic brain.

She sees the enthusiasm in the Trainee Peacekeeper, sees her precise movements fusing into a single blow delivered in strict compliance with protocol. She sees unsteady feet failing the Earth Elemental, hears the crunch of his head on impact with the hard floor tiles, smells the reek of genievre spilling from his shattered bottle.

Anaiya doesn't watch as the situation unfolds in real time. She pivots away from the scene, dragging her finger upwards along her wristplate to increase the sound function's volume and fill her ears with dense, synthetic sounds. Even so, she cannot evade the altercation completely.

The distinctive aroma of the genievre reaches above the musty smell of the tunnel to fill her nose and scratch her throat. She gags unexpectedly, but still keeps her eyes down.

Moments later, the worm slowly pulls into the platform. Anaiya catches sight of standard-issue Peacekeeper kevlars in her peripheral vision and turns her head to block them from view.

She remembers herself as a confident Peacekeeper – assured and decisive in her actions, righteous and incorruptible in her protection of the Orthodoxy. As a Peacekeeper, she had always pushed to be the best, to undertake her duties flawlessly and without question. But now, with the rigidity of her Peacekeeper mind softened by realignment, she feels the threads of doubt coil around her conscience, hinting at the once-invisible line between competence and aggression. She had seen no beauty in the Peacekeeper response to the harmless Earth Elemental.

The dense feeling at her core intensifies as the passengers disembarking the worm exit onto Platform A. She endures the interminable passage of minutes, silently cursing the aimless bumbling of Elementals viewed through the warped glass of the segment's windows. Finally, the doors facing Platform B open and

Anaiya is grateful for the pressing of Air Elementals at her sides and back, cocooning her as she makes her way into the segment.

Two stations on and the connecting worm to Precinct 18 is full. Anaiya stands pressed against the door of the designated Air segment, staring absently out the window as the view shifts from the black walls of the worm tunnel to brightly lit platforms. At each deceleration of the worm, Anaiya's fingers pick at the metal ridge of her wristplate and her gaze darts across the platform, searching for and avoiding signs of conflict. Each time the worm pulls out of the station without incident and back into the darkness of its tunnel.

Thirty minutes and nine stations later, the worm emerges into the soft light of the morning, the muted whirring of its engine a welcome soundtrack. By this time, the segment is mostly empty, but Anaiya remains standing next to the door – keeping vigil as the mismatched, haphazard collection of structures and materials of her new precinct come into view.

ELEVEN

The afternoon air is still and wraps around Anaiya like a keffiyeh. The insistent heat of the afternoon pulls at her to free-run but she tempers the urge, her feet plodding along in slow, measured strides.

Sweat and dust set her skin itching, her discomfort growing with every step. A minor inconvenience. *A simple price to pay for escaping that room.*

Her new accommodation – a modest studio – is located in a rundown, ten-storey apartment complex. Situated near the Northern Border, its rent is cheap and the building is populated by a mixed and ever-changing complement of Elementals. The room itself is large and fully furnished with comfortable Air pieces, but it is not the size or quality that makes it oppressive. It is the waiting.

Three days she had cocooned herself in it – waiting for instructions, intelligence, anything that would kickstart this miserable mission. Hours spent staring at her wristplate, scrolling through her glass screen, maintaining a silent vigil in anticipation of the *ping* that would give her permission to escape her confines.

It had come without warning or fanfare, a simple brief with accompanying coordinates. It hadn't mattered – she had been halfway down the stairwell by the time she had read the full message.

Walking through Precinct 18 takes on a surreal quality – the afternoon heat has stilled activity along the narrow streets and laneways, and for a moment it is as if time has stopped. The Precinct is a hybrid – roads crowded with Air izakaya and galleries intersect with Water administration buildings and offices, overshadowed by tall Earth residential complexes interspersed with large drinking halls. This close to the Edges, Fire izakaya and training gyms are also dotted around the streets. She drags her feet past them all, taking in their differences, their unique identities.

A sudden movement to her left and the cold rush of conditioned air startles her. A lone Border Watcher exits one of the gyms, pausing briefly at the sight of Anaiya. Her breath sticks in her chest, her eyes unable to look away from the Watcher.

"You selling, putain?"

Putain. Whore.

Anaiya blushes. It may or may not be an insult – Sex Workers are among the least respected Air Elementals, but there are many of them and they are popular with solitary Border Watchers. It doesn't matter; Anaiya's neocortex, still governed by her Fire identity, registers the offense and triggers a flood of shame. She shakes out of her stupor and hastens away from the Border Watcher.

"What's wrong, putain?" the Border Watcher calls out after her, her laugh dominant in the quiet street. "Are you playing hard to catch?"

The laugh follows Anaiya, pushing her to walk faster and faster until her feet threaten to lift from the pavement and run. With each thundering step, she feels the tension, like a scream, welling up inside her.

I hate this.

The unexpected emotion, and the vehemence with which it pierces her mind, pulls her up. Her step falters and she stands there, sucking in shaky breaths and looking around at the unfamiliar territory.

The Border Watcher is streets away. And Anaiya is streets away from where she should be. Her neocortex has moved on to telling her to focus on the mission, but the residue of her anger and shame lingers and keeps her from moving.

Move, Anaiya. Just move.

The words echo in her head, but do nothing to motivate her.

If you don't move, you will be stuck here forever.

Slowly her mind clears, the last vestiges of emotion fading enough to be overpowered. Her legs pull her forwards like a synthfly in silicone. Each step is weighted with resistance, but she keeps moving until she reaches her destination.

The silent, still streets of Precinct 18 are immediately thrown into contrast as she steps into the Red Clock Gallery. The space is crowded to capacity. Scores of Air Elementals move and mingle around the small space – talking, arguing, flirting, laughing.

A phantom itch brushes between Anaiya's shoulder blades. She glances around for the other Peacekeeper she knows will not be there.

No. Not other. *There are* no *Peacekeepers here.*

The absence of a patrol partner is accompanied by an unfamiliar sting. She grimaces. And then shakes it off. There is no time for these distractions.

"Midellodioxy? Veniamph?"

An Earth Server proffers a tray of sparkling liquids in tall flutes. Unfamiliar with Air cocktails, Anaiya reaches for the nearest glass. Taking a sip of the sweet-scented liquid, she checks her wristplate to assess the changes to her body chemistry. Elevations in oxytocin and anandamide levels announce it as a feel-good synth – a 'bliss' alcohol. She readily takes another few sips, feeling the tension of the last hour shimmer and liquefy.

The chaotic movement of the Air Elementals slows, finally allowing Anaiya the opportunity to begin her appraisal. While she doesn't have a specific target to monitor, Niamh's intel has provided a general profile – fifth to seventh lustrum, Graphics-based competency, history of Unorthodoxy offences, and socially active across competencies and precincts. The gallery is full of potential targets.

I just have to find the right one.

She scans the room, looking for a *pull* – something that seems a little different, that flashes a little brighter. It is a Peacekeeper tactic, one that Anaiya has used countless times before when managing crowds. There is always something – a tell that draws the eye, a hint of disturbance that alerts the senses. She just needs to zone out and let the signals lift from the white noise.

Except this time there is no white noise – no unremarkable background to provide contrast. Details, vivid and striking, abound. Her gaze flits to the loud male posturing to her left, before being drawn by the tinkling laugh of a younger female. Her focus switches, pulled and pushed with every new distraction – the impatient gesturing, the animated conversing, the playful flirting.

It all calls to Anaiya, every detail demanding her attention equally.

A throbbing begins to pulse at her temples.

This isn't working. This isn't working.

Closing her eyes, she shuts out the chaos.

Inhale. Exhale. Hold. Inhale. Exhale. Hold.

A sudden jolt at her side interrupts the meditation. She struggles not to scowl as three females brush past her, laughing loudly, weaving clumsily through the crowd. Their chaotic journey draws no ire or amusement from the rest of the crowd. To them, it is unremarkable. It is merely the way of Air Elementals – messy, impulsive.

Irrepressible.

It is everything that Anaiya has never been. Will now become. But only if she lets go of the Fire rationality still lingering in her brain.

The thought galls and not for the first time her belly tenses with a kind of regret – an irrational wish that someone else had been chosen.

But then someone else would get the glory.

And Anaiya needs the glory if she is to finally rid herself of Kane 148's shadow. If she is to come out from under Niamh's.

The reminder strengthens her resolve and she lets the scenes in the gallery come back into view. Unable to identify a pull, she tries a different tactic. Starting with the Elemental closest to her – a younger male appraising a wallscreen display – she attempts a speculative profile.

Fifth lustrum – old enough to be confident, young enough to be reckless. Flying solo…which means what? He's conditioned to a more independent competency? Gaming, maybe? Or that he is from another

Area? Has limited contacts in the Northern Area? Or is just confident attending alone? Or…

She clenches her fists and gives up, defeated by the amorphous nature of the Air Elementals around her.

With the other Elements it was easier. A Fire Elemental was easily identified by their respect for authority, dark threads and quiet confidence. It was the same with Water and Earth competencies – each typically announced itself through style, attitude, demeanour and habit.

Air Elementals were different – a Sound Creator was just as likely to attend a Music event solo as they were to attend a Graphics exhibition in a large group; or to stand, quietly contemplative, in front of one piece as they were to passionately debate their interpretation of another; or to gravitate towards solo projects one minute, collaborative pieces the next.

This is futile.

Her Peacekeeper techniques for identifying and assessing targets are useless in this new environment. Clinical observations and rational assessments are just as likely to yield false positives as they are the truth.

Anaiya digs her fingernails deeper into her palms, releasing her frustration into the soft skin. She was naive to think she could spot a Heterodox Elemental as easily as she could a corrupt Administrator or thieving Retail Officer. Naive to think that a Resistor would leave an obvious trail of Heterodoxy in public pieces of art and entertainment, like blood spatters or fingerprints at a crime scene.

Indications of Heterodoxy will be subtle – an offhand comment here, a controversial piece displayed there. Something she won't be in a position to witness standing on the periphery.

As a Peacekeeper, she had always existed on the periphery. Never engaging in the worlds of other Elementals, always watching from her position of authority with an objective eye and cool head. It was cleaner that way. More efficient.

She looks around the gallery again, taking in the messy diversity of Air Elementals, baulking at the chaotic emotions that ebb and swell between them. Reflections of these emotions are simmering inside her, behind her carefully constructed barriers.

The realisation she will have to liberate her own messy limbic emotions leaves a dead weight in her stomach. She is not ready to push aside the only thread connecting her to her Fire identity.

She is not ready to relinquish control.

TWELVE

The rest of the fortnight grinds by in a haze of pain and confusion.

The Task Force is no closer to identifying a lead and Anaiya's daily forays into izakaya, galleries, studios and design hubs yield nothing but the constant conflict between her limbic brain and neocortex. Some days, she dulls the tension with nurozav, but mostly she just tries to get by.

On the sixteenth night, Anaiya heads to the Ravignan Strip, a popular entertainment hub in Precinct 18. Clusters of Air Elementals dance and stumble around her, weaving around each other as they traipse from one izakaya to the next. Anaiya steps around them, finding her escape in an izakaya to her right. Its facade offers no windows, her only glimpse of its inside coming from the regular opening of the large steel door.

A large group of Air Elementals in their fifth and sixth lustrum glide through the entrance and she quickens her step to enter with them. She reaches the group as the last of them steps into the izakaya, the toe of her boot clipping the heel ahead of her. A head of long auburn hair whips around and Anaiya is suddenly confronted by the sharp gaze of orange eyes, their natural colour cloaked by tinted polymer lenses. The scowl rankles, Anaiya's gaze shifting readily to the row of stainless steel rings running along the ridge of the Elemental's left ear and the dark makeup accentuating high cheeks and full lips.

The door slides back into place behind her, pushing Anaiya into the Elemental and earning her another pointed gaze.

Anaiya clears her throat. "Sorry."

The word drags glass shards along her throat. As a Peacekeeper, Anaiya had pushed past, crashed into and shoved between Elementals without a backwards glance, without concern, and definitely without apology.

The Elemental appraises her, running a considered glance down Anaiya's still form. "Nice boots," she says.

Anaiya looks down. Modified from her Peacekeeper boots, they shun functionality with steel rivets and long black buckles that wrap around their girth. They aren't as comfortable as her Peacekeeper boots, but they have an attitude she likes.

"Thanks," she replies. "Sorry they got in the way."

The Elemental laughs. "No harm, no foul. Want a drink?"

Anaiya studies her. There is an openness about her, in the way she flits between annoyance and acceptance, in the way she broadcasts her emotions in her stance and eyes. Anaiya can use this. She nods and follows the bright-eyed Elemental to the bar.

The stranger weaves confidently between the lounges and dense groups of Air Elementals, occasionally leaning in to whisper to some, tapping others on the shoulder to say hello. Anaiya takes it all in on a micro level – she notices the levels of familiarity, filing away faces and relationships, fixating on unique and identifying features.

At the bar, the Elemental pushes to the front of the line and leans over to lock into a passionate kiss with a tall Air Elemental behind the bar. The public display of intimacy surprises Anaiya, but she doesn't look away. The Elemental, the only Air working in the izakaya, grins as the two slowly pull apart, her hand still entangled in ribbons of auburn hair.

"You're here early, Rehhd," she says, her hand disengaging and plucking at bottles and vials lining the shelves to her right.

"Got bored," Rehhd replies. "Issau still hasn't released the specs for the Graphics campaign, so I can't progress the fucking design."

The tall Elemental, who can only be the owner, makes room

on the bar and concocts a tall drink that sparkles purple in the soft light of the izakaya. Rehhd grabs at Anaiya's arm and pulls her in closer.

"And one for my new friend," she says, swiping her wristplate over the inlaid bar terminal to pay.

"Does this new friend have a name, or are you picking up strays?" the owner asks, reaching for the bottles and vials nonetheless. Her voice is flat, but her body language has tightened. Rehhd appears to ignore it, laughing again, long nails tapping against her glass and setting it fizzing.

Anaiya pulls out of Rehhd's grasp and leans on the bar. "Anaiya."

The Elemental looks away from Rehhd to Anaiya. Her eyes draw down in a moment of intense focus. Anaiya maintains her relaxed stance, meeting the bartender's gaze evenly, but allowing her shoulders to fall forwards so she appears lower, smaller. The deference is strategic this time – a conscious attempt to relieve the weight stretching across the bar between her and the stranger.

The Elemental's focus relaxes, her lips releasing a soft sigh. "Here's your drink, Anaiya," she says, pushing the tall glass across the bar.

"Thanks," Anaiya replies, the drink spilling on her wrist as Rehhd grabs her and pulls her away from the bar and back through the crowd.

Rehhd leads her towards an empty table at the back corner, where the crowd is thinner and the music softer, and crashes down onto a cushioned bench seat. She taps impatiently on the tabletop, staring pointedly at Anaiya until she takes the bench opposite her.

Anaiya looks over her shoulder back towards the bar, her line of sight obscured by the incessant tide of Air Elementals moving and condensing around her.

"Don't worry about Yve," Rehhd says, drawing Anaiya's gaze back. "She has a wicked jealous streak, but it never amounts to anything."

"I'm not worried," Anaiya says, lifting her glass to her lips and taking in the strange, bittersweet liquid.

Rehhd watches her closely. "So what is your deal, anyway,

Anaiya?"

The question itself is not unexpected, but the tone is accusatory. Anaiya ignores her impulse to react and forces herself to maintain a slow, sweeping gaze around the izakaya – eyes trained on the assortment of Air Elementals, ears straining to pick up snatches of conversation, to catch forbidden words and thoughts. "What, exactly, do you want to know?"

"Well, you're obviously not from around here." Rehhd waves her hand around. "But you seem familiar…"

And the calmness is gone. Anaiya's mind tickles uneasily with Rehhd's contemplation and she is suddenly, acutely, aware of the way Rehhd is staring at her. It is not impossible that their paths have crossed before.

Surely she wouldn't remember an Eastern Area Peacekeeper…

Anaiya tries to recall the faces of the Elementals she has restrained over the years – but they all merge into one vague memory, a generic face without detail. The Elementals hadn't interested her. Only their crimes were worth remembering.

It is not unusual – Peacekeepers weren't trained to retain such details; once the offences were recorded to wristplates, there was no need for a Peacekeeper's memory. But Air Elementals…particularly those with a Graphics competency…It is unlikely, but Anaiya's heart rate spikes nonetheless.

"I transferred here from the Eastern Area a few weeks ago," she replies, schooling her voice to calm as she replays the fictitious backstory she has learned by rote over the past week. "But I don't remember much of the last twelve months. I was knocked out about a month ago, and I didn't resuscitate for over an hour."

"Hypoxia?" Rehhd asks, leaning forwards, eyes widened, shoulders opened. Her demeanour has shifted from interrogation to curiosity.

Anaiya nods. "So we could have met previously, but I wouldn't know for sure," she finishes.

"You can't remember how you were knocked out?" Rehhd asks.

Anaiya shakes her head. "There were no charges of Unorthodoxy on my wrisplate, but other than that…"

"I bet it was those fucking Fire Elementals," Rehhd interjects, her eyes glittering.

The toxin in her voice is unmistakable. It corrupts the air around them and sets pins in Anaiya's chest.

"See this?" Rehhd continues, pushing her deep red polylehth jacket off her shoulder. A long scar runs ragged across the pale skin of her shoulder. Scars are rare in Otpor. Skin Surgeons and bio-enhancer technologies have practically eliminated them, with only the most injured or agitated patients keeping lasting reminders.

Rehhd trails her finger along the angry white line of skin. "Refusing to cooperate."

The 202 offence is a common one among Earth and Air Elementals, and accounts for the majority of patrol call-outs that Anaiya has attended to in her years as a Peacekeeper. She knows that Peacekeepers have used reasonable force to shut down Unorthodoxy, has often displayed targeted strength herself. But seeing the deep scar unnerves her. It is hard to believe Fire Elementals could have inflicted the irregular, raised line of scar tissue. Unsettling to think Fire Elementals like her could have been responsible for turning a commonplace offence into a permanent disfigurement.

"And this," Rehhd says, pulling the hair back from her right temple. The scar is fainter and, unlike the one on her shoulder, runs a clean, straight line, cutting diagonally just under her hairline.

"After they threw me against the bars of a repentance cell."

"You tried to fight them?" Anaiya asks, careful to keep her voice light.

Rehhd laughs, but it has lost its depth – is shallow and brittle. *Bitter.*

"I'm not the poster girl for Orthodoxy, granted," she says. "But I'm not so stupid as to go toe to toe with trained Peacekeepers, especially when it's three to one."

Anaiya is no longer sweeping her gaze around the room, no longer shifting her hearing to nearby tables. The world has shrunk to the fifty centimetres between her and Rehhd. Blood pumps loudly in her ears, her heart crashing against her rib cage. She downs the purple liquid before her, draining half the glass.

Rehhd is spitting her words out in a rapid stream of vitriol, but Anaiya hears each word in slow motion, each syllable precisely articulated, each hint of emotion clearly defined.

"They'll get what is coming to them. They won't rule forever. They'll pay for their injustices and we'll be compensated for ours."

The izakaya rushes back into her focus. A cacophony of noise assaults her hearing, the motion of the crowd pulls at her vision. She glances down at the four empty glasses lined up along the table's edge and baulks as she feels the full effect of the synth alcohol lacing her neurons.

"Kaide!" Rehhd calls out suddenly, her gaze tracking to the izakaya entry where a new group of Air Elementals has just entered. A tall, male Elemental with broad shoulders waves over to the table.

"Don't let the fire burn you," Rehhd says, looking down at Anaiya as she stands up from the table before making her way across the izakaya to Kaide.

Don't let the fire burn you.

It is too close to the Fire farewell. Too close to her old life as a Peacekeeper.

Anaiya drops her gaze to the table. Suddenly, the emotion in the izakaya is suffocating. She sees it in every glance, every touch. Hears it in the soft tones and raised voices.

She pulls at her wristplate, bringing up her biochemical status. Diethyline, methylate and hexahydrion dominate the readings. Fingers wavering, she presses on each of them, watching as the bars shiver in response. Double tapping her screen brings up the analysis – the cocktail is designed to amplify emotional awareness and heighten emotional response.

Standing up too quickly, she finds herself swaying on her feet. The edge of the table burns in her palm as she grasps it and waits for her vision to clear. To her left, she sees Rehhd in deep conversation with the recent arrivals. Memories of their conversation, of scars and fire, threatens Anaiya's stability and she switches her focus to the entry, glimpsing the twilight of Ravignan Street as the door opens again.

She pushes off from the table, her muscle memory setting her feet in motion towards the door. Half-heard conversations, raucous shouts and musical laughter pierce her concentration and reverberate in her chest, tugging at her heart, settling in her stomach. She quickens her pace, stumbling past groups of Elementals that stand between her and the exit. She reaches out to grab the door handle, jolting short when it starts to slide open.

An Elemental stands backlit against the evening light of Otpor. He doesn't step aside to let her past and Anaiya doesn't wait for his permission to do so. With the door only partially open, she pushes her way into the small gap between him and the doorframe. They both turn side on to fit in the space, but at the last moment he raises his left arm, creating a final barrier between her and the street. She pushes against it; he resists.

"Whoa, butterfly."

Deep green eyes stare down at her, and a small smile teases. "Where are you going in such a hurry?"

"I need to go…" Anaiya says, hearing the strain in her own voice.

He leans in closer, the smile fading.

She pushes again at his arm, a little too forcefully. "Please," she says, the desperation in her voice souring her tongue.

He drops his arm and steps backwards into the izakaya. She turns from him and runs.

Her jogging style is clumsy and slow, made worse by the uneven street and meandering Air Elementals, but it is enough to push fresh blood to her brain. A few blocks away she slows to a quick stride, allowing the blur of her surroundings to coalesce into the random details of the precinct.

Her breathing is steadier and she pulls up the biochemical reading on her wristplate. The enhancer levels have dropped enough to generate a normal reading, but her heart rate is still too high. As she taps on the plate to return to the home screen, she notices a small plus symbol flashing in the top right-hand corner.

She taps on the icon, bringing up three lines of text.

Figured out the rest of the inferno lyrics:
Two eyes stare at the forecourt,

One by one the walls dissipate.

The code word works like a hit of adrenalin, clearing her mind and giving speed to her run back to the apartment. Once inside, she pulls the door shut and turns on the overhead light. It is too bright. Shielding her eyes from the glare, she shuts it off and plunges the room back into a darkness kept only at bay by the soft green glow of her wristplate.

She pulls up the communications portal and types in the number. 24118. She wraps her lifeline around her fingers, letting its smooth links caress her skin as it coils and unfurls. Her eyes track along the links as they pull apart and clasp together along the bend and kinks forced by her fingers.

"Talk to me."

Niamh's voice sends her back in time. She imagines him standing alone on a darkened back street, leaning against the unremarkable wall of a nondescript building, head bent down and fingers pushing the lifeline connection in his ear to block out the background noise. She sees him frown in concentration, the same way he used to when trying to divide his time between competing demands for his attention. Imagines him pulling back the loose hair that has fallen past his temples and across his eyes…

"Ani?" Niamh's voice snaps her back to her dark room in Precinct 18.

"Yeah, I'm here," she says.

"So, talk to me." Blunt. Direct. Typical Niamh.

Something inside her deflates a little, but she shakes the feeling off. "Not much to report," she says. "There seems to be some anti-Fire Elemental sentiment, but nothing more than what I've seen around the streets in the last couple of weeks."

"Give me *details*, Ani," Niamh says.

She hears the contained exasperation in his tone, remembering the same strain of his voice when he patrolled with Peacekeeper Trainees and was trying to keep them on target and in line.

Her cheeks flush and she forces herself to revert to her Peacekeeper standard of communications.

"I made contact with a female Air Elemental, fifth lustrum," she begins, recalling the details of her encounter with Rehhd. "Well known within the localised Air environment, typical behaviour and temperament for Air Elementals. Prenom, Rehhd. Suffix unknown."

"Got her," Niamh announces. "Rehhd 020. Fifteen priors, multiple cases of Unorthodoxy…How did you find her?"

"Where are you?" Anaiya asks, ignoring his question.

"Headquarters, where else?" he replies, shattering the imagined landscape. "How did you find Rehhd 020?"

Anaiya opens her mouth to tell him the truth, but something pulls her back. "She matched the profile."

She baulks at the untruth the moment it reaches her ears, but takes temporary comfort in its necessity. Admitting she had accidentally stumbled upon Rehhd, that she had not thought her worthy of further investigation despite her admissions of prior encounters with Peacekeepers, would have only diminished her in Niamh's eyes. Would have caused him to question her ability as a Peacekeeper and her fitness for the mission.

And she needs this mission – needs to be successful.

"This is good, Ani. This is really good."

He is speaking faster now, his earlier frustration replaced by excitement. Anaiya smiles, and this time allows the feeling to settle rather than shaking it off.

"Her wristplate activity suggests that she will attend either the Lavoir or Veritas izakaya tomorrow night between 1600 hours and 2200 hours. Head to them early and see if you can intercept her. I'll want an immediate debrief. In the meantime, I'll brief the rest of the team and get some intel to you in the next seventy-two hours."

The communication clicks off, plunging Anaiya back into silence and darkness.

The late afternoon light filters through oppressive brown clouds as Anaiya makes her way back towards the Ravignan Strip. She shivers past the long jagged shadows cast by Stricken Core on the ancient bricks of Ruzais Street, her boots slapping the uneven surface as the descent falls steeper and steeper.

Arriving at the start of the Ravignan Strip she stops to survey her target. The Lavoir izakaya rises seven storeys, its pale-brick walls following the sharp angle of the intersection and forming a wedge. Anaiya tilts her head back and stares up at its heights, intrigued by the way its triangular shape is softened by rounded corners that defy the geometric rigidity of rectangular bricks.

The strange perspective pushes her off-balance and she finds herself swaying like the treatment boats in the nearby River Syn. Closing her eyes tightly, she steps back to regain her balance, stopping abruptly when she collides with something behind her.

Spinning around, she is confronted by a smiling Elemental. It takes a moment for the surprise to fade, for her neocortex to kick in and allow her to assess him.

Male. Sixth lustrum. Six feet four inches, maybe five. Traces of skin ink on left arm from mid-ulna upwards. Non-hostile stance. Intelligent eyes.

"Hey," he offers casually, reaching for the entry panel next to the izakaya door.

The door clicks and he pulls it towards him. Anaiya watches as his sleeve recedes further up his arm, revealing more of the skin pattern – thick, dark lines stretch into twisting ribbons, reaching up to cradle a skull.

"Hey," she replies.

He stands there, the door still grasped in his hand.

"Going in, butterfly?" he asks, inclining his head towards the activity just beyond the door.

Anaiya blinks in recognition of the familiar nom de douceur. This Elemental with the interesting ink is the same one who barred her exit from izakaya last night.

She stares at him, trying to gauge his approach, interpret his intent. His body language is neutral, the smile still dancing at his lips. He is teasing her. Anaiya returns the smile involuntarily, enjoying the moment of levity even if it is at her expense, and ducks through into the Lavoir.

Inside, the lighting is dim. A score of ancient incandescent bulbs dangle from plastic cables, throwing soft light around the low-ceilinged, narrow space. Music beats and pulsates, bouncing off the wall and blending with the low hum of conversation. The air is rich with smells and noises.

Anaiya pauses, allowing her limbic brain to revel in the feast of sensations presented before her. The breeze at her back dies as the door to the izakaya clicks shut. She drifts between Air Elementals, slow-dancing a wandering path towards the bar. Her gaze tracks along its architecture; a long piece of graphene, suspended on transparent glass to seemingly float above the polished concrete floor.

The Earth Elemental behind the bar is two generations older than Anaiya, the lines of hard working and hard living marking her handsome face. Beside her, a now-familiar inked arm reaches out to plug its silver cable into the terminal.

"Five lyseracids," he requests.

He looks over to her, eyes glinting in the yellow light.

"Six," he says, amending his order.

The bartender turns her back to fill the order, leaving them alone in the small space buffeted by the throng of Elementals around them.

All Air Elementals possess a certain charisma: A freedom, a spontaneity, that sweats through their pores. As a Peacekeeper, Anaiya had detested it – passed it off as an arrogance and independence bordering on Heterodoxy. Tonight, she envies it.

"Where are you from?" he asks, tapping his fingers against the matte grey surface of the bar.

She runs her fingers along the graphene in a subconscious response, shadows lengthening and retracting under her fingers – her neocortex feeding her an appropriate response even while her limbic mind surrenders to the tactile and audio sensations assaulting it.

"Eastern Area," she says.

"Yeah, you looked green," he says, turning back to the bartender.

Green.

For Peacekeepers, the adjective is used for pups – inexperienced Trainees who don't yet understand the way of the world.

"Why the transfer?" he asks, stacking the shot glasses in a narrow rectangular tray.

"Hypoxic demotion," she says, feeding him the standard response.

He nods, handing her a shot glass brimming with the liquid lys.

"Bienvenue," he says, his voice lilting in the pidgin convention of Air Elementals.

Welcome.

And with that, he retreats from the bar, never looking back, gripping the tray of lys and walking to the far end of the izakaya.

Anaiya shoots the dark liquid, a cloying sweetness coating her tongue. To her left, Air Elementals download their wristplate playlists via one of two terminals attached to the bar. A screen embedded in the bartop flashes with the music's identifier – sometimes a name, other times a visual – before adding it to an updated queue. Bodies sway and dip and writhe in a contorted imitation of Anaiya's free-running; their movements chaotic where hers were precise.

Beyond the end of the bar, a small group hovers around a large table. At its head, a young female leans prostate over it. Her left arm stretches out in front of her, propped up on the bright blue poly surface by splayed fingers. A long, slender baton is cradled between her thumb and forefinger, stretching along the line of her body and grasped firmly by her right hand, which hovers high behind her.

Crack.

In a single, fluid, sharp movement, the baton flicks back before powering forwards to connect with a small white ball. The ball shoots across the table surface, colliding with a red ball and sending it hurtling towards a hole carved into the table's corner.

A shiver runs through Anaiya.

It is well known that Air Elementals, like Earth, are baser in their activities, preferring feeling to thinking. While not eschewing the modern conveniences and technology of Otpor, both groups dengage in more primal activities than their Fire and Water counterparts. But here, in the izakaya, the reverence for the past is palpable. The pidgin slang, the dancing, and the tactile game playing. It is all so far removed from the modernity of Otpor. It appears almost Heterodox to Anaiya's eyes.

The connection registers vaguely in her mind, but does not settle. A cool current is tracing its way through her neural maze; the lys dilating her pupils, raising bumps along her skin and attuning her ears to hidden sounds. The light appears brighter, details sharper, noises clearer, textures rougher. The lys has her in its hold, her limbic brain handing over full control of her mind and body.

THIRTEEN

The hours pass by in a blur of lys. Air Elementals hover next to her at the bar, occasionally engaging her in conversation, buying her drinks and entreating her to dance, but she remains transfixed by the table to her left.

Groups of Elementals flow around it, stopping to engage in the game or merely observe its progression. The single dark baton is passed between Elementals in turn, some players using it to strike the white ball towards one of the red, others towards a yellow, until they run out of a colour and target the lone black ball.

On the surface of it, the game is a simple demonstration of hand–eye coordination she had thought unlikely in Air Elementals. But deeper than that, there is a complex spatial understanding – a desire to create a pattern of impact from hitting the white ball at a certain angle and velocity. And despite the consistent goal of the game, every player approaches the task differently – some are quick to attack the white ball, and others take their time to assess lines and angles.

Anaiya watches as the green-eyed Elemental circles around the table and steps up to one of the long edges. She has watched him play for the last few minutes. He is fearless, never pausing between shots, never hesitating before charging the baton at its target. The white ball is a blur, colliding into the table's edge and sending yellow globes careening off each other into the six holes placed around the table's edge.

The table is transformed into a symphony of noise and movement. He delights in it, erupting in a loud laugh, head twisting to grin at his companions. Straightening from his lazy breach over the table, he navigates to his next point of attack, spinning the baton in his palm and engaging in banter with spectators as he passes.

And then his eyes catch Anaiya's.

His grin settles into an easy smile and, just before he lowers himself over the table to take his shot, he winks at her. The simple, entirely missable, action carries a wasteland of emotion and presumed intimacy.

Deep in her subconscious, where her neocortex is railing against its lys imprisonment, Anaiya is ready to leap over the table and slam him into a clawhold head vice. But something closer to the surface responds to the exclusive familiarity, and she finds herself smiling back.

One by one, the yellow balls disappear from the table, swallowed by unforgiving pockets. When the table is bereft of them, he stands. The new object of his desire, a lone black ball, sits flanked by four red balls butting against the table's frame. She expects him to finally slow down, to assess the table and carefully plan the next shot. The crucial shot.

Instead, he moves almost imperceptibly. The crack of the baton against the white ball reaches her ears unexpectedly and she watches as it hurtles in a straight line towards the cluster of balls. It clips the edge of the black ball, before ricocheting into the closest red ball. The six balls erupt in an intricate, chaotic dance across the blue surface. Each of them flirts with the corners, bouncing against each other and crashing against the sides, but only the black is consumed.

He throws the baton down on the table in triumph as his companions laugh and cheer around him. He ignores them. His gaze is on Anaiya, the same twitching smile that greeted her at the izakaya's entrance playing across his features. He entreats her to join him at the table, beckoning her with the roll of his index finger.

She pauses. He is distracting. Since she first walked into the izakaya, she has remained consciously and subconsciously aware of him. She should have left an hour ago, having still not sighted

Rehhd or any of her Lavoir companions. But something draws her to him: a recklessness to him that hints at her past as a Peacekeeper Trainee; a carelessness that shouts the spontaneity of Air.

Her first steps towards him are leaden, anchored by responsibility, weighted by indecision. Air Elementals move in waves between her and the table, creating a static vision of her destination. Her neocortex screams at her to remember her mission; her limbic brain argues that fraternising with Air Elementals *is* her mission.

"Care to challenge, butterfly?" he asks, twisting the baton towards her.

"Anaiya," she says, taking the baton and balancing it lightly in her palm.

His eyes shine with that familiar amusement, infuriating and endearing. "Seth," he says, stepping to the end of the table where the yellow and red balls congregate with the black in a subterranean opening.

He gathers them by the handful, arranging them in an alternating pattern within a hollow triangle laid flat on the table's surface and slotting the black ball into the centre gap.

Looking up, he tosses the white ball towards her, eyes still shining with anticipation. She plucks the ball smoothly from the air and strides to the opposite end of the table. Leaning over the table, she replicates the motions she has witnessed from him and the other players at the beginning of each game. The white ball runs gently down her fingers onto the azure surface of the table, rolling to a stop on the thin, dark line.

Seth pulls the triangle away from the table with a flourish, the multi-coloured spheres keeping their position on the table.

"Apres vous," he says.

Anaiya positions herself above the table, running her glance along the tapering length of the baton to the white ball and beyond – to the triangle of targets, to Seth's casual stance and intense eyes.

The anticipation and curiosity – the *challenge* – in those eyes connects with something inside Anaiya. She feels a smile spread across her face and, just before she strikes at the white ball for the first time, she surrenders fully to her Air identity. The doubts and internal debates dissipate and she allows herself to be fully consumed by the table and the tinted globes and the attention of an Air Elemental named Seth.

The table is a minimalist graphic of three red balls fighting against two yellow, one black and one white.

Anaiya is suspended motionless above it, entirely focussed on the white ball and its projected trajectory along the table. She clumsily future-searches, the lys still travelling in her bloodstream and bouncing between her neurons, anticipating the point of impact where the white ball will collide with the red.

Her right arm draws backwards, ready to follow through with the baton, when a new sensation alights on the skin of her forearm. She slowly drops her arm and straightens, but Seth's hand remains connected. She stares at him, but his eyes remain downcast, captured by her exposed skin.

His touch shifts something inside her and she is grateful for the lys, which has heightened her senses but dulled her physical responses. She watches as his finger runs up along her arm, pushing the sleeve back with its advances.

"New?" he asks.

In the warm light of the izakaya, red shadows accentuate her skin ink, highlighting its rawness.

"Retouched," she says, the lie thickening in her throat.

His fingers linger a moment longer before he removes them, letting gravity pull the sleeve back down.

They stand there, silently facing each other. The pause becomes too heavy for Anaiya, who breaks the gaze first, returning her focus to the table. She takes a deep breath and resumes her game stance. Her eyes narrow, drawing an invisible line along the angle tracking between the white ball, the far corner pocket, and a lone red ball that sits isolated from the others.

As a Peacekeeper, narrow, rigid focus came easily to her. She could isolate a target – a fleeing perpetrator, a free-running prop, an Unorthodox disturbance – and zone immediately in on it, rendering everything else irrelevant. So she waits, giving more time for her neocortex to ascend and take responsibility. But the lys maintains its hold.

She strikes at the white ball. It careens off course, colliding with the cluster of yellow balls and sending them spinning into the cushioned rails. The red remains untouched. She slowly straightens, never taking her eyes off the red ball.

"It's not going to move, butterfly," Seth says from behind her.

She feels the baton grow heavier in her hand as he tries to take it from her. She holds on to it and turns to face him. The tension between them grows, the silence stretching further than the last, but this time Anaiya doesn't look away. She sees herself reflected in irises that appear black and, for a moment, she is lost in them.

Her grip on the baton loosens and she lets him steal it. He pauses, maintaining the connection between them for a moment longer, before turning his back on her and moving in to take the shot.

The remaining two yellow balls disappear into the nearest holes, leaving only the black, perched precariously on the edge of one of the corner pockets. He strikes again at the white ball, softly, sending it on a gentle trajectory with the black.

As it gets closer, the movement becomes less independent. To Anaiya's eyes it is as if the black ball is pulling the white towards it.

The impact sends both balls into an intimate dance, each of them rotating to pull the other closer. The black shifts in its position to present a gap for the white ball to fill. Its centre of gravity passes over the pocket, its mass falling to the black hole below. The white ball takes its place, filling the void on the table and shivering as its hangs balancing over the pocket's edge. And then it drops.

Seth turns to look at her. Subconsciously, Anaiya knows that she should feel a kind of elation – some sort of satisfaction at winning the game, even if by default. But all she feels is the weight.

FOURTEEN

Anaiya leans against the far wall of the izakaya, watching Seth and the other Air Elementals from a distance. No one interrupts her self-imposed isolation. She is not alone – there are other independent Elementals sitting with heads bent over screens or with eyes closed to revel in non-visual sensations.

She checks her biochemical reading again. All synth readings are normal – the lys left her system more than an hour ago, but her heart rate is still accelerated and the jumpiness in her stomach tells her that adrenalin and norepinephrine are coursing through her body.

After her game with Seth, she hurriedly excused herself, concerned that the same overwhelming chaos that had attacked her at Lavoir would take hold again. For a moment, it looked as if he would protest, but a group of boisterous Elementals surrounded him and Anaiya took the opportunity to retreat.

He is charismatic, like Rehhd – attracting a large and ever-changing collection of Elementals who clamour for his attention. She watches him now, his smile beaming at the Elementals around him, his laugh occasionally rising above the music and chatter. It is a sound that calls to her, distracts her. She stubbornly shoves her hands in her jeans pockets, keeping them from fidgeting.

After a while, a familiar-looking male Elemental catches Anaiya's gaze and peels away from the group. Minutes later he arrives at her table, proffering two short glasses of a clear liquid.

"Mind if I join you?" he asks, filling the space between Anaiya and one of the heavy iron struts that rises from the floor to the ceiling. "Nightshade," he adds, handing Anaiya a glass. "Seth prefers the amp-up factor of lys, but I like my alcohol to dull the edges rather than sharpen them."

Anaiya raises the glass to her lips, tasting the clean, sweetly spiced liquor.

"You were at Lavoir the other night, weren't you?" he asks.

Anaiya swivels her head to look at him. His profile presents high cheekbones and a strong jawline offset by dark hair that falls in thick waves just short of broad shoulders. His face tickles at her memory, but she can't quite place him.

"With Rehhd, yeah?" he clarifies.

And she remembers him. The Elemental that Rehhd had joined just before Anaiya's meltdown.

"Kaide, right?" she confirms, recalling the name her target had yelled out in greeting at the izakaya.

He nods.

"Anaiya," she offers in return.

"I saw you playing pool with Seth earlier," he says, turning his head back to face the crowd. "You were pretty good. How often do you play?"

Anaiya takes a long drink from her glass, giving her time to weigh up her response. Without knowing how prevalent the game is, she is unsure of how many opportunities are available for Air Elementals to play. If it is a game confined to certain precincts or local areas, her answer may contradict her backstory of coming from Precinct 12 in the Eastern Area. But she knows that unless she can offer up some previous experience, she will be unable to explain her sudden competency without attracting suspicion.

"Often enough," she finally responds. "Do you play?"

Kaide shakes his head. "Music is more my thing."

"Composer or Creator?" she asks, surprised to find herself genuinely interested.

"Developer," he replies with a smile, referring to the Air practice of finding and refining new sounds for music integration.

"And recording technology integration. Is Music your competency?"

She nods.

"It's harder after hypoxia, huh?" he says after a while, turning away from her and back to the izakaya crowd.

She looks at him closer. He doesn't have the stereotypical look of hypoxia – the heavy-lidded eyes, the slightly slack jaw. But, then again, neither does she. Someone has been sharing her backstory.

Rehhd or Seth? Each possibility brings its own thrill of possibility.

"It will heal," he says, interrupting her thoughts. "Eventually."

Eventually. Another period of time with no clear end date.

"It won't be the same," he says without sympathy. "It won't be better and it won't be worse. You will heal, but it will be different. You will be different."

"This one came with a dislocated shoulder and two broken ribs," Kaide says, pulling up the sleeves of his shirt to reveal a long, pale scar.

They have migrated from their spot against the wall to a small table nearby. The izakaya has taken on a darker mood, the lighting soft and the music stuck in the lower registers, dense with heavy beats. Anaiya leans forwards, her right thumb running absently along the scar that mars the inside of her left forearm.

"How long were you incarcerated for?" she asks.

"Only for three days," he says, pulling down his sleeve. "Just a minor Unorthodoxy charge."

Anaiya tries to think of a minor Unorthodoxy charge that could result in significant injury. She feels her neocortex strain under the nightshade, failing to come up with an answer. Her frown deepens.

"What?" Kaide asks, smiling.

"Nothing…" Anaiya begins. "I mean, how do you get a dislocated shoulder and two broken ribs from a *minor* Unorthodoxy charge?"

Kaide's smile broadens into a grin. "Pretty easily, if you're breaking into a third-level Water lab to get your hands on some copper wire."

"You *only* got three days for that?"

He laughs. "Well, they got me before I did the breaking in part. So all I got was public nuisance…It was the Protectors' crude extraction methods for getting me off the third level, and the warm reception I received from the Cell Watchers, that left me damaged."

Anaiya's mind flashes to her recent discussion with Rehhd. Thoughts of Rehhd come with twinges of guilt: she has failed to intercept her again. But the twinges are buried beneath layers of nightshade and apathy.

"Rehhd showed me the scars from her time in repentance cells," she says.

Kaide's grin fades into something more sombre. "Yeah, Rehhd has had a few run-ins with Fire Elementals," he says. "They seem to have mutual attraction and antagonism for each other…"

His eyes lift to a point above and beyond Anaiya.

"Not boring the butterfly with your theories on sound structures, are you?"

Seth steps into her vision, standing at the table's edge between her and Kaide.

"Regaling her with my heroic endeavours." Kaide winks at Anaiya.

"Looks like she has her own battle scars," Seth says, looking down at the space where her left forearm is defaced.

"Fire Elementals?" Kaide asks.

"Peacekeepers," Anaiya confirms, shifting her gaze between the two of them.

And, in a way, she is telling the truth. The scar is only four years old, but the memory is fresher. Her race against Niamh to catch the Earth Elemental high on dex had ended with more than a grade three calf tear. Hitting the pavement had carved up her arm pretty good as well.

Anaiya and the Biomechanics had been too focussed on the leg injury to notice the arm damage, and now the scar was permanent. Strange how her leg had healed almost perfectly, save for a slight tinge when the static in the air grew to peak levels, but her arm was left behind as a record.

The three of them fall silent, caught in their own thoughts and memories.

"I'm getting another round," Kaide says abruptly, shaking off his reverie and standing up from the table.

"No more nightshade," Seth says, frowning.

Kaide nods and heads towards the bar, the void left behind quickly filled by Seth, who settles into the seat across from Anaiya. He sits there, just watching her. She returns his scrutiny, with the same level of interest and lack of intensity brought on by the synth alcohol. She tries to remember his eyes as green, vaguely wondering whether her memory of them in the limbo between the street and the Lavoir is accurate. They are still so dark, rendered colourless in the dull light of the izakaya.

"It's harder these days to escape the melancholy," he says, eventually, maintaining his steady gaze. "Even without the nightshade, the world is shifting to a darker place."

Anaiya hears the truth in his unfamiliar words. She has never known melancholy, is unsure of the word itself and what it feels like. But the way he says it reminds her of weight. Reality appears like a mirror glass and she is on one side of it and Seth is on the other. Both seeing the same truth and feeling the same weight, melancholy, but from different worlds and with different understanding.

"The Heterodoxy..." Anaiya begins, and then falters. "It just seems to...*suck*...the life and order out of everything."

The admission emerges from a deep place within her, surprising her with its presence. A sense of dull panic registers under the layers of her mind, warning her to be more circumspect. Reminding her of her mission.

Seth sounds a short, anaemic laugh, stripped of mirth and joy. "That's not Heterodoxy, butterfly."

Anaiya wants to ask him what he means, but Kaide returns with a tray of small glasses brimming with tequila, and the moment is lost.

Anaiya hasn't drunk tequila since the heady days of her

Traineeship. As the last organic alcohol available in Otpor, it is a rarity, with a price point to match. Limited batches are sprinkled through a few of the city's izakaya, a fading reminder of Otpor's organic past. The base plant, a blue spiky-leafed specimen, is one of the few things to eke out an existence in the Wasteland's solitary and sandy environment. But, with Wasteland patrols less frequent, Border Watchers are harvesting it less and less. Soon, tequila – like trees and butterflies – will be nothing more than a memory, a concept for romantics, an unfamiliar reminder of a past never lived.

Anaiya gently reaches out and pulls a glass towards her, upsetting the tenuous balance of the liquid and setting a trickle down the frosted glass and onto her hand. She pulls at the spill with her lips, bracing herself for the raw alcohol's assault. Unlike synth alcohols created to perfect standards in Water laboratories, the tequila distilled by Earth Elementals has a rough aroma that sets pins in your nostrils, and a taste that runs jagged spikes down your throat.

But the assault never comes.

"Salut," Seth says, raising his glass to the middle of the table.

Kaide mimics him, his glass chiming against Seth's, and Anaiya follows suit.

Anaiya lifts the glass to her lips, throwing her head back and letting the liquid sing down her throat. Her belly warms immediately and her tongue lights up with a symphony of flavours from sweet to spicy. A slight stickiness cloys her throat and she can almost believe she will exhale flames at her next breath. It is so different from the tequila she has had before. It is smooth and fiery and delicious.

She looks to Seth and Kaide, who do not seem surprised by the liquor. Kaide is reaching for another glass and Seth picks up two, handing the second to Anaiya.

"Salut!" Kaide shouts, his voice breaking through the frenetic music that now plays over the izakaya sound network.

Anaiya pauses before she shoots the contents of her glass. "It tastes…different," she says, a slight slur entering her words on the back of the natural ethanol.

Seth laughs. "Because Earth Elementals haven't had a chance

to spit in it."

"It's not Earth-distilled?"

Kaide shakes his head. "Yve, Rehhd's girlfriend, distils it offsite and supplies a few of the Precinct 18 izakaya. Being so close to the Wall, it's easier to negotiate with the Watchers before the official trade takes place."

The Unorthodoxy registers with Anaiya, but doesn't surprise her. She briefly wonders if the Northern Area Command Peacekeepers are monitoring the minor transgression or taking their cut. The thought wobbles in her mind, balancing on that precipice that divides the part of her mind consumed with her mission and the part that is rebelling against all thoughts Orthodoxy, Peacekeepers and duty.

"My shout," she says, rising from her seat on unsteady feet.

Anaiya pushes gently against the tide of Air Elementals that crowd haphazardly in the space between the table and the bar. The warmth of the tequila surging through her seems to attract the warmth of the bodies surrounding her, and she crashes lightly into them as a synthfly into fluorescent globes.

At the bar, she waits patiently for an Earth Server to take her order, content to watch the eclectic assortment of Air Elementals mill around her and to listen to the strange music they plug into the bar's sound system queue. After a short silence, the next song begins its domination of the air waves, its rhythm seeming to sync with the intermittent flickering of the lightbulbs above the bartop. Beat, flicker. Beat, beat, flicker. Beat. Flicker. Beat. Flicker.

"You like it?"

Anaiya turns towards the voice. Seth leans against the bar, separated from her by the few Elementals who wait to be served. He extricates himself and joins her at the far end of the bar.

"You're Music too?" she asks, surprised.

"Lover, not a player," he replies. "My competency is Literature."

It is a perfect fit for him. Echoes of the past seem to accompany Seth – dancing, pidgin, tequila. These days, literature is so overlooked and unappreciated, it is almost a relic itself. Elementals watch stories, listen to stories. But no one reads stories –

at least, not anyone Anaiya has ever met.

"But it is from my playlist," he confirms.

Anaiya plugs her lifeline into the terminal, swiping across her wristplate to bring up the download options. The name of the song displays prominently, but the name of the artist is noticeably absent. She taps the download icon, confirming that she wishes to purchase the anonymous track.

"Do you know who the artist is?" she asks, disengaging her lifeline once the download is complete.

"They prefer the anonymity to the money," he says cryptically with a shrug, before waving over a bar server.

"Eight Air tequilas," he orders, swiping his wristcuff across the terminal to pay.

Eight?

Anaiya looks over her shoulder, leaning sideways and craning her neck to get a better view of their table. Kaide sits there with his back to her. Next to him is a female Air Elemental. As if feeling Anaiya's eyes on her, she turns in her seat towards the bar.

Rehhd.

FIFTEEN

"Anaiya!" Rehhd exclaims as Seth and Anaiya return from the bar.

Anaiya smiles and nods her greeting. On the outside she is calmly watching Seth unpack the shot glasses from the tray; on the inside she is trying desperately to pull her brain out of the izakaya's stupor and in to mission mode.

"To Liberty," cries Kaide, raising his shot glass.

"Egality!" Rehhd laughs at the wobbling glass in her fingertips.

"Fraternity!" echoes Seth.

Their eyes turn to Anaiya expectantly.

"Or Death," she finishes roughly, completing the national motto and drowning her faltering voice in a river of tequila.

Closing her eyes, she allows the tequila to take a firmer hold, feeling its warmth reach the depth of her belly and shut down the last of the raw nerves firing in her brain. In the darkness, the sounds of the izakaya fade and she finds herself cocooned in the echo chamber of her mind.

Remember. Remember why you are here. What you have to do.

Rehhd's presence has splintered her joy, casting it as recalcitrance and lazy disobedience. She is an undeniable, tangible reminder of Anaiya's mission. A call to duty.

Niamh's voice floats to the surface of Anaiya's consciousness and she can once again hear the eagerness in it, hear the *delight* at the thought of drawing closer to the source of Heterodoxy. His face flashes in her memories, the angles of his face softened by time and the romanticism of her new Air alignment. And now, in the drunken haze of her Air mind, she wants him. Not what he can give or what he can take away. Just him. It is a silly thought. Frivolous and impossible. But it settles in her mind.

The sounds of the izakaya come back to her and she opens her eyes. It has only been a few seconds, but it feels like hours. Rehhd is deep in a conversation with Kaide and Seth is reaching for the next tequila.

"For you, butterfly," he says, handing her a shot glass.

She holds it steadily, watching the tequila take on a richer colour under the light. She fixes her concentration on the glass, until the rest of the izakaya blurs at the edges. In this moment, she can almost trick her mind into thinking it is Niamh that stands close to her.

"To success," she says, raising her glass higher.

"Or death," comes Seth's reply, sombre as he taps his glass against Anaiya's and drains it dry.

Tequila glasses empty, Rehhd spins to regard Anaiya and Seth. "Kaide and I are going to head over to Scythe's party," she declares, orange eyes sparkling. "Wanna join?"

Seth turns to Anaiya to gauge her response. He stands closer to her, his shoulder resting lightly against her own. This close she can see the shadow of light stubble that grazes his jawline and a slight crookedness to his nose. Details she would have once considered irrelevant now trigger questions and imagined histories in her mind.

The hint of a smile plays on his lips; he is keen to go to this party. No. He is keen to go to this party *with her*. The thought sends another heavy flare of warmth through her, fainter than when she remembered Niamh, but strong enough to remind her of the attraction she felt for this strange, pidgin-speaking charmer just hours ago at the pool table.

She nods, letting her own smile break out across her face. A bubble of guilt begins to rise in her mind, threatening to burst and destroy her uneasy confidence. She pushes it back down.

Niamh told me to engage with Rehhd. I'm engaging. I'll be able to maintain surveillance. Gain exposure to her networks.

The words ring true, but are tinny, lacking depth. But she doesn't have time to dwell on them – Seth's hand is sliding into hers, pulling her behind him through the izakaya crowd in a casual pursuit of Kaide and Rehhd.

The four of them skip and weave through the crowds on Ravignan Strip, heading west, closing in on the border with Precinct 17. Seth's hand is still linked in Anaiya's. The air outside has not cooled, despite the darkness that has descended on the city. The close contact of skin on skin ratchets the heat up higher, feeding off the night's temperatures and the strange new fire building in Anaiya's core.

Ahead, Anaiya spies a tall stone wall rising from the street and bathed in shadows. For a moment, she is disoriented – certain that she is distant from the River Syn and its walls, but unable to account for the ancient barrier that looms up before her.

"Deep peace of the running water to you, deep peace of the flowing air to you," Rehhd's tremulous voice comes to Anaiya, amplified by the reverberations off the stone wall. "Deep peace of the quiet earth to you, deep peace of the warm fire to you."

Anaiya recognises it as an ancient prayer of the Air Elementals. A supplication to their Creator god, recited mournfully at the death rites ceremony of fallen Elementals.

"Deep peace of the life force to you," whispers Seth into Anaiya's ear, his eyes still sparkling with the tequila, his hand still warm in hers.

And she realises that the wall, whose shadow she is now passing under, is the border to the city's necropolis.

For Anaiya, the cemetery is nothing more than the place dead bodies are treated, burned and disposed of. It is the same for all Fire and Water Elementals, who view life and death with a cold, hard logic. But for Air and Earth Elementals, who create bonds, who indulge in affairs of the heart and root, the cemetery is the final resting place of friends and lovers.

She looks over to Seth, his green eyes brighter under the street lights and still focussed on hers. She tries to imagine him as a lifeless, crumbling mass of carbon, disintegrating to an absolute nothingness, forgotten by the world and by her.

And she feels it: a softer, more insidious sadness. *Melancholy.*

Without warning, he pulls at her hand. She falls towards him, submitting to the laws of motion, her other hand bracing for the inevitable collision with his chest. And then his hand jerks upwards, pulling her arm up with it. And she is spinning. The rush of air against her bare skin at her wrists and neck sends her mind tingling and achieves what moments before she could not. Her dark thoughts evaporate.

She laughs. It rushes from her, unfamiliar and unexpected. It reaches her ears as music, rippling through her chest and the Otpor air. And just as suddenly it is silenced. Seth has pulled her into him, her body crushed up against his chest. The two of them drift in the almost-deserted street, Anaiya's hidden Peacekeeper allowing her to walk backwards in his grasp without stumbling.

He is only inches taller than her and he looks down, green eyes meeting hazel. Her heart careens at a hectic tempo; her feet feel light like they have lifted in a dash vault. She lets herself be cradled by his arms at her waist, encircling her own arms around his strong frame to pull him in tightly. He lets out his own short laugh and she catches its hint of breathlessness. And then all thoughts are obliterated. Her limbic brain and neocortex are both silenced as his lips crash into hers.

This is not the frenzied kiss of a Fire Elemental, who yields only to the adrenalin and release of physical need and desire. It is heady and complex – playful yet hinting at a strange desire and unexpected intimacy.

She relaxes into it, her body liquid. New emotions fire along her neural pathways, sending chemical cocktails through her body that push her heart rate faster, dilate her pupils, and run shivers along her skin. She wants this. Her Fire nature slips from underneath the chemical haze of her brain and she pulls him closer, deeper into the shadows of the cemetery's wall. Distantly, she feels her back hit the cold, rough stone, a flash of contrast to the warmth of his body pressed against her.

But, just as suddenly, he pulls away. Dark eyes look down at her, narrowed with unasked questions. She wants to close the space between them, but she remains still, letting the cold stone seep through the thin fabric of her shirt. He regards her silently, seeking out the source of the hunger hidden behind her eyes. A weight settles in the small void that separates them.

The tension does not last long – shattered by an explosion of sound that breaks the silence and echoes down the street towards them.

SIXTEEN

It takes Anaiya a moment to recognise the sound that has shattered the moment. Kaide is shouting for Seth – his voice distorted by the distance and the walls between them, mangled by the sound of other voices, loud and unfamiliar.

She sees Seth's eyes widen and his face, once confused, turn focussed. For a moment she just watches as he tears away and races down the street, and then something inside her reacts and she is following him. Her footsteps provide the off beat to his on beat and, in that moment, she is living two joys – the Air joy at the music of the run and the Fire joy at its physicality. She holds on to the balance, ignoring the pull of her body to disrupt the rhythm and break past the clumsy pace of the drunken Air Elemental in front of her.

Anaiya knows she can overtake him, stretch her stride out and sprint past him. Instead, she hangs back, content with the simple pleasure of her muscles burning and the sight of Seth making his way towards the growing noise. He is an enigma – familiar yet perplexing; high energy like a Fire Elemental, but elegant and inexplicable like an Air Elemental.

He runs straight, despite the tequila, but so slow and encumbered. If he knew how to run properly; could just stretch out those toned calf muscles to hit the pavement in a more efficient rhythm, push that adrenalin to his core instead of just his limbs…But, as inefficient and technically incorrect he is, his movement captivates her. There is poetry in it.

Turning the corner just a few steps behind Seth, her thoughts are halted as she is faced with a mess of colour and movement, a harsh and hypnotic dance of entangled bodies. She picks out the broad shoulders of Kaide first, watches him use his left arm to pull at a body that threatens to stumble to its knees while using his right arm to fend off the advances of a tall figure dressed in dark kevlar.

Anaiya's breath catches and her body jolts to a stop.

Peacekeeper.

Time speeds up, matching pace with the surge of adrenalin that now assaults her. A flash of long auburn hair pulls at Anaiya's eyes, but her gaze stops on the figure that stands in the middle of the melee, casually letting the body of an unfamiliar Elemental drop as she retracts her syringe.

Jenna.

Anaiya cringes as the body falls heavily to the road, gravity crushing it against the hard, uneven cobblestones. An invisible thread in her brain tenses and threatens to snap. The memories of her realignment testing appear as a translucent layer against her current reality. She waits for the rivers of blood to run like an oil slick towards her, her body breaking into a cold sweat that feels unnatural in the persistent warmth of the evening.

Jenna looks up, her eyes sliding past Anaiya and flashing with anticipation at the sight of Seth hurtling towards her in full flight. Anaiya future-searches, her brain clumsily pulling at the potential outcomes indicated by the chaos in front of her. It takes longer than it normally does, and she is less certain of the accuracy of her conclusions. Even so, she breaks out of her stillness and sprints at Jenna.

She sees Seth veering to the left, heading towards what she now recognises as Rehhd thrashing in the vice grip of another Elemental, hurling abuse and vitriol at Jenna and the other male Peacekeeper. Jenna has also shifted in her trajectory, positioning herself to intercept Seth, her right hand at her belt where another three syringes of restraint serum hang glistening in the street light.

Anaiya stretches further, pushing herself to move faster, stride longer. Nearing closer to Jenna and Seth, she pushes off her left foot into a quick series of feints to grab Jenna's attention. Responding to the new threat, Jenna reacts in the calculated way of all Peacekeepers. Anaiya depends on it, watching as the syringe flashes in Jenna's hands as it heads towards flesh.

Anaiya lets her left knee dip lower, pushes her body to a sharp angle and allows her right shoulder to thrust upwards. The sting of the needle breaking skin and hitting bone is overwhelmed by the immense satisfaction of feeling it snap on impact and seeing the look of shock and then recognition on Jenna's face.

The impact of their collision sends them into a warrior's embrace. Anaiya braces against Jenna, buffering her body against the shock of the conflict. Jenna's left arm has instinctively wrapped around Anaiya, the perfect position to support her body for administration of the serum. This close, Anaiya can see the fire burning in Jenna's eyes and feels her own lips curve in a victorious smile.

"Time to back down, Peacekeeper," she whispers. "Zero engagement, remember?"

Jenna stares back at her, a face devoid of emotion. Her eyes narrow in concentration and for that brief moment, Anaiya remembers what it is to be a Peacekeeper. And, in that moment, she knows that Jenna is not angry that she has been bested in combat, but is merely weighing up the gravitas of one order against another. Protect the Orthodoxy. Avoid direct contact with Anaiya.

"Drop," Jenna orders quietly.

Anaiya understands the necessity of the instruction, feels its logic register in her neocortex where her residual Peacekeeper training remains. The only way for the Peacekeepers to disengage is for the combat to dissipate. As a Peacekeeper, Anaiya would have struggled to put on the pretence, but in her new reality she lets her eyelids close, her knees buckle and her body turn liquid, as it had just moments ago.

She slumps to the ground, her fall mimicking the collapse of the unknown Elemental. The cobblestones are cold and rough like the cemetery wall. Jenna's voice floats to her, refracted through the cold, the ease of her deception and the memory of the unfinished moment with Seth.

"Curfew commences in three hours," she says. "Be on your way and keep the Orthodoxy."

A deep-voiced grumble murmurs in the background, the other Peacekeeper protesting at the departure from protocol, but it is quickly silenced. Rehhd is still spouting obscenities, but they come from a quieter place and lack the pure aggression of minutes ago. Anaiya keeps her eyes closed, listening as the echo of fast footfalls recedes. Restraint serum can last anywhere from ten to thirty minutes, depending on the dose administered, so she releases the breath she was holding and lets the cold seep all the way to her bones.

The cold slowly dissipates as warm hands cradle her face and lift her head up. Soft fabric grazes her neck and her head settles against what feels like a hard-cushioned bar. Fingers graze her temples and run through her hair. She lies there, tingling on the inside, motionless on the outside. Her lower back is still in contact with the road, her legs are cramped in the awkward position created by her fake collapse, but her head, neck and shoulders are enveloped in the warmth that comes from contact with another.

"How's she doing?" asks a deep voice she recognises as Kaide's.

"She's a fighter," comes a voice loud and close. Fingers run along her skin and the bar beneath her head shifts slightly. "Just like us."

The voice is Seth's. The fingers are his. And the bar beneath her head is the junction where his legs cross at the ankles, bracing her from the cold stones of the street. She wants to open her eyes and see for herself the scenario she imagines, but she resists.

"What happened?" he asks.

"They were attacking Eamon," Rehhd says, her voice still strained with aggression.

"*Why* were they attacking Eamon?" Seth asks patiently, his fingers tracing circles on Anaiya's cheeks and forehead.

"We don't know – why do they do *anything*?" Rehhd replies.

"We saw him dancing with the male Peacekeeper; they were shouting, we stepped in."

"You stepped in?" Seth asks, his voice softer now. Lower.

"Yes, Seth. We stepped in." Rehhd's voice is tight and clipped.

Seth's fingers slow to a halt against Anaiya's skin.

"Rehhd…"

Anaiya can hear the conflict in his voice, shifting along the line between understanding and unforgiving. She wonders what drives it and why he holds the rest of his words back.

"It was Eamon," Rehhd interrupts. "*Eamon.*"

"And Eamon should know better than to pick a fight with a Peacekeeper patrol," Seth says heatedly. "Should act like the Air he is instead of an undisciplined Earth brute."

Rehhd's voice splutters as she prepares for what can only be a tirade in response, but Kaide cuts her off.

"He's right, Rehhd. It's too dangerous these days; there's too much at stake. We all need to be more careful."

The words seem to hang in the air around them. Seth is impossibly still below her, silent above her. Tension buzzes in the air and weight pushes on Anaiya.

This is not the uneasy weight of Elementals confused and fearful of Heterodoxy, of curfews and patrols. It is a dominant weight, pulsating with a vibrant energy. It reminds Anaiya of the weight that Peacekeepers hold before a patrol, full of anticipation and a tightly coiled discipline that controls the fire. That keeps it a hard, cold flame.

She shivers.

"The serum is starting to wear off," Seth says, registering Anaiya's movement.

"We should get out of here," Kaide says.

Anaiya feels Seth shift below her.

"I'll take Anaiya back to my place," he says. "You help Cress get Eamon back to his."

Arms slip around Anaiya's frame and she feels the tug of gravity as it resists her disengagement from the cold ground of the street. Her leg muscles sing in relief as they are rescued from their unnatural angles and allowed to hang easily over the strong arm that cradles her below her knees. Her chest is pressed firmly against Seth's and her head falls into that beautiful space of vulnerability that Anaiya has only known as a target for slender, silver needles.

She smells the saltiness of the sweat from his brief exertion mixed with the synth and organic alcohol being expelled through his skin. The hint of a spicy note from whatever soap he uses flashes bright and, beneath it all, a familiar scent – sharp and bitter – that she remembers but cannot place.

"I'll go with Kaide," Rehhd says, her voice flat.

Seth's cheek rubs along Anaiya's jawline as he nods, her body pressed closer to him as he starts walking. The sounds of Kaide and Rehhd fade behind them and soon there is nothing but the sound of Seth's constant footfalls and steady breath.

The lack of other sound and movement is conspicuous. Anaiya lets her eyes flutter open, watching as their merged shadow glides underneath them, inking in the already shadowed street.

It is just them, the night and their shadow. Unable to look around without shifting and alerting Seth to her consciousness, she closes her eyes again and lets the rhythm of his steps and the afterglow of the tequila coax her into a soft kind of oblivion.

It is only when the sound of heavy footfalls shifts to sharp and shallow echoes that Anaiya wakes from her trance. Bright fluorescent light follows shortly after, burning into her eyes behind heavy eyelids. She opens them reluctantly, squinting against the glare to make out a mosaic floor of small white tiles cut into perfect hexagons. The floor changes into a black matte expanse and Anaiya watches as Seth's leg reaches out to kick shut the grate of an early-model elevator.

Loud, clunky sounds erupt around them as the elevator commences its ascent. Seth looks down at her. "It's OK. I got you."

He watches her silently and, in the drawn-out passing of a second, she thinks he can see her. See her disguise. See past it.

She closes her eyes, hiding from his searching gaze.

This has gone too far.

Her internal admonishment feels weak, overpowered by a

sense of inevitability that vibrates within her.

I'm drowning.

It is a melodramatic reaction. A decidedly Air response. Rescuer Fire Elementals sometimes rushed to the River Syn, to sections where the walls were lower or easier to climb, to pull drunken Earth Elementals or suicidal Air Elementals from the fast-flowing currents. Sometimes the Elementals were dragged from the dark water back to breathe air, but sometimes they were irretrievable, sinking permanently to the river's depths and lost forever to the other side of the Wasteland.

On her nightly patrols, Anaiya would often find herself atop the river ramparts and staring at the movement below. She would walk the fine edge of the wall's inner facade, wondering what it would be like to cross the water's barrier. To slip beneath the surface and become fully immersed, fully consumed.

She imagined it to be like the soft cloak of the dodecahedrazines she drank as a Peacekeeper – a gradual, yet complete, embrace that turned everything a little more warm, a little less sharp.

"Don't panic, butterfly," Seth says, as the elevator ceases its noisy journey. "It's just the restraint serum wearing off. You'll feel normal soon."

Hollow footsteps and the sound of a door opening echo in Anaiya's self-imposed darkness. Shortly afterwards, she feels the softness and give of cushioned velour as Seth releases her. Finally ready to confront him again, she opens her eyes.

He sits on the floor across from her, knees propped up to balance folded arms, back pressed against a bare wall. He doesn't fidget, doesn't speak. Just sits there regarding her.

"What happened back there?" she finally asks.

She is not sure what *back there* she is referring to. Other questions begin to trip over each other in her mind, their answers hidden under a moving kaleidoscope of new and unfamiliar emotions. The short, stabbing guilt, the mellow and sticky sadness, the fuzzy confusion, the high static of uncertainty. And the sometimes sharp, sometimes soft, shimmering of whatever this emotion is when she looks at Seth.

"Peacekeepers were roughing up some friends –"

"But why?" Anaiya interrupts.

"You know why," Seth says.

The words float in her disoriented mind, gaining weight as they settle. She does know why.

She sees the scars that mark Rehhd and Kaide. She hears the sharp crack as Jenna carelessly drops the restrained Air Elemental to the street surface, his head ricocheting off the uneven stones. She smells the sharpness of spilled genievre as an intoxicated Earth Elemental falls heavily to a worm platform following the flawless execution of just another Peacekeeper Trainee.

And then her unease transitions to something darker. She sees herself dropping the synth-addled Earth Elemental in Precinct 20. Sees herself efficiently dispatching over-confident Trainee Air Elementals.

Recent memories segue into older ones – one Earth Elemental turns into hundreds; the sound of broken bones echoes across a thousand more incidents. She sees countless Elementals – faceless, bruised and broken – all of them damaged because of her.

And worse than seeing it is feeling the new emotions it engenders. It hits her with full force. She is faced with her callousness, her ruthlessness, her hard-hearted perfection. Her force, her aggression, her unyielding strength. Her inability to feel.

And something inside her fractures.

SEVENTEEN

Minutes that feel like hours pass before Anaiya realises that Seth is speaking.

"C'mon," he says, pushing himself up from the floor and walking over towards her. "There's still beauty in this world, you just need to know where to find it."

He reaches down to her and she clings to his arm like a rescue line. He pulls her up and off the lounge, and she follows him silently out of the apartment and into the stairwell. The air is cooler once they exit the apartment building. Threads of the chilled breeze alight on every inch of Anaiya's skin, barred only to the palm of her left hand, which is pressed so tightly into Seth's under-linked fingers that it generates a heat to warm them both.

They head north, walking the straight lines of Rue Jonlaclare towards the boundary of Precinct 17's Edge. The street is quiet and the thought of curfew drifts across Anaiya's thoughts without really gaining hold.

The familiar bloated air recyclers loom larger than they should. She is no longer aware of her feet tracking along the hard ground, of the sticky suction created in the vacuum of Seth's grip, of the increasing urgency to turn around and get inside before curfew strikes.

The recyclers regard her silently, uncaring portents of change and misery. Her eyes flick erratically between them, casting about for glimpses of paint.

Seth remains oblivious to her inner turmoil, casually weaving between the concrete structures. He pulls her easily along in his trajectory, his gaze steady on the path ahead.

Anaiya tries to calm her thoughts, her breath, her heart. She lets her grip tighten slightly in Seth's hands, as if his quiet confidence can transfer to her via osmosis.

When he stops suddenly, she whips her head around, expecting to see the images that have plagued her last two trips to the Edges. Instead, she is faced only with the greyed surface of just another recycler.

"Are you scared of heights?" Seth asks, dropping her hand gently and moving closer to the recycler.

He turns to look at her, waiting for her response.

"No..." she replies hesitantly.

A small smile widens across his face, but he turns away from her before she can witness the full transformation. She watches as the muscles in his forearms flex, reaching up to run his hand over the recycler's surface and stepping around its circumference. She follows him, her anxiety replaced with curiosity.

Tracking around the lazy arc of the recycler's circumference, she watches with interest as Seth pulls to a stop. The surface here is mottled, a flaw in the concrete mixture succumbing to cancer generated by decades of pollution concentration and absorption.

Seth bends down to pick up a large piece of fragmented concrete lying rejected on the blanket of gravel. He runs it across the corroded surface, digging and gouging, sending concrete abscesses scuttling to the ground. When he is finished he reaches higher, to repeat the process at another stained spot slightly to the left.

"Follow my lead," he calls out over his shoulder.

And then he slots his right foot into the lower niche, using the leverage to push himself up to grip the higher niche. With his free foot, he kicks and scrapes at nearby surface pits, finding purchase and creating new footholds. With his free hand he uses the concrete shard to claw new grip holes higher on the surface. And he climbs.

Anaiya moves closer to the recycler until her palms lie flat against its cold exterior and her T-shirt fabric grabs at the elbows.

She tilts her head back and her eyes alight on Seth as he scales at a constant pace, heading towards a horizon where the shadowed grey of the recycler meets the charcoal grey of the sky. This close, she can smell the sharp, dusty aroma of the crumbling concrete. A hailstorm of concrete gravel rains down the surface, skipping into her hands and falling harmlessly at her feet.

Seth doesn't look down, just keeps on climbing. Never slowing, never accelerating. He never falters.

A sense of excitement, a small thrill of adrenalin, rises in Anaiya. No longer content to just watch, she takes a few quick steps back from the recycler before lunging towards it, pushing up into a vertical vault and gripping at the deep indentations. She loses herself to the motion of ascending higher and higher.

The indented collar of the recycler sits less than three metres above her. One metre high, the void stretches around the girth of the recycler topped only by the solid concrete ceiling of the structure that rests one metre above the collar. Air rushes into the gap, sucked by powerful turbines ensconced below ground level. She feels it careen over her skin and pull her hair into a maelstrom around her face as she draws nearer.

She is close to Seth now. Can clearly see the path he intends to take to reach the summit. Caught in the moment, she doesn't wait for him to crest to the ceiling. She spies a smaller grip hold, a natural flaw in the corroded surface of the concrete, and uses the foundation of the collar to pull down into a deep crouch before springing up to find purchase in the crumbling dimple.

It all feels too easy, her body instinctively positions itself in preparation for the layout, drawing on the kinetic energy floating across and through her, ready to lift her to the top of the recycler in one fluid movement. She almost gives in to it, almost succumbs to the temptation, almost falls back into her free-running Peacekeeper habits.

The small voice in her subconsciousness screams for her attention, and before she lets momentum and strength carry her to the peak, she listens to it.

You'll be discovered. Your secret uncovered.

The warning should pull her up immediately, but instead she

lets it wash over her. Seconds pass and the urgency to move into her upwards twist or downwards swing becomes stronger. No decision will mean a painful ten-metre drop to the ground.

She feels the fingers of her right hand tingle and begin to twitch as the indention resists her grip. Still she delays her decision.

Her left foot scrabbles across the lip of the collar, desperate to stabilise her body as it rapidly moves out of alignment.

And when time is about to make Anaiya's decision for her, she clenches at the concrete beneath her right hand, pushes firmly against the surface at her feet and looses herself in a final movement.

Her body repels off the recycler's surface, before settling into a long curve that lands her back on the collar's platform. Dropping in a deep crouch to stabilise her shaky dismount, she pauses to let the air swirl around her.

She steadies herself, placing her right palm against the fine mesh that separates the collar from the yawning gap to the turbines below. She flexes against it, testing its resolve as a barrier between her and the unseen depths of the recycler. It holds steady, the mesh pushing deep into her skin.

Straight ahead, she can see the other side of the recycler frame the moonlit sky. Sheltered by the collar's overhang and protected by the mesh, Anaiya lets it all wash over her.

How did I get here?

She is not as weak as she was back at Last Defence, not as distracted as she was at the izakaya. Here in the Edges – in the dark, in the isolation – the question finds a direct path to her consciousness.

What am I doing here?

The questions are clear and loud, the answers lost in a tangle of confusing and contradicting thoughts, sensations and fears. Fear is a new emotion for Anaiya, one that sits off-centred. She hates how it makes her feel, how it unveils her shameful vulnerability. But, mostly, she hates how it catches her unaware, how insidiously it attaches itself to her in simple, unguarded situations. Like now.

"Anaiya?" Seth's voice distorts and echoes in the small space within the collar. "Are you all right?"

Simple questions. All of them. But no easy answers.

"Stay there, I'm coming to get you," he calls.

Anaiya turns around as Seth swings himself down onto the floor of the collar.

"Hey, butterfly," he says softly, barely audible above the hum of the turbines. He advances slowly, crouching down to fit within the confined space.

"Hey," she replies, sitting down on the platform.

Seth shuffles further into the air vent and settles down beside her. "Whatcha doing?"

Anaiya shrugs, bowing her head against the rush of the oncoming wind.

For a while they just sit there, backs up against the mesh barrier, subjected to the incessant air. When he finally speaks, Anaiya almost loses it under the drone of the recyclers and the echoes of the air beating against their vulnerable enclosure. But then he turns towards her and his lips, only centimetres away, spill the words into her ear.

She doesn't hear it all, only catching the last part, but to her, it feels as though it is the most important.

"...you know there's nothing to be afraid of. I won't let you fall."

In the dark, small space, his hand reaches for hers. As they link, Anaiya is not sure whether the small action has removed the fear or merely eclipsed it. Regardless, it is enough.

"Let's climb," she says.

She doesn't see him smile, only feels his grip squeeze her hand and his body shift beside her. He pulls her up, their bodies too close in the too small space. But she doesn't mind, just follows him as he leads her towards the edge of the platform.

"You go first," he says, raising his voice so that she can hear him. "I'll give you a boost and then follow."

He stops and turns, urging her to stand next to him at the lip.

"Like a safety sheet," he says, smiling.

Anaiya can't help but smile back. As a Peacekeeper, she had

laughed at the Earth Elementals who toiled at cleaning building exteriors, at their nervous gazes downwards, despite the failsafe protection of the large elastoplastic sheets suspended below them. Safety sheets were for second- and third-lustrum Fire Elementals. Before tonight, the thought of her needing a safety sheet would have insulted her, but tonight…Well, tonight was different.

She banishes the train of thought before it gains traction and lets herself lean into Seth. Her hands reach hesitantly for his shoulders, her thumbs finding the ridges of his collarbone. His eyes never stray from hers.

"The grip holds are in place, just follow them and I'll meet you at the top."

His hands come to rest lightly on her hips. She shivers in the cold air.

"Ready?" he asks.

She nods.

Her grip on him tightens, compensating for the loss of his hands at her hips. She lifts her right foot into the foothold created by his clasped hands. There is a weakness in doing this. In relying on someone else. In trusting them.

Pushing up, she reluctantly trades his warm, solid form for cold, crumbling concrete. She takes her time scaling the wall, following the path Seth created only minutes ago. She can't hear him following over the oppressive noise of the recyclers, vibrating below her. But she knows. Knows without looking down, without stilling the noise of the Edges, that he is there.

It doesn't take her long to reach the top of the recycler. As she pulls herself up over the edge, the distant city lights of Precinct 17 bleed into the night sky. She stands slowly, feeling the fibres of her muscles stretch taut and tingle, her eyes drinking in the far glow. The rustle of movement against the concrete surface pulls her gaze from the city.

Seth clambers onto the platform easily. There is such a look of pure enjoyment and satisfaction on his face that Anaiya momentarily forgets her earlier crisis of conscience, lets herself enjoy the simple pleasure of standing ten metres above the ground and surrounded by the dark blanket of sky. It is so easy to forget her past, her future, out here in the isolated darkness. Except for Seth, who pulls at her fire while constantly reminding her of her new identity and mission.

"Always such a rush," he says with a breathless laugh.

Anaiya laughs back. Typical Air Elemental; they were always searching out new emotions, heightened feelings, untapped experiences.

"How often do you come here?" she asks.

"A couple of times a year," he replies, turning to look over his shoulder at the view behind his back. "Whenever I need some perspective or want to lose myself in my thoughts."

He pivots and crouches down until he is sitting on the edge of the recycler, legs dangling down the side. She imagines him here alone, just staring out at the darkness and beyond.

"Want to join me?" he asks.

Anaiya sits close to Seth, their bodies converging on each other to fight against the cool insistence of the night breeze. For a long time they don't speak.

Anaiya's eyes drink in the sight of the sky. From up here, the Wall, though imposing, does not block the Wasteland sky. From here, she sees the midnight blue travel endlessly, punctuated by more stars than she has ever seen in her glimpses of light-polluted skies above the city. They are brighter over the Wasteland, and arrayed in a tangled, complex, random pattern of clusters – small stars like freckles interspersed against the shining beacons of larger stars. She sees music in them, a dark melody with bright notes.

"What song is that?"

Seth's voice, clear and strong in the night, interrupts her reverie.

"Hmm?"

"The tune you were humming," he says, turning his head to face her. "What song is it?"

Anaiya starts at the realisation she has been giving voice to the night symphony she found in the stars. "It's nothing," she says. "I was just messing around with some sounds…"

She lets her words hang in the silence, fighting back the confusion and embarrassment threatening to rise up and swallow them.

"I liked it," Seth says simply, turning back to the view before them.

She smiles into the darkness and lets herself lean back to lie flat on the recycler's roof. Seth lies down beside her and the two stare up at the black canvas above them.

"Do you miss life in the Eastern Area?" he asks.

Anaiya knows he is referring to her cover story, but she lets her mind drift over her life as a Peacekeeper. Does she miss it? As a Fire Elemental, she had never built emotional attachments to the things in her life. The buildings, locations, possessions and Elementals – they were all functional items that either helped or hindered her in being the best Peacekeeper. There was a familiarity to them, which was comforting, but does she miss them?

She closes her eyes, trying to tap into her heart's desires, the things she longs for when she is alone in her room at night. "I miss the feeling I used to get when I was lost in a job," she says, thinking of the rush that always came with free-running. "And the satisfaction of knowing I was good at it. I miss being able to navigate the streets and laneways without thinking. But I like the thrill of wandering down unfamiliar paths in the Northern Area precincts and finding something unexpected. I miss cola-roasted pigeon at the Samedi Markets," she says with a laugh, imagining greasy fingers and lips, her stomach growling at the memory.

Seth laughs quietly beside her. She feels the movement tickle against her side, like a thousand rapid caresses.

They fall silent again.

"Do you miss anyone from your old life?" he asks after a while.

Anaiya forces her eyes open and looks up at the sky, seeking out hidden details in the dark underlay. "I wasn't that close to anyone," she starts hesitantly, surprised, and somehow not, at how hard it is to answer his question. "At least I didn't think I was."

She thinks of Niamh, and a whole new torment of emotions attacks her. Who is he to her? Are her feelings mutations of the relationship she used to have with him or new feelings she is building and discovering? She sighs, frustrated at not being able to make sense of her emotions, let alone articulate them. "Coming here has been confusing," she says finally.

She lets her head roll to her left, glancing at Seth. She knows he can see her looking at him, but he maintains his gaze straight up at the sky. Seconds later, warm fingers find hers and interlock in a tight grip.

Anaiya sighs again, softer, more resigned. "I thought I had lost myself when I moved here," she says, forcing down the barriers in her mind to let the words flow unencumbered. "Now I feel like I've been torn in two: one part of me pulls me back towards the Elemental I used to be, and the other pulls me towards the Elemental I can be, and I'm not sure which one I want to be or which one I should be. Sometimes I hate myself for being different and sometimes I hate myself for *liking* the different me, and sometimes I just get so lost in being me that I forget who I actually am."

It's a messy tumble of words, an unfiltered stream of consciousness thrown out with no inhibition. The rawness of her admission pricks at her throat. She has voiced a truth she has so far kept hidden from even herself; it brings no welcome relief, no much-needed clarity, just an emptiness that reverberates with her harsh reality.

"Don't hate yourself for liking who you are now," Seth finally says.

The night above them grows deeper and the air around them colder.

"I like who you are now."

The compliment catches Anaiya off-guard; she hears the simple honesty in it and is comforted.

"I also like cola-roasted pigeon," he says, turning his head a little to smile at her.

Anaiya laughs. "Yeah?"

"Definitely. The Samedi Markets have the best, but there's a pretty good vendor along the Canal Delourq," he says. "We should go sometime."

"We should," she agrees, closing her eyes and smiling.

"We'll have to keep it quiet from Kaide, though," he says. "If he finds out I've given away the best-kept secret in the Northern Area, he won't be happy."

Anaiya laughs again and is giddy with it. She has never laughed so often as she has since her realignment. She wonders if her previous life was joyless or whether she was just incapable of feeling it. "How did you two meet?" she asks.

"We met about five years ago. I'd met a girl in one of the Ravignan izakaya and we were sort of connecting with each other."

Connecting with each other. It was a uniquely Air colloquialism for a concept specific only to Air and Earth Elementals, both of whom were notable for the regularity with which they formed long-lasting, if emotionally unstable, connections with others of their Element. Earth Elementals, who craved and thrived on the mundane, often took the arrangement to its extreme and declared ongoing monogamy to each other in front of Air Priestesses.

As a Fire Elemental, Anaiya had found the whole idea ridiculous and almost unfathomable. Tonight, however, shielded from the wind by Seth's body lying beside her and comforted by his hand still grasping hers in the crushed void between them, she can understand the appeal of being emotionally attached in a deep and lasting way to someone else.

"She was an Experimental Musician, did freaky stuff with sound mixing and wave distortion," Seth continues. "She was actually pretty good. Although Kaide would tell you that she had a genius for a Sound Developer."

"Ah," Anaiya murmurs.

"She introduced us one night. I remember he was commandeering the music uploader at the bar, playing all of these chaotic sound mixes. I insulted his taste in music, he insulted my taste in fashion – I wore a lot of black back then – and then reminded me I was dating an Experimental Musician – who had overheard my insult and was rather less than impressed with my genius wit."

"Smooth," Anaiya teases softly, her voice floating in the darkness.

"Yeah, not so much. So unimpressed was my Experimental Musician that she left me to hook up with another guy at the izakaya. Kaide felt bad and, in his typical style, bought a round of drinks to apologise. We drank till morning, stumbled down to Precinct 19 to hit up some cola pigeon to fight the hangovers, and have been hanging out ever since. He was the one who introduced me to Rehhd, and Rehhd introduced us to Cress, Eamon and Yve, and practically everyone else in the Northern Area."

Rehhd's name brings with it the inevitable and now-familiar guilt. "What is her story?" Anaiya asks, struggling to keep her voice casual.

"Rehhd's a bit of an enigma," Seth says. "She makes friends with everyone but is close to no one. Kaide is probably the closest to her, even though they've never been involved. They've shared a few battles together. Kaide was the one who saved her from bleeding out after a Peacekeeper attack a few years back."

Anaiya realises her grip has tightened uncomfortably on Seth's hand and she releases it quickly.

"Bad memories?" Seth asks quietly.

Anaiya opens her eyes and shakes her head. "No. That's not it…" she says. "It wasn't that bad in the Eastern Area."

"What do you mean?" Seth asks, rolling onto his side and propping up his head with his hand.

She stares up at him, a dark shadow beneath a dark sky. "Just that it never got that bad where I was from. There were no clashes between Fire and Air Elementals. No Peacekeeper attacks."

The words are acrid in her mouth. *Peacekeepers do not attack. Peacekeepers enforce. Protect.* Her thoughts ring loud in her head, but hollow.

Seth looks down at her. "You've never seen Fire violence before?" he asks softly.

Anaiya shakes her head.

"Tonight was your first encounter?"

Anaiya looks up at him confused. *But there was no violence tonight.*

Seth's eyes don't move from hers and under his scrutiny she replays the events of the night. Replays the encounter with Jenna and the other Peacekeeper. It was calculated. And it was clinical. But was it violence?

"Is it always like that?" she asks instead.

She watches as he rolls back down to lie flat beside her.

"Sometimes," he says. "Usually it's worse."

"What does worse look like?"

"Unprovoked. Targeted. Unjustified. Excessive…"

The words wrap around them like dark spectres.

"Tonight wasn't that. Not really," he says. "Peacekeepers are easy to provoke – show them the slightest hint of Unorthodoxy and they'll jump into action."

Anaiya's fire flares at the insult, but she ignores it and forces her body to stay still.

"In some Peacekeepers, the fire burns hotter, it seeks out the fight. And in some Air Elementals, there is a lust to spark the flame, to engage in the dance. Eamon's like that."

Eamon. The Elemental who had gone down to Jenna's restraint serum.

"He probably called for the Peacekeepers' attention. And no doubt they were all too happy to oblige."

"Is Rehhd like Eamon?"

"Yes…No…" He sighs. "Mostly, I guess," he concludes reluctantly. "Rehhd loves the thrill of the chase, loves the attention. In that way she's a lot like Eamon and Cress. The three of them love finding the drama, rather than waiting for it to find them. But Rehhd doesn't chase it just for the thrill. The thrill is a definite bonus in her eyes, but it's not the only reason she does it. She's damaged. She suffered, and she's changed because of it. Plus, she doesn't have to look as hard for the thrill as Eamon and Cress. Trouble loves finding Rehhd – it's attracted to her past. It makes her a target. She caused some real headaches for the Peacekeepers up here. They don't forget easily."

Seth falls silent and Anaiya is grateful for the pause. Jagged-edged thoughts are grating along her synapses; her mind struggling to make sense of Seth's words, faltering under their weight and fracturing under their impact.

"Real Peacekeeper violence comes from a darker place." His

voice pushes its way into her already too-full consciousness. "It's unpredictable. Unmerciful. Invincible."

EIGHTEEN

Anaiya doesn't remember how long they stayed lying up there on the recycler in the dark and silence afterwards. There were no more words left in either of them. Only when the sky above and the concrete below had completed a full circle of numbing cold, fully enveloping them and their dark thoughts, did they wordlessly shift and commence their descent back to terra firma.

They don't hold hands on their way back through the Edges, suffering through their own torment alone and without comfort.

Anaiya's torment takes many faces. The distorted reflection of a Peacekeeper seen through Seth's eyes. The hints of personal experience with Peacekeeper violence. And the difficult acceptance of an unimagined possibility – that it could be true – that Seth's 'Peacekeeper violence' is just another name for the hot, mutated, undisciplined fire in Heterodoxy-affected Fire Elementals.

The silence accompanies them right up to the boundary streets of the precinct. The purple bruise of light in the East announces the darkest part of the night is over, that the curfew is lifting and another day is being thrown at Otpor.

Seth turns his back to the light, taking a step towards the east.

"I'm this way," Anaiya says, nodding her head towards the south.

Seth pauses, glancing between the two paths to be taken.

"Want some company?" he asks.

Yes.

"No, I'm good," she replies.

His face falls, but he recovers quickly. "OK..."

"OK..." she repeats.

They both are stalling, unwilling to accept the end to the night.

But, there is nothing left to be said and so she pulls at her reluctant feet and starts towards Rue Leibniz.

"Hey Anaiya?"

She turns around. He still hasn't moved.

"Yeah?"

"A few of us will be at Soylent tomorrow night. For a Sound event..."

"Soylent?"

"This izakaya on Rue Dayroses." There is a question in his eyes and the tilt of his head. "Every Fourth night they hand control of the amps over to Elementals with a Music Competency who are working on new sounds. Sort of lets them beta test it to a live audience."

He pauses again, seemingly uncomfortable with Anaiya's lack of response. "So, anyway, if you're interested...It would be good to see you there."

It is an intriguing invitation, and an excellent opportunity to gather more intel on Rehhd and gain exposure to her network.

And to see Seth again.

She brushes away her limbic brain's accusation with a frown.

"OK..." she replies hesitantly. "Maybe I'll see you there."

A small smile plays across his features. "Great. I'll keep an eye out for you."

Another heavy pause settles between them and, for a moment, Anaiya expects him to say something else. A strange sensation takes over her body – an unfamiliar tension, an unexpected anticipation. It sets her heartbeat to an unsteady rhythm and stretches time like pitch succumbing to gravity.

The smile broadens on his face. And then it is just her, watching him as he turns and walks westwards, setting the path for the sun.

It is late afternoon by the time Anaiya wakes. Her eyes spring open and her heart clenches in a sharp state of panic. She swipes at her wristplate with urgent fingers, trying to locate the inevitable demand from Niamh. The messages scroll past in a blur as she flicks her fingers upwards and then downwards, skimming, and then more thoroughly scanning, the contents of her inbox.

Slowly she sits up. Her heart rate slows to a more measured beat as her mind works to make sense of the puzzle.

No doubt Jenna would have reported the run-in from last night. Niamh would have avoided messaging her while she was likely to be in the presence of a target.

She glances at her wristplate again. More than fifteen hours have passed since the encounter.

What game are you playing, Niamh?

Her fingers hover over her wrist, phantom strings pulling at them to send the proactive communication. She knows it is a test. That Niamh is deducing all kinds of conclusions from the time it takes to contact him, from the amount and type of information she presents to him.

What will I tell him?

It is a question without an answer. What can she tell him? That she spent an entire night with a known associate of Rehhd, spent a large chunk of that night with Rehhd herself, but has no information on either of them that will help to uncover or dismantle the Resistance. She knows the questions he will ask, the results he will demand. And she knows that she is unable to answer or provide them.

For now.

It is the motivation she needs to put aside the messy, limbic-dominated thoughts that cloud her mind when she remembers her time with Rehhd and Kaide. And Seth. Forcing her brain to compartmentalise her memories and desires, she buries her newfound Air tendencies and sharpens her Fire instincts.

She needs to gather useful intel immediately – something she can pass on to Niamh that will excuse her late reporting. Conversations of the night before tickle at the back of her mind, resisting her attempts at forcing them into focus. Snatches of dialogue and random phrases filter through her brain, none of them presenting a useful lead.

The room is becoming oppressive, its vacant walls mocking her inability to find the answers she needs, that Niamh expects.

Enough.

She dresses quickly and heads out into the streets of the Northern Cardinal Area. Unable to run, she sets a brisk pace, losing herself in the rhythmic slap of her feet and simple pleasure of exercising. Her mind wanders in an unfettered stream of consciousness, looking for a solution somewhere in the mess of chaotic thoughts and emotions.

Wide streets shift into narrow laneways; hidden arcades widen and stretch into broad avenues and boulevardes. Food stalls and meal kiosks dispense pre-packaged synth food parcels to waiting customers, a cluster of Air Elementals here, an impatient Border Watcher there. Earth Cleaners scrub at building windows and wash down dusty coordinate plates.

The air cools as the brown sky darkens and a new wave of activity washes over the precinct. Coloured lights emerge and windows are flung open to eject stale warm air and a hundred individual soundtracks. Air Elementals begin their evening pilgrimage to various entertainment hubs and Anaiya finds herself caught up in the procession.

Ahead, she spies the familiar entrance to the Ravignan Strip and peels off towards Veritas, the izakaya where she first ran into Rehhd. Inside, the space is busy without being crowded. Younger Air Elementals dominate the izakaya, filling the tables and lounges scattered around the performance space. A few older Elementals, faces gaunt with the inevitable synth toxin buildup, stake out solitary places at the bar.

Anaiya finds a spare stool at the bar and takes a seat. An Earth Server wanders over to take her order, but she waves him away. A few minutes later the tall Air Elemental Anaiya has been watching wanders over.

"Anaiya, right?" Yve says, running her hand through short, spiky hair. "What can I get you?"

"I was thinking of trying a new concoction – any recommendations?"

It is a simple strategy to keep Yve around, get her talking.

"I'm working on a sour-based alcohol with a slow-release enhancer, a kind of cross between a jaydeedioxy and a genemoly. Interested?"

Anaiya has never heard of the synth alcohols mentioned. "Sounds great."

Yve turns her back and busies herself grabbing various bottles and vials from behind the bar. The silence between them grows and Anaiya lets it stretch.

"Heard you had a rough one last night," Yve eventually calls over her shoulder.

Anaiya smiles. At least in some ways, Air Elementals are predictable.

"Yeah, too many tequilas," she replies.

Yve laughs and returns to the bar with Anaiya's drink. "The organic stuff is a bit more potent."

"I hear I have you to thank for that."

Yve shrugs, but her smile lingers.

Anaiya unravels her lifeline and reaches for the payment terminal, but Yve waves it away.

"On the house," she says, pushing the tumbler of clear fizzing liquid towards Anaiya.

"Thanks," Anaiya replies, taking a long sip from the frosted glass. "So, how was Rehhd afterwards?"

"Amped up," Yve says with a laugh. "But then again, she's always amped up with Eamon."

"He was the one that the Peacekeepers…dropped?"

Anaiya stumbles over the Air colloquialism, but Yve doesn't seem to notice.

"Yeah, not his first time," she confirms. "What about you? Have you been dropped before?"

Anaiya shakes her head, abruptly stopping when she realises the implications of her answer.

"Me neither," Yve says. "I prefer to keep my Fire relationships all about business. So, how did it feel?"

"Disconcerting," Anaiya replies.

Wait. Something is not right here.

The thought comes too late, her words already unleashed. She stares down at her glass, the tumbler close to finished. That the enhancer is a disinhibitor is no longer in doubt, but Anaiya has never come across one as strong or as rapidly acting.

You said the enhancer was slow-releasing…

"You were lucky Seth was there to look after you," Yve says.

Anaiya has picked up on Yve's pattern and knows a question will follow. "How long have you known him for?" she asks, cutting in before Yve gets a chance to continue.

"Rehhd and I started to connect about six months ago; Seth and Eamon seemed to come with the territory."

The timeframe is interesting, but Anaiya needs to keep Yve talking lest she start asking more questions. "Six months. Things getting serious?"

"Why?" Yve's voice turns sharp. "You looking to cut in?"

Anaiya recalls Rehhd's words at their first meeting.

Yep. That definitely is a jealous streak.

Anaiya raises her hands in submission. "No, no, no."

Yve narrows her eyes briefly, but eventually relaxes.

"Rehhd doesn't do serious," she finally concedes. "Unless it's work."

Anaiya hears the tightness in Yve's voice and is surprised when she finds her thoughts softening in response.

"You want another one?" the bar owner asks, looking down at Anaiya's empty glass.

The opportunity for more intel is tempting, but the risky chemical concoction is already causing her problems. And she can't afford to let anything slip so early in her mission. Besides, she has somewhere to be. "No," she says, standing up from the stool. "I've got work of my own to do."

The walk to Soylent is an easy one. Anaiya constantly glances at her wristplate, checking as her vitals return to sobriety, seeking out any new communications from Niamh. The lack of intel gathered from

Yve compounds the anxiety that rushes over her every time she thinks of him waiting for her call.

Ahead, the neon green lettering of the izakaya casts a garish aura around the Elementals nearby. Anaiya looks around for Rehhd, finding her in a group of unfamiliar Air Elementals. As she walks towards the group, Rehhd looks over. A scowl briefly appears on her face, but it quickly fades, replaced by a brittle plastic smile.

"Anaiya." Her voice is a glucose-covered barb. "I didn't know you were coming tonight."

It sounds as an accusation, and a reprimand. Anaiya frowns, but doesn't bite. "Seth invited me." The words are out before she can reconsider them. Inwardly, she cringes at the sound of her explanation, her deference.

"Did he just?" Rehhd counters. "How very *cordial* of our Seth."

"Did you expect any less?" Seth saunters towards them, stopping next to Anaiya. Grinning, he winks at her before turning his attention to Rehhd.

"Not at all," Rehhd says, her smile still tight.

"How's Eamon doing?" he asks.

"Not as well as Anaiya," she replies, a shadow of her scowl reappearing. "He's still recovering, but he'll bounce back soon enough."

"No doubt," Seth says. "He always does."

The words seem to hang in the air. Rehhd opens her mouth as if to say something, but closes it with a sigh.

"Did he say how it all started?"

Anaiya's question draws a sharp look from Rehhd and she wonders, not for the first time during this encounter, what has happened since their first meeting to draw this newfound ire.

Seth interrupts, drawing her attention away from Anaiya. "What *was* he doing out there, Rehhd?"

She shakes her head, seemingly exasperated. "Nothing *official*. By his account, he was just heading to Scythe's when he saw the Peacekeepers."

"No provocation?" Seth asks.

"Of course not," Rehhd snaps, her frustration clearly showing now. "He may be reckless. He's not stupid."

Doubtful. "What restraint charge was recorded?" Anaiya asks.

It's an answer she would already have if she had spoken to Niamh. She glances surreptitiously at her wristplate. Still no communication.

"It doesn't matter what they recorded," Rehhd seethes. "With Eamon's history, they could have uploaded any charge and he would struggle to challenge it."

She's right. Challenging a restraint charge is difficult enough in ideal circumstances; Elementals with long Unorthodoxy records have almost no chance at being granted deletions. But Peacekeepers do not record false charges. They might err on the side of caution when assessing intent, recording a murder instead of a manslaughter. Or they might pre-emptively restrain Elementals based on an association with known perpetrators or an imminent threat to Orthodoxy…

As a Peacekeeper, it had all sounded so rational. So *necessary.* Now it sounds hollow, hinting at a wrongness that sours her memories.

"What did they record for you?" Rehhd asks.

"Interfering with an enforcement action," Anaiya replies, recalling the offence she would have been charged with if her restraint had been real. It is a low-level charge, a common slap on the wrist applied in most misdemeanour situations.

"Really?" Seth asks, frowning. "That's all they gave you for rushing a Peacekeeper?"

Rushing? I didn't rush Jenna…

And then she sees it as he would have. An Air Elemental running to confront an on-duty Peacekeeper in the middle of a restraint action. She *had* rushed Jenna. And just as quickly, she realises that her interference charge is too lenient. "Maybe because it was my first charge? Or my hypoxia?"

Seth tilts his head thoughtfully, and Anaiya thinks he might just believe it, but Rehhd folds her arms and regards Anaiya coldly.

"Your first charge?" Rehhd's voice is soft. Deadly.

Anaiya nods, her mind racing for ways to diffuse the situation and redirect suspicion away from herself.

"You tarnished your record in a fight that wasn't yours."

Rehhd leaves the statement hanging in the air. Like an accusation. "Why?"

"Tequila?" It is a poor attempt at humour.

Seth rewards her with a grin but Rehhd's not letting her off so easily. Eyes narrowed and lips pursed, Anaiya can see that she will pursue this unless she gets a satisfactory answer.

Her mind races to manufacture a reasonable justification, but she knows that each passing second only serves to heighten suspicion. With her pulse racing, she makes a snap decision to tell a kind of truth. "I didn't want Seth to get dropped…"

The confession earns a smile from Seth.

"…and I really needed to wipe that smug, self-satisfied smile off the Peacekeeper."

Seth barks a short laugh and even Rehhd's face softens.

"I haven't seen her before," Seth says, addressing Rehhd.

"None of us have," Rehhd replies, her interrogation of Anaiya forgotten. "Figure she must be a transfer."

Seth frowns, nodding his agreement.

"The whole Area is being overtaken by outsiders," Rehhd says, flicking a pointed glance at Anaiya, before turning to head into the izakaya. The ire is still there, but it has lost some of its sharpness.

"Play nice, Rehhd," Seth calls after her.

Rehhd flashes a wicked grin over her shoulder. "You're no fun any more, Seth."

"Rehhd seems…feisty tonight," Anaiya says, glancing around the izakaya.

It is a smaller space than the other izakaya she has been to since her deployment, but the sheer volume of patrons makes it impossible to focus on anything, or anyone, for too long. The room is a mayhem of Air celebration and debauchery. She waits for her usual Fire disapproval to emerge, but it never comes. Seth grabs her hand and instead she revels in the thrill of anticipation that skips along her skin.

Stay focussed, Anaiya.

But the call of the izakaya already hints at intoxication. Lights bounce and reverberate off mirrored walls as loud beats and sweet melodies swell through the packed room.

"Don't pay any attention to Rehhd," Seth replies. "She's been a little high-strung lately."

Don't pay any attention to Rehhd.

He means it to be a comfort – something to alleviate her concerns – but the words circle in her mind, becoming a reprimand.

The only thing she *should* be doing is paying attention to Rehhd. It should be the thing that consumes her thoughts, fills her hours, directs her movements. *That* is her mission. Yet, here she is. Captivated by an entirely different Elemental.

A dense feeling, like shame but *brighter*, bubbles up inside her. She pushes it away, letting Seth lead her through the crowd.

The line to the bar is four rows deep – a compact collection of Elementals laughing, swaying, gossiping, flirting. Anaiya and Seth take their place amongst them, their bodies pressing together as the crowd pushes against them. The absence of personal space – the familiar no-go zone she had strictly maintained as a Peacekeeper – is immediately noticeable. She doesn't step away, instead taking comfort in the stability of Seth against the crush of the crowd.

There is something about him – the quiet confidence, the way he inhibits a space. The way energy seems to gravitate to him. Swirl around him.

"Here." Seth's voice breaks into her thoughts. He holds out a tall glass fizzing with a black liquid.

Anaiya hesitates.

"It won't hurt you, butterfly." He is smiling again. Teasing her.

And just like that, complex thoughts and emotions are dispelled by the simple need to prolong this moment. Anaiya takes the glass from him and follows him to the nearest table. Reaching it, he pulls out a chair with a flourish, beckoning to her to sit down. It is a decidedly Air gesture that she finds oddly charming.

"So, where are the others?" she asks as he takes a seat next to her. "I thought this was a group rendezvous."

Seth glances over his shoulder. "A few of them are with Rehhd…"

Anaiya follows his gaze to where her target sits, deep in conversation with a small group of animated Elementals.

"…Eamon is out of commission, obviously. And Kaide and Cressida are doing some last minute additions to a project they are working on."

"So, it's just us?"

"It's just us." He watches for her reaction, holding her gaze as that trademark curve of a smile grows on his face again. "Is that OK?"

No. It's not OK, Anaiya. How will you keep track of Rehhd? How will you get useful intel for Niamh?

Seth quirks his head to the side. Watching her, waiting for her response.

How will you progress this mission if you're sitting here all night with Seth? Staring into those eyes…Fixating on that irrepressible smile…

"It's perfect."

"Wow," Anaiya breathes.

The room has fallen silent, or as silent as a packed izakaya full of vibrant Air Elementals can be.

A soft, melodic buzz still vibrates as the last notes of the performance fade to memory. A rush of dopamine floods her brain, and she rubs at her arms vigorously, shaking off the remnants of pleasure that continue to give her chills.

"That was amazing."

Amazing. It is a word she has heard, but never used. Never felt. It comes with a lightness – an exhilaration that is as close to free-running as she has felt since her realignment.

"How do you feel?" Seth asks. "*What* do you feel?"

"Light," she replies. "I feel as if I could float."

Seth laughs. "Then I guess it works."

Anaiya laughs, the synth alcohol making her loose, uninhibited. "What works?"

The noise in the izakaya starts to build again and Seth leans in close in order to be heard. "Kaide's project. He's been working on it for years…*years.* It's like…like a phylogenetic tree of sounds."

"*Phylogenetic,* huh? Someone paid attention during their conditioning."

"Ha, ha," he replies in good humour. "Yes. *Phylogenetic.* You know, the branches of genetic similarity."

Anaiya does know. It is the basis upon which the Cooperative engineers new generations – merging the best genetics from donated sperm and eggs to create the required diversity among Otpor's Elementals. Peacekeepers use their knowledge of it to understand criminal profiles and enhance future-searching. It is surprising to hear an Air Elemental use the term with familiarity.

"He's developed some sort of application or device to group sounds based on likeness – to create aural haplotypes. It's completely visionary. He's spent the last year working on linking those haplotypes to emotional responses…Testing how certain alcohols and enhancers affect the raw response."

Anaiya glances down at her half-empty glass. "This?"

"A pituarmagn," he confides. "To amplify dopamine triggers."

"And the performance?"

"Ella has been working with Kaide for the last three months, trying to build a piece that would work musically and biologically. Tonight was her debut."

"So the music is a manipulation?"

It is a simple conclusion for Anaiya to make, but Seth frowns, that smile of his faltering. "A manipulation? No…"

The pause lengthens, his frown deepens. Anaiya watches uncertainty trace lines across his face. Her chest feels hollow. She recognises his affliction – understands what it is like to have your reality shattered when it collides with someone else's.

"No?" she asks gently.

"No." He is more adamant, now. More certain. "Not a manipulation. An encouragement. A *catalyst*. Not a manipulation."

Seth stares at her intently, each word spoken in earnest. As if to convince her of their truth.

She shrugs, unconvinced but unwilling to press further. Manipulation or catalyst – either way it makes her feel something she wouldn't have otherwise. Just like her realignment has.

"All art is a catalyst, no?"

That makes him smile again. "Oui, butterfly. All art is a catalyst. All art triggers a response – raw or enhanced."

He runs his finger down his own glass of pituarmagn, sluicing off beads of condensation that have formed on the chilled surface. Reaching across the table, he takes her palm in his hand and traces lines across the skin, leaving wet trails that glisten in the muted izakaya light.

Anaiya shivers in spite of herself, the sensation eclipsing the warm and fuzzy feeling left behind by the flood of synth alcohol in her bloodstream. Desire, thick and heavy, spikes through the dulled edges of her mind. All thoughts of Rehhd, Niamh and her mission obliterated. It is not the desire of a Fire Elemental, which burns hot and fast, dying quickly and cleanly. It is denser, more complex – pulling at her mind and not just her body, a heady mix of competing thoughts and emotions and sensations.

She craves it as much as she wants to run from it.

NINETEEN

It is late by the time Seth and Anaiya leave the izakaya and head home. Anaiya had lost sight of Rehhd early in the night, too distracted by Seth to notice, too inebriated to be concerned. But, now, with the sobering night air brushing against her, the gravity of her situation begins to weigh heavy.

So wrapped up in the tangled threads of her mind, Anaiya doesn't see the dark-clad figures melding into the shadows ahead until they are less than two blocks away. Following the trajectory of her thoughts, her brain screams *Peacekeepers!* and she knows without glancing at her wristplate that curfew commenced hours ago.

In one fluid movement she flattens herself against the wall of the tall, terraced building to her left. In the next, she grabs at Seth's sleeve and pulls him roughly to her. He stumbles and grunts, but she catches him before he catapults over his own feet and jams her palm over his mouth. Her right-hand grip has moved from his sleeve to his chest and, without moving her left from his mouth, pulls him closer. Confusion registers in his frown.

"Shhh," she whispers tightly, slowly drawing her hand from his mouth.

He grabs hold of it, placing it next to the one on his chest.

Something else flares in his eyes and Anaiya's belly warms in unconscious response. She shakes her head and looks pointedly to her left, to where the two concealed strangers still loiter.

Seth turns his head to follow her gaze. His reaction is unexpected. No shock or exaggerated stillness overcomes his posture. Instead, his fingers reach up to pull her face back towards his.

Anaiya shakes her head again, sterner, more urgently. They need to be still, avoid detection, become invisible. But Seth merely leans in closer, his forehead touching hers. His body presses heavier against hers, testing the barrier of her arms levelled against his torso. His hands brush over her scapula and run down her shoulders. In other circumstances, normal circumstances, she would hardly be aware of them. But her whole body is tense with anticipation and attuned to the slightest stimulation. She feels the light touch of his hands, smells the musty aroma of the building's facade mingle with the clean citrus smell of his skin. And when he kisses her, she can taste the alcoholic echoes on his tongue.

The pure, perfect pleasure of it is distracting. A furtive glance to her left confirms the two figures are still ahead of them. "Seth," she whispers insistently. "Two Peacekeepers are –"

Impossibly, he shakes his head. "They aren't Peacekeepers, butterfly," he says, before leaning in to kiss her again.

This time his grip tightens on her hips and, with slow and steady steps, he pulls her with him as he steps backwards into the muted light of the street. At first she resists, gripping his shirt and pulling him towards her, desperate to maintain their cover. He laughs, all the while continuing to pull her out into the street with him.

Moments later he breaks away and finally pauses to look down the street to the strange figures that have been haunting Anaiya's peripheral vision. They are moving closer, gaining in size and definition with each stride they take. Anaiya grips his hand tightly, ready to run. Her feet itch with the need to escape, to remove herself from this dangerous situation and never look back. Seth maintains his casual stance and stillness.

Anaiya's eyes are fixated on the advancing figures. Their dark kevlar makes it difficult for her to make out distinct movements and they almost appear to be floating towards her. Something about the vision settles uneasily in her mind, tickling in its unfamiliarity and wrongness.

And then it registers. They aren't moving like Peacekeepers. They are too light on their feet, not so much striding towards Anaiya as they are drifting…dancing.

They aren't Peacekeepers.

The fact is as simple as it is shocking. She watches them both closely as they step nearer, trying to decipher the true identities of the shadow dancers. The one to the right appears male and angles his shoulders forwards as he advances. There is something familiar in the action, a sense of disguising the true dimensions of the solid form it shields. When he quirks his head to his right, Anaiya gasps.

"Hello, Anaiya," the soft voice sings to her in the quiet street.

Beat. Beat. Beat. Her heart betrays her panic.

"Hello, Kaide," she manages to strangle from her constricted throat.

"What is this?" she asks Seth, her voice trembling with confusion, betrayal and the worst emotion that has yet to torment her. Harsher than jealousy. Deadlier than guilt.

Fear.

Kaide and his companion have arrived at the corner of the block where she stands, stiff and tense. Seth moves to greet them, Anaiya's question left unanswered. She watches as he and Kaide engage in a familiar playful jostle before Seth picks up and swings the diminutive female Air Elemental around in wide circles. Anaiya works to calm her racing thoughts, trying desperately to rationalise the situation.

The breeze shifts, bringing with it a sweet, bitter scent she has smelled before. It radiates from the two kevlar-clad Air Elementals, dripping down Kaide's wrist and scattered as invisible droplets in his companion's hair.

"Cress, this is Anaiya," Seth says, lowering the female to the ground and motioning back to Anaiya. "Anaiya, this is Cressida."

She doesn't respond. Her Fire identity is rapidly asserting itself, her mind reverting to a clinical observation of the scene before her. Cressida is a lustrum younger than Anaiya, the five-year difference noticeable in the giddy excitement emanating from the Premie's presence.

At the sound of her name, Cressida falls into an exaggerated bow, arms flourishing before her.

"You didn't tell me she was a Dancer," she says to Kaide once she has righted herself.

"She's not," Kaide says with a slight frown, confused but drawn to Anaiya's poised stance and soft feet.

Seth laughs, redirecting attention away from Anaiya.

"Anaiya is Music," he says, a bright pleasure tingeing his words.

Cressida smiles widely and nods.

"Of course." She laughs. "Music and Literature are the greatest companions." A sly look flits across her features as she shares her gaze between Seth and Anaiya. "Although, Music and Dance are the most fun."

Cressida and Seth laugh. Anaiya smiles tightly before she sees Kaide's thoughtful gaze still on her athletic frame.

"What are you two doing out here?" she asks abruptly, keen to keep the focus away from her.

"You haven't told her?" Kaide asks too loudly, shifting his stare to Seth.

Cressida's smile falters.

"Told me what?" Anaiya asks, her soft voice a deadly counterpoint to Kaide's.

"Kaide." Seth squares off against the larger figure, his voice low and harsh. "Not now."

"You haven't vetted her, have you?" Kaide accuses.

"Told me what?" Anaiya repeats, her voice shifting to a lower register.

Cressida steps smoothly between them, blocking Seth from Anaiya's gaze. "I think it's better that we show her."

Anaiya steps to her left, giving her room to view all three Air Elementals. Cressida, despite her small frame, stands tall and unflinching before Seth. Seth is tense, his right hand dragging trenches through his hair. Kaide, however, is completely focussed on Anaiya.

"Do you trust her?" he asks Seth without disengaging his focus.

Seth doesn't answer immediately. His eyes shift from Cressida to Anaiya. She forces her heart to slow. He is looking for that thing inside her, the part of her that signals who she is and what she wants.

Anaiya's breath becomes slow and shallow, waiting for him to see her Fire identity raging hot within her.

And then he simply nods. "She is one of us."

Cressida leads them through the softly lit streets, away from the Edges and towards the invisible boundary line that separates Precinct 17 from 18. The buildings begin to take on the eclectic feel of a hybrid precinct, where no one Element dominates. Galleries, bars and restaurants sit alongside functional administrative buildings and a handful of multi-storey residential apartments. Deep in curfew hours, the buildings and streets are dark and quiet, punctuated only by the occasional glow of light or snatch of raised voices from an opened apartment window.

The four of them stick to the shadows, Kaide walking with Cressida and regularly casting furtive glances back towards Seth and Anaiya. Cressida leans into Kaide to whisper something beyond Anaiya's hearing, but otherwise they move silently.

Anaiya keeps her eyes firmly ahead, despite the occasional tug of Seth's glances in her peripheral vision. The panic that rushed at her earlier has dissipated. It is replaced by a heavy awareness that comes with teeth, gnawing at her insides like rats at rotting meat.

At this deeper level is the knowledge of exactly what Seth hasn't told her and of where Cressida and Kaide are taking them. Knowing what she will find at the end of their journey, however, does not prepare her for the visceral reaction when she sees it.

Cressida and Kaide halt their progress at the end of a darkened laneway lined with shopfronts and restaurants that will soon fill with the morning rush. With the ghosts of these future Elementals brushing against her, Anaiya's step falters. Seth reaches for her, keeping her from tumbling. She leans gratefully on him as she regains her balance. Straightening, her eyes lift to where Kaide and Cressida are standing to attention either side of a black wall.

She realises, belatedly, that they are waiting for something. The incriminating scent that has followed them is denser here, clinging to Anaiya's nostrils and making her eyes water. Seth glances at her, checking she is OK. A slight squeeze of her hand is the last thing Anaiya remembers before her world is thrown, again, into chaos.

Releasing her, Seth taps at his wristplate and the harsh white light of the diode explodes around them. Anaiya doesn't see how the light creates deep shadows on the faces of her companions or obliterates the subtlety in the details of the buildings around them. All she sees is the nightmare vision in front of her.

The mural is immense, scaling almost the entire height of the four-storey facade. Instinctively, Anaiya knows that the details must be different, but all she can see are the same motifs that have plagued the other cases of Heterodoxy. Black fire scorching the other elements, turning them to ash that crumbles and disintegrates at the edges. And the forbidden word. Painted in metre-high lettering, it runs the full length of the ten-metre wall.

RESISTANCE.

TWENTY

Anaiya clenches down on the bile that threatens to erupt through her system. She closes her eyes, seeing the mural painted in negative on the inside of her eyelids. Her body tingles with the effort of staying still; she wants to scream, to rail.

Pulling in deep breaths, she concentrates on counting the supersonic beats of her heart. Lets the chaos consume her.

And clears it.

The torrent of emotion freezes inside her mind. Still there, but no longer active. She feels her neocortex navigate around it, pushing forward to assert its dominance.

Opening her eyes, she is confronted again with the mural. But this time, her heart is hardened and she can appraise it with cold rationality. The details of the mural are more complex than in previous instances, leading her to conclude that the perpetrators have had more time to complete their Heterodoxy. She realises that they are using the curfew to their advantage, turning the Cooperative's efforts against them.

She laughs.

The sound is too loud: it reverberates off the defaced wall and down the streets, a globule of lys travelling and diluting along a network of veins. Cressida startles at the sound before relaxing into a relieved smile. Anaiya turns to Seth. Unlike the other two, his face is harder to read.

"So you like it?" he murmurs.

She looks back to the mural. Despite her newfound clarity and calmness, she finds it easier to face the crime than the traitor. The traitor who only moments ago…

She shuts down the memory before it can consume her, before it can distract her from the situation at hand. She will not be distracted again. Despite her own failings she has been given a second chance to succeed in her mission and she is adamant she will not need a third. Her neocortex maintains its primacy, containing the trembling limbic brain that continues to seek out Seth's presence like a synth-addled addict. It pushes down the conflicting emotions and vulnerable memories to plan her next move.

"It is perfect," she whispers.

Moments later, with thoughts of curfew and extra Peacekeeper patrols, the four of them tear their respective gazes away from the mural and begin their retreat. No words are spoken as they slink through the empty streets.

After ten minutes or so, Cressida peels off down an unmarked street alone and Anaiya is left with the two males. The streets are growing wider, lined with blaring street lights and well-lit administrative buildings; it is harder for the three of them to stay shadowed and obscured. Anaiya presses in behind Seth, recoiling internally at the intimacy. She feels Kaide follow suit, catching flashes of connecting skin and a shallow breath at her neck. Hand clenched at her sides, she endures the shame, desperate as they are to remain hidden from unannounced Peacekeeper patrols.

Finally seeing a familiar street that will lead her to her apartment, Anaiya exhales and breaks away from the two males. A strong grip wraps around her forearm, halting her in her tracks.

"Where are you going?" Kaide whispers.

Seth turns around, frowning at Kaide and then Anaiya. Kaide drops his grip, but moves to block her path.

"I'm going home," Anaiya whispers back, glancing at Seth before stepping to move around Kaide.

Kaide mirrors her movement, continuing to block her path.

"We can't let you do that. It's too dangerous."

"Kaide's right, butterfly." Seth has moved closer to make his hushed voice more easily heard. "Peacekeeper patrols are too prevalent in this area. You'll have to come back to my place until morning."

She looks from Seth to Kaide. Kaide's arms are crossed loosely against his chest, reminding her of confident Peacekeepers who anticipate resistance from deluded perpetrators. She is caught – there is no time to try and reason her way out of it: every minute they stay there in the half shadows and silence increases the risk of their detection. Attempting to evade Kaide will only create disruption and suspicion, neither of which she can afford.

There is nothing for it. She shrugs her shoulders and turns back to Seth. "OK."

When they finally reach Seth's apartment building, Anaiya's wristplate flashes 0411. She should be tired, but the adrenalin of the night is unrelenting and she climbs the stairs to his unit with purpose. Free from the threat of capture and detention, Kaide and Seth also seem less tense, although Anaiya senses a new weight about them.

Once inside the unit, she settles down on the lounge that had cradled her hours ago and waits. Kaide comes to join her, perching on the lounge's arm, while Seth takes his spot on the floor across from them.

For a moment, Seth just looks at her. She forces her body to stay neutral, not engaging him, not giving anything away. She can't afford any more missteps, any more flashes of unrestrained Air or Fire emotions.

A shrill beep interrupts the silence.

"Cress made it back OK," Kaide announces. "Rehhd's pissed."

Seth sighs. "Nothing new there."

"Does she know about this?"

Anaiya glances up at the change in Kaide's tone, catching his eye before he looks away. Seth drags his hand through his hair, refusing to look at either of them.

Kaide curses. "Seth…"

"I know," he replies. "I know."

"Do you?"

Seth looks up sharply, his retort dying on his lips. He pauses. "How are you doing, Anaiya?" he asks instead.

Surprised by the sudden diversion, she forces herself to wait before answering. Things are getting out of control and she feels as if everything hangs on a precipice. "Confused…" she begins. "I'm not sure whether you want me here or not."

Before Seth can reply, Kaide shifts next to her and speaks. "What did you think of our protest?"

The forbidden word rolls easily off his tongue. It registers no response in Anaiya, she wonders if she will ever be shocked by Heterodoxy again. "The mural? It wasn't as creative as others I've seen."

Seth barks a short laugh, but Kaide is unmoved. "Did you have much exposure to the resistance movement in the Eastern Area?"

"Not personally," she replies.

"What does that mean?"

"It means I didn't get personalised, post-curfew viewings by the artists themselves," she says. Too quickly, too harshly.

Kaide raises an eyebrow, but the interrogation halts.

Play it smarter, Anaiya.

She knows she has to be more careful; knows she has to give them the impression that she is open to this rebellion, that they can trust her. But in her current state of chaos there is no way to guarantee it will be her neocortex, and not her limbic brain, that will respond first.

She looks over at Seth. "It's been a big night. I'm going to try and get some sleep before curfew ends."

He blinks out of whatever reverie she has caught him in and stands up. "You can take my room for the night," he says. "Kaide and I will sleep out here."

Settled in Seth's bed, Anaiya stares into the darkness, straining to hear more clearly the muffled conversation that leaks into the room. The tension between the two males occasionally swells, and she catches brief bursts of dialogue, but never enough for her to piece together a coherent exchange.

She fights the growing heaviness of her eyelids, straining to stave off sleep, but in the end her efforts are useless and she falls into a tortured slumber.

Two hours later, shafts of golden light stream in through Seth's bedroom window. Anaiya lies still as the memories of the night before disentangle themselves from the dreams that followed.

In the soft-tinted light, the room is a strange balance of hard lines and soft shadows that reminds her of Seth himself. His mark on the room is immediately obvious – an aesthetic counterpoint to its functionality. Market trinkets are scattered on geometric chairs and hung in ribbons from the window lintel. Construction materials are fused together to create arresting sculptures that serve as shelves, stools and doorstops. The far wall is a jumble of small, low-voltage screens that play music visualisations, game scenes and clips from vintage movies on endless loops.

But it's the ceiling that captivates her. The material is a soft polymer. An inconsistent tint sees the grey darken and mottle in some places and shift from gloss to matte in narrow strata. In spite of how interesting the actual material is, how contradictory and utterly Seth it is, its crude vandalism interests her.

Shallow grooves are carved into the surface, running in slanted lines across the ceiling. The harsh gouges unnerve her, but she finds the words themselves beautiful, and familiar.

Liberty…Egality…Fraternity…Or Death.

Staring at the engraving, her mind works to understand this intimate stranger who is capable of carving the state motto on his ceiling while working to undermine the state through the ultimate crime of Heterodoxy.

Why, Seth?

It is a question she wants to scream through the walls. Lacking an answer, the question quickly morphs into a simpler enquiry.

How?

How could someone like Seth be corrupted? Who recruited

him into this madness? What lies have they fed him?

These smaller, subsequent questions repeat on a constant loop through her mind, stirring up and consolidating all of her uncomfortable feelings, shaping them into one dominant emotion. Anger.

And with that emotion comes a target for it.

Rehhd.

"Morning," Seth greets her as she wanders from his bedroom to the lounge room. "How did you sleep?"

His eyes are red-rimmed and dark shadows make him look older, more rugged. Her heart twinges, but she roughly shoves the feeling aside.

No. No more, Anaiya. No more distractions.

"Better than you, it seems. Where's Kaide?"

"He left as curfew broke – he lives on the other side of the Area, so he has a fair way to travel."

Seth is making unnecessary excuses for him.

Anaiya is not interested. "I'm going to head out, as well," she says, moving towards the door.

Seth sighs, dragging his knuckles across his cheek, and nods. "Will I see you again?"

It is a question loaded with a dozen more. Can I trust you? Have I scared you away? Are you on our side? Are you really one of us?

She cannot answer the unspoken questions and so she ignores them.

With Rehhd and Kaide less than enthused about her presence, she needs to maintain contact with Seth. He is her only link to the Resistance leadership, her only opportunity to gain more intel on Rehhd.

"Yes. I would like that."

A weary smile emerges from his tired face. "There's a curfew lockdown party at Yve's izakaya next weekend," he says. "You should come."

"I wouldn't miss it."

TWENTY-ONE

The early morning streets of Precinct 18 are quiet. It is the Seventh day – the day of recovery for debaucherous Elementals, of religious observance for the pious. The brown sun, shadowed by a dense haze, is still too bright for Anaiya. She closes her eyes against it, fragile from the night's encounter.

A shrill beep shatters the silence. Anaiya startles and opens her eyes. Her arm shivers with the vibrations of her wristplate and the panel illuminates with the new message icon. She taps on it, her heart racing as the text materialises, the code immediately recognisable.

She stares at it for a while, organising her thoughts, before entering the six-digit number into the communication module and plugging her lifeline into her ear. The low-pitched rumbling of the dialling tone is quickly terminated by the sound of Niamh's voice.

"Ani, where are you at?"

It's tight; perfunctory.

"Heading to ground zero," she replies. "Should I call you back?"

"No need," he says. "Can you meet at Peacekeeper HQ for a briefing in thirty?"

Scenarios and second-guesses assault Anaiya's mind. It has been too long in between communications. Why is he calling now? What isn't he telling her?

"See you then," she says, clicking off the communication before Niamh can throw her into further chaos with his words or voice.

Standing still in the busy street, Anaiya lets the crowd rush around her, anchoring herself against the ebb and flow of Elementals oblivious to her panic and despair. She tries to focus her mind on more rational thoughts, like getting her feet to move. Instead, inane and irrelevant comparisons of Niamh to Seth jostle alongside contingency plans to keep both of them from her secret mission.

Disturbingly, she finds herself unsure of which would be worse – conceding to Niamh her intimacy with the Resistance or confessing to Seth her true nature as a Peacekeeper.

Standing outside Mission headquarters, uninvited memories of Anaiya's last visit flood her mind and the hesitancy that overwhelmed her then threatens to re-emerge. She forces her limbs to stand straighter, arches her back and trains her eyes calmly on the sight in front of her.

Using her mind-clearing technique, she banishes all limbic thoughts and sensations and brings her neocortex to the fore. Her breathing regulates, her heartbeat slows, and she doesn't need to look at her wristplate to know that her endorphin levels have dropped and chemical stats normalised.

She is ready.

Arriving at the briefing room, she finds Niamh standing alone, staring out a window that takes up the entire wall. He has his back to the door, but Anaiya knows his ears are alert to any unexpected presence. He doesn't react when she steps into the room.

Anaiya moves slowly towards him, not distracted by the expansive vista. With her limbic brain silenced, her appraisal of Niamh is considered. Memories of their time together mix out of order with numerous reports and conversations, forming a rough and organic perspective of the Elemental before her. He is the consummate Peacekeeper – fearless, disciplined, committed, confident.

But there is more than that: a self-assuredness that announces itself in his casual stance, a challenge in the way he dismisses her until he is ready to engage.

There is an economy to Niamh. A cold calculation of how much you can offer him against how much he needs to offer back. A balance sheet where he is never in debt and never pays more than market value.

"Hey, Ani," he says abruptly, keeping his eyes ahead.

Anaiya flinches. Grateful he is not facing her to see it, she crosses the gap between them.

"Hey, Niamh," she says, reaching the space next to him.

"Long time, no speak." His voice is heavy with a hidden challenge.

"Nothing new to report," she says carefully, glancing at his profile to gauge his fire.

"Not what I hear," he says, turning his head to regard her.

Grey eyes glitter black, cold despite the warm-tinted light. A clenched jaw and still posture threaten to break Anaiya's resolve and her mind races with the likely consequences of telling Niamh everything.

She wants to shrink under his gaze; instead, she forces herself to calmly return it.

"Anything you want to tell me, Anaiya?"

Anaiya's thoughts are a swarm of synthflies. What does he know? And how much of it?

A new but familiar voice calls out. "Like, how close you've become to your targets."

It is a flat statement, no question or curiosity in it. Anaiya knows without turning around that Jenna has joined them, so she continues to watch Niamh, looking for clues about what exactly is contained beneath his schooled features.

He turns to Jenna.

"Back down, Jen," he says sharply.

Anaiya is satisfied with his tone, but feels a bitter edge; wondering whether Niamh gives nicknames to all the Elementals he is intimate with.

"Ani?" he asks, the toxin still lacing his voice.

"What?"

"Are you getting too involved with the targets?"

She shoots a quick glance over to Jenna. The Peacekeeper shares the same confidence as Niamh, but her stance is combative where Niamh's is calm.

Anaiya lets her thoughts dredge up the memory of the confrontation with Jenna, trying desperately to isolate it from the events that preceded and followed it. It seems almost impossible that it took place only three nights ago.

Visions of Jenna dropping Eamon to the ground, the fire in her eyes, the thirst for conflict with Seth and with her – they all play out in a jumbled, fractured memory. The sweet feeling of triumph tingles along Anaiya's neural pathways and a cold smile plays on her lips.

Jenna's eyes narrow at the sight.

"No," Anaiya says, her voice as hard as her smile. "I am not getting too close to the targets."

Niamh nods, satisfied: her voice rings with a truth she's only just discovered for herself. A small corner of her mind marvels at how, just a few hours ago, the same words would have marked her as a liar.

"Jen, give us a minute."

The Peacekeeper scowls, but leaves the room.

"Then what happened out there?" Niamh asks once they are alone.

Anaiya chooses her words carefully. Her time at the izakaya is quickly glossed over as standard surveillance and reconnaissance, slanted as a story of how she had identified Rehhd and attached herself to the group.

Her retelling of the confrontation with Jenna in the back streets near the necropolis comes much easier. Anaiya draws out the details, turning a three-minute skirmish into an epic tale. With each word, she drives the needle deeper, relishing the pleasure in imagining Jenna's face contort into tight grimaces as Anaiya hints at her lack of restraint and the risks her cavalier attitude had posed to the overall mission.

Niamh, oblivious to or uninterested in the tacit conflict

playing out in the room, nods his head and waves his hands around, impatient. "So, what happened afterwards? Were you able to obtain any valuable intel?"

Anaiya's mind falters, unsure how to spin this particular part of the story. Her earlier instinct to tell Niamh the truth, or at least part of it, has quickly evaporated in Jenna's presence. "I've gained some credibility," she says. "Rehhd seems to trust me and her acquaintances have raised no objections or concerns."

The substitution of Rehhd for Seth is a simple one and, to some extent, she is confident that the Resistance leader has in fact accepted her backstory. The lack of concern from the rest of the group is a harder untruth to speak. Anaiya's memory revisits the tension between Seth and Kaide and she sees again the concern and distrust in Kaide's eyes. She'll need to fix that.

Niamh rubs vigorously at the frown creasing his forehead. Bringing up his lifeline, he calls Jenna back in. She glances momentarily at Anaiya before taking a seat near Niamh.

"Who are the acquaintances?" Niamh asks. "What do we know about them?"

Jenna plugs in her glass screen and taps on the wall, bringing up a high-definition photograph of Rehhd that zooms large before shrinking and shifting to the centre. She swipes and taps on her glass and a new photo appears.

"Eamon 801," she says. "Fourth lustrum Air Elemental, Graphics competency. Primary offender in recent conflict. Substantial Unorthodoxy record. Known connection to Rehhd 020 dates back two years. Both were detained for 93C, 150 and 195 offences."

Anaiya translates the offences in her head. Affray, stealing manufactured goods, destroying or damaging property.

"Analysis of data movements confirms regular interaction."

Eamon's photograph shrinks in size and falls into position beside Rehhd's, a thick, dark line connecting the two images.

Jenna taps again and another image appears on the screen.

"Kaide 177. Present at the recent conflict. Multiple Unorthodoxy offences. Seventeen co-location instances with Rehhd over the last six months."

Seventeen?

"Ani?" Niamh questions, halting Jenna's narrative.

"Yes," she replies, losing her train of thought. "He's a known associate. He's been present the last few times I have monitored Rehhd."

Niamh nods. "Add him to the list of potential targets," he directs Jenna.

Jenna nods and begins tapping on her glass screen. She is not finished. A blank space flickers on the wall: the spot where a third associate will be located. Anaiya's body tenses and a strange tingling affects her clenched fingers.

"Unknown Elemental," Jenna announces, looking up to the wallscreen. A question mark appears in the space. "We're confident that for an operation of this scale, there would be at least three core associates. There are just too many potential candidates based on the data analysis alone. Surveillance has managed to narrow it down somewhat, but our primary target interacts with a wide range of Elementals."

"Give us a name, Ani." Niamh's voice is flat and harsh.

Anaiya is careful not to pause, or take a deep breath, or engage in any behaviour that would betray her knowledge. She answers as if without thought or pretence. "It's too early to identify a third candidate. I've had some exposure to Kaide but have yet to make contact with Eamon, let alone others of the circle. I'll need more time. And opportunities."

Jenna's fingers flicker across the glass screen in immediate response. "Eamon's movements suggest that he'll be present at the Rabid Dog izakaya from 1800 hours tonight."

"Good," Niamh says. "Get what you can tonight, Anaiya. I want an update tomorrow."

The worm is quiet as it makes its way through the lower-numbered precincts to the Eastern Area. Anaiya sits stiffly, the polyurethane seat resisting her slightest movement.

It hadn't surprised her that Niamh had directed her to meet him after the briefing session. *Interrogation.* He knew Anaiya's competitive streak intimately and was observant enough to notice that she was providing bare details with Jenna in the room. What had surprised her was his invitation to meet at the Wild Rover.

Memories of her last foray into the izakaya hangs heavy in her consciousness, inextricable from those of the realignment testing and all that came after. Despite her limbic control, echoes of his betrayal trip the wires of her heart. She doesn't fight it, instead using the opportunity to explore her feelings for him.

She cedes control of her neural pathways slowly, careful to manage the transition from the stable and rational neocortex to the impulsive and unpredictable limbic brain. Immersing herself in simple Peacekeeper memories, she lets emotions attach to them. The easy, predictable ones develop first. Her awe at Niamh's abilities, her trust in his leadership, her satisfaction at his recognition of her own worth.

Encouraged, she delves deeper in the memories, opening up the limbic pathway for more emotional responses. Darker feelings pick at the edges. Anaiya doesn't swat them back, letting them attach to the memory and grow.

Frustration and envy shatter in her mind at the memory of Niamh's athletic superiority and irritation grates at his imperiousness and egotism. Rage simmers at the way he can so easily overlook her or dismiss her. And hurt, at the way he has so easily replaced her.

She swipes at the entrance panel by the Wild Rover's door but it is only when the unnatural fluorescent light assaults her eyes that she realises she has arrived. Her brain switches into rational mode and tries in vain to recall disembarking the worm and walking through Precinct 13's streets. But whatever latent memory she has of the journey is now obscured by the heavy shadow of her feelings for Niamh.

She glances around the izakaya, suddenly unprepared to see him again. The familiar spartan space is occupied by a typical mix of Fire Elementals. Its lack of colour and activity is stark in comparison to the Air Elemental izakayas of her new life. The difference distracts her and she doesn't immediately notice how the other patrons are eyeing her.

As she works her way towards the bar, she senses the attention, and looks around. In each face, in the slight frowns and set jaws, is judgement. In some it is suspicion, in others disgust. Some are conspicuous, others less obvious; but they all let her know that she is not welcome there.

The realisation puts a stumble in her step and her posture becomes rigid under the weight of their collective focus. She wonders if it was the hint of amble in her gait, the loss of focus in her gaze, or the non-utilitarian style of her threads that has triggered their assessment. And in wondering she becomes immediately self-conscious.

Gratefully, the Earth Bartender is oblivious to it all, and she quickly paces to the bar to order her drink.

"One dodeca," she says, her voice straining and the skin on her neck prickling. She doesn't let her eyes waver from the sight of him pouring the drink and, as soon as it is within her grasp, she downs it in three large gulps.

"Another," she rasps, her throat thick with the synthetic alcohol.

The second one goes down slower and smoother, her body reacting to the heady cocktail of alcohol and enhancer. She waits a little longer, savouring the rush of courage and indifference flowing through her veins.

By the time Niamh arrives at the izakaya, Anaiya's blood is buzzing with dodecahedrazine. He saunters in alone but is immediately captured by a loud group of Peacekeepers at the bar. Anaiya is too far away to hear the conversation, but she sees Niamh glance around the izakaya and watches as his companions turn their attention along the same trajectory.

A soft click sounds in her mind as his eyes meet hers. He nods to himself and turns back to the others. As expected, he doesn't excuse himself straight away. Anaiya barks a short laugh to herself, remembering her recent spikes of irritation and rage at memories of this exact behaviour, and grateful for the dulled edges of her thoughts.

Ignoring the snub, she takes another sip of the dodeca before her and lets her eyes roam the room in search of some eye candy. The izakaya is fairly packed, with a strong showing of both male and female Fire Elementals, most between their fourth and seventh lustrum. Her eyes sweep from one to the next, scanning randomly for a face or physique that will seduce her from afar.

This should be easier.

And it is true. An inebriated state and a full izakaya of Fire Elementals in their prime present the perfect conditions for entering a state of lust. Yet, Anaiya keeps searching, finding the faces too harsh, the stances too rigid. Below the haze of the dodecas, a question starts to form in her mind, but before she can rescue it, her view is cut off.

"Find anything to your liking?" Niamh asks dryly.

Anaiya tilts her head to take in his presence, running her eyes up and down his body in a considered appraisal, re-acquainting herself with the details she had touched in a previous lifetime. She halts her inspection at his face, pausing at the crooked grin and knowing eyes.

"No," she says, squarely meeting his gaze.

His smile falls brittle and his eyes glitter with the acceptance of a non-existent challenge, but he doesn't speak and contents himself with settling into the seat next to her. Her view clear again, Anaiya returns to perusing the room.

"So," Niamh says after a while. "Let's finish our earlier conversation, shall we?"

"Which particular conversation did we leave unfinished?" Her voice is flat, singing with a lazy indifference.

"You hold little esteem for Jenna, no?"

The word "esteem" sounds discordant. It strikes her as strange that he has assessed her dislike of Jenna as disrespect, until she realises that dislike is a decidedly Air feeling.

"I hold little *esteem* for her amateur approach to complex missions that directly impact on my life."

Niamh emits a heavy sigh, thick with exasperation. "We're all on the same side, Ani. We all want to find and dismantle the Resistance, restore the Orthodoxy. And we all have a part to play."

Anaiya isn't in the mood for one of Niamh's lectures or a detailed discussion about Jenna. "There are no problems between me and Jenna," she says flatly.

"That's not what she says."

"Then maybe it's Jenna with whom you should be having this conversation."

Niamh does not counter and the two of them fall into an uneasy silence. Anaiya finishes her drink and finally gives up on searching for some visual distractions.

"Another?"

The voice belongs to her favourite Niamh. The Niamh from her earliest memories of him, where they were equals and could lose hours in simple pleasures and playful challenges. She knows the reappearance will be brief and that Niamh will resort to his normal superiority and hubris, but she allows herself to ignore the inevitable, if only for a moment.

"Another."

An hour later, Anaiya makes her move to depart. A group of Fire Elementals has since crowded the small table she shares with Niamh, jostling the conversation between themselves. Anaiya touches Niamh on the elbow, catching his attention and interrupting the competitive dialogue.

"I'm out of here," she says, standing up to vacate her seat.

Niamh halts his train of speech and excuses himself from the group. "I'll see you out," he says, standing up beside her.

Anaiya shrugs and leads the way through the izakaya to the exit. As she reaches the door, Niamh pulls at her arm, dragging her to a spot against the adjacent wall.

"I've missed you, Ani," he says unexpectedly, his words syrupy with dodeca.

Anaiya rolls her eyes at him, dismissing the sentiment despite hearing the truth in his voice. Niamh chuckles softly, his hand reaching up to play with errant strands of hair falling around her face. "Our fires had a good compatibility," he says, fingers flicking around her face, raising shivers along her skin. "And no one else does that thing…"

Of course he was talking about the sex. With Fire Elementals there were no deeper feelings, no complex attachments.

His eyes drill into hers, forcing her to see and acknowledge the desire in them. He leans in close until his lips are brushing against her earlobe. "Come back to my place," he whispers.

Anaiya disentangles herself from his grasp. Her eyes return his gaze, her own will projecting deeply into his. Time shudders into a lower gear and the world shrinks.

"I have to go," she says. And without waiting to see his response, she pulls away and exits the izakaya.

The air is cooler outside, the light softer. Anaiya's footsteps fall comfortably on the bitumen and her heart beats a calm tempo. She is unhurried on her approach to the worm station and the journey rings clear in her consciousness. Despite all the conflicting emotions Anaiya still holds for Niamh, her need to be wanted by him is no longer one of them.

TWENTY-TWO

The Rabid Dog is more subdued than Anaiya expects when she steps into its music-filled belly. A few individuals hover at the bar and a handful of small groups occupy the lounges and tables scattered around the izakaya.

"Anaiya!"

Cress waves to her from a table close to the door, standing to grab Anaiya's attention. Her three companions swivel in their seats to regard Anaiya and she braces herself for the same judgement that confronted her at the Wild Rover, but they merely smile in greeting and turn back to their conversation.

"Come join us!"

Anaiya smiles too. "I'll just grab a drink."

The effects of the dodecahedrazine have largely worn off, the chemical's soft and scratchy fuzziness now faded and faint. Stepping up to the bar she orders a low-level paramethylate, something that will file away the edges of her thoughts while keeping her alert and focussed. The Earth bartender busies herself with the order and Anaiya turns her back to lean against the bar and survey the room.

More Elementals are entering the izakaya and the noise level is picking up. The mellow music track ends and a more chaotic sound of fuzzy wails and off beats introduces the next tune. Anaiya connects her lifeline jack to the sound terminal and downloads the track.

"You like it?" a deep voice asks beside her.

Anaiya glances to her left, encountering familiar grey eyes shining in the bright bar lights.

"Yeah," she replies to Eamon. "Yours?"

He shakes his head, his hand pushing back the sheaves of bronze hair and scratching the stubble at his jawline.

"No, I'm just keen to download it next," he says grinning. "I like the bass line."

The music terminal promptly clicks as it ejects Anaiya's lifeline and she moves aside to let Eamon insert his own. The bartender hands over her parameth and she plays with the glass while she assesses Eamon. He leans casually on the bar, showing no signs of recognising her.

Why would he? It's not like he's just come from a Sec Level 5 briefing with my face lighting up a wallscreen...

"You here for the spoken word?" he asks, looking up at her.

Vibrancy and energy and vitality seem to pour from his skin. He doesn't fidget or issue rapid-fire conversation, there is no nervous energy or barely restrained hyperactivity skimming along his skin. But the glitter in his eyes and the pure expression on his face are irrepressible...and contagious.

"Yeah. You?" she asks, taking a sip of her drink.

"I am," he confirms. "If you're not here with anyone, you should join us."

His lifeline is ejected from the sound terminal and another track fades in. He turns to face Anaiya, absently wrapping his lifeline around the cuff on his left hand. Charm and charisma radiate from him, qualities not visible in the two-dimensional photograph that flashed on Jenna's wallscreen.

"I'm catching up with someone," she says, indicating the direction of Cress's table with a tilt of her head. "But maybe later?"

"Later, then," he says, still smiling.

Anaiya turns to make her way across the room to Cress's table when his hand shoots out to grab her arm. It is not the action itself that surprises her – as a Peacekeeper, any unannounced contact would have ended with a sprained wrist, broken fingers, or worse.

She turns back around; a simple movement, unaffected and calm. A second later her neocortex kicks in with the fight response, surging adrenalin to her limbs, but the moment has passed. She faces Eamon, who remains oblivious to her racing thoughts.

"I'm Eamon," he says, releasing his grip on her arm and running his hand down her sleeve.

"Anaiya."

Eamon blinks.

"Seth's Anaiya?"

Anaiya feels her face harden and Eamon cocks his head in interest.

"So, *not* Seth's Anaiya," he says slowly, rubbing his knuckles under his chin. "You don't remember me, do you?"

Anaiya neither confirms nor denies. "It was you, wasn't it?" she asks instead. "You went down during the run-in with the Peacekeepers the other night?"

"I heard I wasn't the only one," he says, smiling. There is a playfulness to that smile, a recklessness.

"Couldn't let you have all the fun, now could I?"

His laugh is husky, a rustling of corduroy against bare skin. "I guess not," he says. "Are you here with Cress?"

Anaiya nods, looking over to the table, where new arrivals have gathered.

"I'll come with you."

Anaiya watches Eamon closely as he bends his head closer to Cress, sending her into another fit of giggling. The izakaya is now full to capacity; voices, conversations and music rise and fall around them. Anaiya's third parameth has kicked in and she reclines in the worn polyester armchair, calm and focussed.

For the most part, Eamon is a clear screen, a simple narrative. Over the last hour he has engaged easily with the other Elementals at the table; flirting, laughing, joking and debating. In so many ways, he reminds her of Rehhd – his dark anger and rebelliousness hidden beneath a bright layer of magnetism and levity.

"What about you, Anaiya?" Cress asks, turning away from

Eamon with flushed cheeks.

Anaiya frowns, recalling fragments of the conversation she had half-heartedly been listening to. "Hmm?"

"What is your alternate competency?" Cress repeats.

They are speculating. As Anaiya knows, from both of her alignments, competencies are inevitable – uncovered rather than chosen. It is a sentimental game, a relapse into the idle musing of childhood when competencies were unknown and there seemed a world of possibilities, a thousand paths that one's life could take. Rather than scorn their sentimentality, Anaiya understands it.

She smiles wryly. "Border Watcher."

The Elementals around her break into laughter at the irony and wait for her real answer. So, she chooses the Air competency that, in her mind, is closest to Peacekeeping. The one she was confident the Water Technicians would have assigned her.

"Dancer."

Cress's face lights up and she claps her hands in delight. Anaiya grins despite herself. But then she catches Eamon's steady gaze and her smile falters.

"I would have been a Trinketeur," the diminutive Elemental beside Eamon announces. The laughter builds again, the others entertained at the thought of Scythe, the night's orator, being a low-level creator of market knick-knacks.

"I would have made gaudy yellow baubles and synthfly sculptures as big as a fist," she continues, revelling in the attention.

The light-hearted banter swells around her, but Anaiya and Eamon are both oblivious to it. She meets his gaze evenly, despite the quickening tempo of her heart and the light sheen of sweat on her palms.

What has he noticed?

The paranoia itches along her skin.

It's just the parameth. It's just the parameth.

She forces herself to breathe normally and holds his gaze until he raises an eyebrow, and she realises immediately that she is displaying very atypical Air behaviour. She drops her head quickly, but it is too late. Moments later, the scrape of the seat next to her against the polished concrete floor announces his arrival.

He sits casually next to her, legs outstretched and crossed at the ankles, his left arm propped up on the cold metal of the chair, cradling his head. His fingers disappear into his hair, his head cocked towards her as he regards her, eyes shrouded in the dim light of the izakaya. "You have that look, Anaiya," he murmurs.

She looks away from him. "What look?"

In her peripheral vision, she sees him shrug non-commitally, his flippancy betrayed by the rigidity of his frame and steadiness of his gaze. "Of rage…" His voice is soft and viscous, grabbing at the air around her and decelerating time. "Hunger."

She turns her head slowly to face him again. He is smiling, his angled face turned into something dangerous. He leans in to her and her head bows to meet him. He is close, now, his lips at her ear, his soft breaths amplified and hypnotic. "The thing that drives you to take on a Peacekeeper in a dark street," he murmurs. "That rebellion that makes us the same."

The forbidden word is whispered, rippling from his lips to her core. She shivers. At the sensation, at the intimacy, at the word and its consequences. He is opening himself up to her, revealing himself, giving her an in, an entry into the Resistance.

She turns her head slowly, his lips grazing her ear and cheek as she does. She doesn't pull back, keeping the distance between them minimal. This close she can see anticipation and hunger in his eyes. He trails a finger down her cheek and smiles. "We're the same, Anaiya."

Anaiya opens her mouth to respond, but the words die on her lips as the izakaya's soundtrack is abruptly silenced. The secondary sounds of the Rabid Dog's patrons hush in response and everyone looks to the figure lit by a soft, golden spotlight. Anaiya and Eamon reluctantly pull away from each other and turn to the corner of the izakaya where the beam of light has singled out a lone Elemental.

The first orator begins with a tremulous note. It shifts and shatters against the walls of the izakaya before gaining strength and stabilising.

"I walked along the edge of my Syn,
and looked down.
The reflection was mine, but it was not me,

and I drowned..."

The words, and the haunting, hollowness of the voice, arrest Anaiya. With the parameth softening the otherwise sharp transition, she forgets about her fixation with Eamon and drifts in the words of the orator, and their rhythm. Time loses its form as a reference, and minutes pass as both brief moments and long, epic journeys.

And so it goes. Other orators stand to bathe in the spotlight, their words spilling over the attentive audience. It has music, and a hidden, evocative beauty that rises and swells with the emotions of the crowd, pulling at Anaiya and dragging her away. She does not resist, does not analyse or assess. She closes her eyes to the izakaya and simply experiences it.

"...and I will wait."

The orator's voice, this time the deep and husky tone of an older male Elemental, comes to a dramatic conclusion. The words are dredged up from his lungs and pulled from his mouth, his face twisting with an unseen torment. As they are released into the crowd, his shoulders slump and his head bows. He falls into his seat heavily and silently.

Movement flashes behind him, immediately noticeable against the stillness of the room. Two figures stand close together, their heads bowed in deep conversation. The one on the left nods his head and the two break apart, Anaiya recognising the taller one as Seth.

As if sensing her attention, he turns to her. Their eyes collide and a heavy stone lodges in her stomach. A smile plays on his lips, but it disintegrates before fully engaging, his eyes now focussed on the Elemental beside her. She waits for him to walk over, but he remains where he is. Moments pass like this, with him shifting his gaze from Anaiya to Eamon. Finally he looks away, glancing around the room and occasionally leaning in to speak to the unfamiliar Elemental.

The rock in her stomach falls heavier. She looks away. Beside her, Eamon reclines in his chair, arms folded across his chest and eyes unmoving. Anaiya doesn't need to follow them to know their target. So, instead, she watches Eamon. A contradiction of emotions plays across his body: he's openly calm, but his eyes glitter. His right foot taps rapidly against his left; his legs are rigid despite their languid stretch.

The tension she heard in Seth's voice the night of their encounter with Jenna has obviously developed into something more tangible. Coupled with the conflict between Seth and Kaide, she wonders how involved Seth is with the Resistance, whether he is on the fringe and drifting outwards. The rock lightens.

She lifts her head to seek Seth out again, but the spotlight blinds her; she shields her eyes and turns away. Less than a metre away, Scythe stands up, blocking the harsh light and Anaiya's view of Seth. Frustrated, she leans towards Eamon in the hopes of improving her view.

"I am a person, not an Elemental."

The words, spoken in Scythe's familiar high-pitched, lilting melody, register a few seconds later in Anaiya's mind, their reception delayed as her neocortex struggles to make sense of them. Her body snaps back to its original place in the armchair and her gaze fixes, unwavering, on the orator.

"A citizen without a government,
a scorched and barren land."

She glances down at her wristplate, desperate to bring up the recording function, but knowing that Eamon, if not other Elementals, will see the movement and question it.

"My voice will be mine again,
and I will coat my tongue with the ashes of fallen Fire.
I will bleed in colour,
and paint my blood on Otpor's walls."

If not for the parameth still coating her mind, Anaiya knows that she would be visibly reacting, openly betraying the shock that sours in her mouth. As it is, her fingers grip tighter on the chair's armrests and her legs ache with the strain of not shifting, not standing, not striding through the golden glow to Scythe and…

She bites the inside of her cheek, increasing pressure until her tongue is pricked with the taste of iron.

Later, she will struggle to remember the exact words, the

precise inflections, with only the intensity of her emotions and the first stanza searing into her memories. For now, in the haze of her revulsion, she looks past Scythe and over the faces of those in the crowd. She takes in the expressions of intrigue, adoration and amusement that shape them.

Scythe shifts her balance, stepping back to lean against the table as she continues her monologue. The movement affords Anaiya a clear view of Seth. As always, he stands apart from the crowd, despite the bodies pressing against him. There is none of the room's rapture in him. Just a deep stillness. He doesn't murmur, doesn't move – a small frown the only outwards sign that he is present and attentive.

Scythe is coming to the conclusion of her oration, her voice dropping in decibels, morphing into a harsh whisper. As the words die, Seth glances towards Anaiya. She waits for his face to change, his stance to shift, but he merely turns and disappears through the crowd.

Her gaze sweeps the room for his path and seconds later she sees him exit the izakaya, just as Scythe drops into a flourish and settles back into her chair at the table.

Two innocuous monologues later, the table where Anaiya sits is enveloped in the noise of rapid chatter set against the backdrop of a mellow song track. Mostly the conversation centres on praising Scythe for her brilliance, her rawness, her insight. Anaiya feels sick. But then parts of the conversation break apart and when she hears Cress mention Rehhd's name, she turns subtly towards the smaller group.

"Rehhd would have been proud of you tonight."

Scythe smiles broadly.

"Where *is* Rehhd?" Anaiya asks Eamon, who has taken to perching on one of her armrests.

His right arm dangles in the space between them, his fingers pulling absently at the fraying strands of torn upholstery.

"Rehhd's working on another project," he says, dragging at a particularly long thread and idly wrapping it around his index finger. "I doubt we'll see her."

"A solo project?" Anaiya asks, frowning.

"Not exactly," he replies, snapping the thread and discarding it from his finger. "More like a group project she's spending some alone time on."

Anaiya wants to ask more questions, but she displays restraint, careful not to rouse Eamon's suspicion. "What about your projects?" she asks instead. "What are you working on?"

She keeps her voice light. Playful.

Eamon smiles down at her. "I've got a few Graphics projects going," he says, swiping across his wristplate.

He leans closer to her, his left arm wrapping across his body to place the wristplate in Anaiya's line of sight. His chest presses against her left shoulder and his nose brushes lightly against her cheek. She can feel his breath on her face, but she ignores it, focussing on the images taking up and flashing across the screen panel of his cuff.

The images are monochromatic and abstract. Clean lines and flat colouring speak of a simple technique, but the designs themselves are intricate and complex.

The next image that flashes up on the screen is familiar. A perfectly detailed skull adorned with extinct butterflies and delicate flowers sits in quarter profile, the hollow eyes gazing lifelessly over Anaiya's right shoulder. It's sketched entirely in black; dark shadows pull at the gaunt cheekbones and the petal folds of twisted blooms.

"I've seen this one before," she says, turning to look up at Eamon.

He pulls his arm back and switches off the screen with a double tap.

"Seth bought it off me a year ago," he says. "He had it inked on his forearm an hour later."

"How did you two meet?" she asks, remembering Seth's version but wanting to hear the story from Eamon's perspective.

"We met the night he bought the ink design off me," he starts, shifting on the armchair and leaning his body closer to Anaiya's. Together, they stare out over the izakaya crowd. At groups of Air

Elemental talking and laughing, at lovers embracing in dark corners and under soft, golden lights, at Cress dancing with Scythe, spinning her around in leisurely circles and caressing her face.

"Rehhd and I had met the year before. We had been working on a project together and it had all been pretty intense. We both moved in different circles – she was more eclectic in her selection of friends; I tended to stick with the Graphics crew. But we kept in contact and occasionally collaborated on other joint projects. I had seen her out and about – but you know Rehhd, she moves between groups like a synthfly between corpses – so I never really met her other friends until a year ago."

His voice is deep and husky, combining with the paramethylate to become hypnotic. Anaiya settles further into the armchair, letting the words tumble around her skull, her fuzzy brain catching on one word: *Rehhd.*

"We were at Veritas, an izakaya not far from here," he continues. "Cress was performing that night, so I was just hanging around. Rehhd arrived with two males I had sometimes seen her with. She came over to the bar and they followed. Kaide was the talkative one, but Seth was the more interesting."

Eamon pauses. "He had this *intensity* back then," he says. "A fire…"

The word snatches Anaiya out of her trance.

"I always thought it would develop into something bigger. Like I was standing before this prodigy whose genius would just continue to grow until it blocked out the sun…" He laughs hoarsely – a cold and broken sound. "I worshipped him back then," he says, hooking his right leg over Anaiya's, tangling her up in him. "I would have followed him anywhere into anything…And for a long time, I did."

"What happened?" she asks softly, staring at the way their legs are intertwined in the foreground of her vision.

The sound system pauses as one track shifts into another, providing an almost silence that allows her to hear his next words, even though they are whispered.

"He stopped being the god I thought he was. And I outgrew him."

The next track swells in the stale air of the izakaya. The melody is dark and heavy, interspersed with a bright, quick tinkling. It falls into a repetitive beat, then skips, diverges on a different beat, then skips again and returns.

"You just walked away?" she asks after a while, hooking her right leg over his to form a tighter weave.

"No one just walks away from Seth," he replies, smiling down at her as he hooks his left ankle over the weave to complete it. "Or Rehhd, for that matter."

"It's strange," she says. "Them being friends. They seem so different."

"They are in a lot of ways. But they're the same in the ways that count."

Anaiya is about to ask what are these ways, the ones that count, when he speaks again.

"And with both of them being so close to Kaide, it was inevitable that they would end up being thrown together."

As if at the mention of his name, the tall and broad figure appears at the edges of the izakaya's shadows. Unlike Seth, he does not pause at the border between light and dark, his even stride bringing him across the small distance to their table. He stops at Cress's chair, reaching down to tickle at the exposed skin under her ear and sending her into a fit of laughter. He smiles at the sound, but his gaze rests on Anaiya and Eamon and their interlinked limbs.

For a moment, Anaiya feels a sharp desire to pull them free. It passes and, instead, she returns his gaze. Nonetheless, her legs spring back when Eamon disentangles himself and stands up.

"Drink?"

Anaiya looks up at him, her assent poised on her lips. But Eamon is looking at Kaide. And Kaide is looking at her.

"Tequila," he says.

Anaiya ignores the taunt and watches as Eamon retreats from her on his way to the bar. Kaide pulls up a stool next to her.

"So, you found Eamon?"

His voice is light and casual, but Anaiya isn't entirely convinced this conversation is one without motive.

"He found me."

"Oh?"

"I like drinking. He likes drinking. The bar is the place to procure said drinks. Ipso facto, we met at the bar."

Kaide laughs softly. The sound hits Anaiya as genuine and she relaxes.

"What are you doing here?" she asks, turning to face him. "You missed the main part."

His smile falters at that, but he quickly recovers. "I'm actually looking for Rehhd..." he replies, casting his gaze around the izakaya.

"She never showed," Anaiya says. "Eamon said something about her working solo tonight."

A tight grimace pulls at the strong features of his face, hinting at a sharper emotion beneath the barely restrained facade. "Eamon said that?"

Anaiya nods, intrigued by this emotional shift in the otherwise steady and controlled Kaide. She watches him carefully.

Kaide stands up slowly, the stool barely moving as his solid frame extends to full height. Wordlessly he turns his back to Anaiya and stalks over to the bar, where Eamon is placing his order with one of the Earth Elemental servers.

The conflict is not the kind of physical fight Anaiya would expect at a Fire izakaya. The angst here is all quiet and coiled.

The two of them huddle close together, not opposites, but noticeably different.

Following what Anaiya can only conclude are terse words, they both leave the bar, tequila glasses left glittering in the soft light. Kaide strides purposefully towards the exit, unmoved by the distractions surrounding him, focussed only on his destination. Eamon follows, his self-assured saunter more guarded, less casual.

Something is happening and it is happening because Anaiya mentioned Rehhd. She moves to stand up, ready to follow them, when Cress appears at her side.

"Be careful of that one, Nisha," she says, sliding onto the spot Eamon has only recently vacated. "He burns hearts like they're corpses."

She laughs, a tinkling that mingles with the melody streaming through the izakaya. Its contagious pull passes Anaiya by; her eyes are still firmly trained on the exit that has swallowed Kaide and Eamon.

"And you don't want to be burned…" Her voice fades, blending with the music until the words become part of the lyrics.

Anaiya nods absently, the words barely registering. "Got it. Thanks, Cress," she says, standing up.

Cress's laugh follows her as she makes her way to the izakaya exit. "Don't let the fire burn you, Nisha."

TWENTY-THREE

The next morning, Anaiya tingles with restrained excitement as she leaves her apartment. Her earlier debrief with Niamh had elevated Kaide to a primary target and she is keen to commence surveillance. Anticipation is a hand around her throat, making her flush with excitement and nervousness and desire. The thought of reaching her goal, of finally uncovering the Resistance leader and ending this deception, feels almost tangible – a synthfly buzzing in her brain, sending off waves of energy.

As she makes her way through the connecting streets and laneways to the riverside area of Precinct 19, something deep in her subconscious spurs her to break into a free-run. The pull is strong, but she resists, taming the wild energy inside and forcing her feet to beat out a slow but consistent rhythm on the esplanade stones.

Her body relaxes and her mind quietens, allowing thoughts of the morning's debrief to drift and weave along her neural pathways. Niamh's voice echoes in her memory. In spite of the noisy morning sounds, she can still hear the excitement in it. The thirst. The *hunger*. She instinctively knows he has always been like this and wonders why she never saw it. Having spent so many years with him, running the same streets, working the same shifts – had she really failed to see this part of him?

The sounds and smells of the river market shake her out of her introspection and she slows to a steady stride. Water analysis of

Kaide's communications and wristplate transactions suggest she will find him here, somewhere in the microcosm of Elemental activity. Air Elementals dominate the riverside bustle, but a few Peacekeepers linger nearby and Earth Elemental sellers call their wares and tend to their stalls. A familiar smell lingers in the air.

Cola-roasted pigeon.

Her mouth starts salivating before she can finish the thought. Memories, good memories, happy memories, flood her cerebral cortex. Her feet propel her along the scent pathway before her neocortex can catch up.

She sees the crowd before she sees the vendor. It is early enough in the morning to catch the workers, late enough to catch the recently roused and hungover nightlovers.

The crowd around the pigeon vendor is dense. She manoeuvres carefully, but a careless jostle at her side sends her stumbling into the dark-shirted Elemental in front of her.

"Hey, ease on," he grumbles, and turns to continue his rant, but stops abruptly when he sees her. It's Kaide. "Anaiya?"

Well, that was easier than I expected.

Now, two faces have turned to regard her.

Kaide and Seth.

Or not.

Kaide frowns at her. Anaiya meets his gaze evenly, keeping her stance casual. She glances to Seth, finding it harder to meet his eyes. Her feet shift uneasily and she jams her hands into her kevlar pockets to keep them from fidgeting.

"Hey," she says. Lightly. Casually. "I didn't expect to see you here."

Which is true. For Seth. "You both left the Rabid Dog in a bit of a rush last night," she continues. "Everything all right?"

A flash of surprise crosses Seth's face and he turns to Kaide. "You went to the Rabid Dog last night?"

Kaide nods, but keeps his gaze on Anaiya. "So, what brings *you* here, Anaiya?" he asks.

Seth looks to her expectantly, head tilted and right hand pulling at the back of his neck. The chance encounter is obviously causing him some level of stress, but Anaiya is unsure why.

Interesting and more interesting.

"Same thing as you, Kaide," she replies, the smell of roasting pigeon growing stronger as the line grows shorter.

She is not ready for the curse as it explodes from Kaide's lips. He glares at Anaiya before flicking his head to Seth.

"Eamon," he spits.

Seth nods, frowning. When he looks at Anaiya, he draws himself up. He is calm and composed.

"You were talking to Eamon last night?" he asks softly.

Anaiya's mind is racing. This reaction is obviously not over her penchant for cola-roasted pigeon. She runs through the events of the last few minutes. Their surprise at seeing her, Kaide's antagonism, Seth's ignorance of Kaide's visit to the izakaya last night, Seth's heightened unease. *What are you doing here? Same thing as you.*

Same thing as you...

What *are* they doing here?

"I talked to a lot of Elementals last night," she answers slowly. "Except, of course, to you..."

He dismisses the bait with a shake of his head.

"What did Eamon talk to you about?" Kaide asks, stepping in.

"Nothing."

"You two were looking pretty cozy to be talking about nothing."

"No *cozier* than you at the bar or as you both stormed out of the izakaya," she retorts. "If you were so desperate to know what we were talking about, maybe you should have asked him after you dragged him out to the street."

"How did you know about this, if Eamon didn't tell you?" asks Seth, his voice quiet and hard.

"Because *you* told me," she says darkly, enjoying the shift in the pair's body language.

Kaide's eyes fly to Seth, who, Anaiya notes with satisfaction, stares dumbfounded at her.

"I did not," he eventually manages. "I didn't," he repeats to Kaide, shaking his head furiously.

"You did," Anaiya insists, pulling her hands from her pockets and crossing them across her chest. She may not know what the two of them are here for, but it's clearly significant; she is happy to feign ignorance if it causes them to panic and reveal some of their secrets.

"You said not to tell Kaide, because he would never talk to you again."

The line behind the two of them has dwindled and a large space has opened up before the street vendor. She moves to pass by them but Seth grabs her arm.

She looks down at it and then slowly raises her eyes back to him. A look of indecision flits across his features and he softens the grip, but doesn't release it completely.

"Butterfly, this is not funny."

His voice is low and dangerous. She runs her free hand down his forearm, over the ribbons of skin ink, and circles her fingers around his wrist. She keeps her eyes locked on his.

"I agree," she says slowly and tightens her grip, finding target pressure points, fingers pressing into his heart point and pericardium six.

His eyes widen in pain, and his grip slackens slightly, but he grimaces and maintains his hold. "Anaiya…"

"Seth."

Finally he releases her arm.

"There are easier…and more enjoyable…ways to touch me," she says quietly, refusing to rub circulation back into her arm where he had gripped it, impressed to see that he too is refusing to show the same weakness. "If I had known keeping your cola pigeon secret was so…*imperative*…I would have just waited for next week's Samedi Markets."

She brushes past him and strides up to the vendor. "Two pieces," she says, plugging her lifeline into the antiquated pay terminal.

"You're here for the pigeon?" Kaide asks quietly, stepping up to counter beside her.

She glances over her shoulder to where Seth still stands. He regards her silently, a slight frown creasing his forehead, his hand back to worrying at the nape of his neck.

"Isn't that what you're here for?" she asks innocently, taking the pieces of pigeon the vendor offers. She watches him, shifting the hot meat between her hands till it cools.

"What game are you playing, Anaiya?"

"No game," she says as Seth steps up beside Kaide.

They pause, time stretching into a moment where something seems to hang in the balance.

"Can I have a minute to talk to you?" Seth asks.

"Seth –" Kaide warns.

"No," he replies steadily. "I need to talk to her."

Kaide shakes his head and turns away from them.

"So, can I?"

"Want one?" Anaiya asks, offering him a piece of her pigeon, as Seth leads her towards an unoccupied bench.

"Thanks," he says, his fingers brushing hers as he reaches for the dark brown flesh. "I've been thinking a lot about the other night," he continues as they reach the bench.

Anaiya nods absently. Though she has been trying to forget the more intimate details of that night, flashes of it have still plagued her dreams.

She expects him to say more, but he falls silent. There is a moment when they just look at each other and Anaiya wonders, not for the first time, what thoughts are raging in the mind of this rare Elemental before her.

He breaks their eye contact first and sighs as he falls onto the cold stone of the bench. She follows his lead, sitting close enough to feel the brush of his thigh against hers and the radiant heat of his body combatting the chill of the river breeze. She looks out over the crowd, catching a glimpse of Kaide still staring daggers at her. The two of them distract themselves with the pleasure of sucking pigeon flesh off brittle bones.

"What's Kaide's problem?" she asks mouth full with the final bite.

"He has some trust issues…"

"With Eamon or me?"

"With everyone."

Anaiya steals a glance at Seth in her peripheral vision. He has pushed his sleeve up his forearms and his right thumb dances over the dark patterns twisting around his forearm.

"I'm sorry about the other night," he says.

She was expecting a confession of sorts, or at least more intel, but not an apology.

"Which night?" she asks, genuinely confused.

He barks a short, rueful laugh. "They've all been a bit of a disaster, haven't they?"

She twists to look at him properly. He has stopped his absent fidgeting and stares down at his still arms.

"Not completely…" she replies, hesitant to get drawn into a conversation about their earlier encounters, their abandon and intimacy still unsettling.

He gives her a grateful smile. "I didn't mean to ignore you last night," he says.

She resists the temptation to interrupt him and ask one of the hundred questions that have flitted across her mind since she saw him stride out of the izakaya.

"I didn't expect to see you there…Not with Eamon."

"My unexpected appearances and Eamon seem to be a bit of a problem. Why is that?" she asks, debating whether or not to continue her light interrogation. "Does it have something to do with the Resistance?"

He pauses and Anaiya thinks that he will actually start giving her the answers she needs. Instead, he replies with a question of his own. "What did you two talk about last night?"

Anaiya resists the impulse to sigh. Perhaps if she gives him some intel, he will return the favour…

"Not much," she replies, glancing over to Kaide. Another Elemental has joined him at the pigeon stall. With their backs turned and a moving crowd of Elementals between her and them, she has no way of knowing who the mysterious arrival is.

"I arrived not long before the spoken word started and he left not long after they finished, so there really wasn't a lot of time to talk. We laughed about both of us going down to the Peacekeeper restraint the other night, he showed me his works in progress…"

She pauses looking down at the replica of Eamon's work covering Seth's lower arm. Seth catches her glance and looks down at it as well.

"Seems like a lifetime ago that I got this," he murmurs.

"I like it," Anaiya says and is surprised to realise that she means it.

"Me too," he says, smiling.

A crowd is beginning to gather along the riverbank and the brown haze of the sky shifts in the dominant Easterly, sending shards of bright light down to illuminate their faces. It is a pleasant day, one she would have loved as a Peacekeeper – with nothing else to do but free-run in the breeze and untainted sunlight, with the taste of cola-roasted pigeon on her lips and the promise of a long night at the Wild Rover in her future.

"Did he talk about Rehhd?"

His question sharpens her mind back to the present moment.

"I asked him where Rehhd was – I was surprised that she wasn't there. He said she was working solo that night."

Seth frowns and Anaiya's heart rate quickens. First Kaide stalking off with Eamon at the izakaya and now Seth fretting, all because of Rehhd working solo on a project. Or because Eamon told her about it.

What is Rehhd up to?

"Is Rehhd...in trouble?" she asks hesitantly.

"Not yet," he says darkly and then catches himself.

His frown fades and he shoots her a grin, but it is forced and fake and does nothing to ease the jittery fire rumbling in her core.

"What is Rehhd working on?" she asks, less hesitantly.

"Nothing," Seth replies, shaking his head. "It's nothing."

A buzzing at her wrist distracts Anaiya from pushing further.

Impeccable timing, Niamh.

She stands up from the bench. Seth stands quickly in response.

"I have to go," she announces, too loudly. Her first thought is to suppress the spiky feelings Seth provokes, but she lets them linger, her mind exploring ways she can use them.

"I'm sorry, Anaiya –" he starts, but she cuts him off before he can continue.

"I don't care," she says heatedly. "I don't know what's going on or what it has to do with me, or what you *think* it has to do with me –" Seth opens his mouth to interrupt, but she throws up her hand, palm flat. "No. I don't care. Whatever *is* going on, it is clear you don't trust me. It's obvious you find it easier to blame me, ignore me or accuse me than actually talk to me, so I'm done."

Her performance is flawless and she can see in his defeated stance and downcast eyes that he is on the pivot point, that he is considering ignoring the good advice of Kaide and his own neocortex and actually confiding in her.

She waits, letting her body lean subtly towards him and softening her eyes.

Come on, Seth. Open up to me.

He looks at her and takes a step forwards.

This is it, this is where Anaiya will get the intel she needs to confirm Rehhd as the Resistance leader, to prove herself as a Peacekeeper, to end this mission and return to her life.

A shout rings out and echoes off the river ramparts. Anaiya spins around, her eyes scanning the crowd. She spies Kaide, still in his original position near the vendor stall, but the mysterious Elemental beside him has disappeared. He is no longer staring towards her and Seth; his gaze is now fixed on the spectacle unfolding in the centre of the crowd.

Anaiya moves closer to the crowd that has gathered to watch, weaving in between and around the Elementals until she finds a clearing near the front.

At first, all she sees is a troupe of Dancers: Air Elementals twisting and turning and curving in on themselves and around each other, flashing black and grey and red with their long, hooded cloaks and rapid movements. It is strange to see them dancing in the flesh, instead of via a wallscreen. The organic appeal of it reminds her of the Lavoir and the throwback to activities that require no technology.

The association tickles faintly along secondary neural pathways, but she pays it no heed – consumed by the performance.

Her gaze follows every movement, spellbound as the kaleidoscope fractures and coalesces before her. Still her nape pricks with warning and she raises her left arm to record the performance on her wristplate.

The crowd grows as the performance continues, swelling to make movement along the riverbank almost impossible.

Without warning, the dance changes. With a swift and seamless flick of their hands, all five Dancers rip back their hoods to reveal their faces. Except there are no faces. Only masks. Harsh and angular surfaces, each tattooed with a single flame on the cheek.

Whispers in her mind turn to shouts.

The Dancers let out a piercing wail, dropping their cloaks in unison and falling dramatically upon them. Their forms continue to writhe, the deep red lining of the cloaks twisting and splaying on the ground like pools of blood. Anaiya steps closer, pushing urgently into the small gaps left by Elementals in front of her, and stares at the central figures, free of their cloaks and revealed in dark kevlar jeans, tight cottonex shirts and heavy boots.

She is no longer looking at a troupe of Air Elemental Dancers. She is looking at the death throes of a Peacekeeper corp.

Another shout rings out from somewhere in the crowd opposite her. Arms shoot up in the air, hands curled into fists. Again, a distant voice rises above the excited chattering of the crowd. High-pitched and melodic, it carries clearly to Anaiya, a single wail.

"Resistance!"

The word sets off a flurry of movement: the troupe spring to their feet, disband and melt into the crowd. Anaiya screams at herself to follow them, any of them, but her feet remain rooted to the spot.

She closes her eyes, blocking out the sight of the crowd and their reactions. Slowly a smile creeps at the corners of her lips. She lowers her arm and taps the screen of her wristplate to conclude her recording.

She doesn't need to follow the Dancers. They are irrelevant. She has caught something much more important. She smiles because she has recognised that voice, that unique, rebellious,

Heterodox voice.
    It is Rehhd's.

TWENTY-FOUR

The run to the Western Cardinal Area and Peacekeepers'
headquarters is a buzz of plans and ideas, opportunities and
expectations. Anaiya did not linger at the scene of the performance,
her exit assisted by the rapid dissipation of the crowd. She briefly
looked around for Seth and Kaide – feeling shades of
disappointment, relief and curiosity at finding neither.

The conflicting emotions fade as she moves further away from
the riverside, closer to the Peacekeeper headquarters. Reaching it,
Anaiya barely glances at the imposing facade as she strides through
the crowded courtyard and into the foyer. Forsaking the lift, she
takes the service stairs two at a time, relishing the fever in her legs
and her lungs.

She is early. Her wristplate message to Niamh was sent ten
minutes ago, telling him she would be there in twenty. It doesn't
matter; she will use her time alone to collect her thoughts and
sharpen her plan of attack into something coherent and failsafe.

As she advances towards the door of their assigned meeting
room, she works over the facts her mission has uncovered.

She knows that Rehhd is the leader of the Resistance. And that
Eamon, Cress and Kaide are involved. Seth, too, possibly – although
not as deep. He holds less angst than the others. Is more thoughtful.
Less likely to be intimidated or enamoured into staying with a
doomed rebellion. Too independent to follow Rehhd's, or anyone's,

lead. The tension between him and the other three all but confirms his distance from the Resistance's core.

She steps into the meeting room with her thoughts full of Seth and it takes a moment for her ears to pick up on the low-pitched, muffled sounds. She pulls her mind from its reverie and looks around. And then she sees Niamh. With Jenna.

It's easy to ignore their intimacy, to pass it off as another Fire flirtation. She opens her mouth to announce her news, when Jenna looks up.

It is not the way her arm drapes languidly over Niamh's shoulder. Nor is it the way his eyes are clouded with desire. It is her smile. That self-satisfied, smug, arrogant, intimately infuriating smile, that pricks at Anaiya's neurons.

She will not share her finding with Jenna.

"Ani." Niamh's voice is deeper and softer than what it was radiating down the silver links of her lifeline. "What have you got?"

He is so casual. So certain that she will play her usual role of obedient subordinate. The one who always comes second.

Not this time.

If nothing, her regular betrayals – by Niamh, by Seth – have taught her to be a little rebellious.

"There's been an incident in the Northern Area," she states perfunctorily. Like a good little Peacekeeper.

"We've heard," he says, his hand running down Jenna's back and gripping at the soft convex between her ribs and hip. "Jenna's Peacekeepers were able to detain some spectators – view the recordings on their wristplates."

So, they have some intel.

"Any identity matches?" she asks casually.

"No," he says. "We were hoping you could fill in the blanks."

Anaiya feels a small spark of satisfaction seeing Jenna's face sour at Niamh's admission, but she resists showing it openly.

"I retrieved the same intel," she says instead, the lie sweet on her lips, her wristplate heavy with secrets.

Niamh nods, as if that is to be expected. "OK," he says, finally stepping away from Jenna. "We need to identify the Heterodox."

He moves to the wallscreen, bringing it to life with a cursory swipe against its surface. The other Peacekeepers, the ones in the initial meeting whose names Anaiya promptly forgot, saunter into the room. Identical in their kevlar and nonchalant expressions, they seem an extension of the Dancers Anaiya had just gazed upon.

Niamh is speaking, his authoritative voice reverberating against the walls of the small room. He is outlining his plan. Anaiya is not listening. She is developing plans of her own.

Sitting alone in her apartment, Anaiya plays her wristplate recording over and over again on the small wallscreen. Not the whole recording: the first three viewings had confirmed that there was no way of identifying the street performers.

"Resistance!"

The five-second sample runs on an infinite loop. Again and again, Anaiya hears Rehhd's voice ring out over the crowd. Watches as the crowd startles and the performers disband.

The forbidden word still sits uneasily with Anaiya, but it no longer causes her body to respond so violently. She lies back on her small bed, closes her eyes and lets the voice bounce around her, forming the soundtrack to her coalescing thoughts.

Entering the Lavoir an hour later is like exhaling a deep breath. She immediately acclimatises to the familiar environment, her senses soaking up the cool air and soft light, her mind and body shifting to a calmer mode.

With each step she makes through the space, her eyes sweep the izakaya crowd, appraising the scene and its players with a cold and calculating eye. She is here for Kaide. Mostly. Other motivations lurk in the deeper recesses of her mind, but she keeps them at bay while her neocortex sifts through more urgent information.

She spies him at the far end of the bar, running a hand absently over the smooth graphene countertop while holding court with a small group. Scythe leans next to him, while Cressida sits fiddling with her orange tunic on the sole bar stool. Scythe sees her first, elbowing Kaide in the ribs. He pauses mid-sentence to frown at her before following her gaze to Anaiya's approach.

At the interruption, the others follow Kaide's gaze. The unfamiliar Elementals – an older male in his seventh lustrum with sharp features, a female in her fourth lustrum with lazy, drug-hazed eyes, and another fourth-lustrum Trainee still in the grey-tinted threads of his Premie uniform – seem unconcerned with her.

The others are clearly more moved by her unexpected appearance. Scythe wrinkles her nose as if assaulted by a foul smell. Cress's fingers lock together in a fierce grip, belying the faint smile that feathers at her lips. And Kaide. Kaide blinks away his obvious surprise and attempts to welcome her with a smile. It ends as a grimace.

"Anaiya," he says, his typically deep voice pitching high.

"Hi," she says calmly, smiling at him and the others.

He throws a quick glance at Scythe, who sighs openly and announces too loudly, "I tire of this place; who wants to go to Penultimate?"

The others nod their general assent and take their leave of Kaide. Cress touches Anaiya's arm as she passes. "It's good to see you again, Anaiya." Her voice is small, and while the words seem genuine, they are cold and empty without the familiar 'Nisha'.

Anaiya feels a small twinge grab at her core, a prick in the space between her heart and solar plexus. She nods gently at Cress and pauses in her one-eyed mission to watch her follow the others through the izakaya. For some reason the horror she feels for the Resistance does not extend to this pixie.

"So," Kaide says, pulling her attention back to him. "How're things?"

Anaiya laughs lightly. "Since our very awkward meeting at the riverside?"

Kaide surprises her by smiling. "Yes," he says. "Since then."

"Where did you and Seth go? I went to look for you after the performance, but it was chaos out there."

"We got caught up in the crowd as well," he replies, the small smile fading to a shadow.

Anaiya shrugs, nodding her easy acceptance. He could be telling the truth or it could be another deception, but either way she is unconcerned. She is not here looking for intel. "I love this song," she says, tilting her head towards the ceiling.

It is a lie, of course. She has never heard the song before. Although listening to it now, she feels her body move imperceptibly to its rhythm and melody. "That one sound," she says, finding a quirk in the music she can exploit. "It sounds so familiar…"

Kaide frowns in concentration, lowering his head to eradicate other sensory distractions so that he can focus on the soundwaves.

"Shame there isn't a wristplate app that lets you compare sounds and search for matches…" She says it softly, letting it hang between them, waiting for him to hear it, to process it.

He raises his head and looks at her. "Maybe not a wristplate app…But I do have a prototype sound development device that needs some more beta testing."

Kaide leads Anaiya through the streets marking the western border of the precinct. The buildings are eclectic, a random mix of high-density residential and Air-dominated commercial. As they pass a six-storey apartment block, coloured baubles hanging from window lintels, shiny curtains rustling in the faint breeze, Anaiya spies a flash of red at the base of the facade. Kaide keeps walking undeterred, but Anaiya looks more closely. It is a remnant of a Heterodox mural, a spot the Special Ops Forensics have missed.

"So this device," she starts. "Have you been working on it long?"

"A few months," he says. "In between commissions."

"It's a private project?"

"Of sorts…What sort of jobs are you working on at the moment? Any interesting commissions?"

The question takes her by surprise. It is a simple question and on any other day, with any other Elemental, she would not have thought twice before doling out her backstory response. But the circumstances are not simple. This is Kaide asking her, smiling at her and helping her out. The same Kaide who for a week has been scowling at her and judging her with a wary eye.

Anaiya glances at him sideways. Is he playing her? What

exactly does he know?

"I've got a small commission for a Water company in the Western Cardinal Area," she says, testing his reaction. "An advertising piece."

Kaide nods his head but doesn't say anything; either he buys it or he's waiting for her to say something. It's a classic interrogation technique used by Truthseekers.

I wonder how many times he was interrogated before he learned it...
She lets the silence hang for a little bit.
OK. I'll play.

"It's pretty average..." she continues, turning to look at him. "Do you ever get the feeling that you lost a part of your...identity after hypoxia? That you'll never be as *good* as you used to be?"

Kaide's cool demeanour fails, but he recovers quickly. He slows his pace and turns to look at her. "Is that what you think?"

"Sometimes. Maybe. I don't know..." And, strangely, she is telling the truth. "What did you do before your hypoxia?"

"Pretty much the same. I just do it for different customers."

He points out a squat, rubber-clad, three-storey building ahead. "That's my workspace– we'll grab the prototype and then we can head out to test it."

"How exactly does it work?" she asks as they enter the building's foyer.

The door slams behind her, and the sudden transition between the afternoon light and windowless interior renders Anaiya blind. Slowly her eyes adjust to the dim lighting, peeling back the darkness to reveal the room's details.

And in that moment, she forgets everything. Forgets her question and the fact that she is still waiting for Kaide to answer it. Forgets her suspicion that Kaide is interrogating her. Forgets that Kaide is even there with her.

In front of her, a mosaic of tiny photovoltaic cells is amassed on the distant wall. Streams of muted light, amplified by convex glass lenses pitting the opposite wall, run in haphazard patterns across the tiles. The pathways of light, created by the movement of the lenses within their sockets, light up the cells they hit, sending them flashing to a new colour and pattern.

As they walk closer, heading to the nearby stairwell, Anaiya realises that each cell is a glass screen, broadcasting a random selection of static Graphics, music visualisations and digital stories. Each cell fragmenting to a new display with each new hit of sunlight.

She stops, transfixed – her eyes roaming the cells and delighting when they catch the light triggering a new offering.

"Pretty cool, huh?" Kaide says.

Anaiya tears her eyes away from the sight before her, looking over to where Kaide has already ascended the first few steps.

"Very," she says, looking back one last time before joining him.

A clattering above warns of someone descending towards them and they move to the far left of the stairwell. An older Elemental, of short stature and dressed in the neutral polyester tones preferred by Water Elementals, brushes past them without greeting.

Of course.

The building is a shared workspace for Air and Water Elementals, perfect for collaborations that meld artistic vision with technological advances.

Which would explain the foyer piece. And the soundmatching prototype.

Armed with her new understanding, Anaiya peers into the rooms greeting them as they exit the stairwell. Open doors afford glimpses of tricked-up three-dimensional printers, choreography tracking operations, and holographic experiments. Sounds of excited chatter from Air Elementals and sober murmurings of Water Elementals follow her and Kaide as they approach the room at the far end of the hallway.

Unlike the others, the door to this room is closed, hiding its contents securely away. Anaiya's eyes scan the adjacent area, seeking the swipe panel out of habit, but finding nothing.

"Synthflies flutter beyond the Border Wall."

Anaiya flicks her head back to Kaide, a frown creasing her brow and question forming at her lips.

"What did –?"

She doesn't get a chance to finish. A loud click sounds and the heavy door swings inwards.

Kaide strides in and Anaiya mutely follows, turning her head to stare at the interior wall, her eyes finding a familiar electronic gauge lit with the moving line of a sound visualisation.

"Oooof!" she exclaims, running into the solid, unmoving mass of Kaide's back. "What the fuck?"

A deep chuckle erupts in the room.

"Tch, tch, tch. Language, butterfly."

Kaide steps aside. Sitting on a deeply recessed windowsill, feet propped against one side, back resting against the other, is Seth.

"What are you doing here?" Kaide asks, voicing the same question pinging in Anaiya's mind.

"I'm here to see you," Seth replies before nodding towards Anaiya. "What are *you* doing here?"

Anaiya pauses, wary that Seth will see through any attempt to lie. "Kaide's helping me with a project."

"Is he?"

Kaide grunts as he moves towards a long table pushed up against the adjacent wall. "You asked me to play nice. I'm playing nice."

Anaiya raises an eyebrow at Seth who matches her gaze evenly.

"Here," Kaide interrupts, handing her a small black box. The glass of its upper face is split in two.

"Double tap here to record the sound you're interested in," he says, tapping on the left-hand segment. The screen comes to life and a soundline appears, undulating to the sound of Kaide scratching his fingernail on a nearby tabletop. A single tap on the line ceases its movement, capturing the wavelength's unique pattern.

"And then double tap here to record possible matches," he says, tapping on the right-hand segment. Again the narrow flatline appears, sparking to life as Kaide rubs his hand along the rough material of his jeans.

"Merge the two together," he says, pinching his thumb and index finger across the screen, dragging the two wavelengths together. They shimmer together as one double-line extent across the full screen.

"Eighty-two per cent," Kaide says, stating aloud the number that has flashed on the screen.

Anaiya is silent. Her heartbeat threatens to escape its cage. She fears looking at either Kaide or Seth, certain they will see her unparalleled joy, the culmination of her mission, her impending success.

She stills her thoughts, willing herself to focus on the one obstacle still in her way. Her hand itches to grab it from him, to secure it in her sweating palms and retreat with it in search of Rehhd.

How am I going to do this?

Her original plan had been to break into the workspace with her Peacekeeper access and retrieve the device after everyone had left, but the sound recognition entry has killed that option. Now, her only other alternative seems undone by her own cover story. It would be so simple for Kaide to ask the name of the song Anaiya had chosen at the izakaya, to search out the soundmatches himself. She needs to give him a reason for her to take the device – a chance for her to experiment on her own.

"Here," he says holding the device out to her.

She looks up at him, surprise evident on her face. He takes her hand and deposits the small box in her palm.

"Have a play around with it. See what you think," he says smiling at her. "I'll get it back off you at the lockdown party."

She forces herself to breathe, subtly exhaling the air she hadn't realised she had been holding. She works her tongue, pressed tightly to the roof of her mouth, forcing it to make the words she so desperately needs to voice. "Thanks." Breathy, but not shaking. "I'll take good care of it."

Kaide nods and turns back to Seth. The small movement is a release for Anaiya. Her shoulders relax and her grip on the precious device loosens.

She looks over to Seth. He has shifted on the windowsill, his feet now firmly planted on the floor, his back resting against the glass of the window. It is an arresting sight, his sculpted form backlit and the endless view of the precinct beyond.

And then she sees the slight frown pulling at his eyes. Notices the way he worries at the tattoo on his forearm, running his thumb in endless circles of pressure. A question forms in her mind but dies on her lips.

I need to get out of here.

Before they see the elation in her eyes. Before they uncover her secret.

"I'll leave you two to it," she says, indicating the door.

Kaide nods. "I'll let you out."

Anaiya doesn't look back as the door slides open, doesn't wait for it to close behind her. She passes without a cursory glance at the photovoltaic wall that had captivated her only minutes ago. She doesn't hurry, she doesn't stop. She maintains an even, steady pace, free of detour and free of thoughts. All thoughts. Except one.

Game over. I win.

TWENTY-FIVE

"Her last access swipe was four hours ago, but her lifeline hasn't engaged for at least three hours," Niamh's voice echoes into Anaiya's ear via her lifeline.

"OK. I'll head to the Lavoir. Contact me if she checks in somewhere public."

Anaiya disconnects the communication and wraps her lifeline in place. Her hand free, she immediately feels for the hard planes and corners of the device tucked safely away in her kevlar pocket.

After leaving Seth and Kaide she ran straight to her apartment, unconcerned with how strange it must have looked to see an Air Elemental run anywhere. Shutting the door behind her, she had settled on her uncomfortable bed and played with the soundmatcher for hours, recording and matching random sounds, until she was satisfied she had mastered the technology.

She had tried matching her own voice at different decibels and across like-sounded words – learning that volume did not factor in the match and that word approximations would impact on the result. If she tried matching 'synthfly' to 'synthetic', the wavelength comparison was thrown out by the different ending. After a few tries, however, she learned to concatenate both recordings to match the first syllable only. The result had been a ninety-nine point two per cent match.

And then she had tapped on the recording of the street

performance.

"Resistance!" Three syllables. Three opportunities to match Rehhd's voice.

The words play on repeat through her mind as she makes her way to the Ravignan Strip. They branch off into potential conversations she can use to lure Rehhd to say the sound that will damn her.

I just need to find her. And get her to talk.

The fingers of her right hand twitch at her wristplate, her fingernails plucking at the thin metal edges. Tink. Tink. Tink.

It is only when she sees the familiar sight of the Lavoir that she stills her fidgeting. Even now, weeks after her first visit, the same feeling of unsteadiness and imbalance plague her when she looks along the lines of its facade.

Shaking her head, she closes her eyes tight. When she opens them, she stares resolutely at the entry door and strides towards it. She disregards the Elementals congregating in the street, ignores the ones milling about inside. She brushes past them, bypassing the bar and taking up residence at a vacant table.

The izakaya hums with chatter, laughter and music. A few familiar faces fill the small space, too caught up in their own realities to notice her. Except one.

"Nisha?"

Anaiya looks up as Cressida's shadow falls over her table. Her eyes are dull with enhanced alcohol, her speech husky and slurred at the edges.

"Hey, Cress."

Cress looks around before settling into the chair opposite Anaiya. A familiar conflict begins to simmer in Anaiya's mind. She crushes her limbic brain's emotions, pulling the rationality of her neocortex to the fore. Cress's smile is tremulous, uncertain.

"I just came over…I just wanted to…to, um, apologise." Her eyes search Anaiya's, seeking understanding.

Anaiya shifts her body language, relaxing it, encouraging Cress to continue.

"You know, for yesterday?"

A table nearby breaks into raucous laughter, startling

Cressida.

"No problem," Anaiya says. "What was with that, anyway? You all looked so sombre. I thought someone had died."

Cress shakes her head. Rueful. "Just the usual ego battle. The resistance has us all a little fired up."

Anaiya's skin tingles with the unsaid subtext of Cress's words. Forbidden words thrown out easily among familiar. Resistance. Fire.

She forgoes her usual restraint. "How did you get involved in it? In the Resistance?"

She hears her capitalisation, where Cress had none.

"Seth says there is no resistance," she says. The words cause Anaiya's heart to lurch. "Just consciousness."

The music in the izakaya swells and fades.

"But others. They see the resistance. See the need for it. And the need for it to do more than just exist. To grow. To do *something*."

It is more than Anaiya is expecting. Overwhelming.

Her mission had been simple. To find Rehhd. To have her murmur a sound, any sound, that would approximate three simple syllables.

But here is Cress. The sprite with a spark, a daring and youthfulness that pulls at Anaiya. A Heterodox Air Elemental.

"But why did *you* get involved?" she persists. She wants to hear Cress say it – to confirm Rehhd's treacherous pull on vulnerable minds.

Cress shrugs, throwing a cautionary glance over her shoulder.

"It's never felt right. This," she murmurs, throwing her hands in a vague clarification. "This has *never* felt right."

Something crumbles in Anaiya.

There is the raw honesty of Cress's statement. But it is more than that. There is a part of Anaiya that responds. That echoes the sentiment.

It doesn't feel right. *She* doesn't feel right.

Recognising it, she immediately thinks of Seth. And then stops herself thinking of him.

Chaos everywhere. What she needs is clarity. The simplicity of her mission.

She bows her head and closes her eyes, keeping them shut

even as the chair opposite her scrapes backwards along the polished concrete.

"Don't let the fire burn you, Nisha."

The words are mournful. A melancholic echo of the words Rehhd had casually thrown to her on their first encounter.

Anaiya opens her eyes. And Cressida is gone.

Suddenly, the izakaya feels larger. Anaiya, smaller. Her newly minted resolve starts to waver.

What am I doing here?

Beat. Beat. Beat.

Who am I?

The world seems to tilt. Anaiya places her hand on the worn tabletop, steadying herself before she stands.

And then the door to the izakaya opens.

And Rehhd saunters in.

Rehhd's burnished hair flares bright under the warm lights of the izakaya. Despite her obvious Heterodoxy, she is still impressive. Anaiya lets her centre of gravity fall back into her chair.

I can do this.

Her limbic brain voices its doubts, unheard in the power of Anaiya's resolve.

"Rehhd," she calls, her voice tilting over the thrum of punk beats.

She turns, recognition and then confusion carousing across her features. Nonetheless, she wanders over, shifting from her original trajectory, caught in the curiosity of Anaiya's implicit command.

"Ah, Anaiya." She draws out the words, like a languid stutter. "We meet again. You've certainly caused a stir since your arrival."

Anaiya ignores the barb, tapping the recording function of her wristplate hidden under the table. "The world's a chaotic place," she replies. "Causing a stir is no difficult feat."

Rehhd laughs, a light tinkling of champenois glasses, set in sharp contrast to the dense beats of the izakaya soundtrack. "And we all love a good stir, don't we?" she says, taking the seat only recently vacated by Cressida.

"I haven't seen you around," Anaiya says. "Eamon mentioned you were working on a solo project."

She takes some satisfaction when Rehhd's eyes narrow slightly, but keeps her own features schooled.

"I've got a few works in progress," she says, before laughing. It is a brittle sound. "What about you, Anaiya? Any interesting projects?"

"A couple. I find the more promise they show, the more they frustrate my efforts at finishing them."

"That's the way with all art. The more you pursue it, the more it resists."

The word flares in Anaiya's mind. In the end, it was easier than she imagined. The sense of triumph urges her to take her prize and return to her apartment for the analysis, but she stays where she is. "And resistance leads to failure," she says.

Rehhd's expression hardens for a brief moment, but then she shakes her head, her features softening. "No, Anaiya. Resistance leads to growth."

They are both talking in code, layering their words with enough subterfuge to protect themselves, but grounding them with enough truth to voice what they truly wish to say. The realisation sends a thrill through Anaiya and she leans forwards, folding her arms over the table.

"But, fighting the...*art*...It weakens it," she says, encouraging Rehhd to engage.

Rehhd pauses. Anaiya sees her indecision in the slight frown at her brow. And, for a moment, Anaiya thinks she has pushed too hard, too fast.

Rehhd sighs, relenting. "No," she says. "Fighting the art is about restoring the proper order of things. The Elemental creates the art; the art doesn't direct the Elemental. Fighting the art strengthens the artist. And it is the artist, and not the art, who needs to be strong."

An uneasy stalemate settles between them. Anaiya looks at Rehhd, trying to understand her words, gauge her motivations. But the code refuses to translate.

Rehhd stands up, breaking the connection. "Don't let the fire burn you, Anaiya," she says, before disappearing into the izakaya crowd.

Streets and alleys blur as Anaiya makes her way back to her apartment. She treads the familiar path with heavy feet, oblivious to everything but the maelstrom within her brain. Over and over, it repeats just one word.

Resistance.

Over and over it echoes. Spoken by Rehhd. Spoken by Cress. Spoken by her. And somewhere, layered underneath, kept quiet but not silent, is a dangerous question. *What is Resistance?*

"Anaiya?"

Seth's voice comes crashing into her thoughts. She stops abruptly, finally taking in her surroundings.

The narrow street is uneven underfoot, the bitumen surface cracked and pitted. Stark, blank walls rise either side. Simple, unadorned doors provided the only relief: it's a service lane. Ahead, the view opens onto a sunlit boulevarde, full of life and activity. But, here in the deep shadows of the laneway, there is none.

Anaiya turns around slowly. Seth stands backlit at the laneway entrance.

He moves towards her, each step bringing more details into focus. He's tired – she sees it in the set of his shoulders and lines on his face.

"Hey," she says softly.

"Hey," he replies.

He stands only a few feet away from her. They stay like that for what seems like minutes, silently observing the other.

"I've been thinking about you," he says eventually.

Anaiya's throat closes painfully around the words, feeling them grate against the soft flesh as she swallows.

Walk away, Anaiya. Don't let him complicate things. You have your evidence. Your mission is almost complete.

But she remains still.

"How is your project coming along?" he asks, raking his hand in a familiar gesture through messy hair. "The one with Kaide's soundmatcher?"

Instinctively she runs her fingers over the hard planes of the compact cube buried in her jeans pocket. "It's almost complete…" she manages.

Seth nods, his hand moving to grip the back of his neck. Anaiya can see that he is trying to establish a connection, can see the pained frustration that every pause and shut-down conversation triggers.

Something within her wants to engage, to open up the dialogue and let him in. She pushes her fingers harder against the outline of the soundmatcher, resisting the temptation.

"Is it working out the way you wanted it to?" he asks, still clinging to the bare-thread conversation.

She thinks of the Heterodoxy, of Rehhd and of erasing Kane's shadow. But the clarity and strength of her usual self-righteous rage has diminished. Tarnished by the unwarranted aggression of Peacekeepers and her growing disconnect with Niamh and the Fire Element. Subdued by her irrational Air attachment to Seth.

Anaiya sighs. "It's complicated."

"Good art always is."

He smiles sadly, the expression causing Anaiya's heart to tighten. She wonders how her mind will remember these moments once it is realigned back to her Fire Element.

Thoughts of the impending return to her old life flick across the surface of her mind. She realises she will never hear music the same way, or look at a simple object and see a complex beauty. Will never again climb air recyclers to just sit and reflect. Will never again savour cold mornings or quiet moments. Will never again see Seth.

And while it is unlikely that her Fire-aligned brain will miss any of that, the thought of losing it creates a melancholy within her.

"Are you still going to the lockdown party?" she asks.

The grin that brightens his face sets an edge to her melancholy. Her betrayal, a dark shadow that lends weight to her fragile shoulders.

"Yeah. Yes." He ducks his head and gives a short laugh.

Anaiya smiles despite herself.

"Yes, I am still going to the lockdown party. Does that mean you will be joining me?"

The smile turns cheeky. Seductive.

"I told you," she replies. "I wouldn't miss it."

TWENTY-SIX

"This is a recording I appropriated following the performance
Heterodoxy."

Vision from that afternoon in Precinct 19's riverside area fills
the wallscreen of the small briefing room that Anaiya shares with
Niamh. She watches his face closely. He looks non-plussed.

"How does this help us, Ani?"

"Wait," she says.

Niamh frowns, unfamiliar with delayed gratification,
unaccustomed with being told to do anything by Anaiya.

She ignores him and watches the screen. As they did that
afternoon, the Dancers let out a piercing wail and begin their
dramatisation of death throes. Anaiya holds her breath. There is the
shout, and the raised fists, and then the voice. The voice she has
listened to over and over again in the isolation of her apartment.
That high-pitched, melodic projection of three syllables. Resistance.

The recording stops.

"Ani, there's nothing we can use. There are no identifying
marks, no facial data points. How does this help us?"

"We can identify –"

"We can't identify anything, Ani."

She ignores the interruption – the terseness in Niamh's voice,
the lines of frustration on his face.

"We can identify the voice."

Niamh falls silent, letting Anaiya's words sink in.

"We can identify the voice?"

A smile spreads across Niamh's face. Anaiya can't help but smile back even as her stomach tightens.

"Show me."

Using some basic sound software, Anaiya strips away the background noises of the riverside and the izakaya so only Rehhd's voice remains. In the perfect acoustics of the briefing room, the identical nature of the two samples is undeniable.

"One hundred per cent match."

It sends a shiver through her, as it has every time she has read it aloud.

"We'll need to verify the technology," he says.

"Get your Water Developers on it."

His smile slips a little at her tone, but he nods. "It will take a couple of days."

He starts tapping away on his mobile screen, bringing up a mission spec sheet on the wallscreen. "I'll put Jenna on exclusive surveillance of the target, get her to identify the ideal detention opportunity."

"No." The word comes out harsher than she anticipates, but she doesn't retract it. "This is mine, Niamh. My intelligence. My mission. I'm the one who will take Rehhd down."

"Anaiya –"

"No. This is mine."

Niamh frowns at her. She knows the exchange presents a shift in their dynamic, can tell he is not entirely comfortable with it.

"There is a curfew lockdown party in Precinct 18 on the Sixth Day," she begins, feeding Niamh the details of the plan she has been developing for the past twenty-four hours. "Rehhd will be there. Get your technology verification before then and we can detain her when curfew lifts. I'll message you the location of the party and confirmation of her attendance. I'll lead her to a suitable detention place after curfew lifts – separate her from her supporters, minimise complications."

"You'll need backup."

The thought of Jenna being there to assist grates at Anaiya, but she needs Niamh to approve her plan. "Fine. Jenna and the others can provide backup," she concedes. "But I'm lead – I'm the one to restrain her."

Niamh shakes his head. "This Air attitude is not attractive. The sooner you're realigned back to Fire, the better."

"So can I have the lead?"

"You get one chance, Anaiya. Mess it up, and Jenna takes it."

Anaiya hears the lockdown party long before she turns into Beauvoir Lane. Unlike other izakaya whose bellies are being emptied of patrons and sound, Veritas has a steady current of Air Elementals disappearing behind its door, a cacophony of music and shouting spewing into the street with every gape of the entrance.

The sight of the izakaya, her first meeting point with Rehhd, forces her to pause. The moment grows heavier, full of meaning and inevitability. It has come to this. Her mission – her madness – has arrived at its destination.

Tonight, before the curfew lifts, before the new day is born, she will have her victory.

A jostle at her side forces her back into the real world of sounds so dense she could swim through them, sights so vivid she could clutch them. Around her, the final thrum of Air Elementals are making their way into Veritas, their levity singing through the emptying streets.

Curfew will begin in less than ten minutes; the Peacekeepers are already amassing on street corners to enforce the Orthodoxy. They survey the spectacle with stony faces and relaxed feet.

And for a moment, she is caught – suspended between her past, her present and her future.

She stares at the kevlar-clad Peacekeepers, wanting to see herself there – to see herself again as one of them. The one on the left, a female in her fifth lustrum like Anaiya, catches her staring. A quick nudge to her partner and both pairs of eyes regard Anaiya coolly. And just as quickly, there is weight.

Anaiya blinks at its sudden appearance but does not look away. Instead she squares her shoulders, turning to face the

Peacekeepers more directly. The action awakens old memories. Of the street party in Le Maraias. Of loud music and lounges. Of the Samedi Markets. Of weight. Of a defiant Air Elemental who refused to look away under her Peacekeeper scrutiny.

The Peacekeepers shift, a glance at their wristplates confirming that curfew is only minutes away. Anaiya is the only Air Elemental still in the street. With a curse under her breath she turns and hurries into the izakaya.

Her arrival into the dimly lit space is halted almost immediately, her body colliding with another walking at pace towards the exit. The impact sends her stumbling back, her back grazing the cool metal of the door. Laughing eyes dance over her and strong arms grab her by the shoulders. "You had me worried there, butterfly."

She is given no time for a response, relieved of needing to come up with a poorly constructed excuse for her tardiness. The same strong arms drop to her waist and pluck her from the ground, cinching her securely and spinning her in dizzy circles until she is weightless and laughing despite herself.

Guilt threatens, but she squashes it. She can have this moment. She can be happy. *I've completed my mission. I can celebrate.* She allows herself to relax against him, savouring the faded scent of aftershave and tequila. "You started without me?"

Seth sets her down gently, grinning broadly. "Only just. Come on – let's get you a drink."

He pulls her towards the bar. The feeling of her hand in his reminds her of their time in the Edges. It feels solid; it feels *right*. Their progress through the crowd is halted a few seconds later when the shout goes up.

"Ten! Nine! Eight!"

Elementals take up the chant as the numbers flash down on a large wallscreen above the bar. A large Elemental pushes past her and Seth to take up a position by the door.

"Seven! Six! Five!"

Seth is beaming at her, pulling her closer until they are pressed tight against each other, a single unit against the tide of Elementals around them.

"Four! Three! Two!"

He leans his head forwards, their foreheads touching. She looks down at his lips. Fixated as he whispers the word that otherwise echoes in a loud collective voice around the izakaya.

"One."

A cheer erupts in the small place, the explosion of sound a poor imitation of the sensation that takes Anaiya when Seth tilts her chin up and presses his lips to hers. Her mind teeters on a precipice, caught between wanting more of the ecstasy and wanting to shun anything that marks her as something other than a Fire Elemental.

But for tonight, if only until the curfew lifts and the doors open, she is not a Peacekeeper. She is not a Fire Elemental. She is another tripped out, heady, careless Air Elemental wrapped in the arms of a kindred spirit who sets her nerve endings on fire.

It is a second chance. A last chance. A caution where, in typical circumstances, a penalty would otherwise be imposed.

It is the reprieve she needs to relax into the moment and kiss him back.

"Anaiya."

The voice breaks into the moment, pulling them apart. Anaiya looks over Seth's shoulder to see Kaide advancing.

She smiles, despite the intrusion, and reaches into her jeans pocket to retrieve the soundmatcher. The hard planes dig into her palm as she squeezes it tightly one last time, a silent thanks to this technological accomplice.

She offers it to Kaide, palm upwards, watching it glitter in the izakaya lights. He smiles in return, the hint of tequila softening his typically sharp eyes. "You find your mystery sound?" he asks, plucking it from her hand and rolling it in his.

A hidden question lingers under the surface of his query. It calls to the uncertainty of her unsettled mind. She is not sure whether he put it there or whether it is only her ears that can hear it.

Relax. It's over. You've won. Enjoy the moment.

The truth of her exhortations is clear, but still her limbic mind nags.

What have you won? What will you lose?

Once upon a time, the incendiary whispers of her limbic brain would have caused her untold grief. But no longer. She has mastered the workings of her paradoxical brain. Can manipulate the switches that erect and dismantle the barriers between the two minds. So she shuts down the limbic brain, muting it behind the dense structures of her neocortex. And smiles. "Yes. I found it."

"Out of curiosity," he says, "what was it?"

She turns her mind to the afternoon in the bar, replaying the encounter with Kaide, working through the microcosm of details to remember the song she had chosen as her cover story. It comes to her with effort, initially through a haze of white noise and static, but slowly crystallising into an exact replica of the sound. The high-pitched rumbling that filled her ears that night at the air recycler with Seth. Dense and light all at the same time. So like an air recycler, but different – more timid, more vulnerable.

Beat.

"It was a synthfly," she says.

It doesn't take Anaiya long to find Rehhd in the crowd. She stands at the pool table, slender arms draped down a cue. Around her, Elementals weave and jostle, electric in their movements, extreme in their emotions. But Rehhd just stands there.

There is an atypical calmness to her – as if the hunger has drained from her and she is sated. It bothers Anaiya, even as Seth drags her in the opposite direction to a calmer corner of the izakaya.

"I'll grab drinks, do you want anything in particular?" he says, shouting to be heard.

Anaiya shakes her head and leans back against the velvet-clad wall. The tables and assorted chairs scattered around Veritas are already occupied. She doesn't mind – her position against the wall affords a generous view of the izakaya and its inhabitants, allowing her to survey the scene while protecting her from similar scrutiny.

From here she can see Seth, three lines deep at the bar, idly chatting to a small group of Elementals; and Kaide, sitting at a table with his usual crowd, deep in discussion; and Rehhd, still at the pool table, patiently waiting for her next turn, a small smile dancing at the corners of her mouth but never directed at anyone or anything.

Anaiya frowns. Seeing Rehhd so preternaturally calm has unsettled her. She had wanted to come tonight and see Rehhd her usual buoyant, gravitational, impossibly charismatic self. To see her brought low from her lofty heights. To take that pleasure from Rehhd and make it hers.

But there is no wild delight to siphon from, no ecstasy to steal. It blurs Anaiya's anticipation, dulling the edges, draining the brightness.

Snap out of it.

The words bounce uselessly in her mind, unable to break the fixation.

"Hey, Base to Anaiya…"

She blinks, dragging her gaze from Rehhd.

"I figured we could start with lys and end with tequila," Seth says, handing her the narrow glass tumbler.

She throws a quick glance to the bar she had just seen him standing at. The crowd has shifted – new faces, different patterns.

"Everything OK?" Seth asks, pulling her gaze back to him.

"Yeah," she says quickly. Too quickly.

She takes a sip of the lys, the slick alcohol lightened by a second, effervescent liquid. The tiny bubbles tingle in her throat as she swallows, accelerating the enhanced alcohol through her bloodstream.

Seth leans into the wall next to her, their shoulders grazing. She leans a little closer, finding comfort in at least the immovability of this, and him.

"Good?" he asks.

"Yeah," she replies, slower. And this time she means it.

An hour into the curfew and the lyseracid has settled in to coat Anaiya's neural pathways. The lights seem warmer, colours more vibrant and a generic feeling of happiness, of some tinny brightness, moves across her body in long waves.

She waits patiently at the bar, content to trail her fingers over the solid countertop. A shiver runs down her neck, solidifying into a general pressure. She leans into it before looking up at the source, expecting to see Seth. Instead finding Eamon.

"Anaiya."

His voice is low and gravelly. It seems almost unbearable in the lightness of the izakaya.

"Eamon."

"I'm surprised to see you here with Seth," he murmurs, fingers still lingering at the base of her neck, pressing softly at her clavicle.

Anaiya looks over her shoulder, past Eamon's fingers, to where Seth is absorbed in a multi-player game of pool. She remembers her encounter with him at the Lavoir, the initial attraction, the strange weight that had interrupted their own game.

"I thought you were more like me, Anaiya – hungry for something a little more challenging."

She looks back to Eamon.

"I have my challenges," she says, disengaging from his touch and walking away.

"Artistic challenges don't count," he calls after her. "We all have those."

She heads towards the pool table, her path a sine wave between izakaya debris and microcosms of Elementals, to where Seth still lingers. He looks up as she approaches and instantly she is transported back to that afternoon in the Lavoir. It seems like a lifetime ago and, tonight, in a way, it is.

"Care to challenge, butterfly?" he calls to her when she gets closer.

She plucks a stray cue leaning against the table.

"Losers first," she says, pointing the stick at him.

The table is a mosaic of coloured balls in motion. One by one, they tumble towards their own dark abyss, some falling heavy, others teetering before they disappear.

The game is different to the last. Seth is more hesitant, playing with more focus and structure. Anaiya is less confident, her Peacekeeper brashness dulled – inviting missteps and rookie mistakes. She hits the red orbs, instead of her yellow, and two shots running she sends the white ball tumbling into a dark hole after her target.

Throughout it all is the steady exchange of teasing. Seth brushes past Anaiya to take his shots, whispering playful jibes in her ears. She retaliates by rapping his knuckles with her own cue, darting out of reach when he stands to respond.

They laugh, touch, tease, until there is only the black ball left. And like last time, Anaiya doesn't feel the weight until she has taken the shot and the black ball sinks into the depths of the far pocket. She lets her baton fall back against the wall behind her, no longer wanting to touch it.

Seth is grinning, bending in a mock flourish as he walks towards her. She can't avert her eyes, watching as he draws nearer, her faint smile a pale reflection of his. She turns her back to the table as he rounds on her, stopping just centimetres away.

Beat. Beat. Beat.

The pause is interminable. Until it isn't. He sets his hands either side of her on the table, trapping her against the edge. He opens his mouth to say something, but she jumps into the space before he can claim it.

"What happened that night after Soylent? With Kaide and Cressida?" The words tumble out of her mouth unbidden, riding on the wave of lys sedating her neocortex. She continues before she can regain focus and stifle her inhibited tongue. "Everything changed after that. Why? What happened that night?"

For a moment, he just looks at her. No surprise flits across his face, no resentment or anger. Just resignation and something softer, something heavier. His face transforms with the weight of it, yet he still offers her a tired smile. "This week has been so long," he starts softly, his gaze lowering to where the toes of their boots touch on the izakaya floor, sticky with spilt drinks.

And she knows he is talking as much to himself as to her.

"So much longer than seven days…It's strange to think you can fit several lifetimes into such a small slice of time. In the scheme of things, this week is a grain of sand in the Wasteland…but even a grain of sand holds more atoms than there are stars in the universe."

He looks up, his forehead creased, his eyes imploring her to understand.

"Seth, what happened?"

Finally, he shifts his hands, raking the right through his hair in that familiar tell of his. "They never trusted you like I did. They couldn't see you were one of us."

He shrugs, green eyes flashing, hands still agitated. "You were different. God, you were different." His laugh is light. It sounds wrong against the heaviness of the words. "But being different is kind of a revolutionary act in itself, no? And I liked you. I really liked you. And I haven't liked anyone in a really long time."

The words are coming faster, his confession tripping over itself. Her heart tightens; she knows this is building to something terrible.

"I was supposed to have vetted you. As a precaution. To gauge your reaction before…before you saw the mural. Before you knew…"

"Before I knew what?"

His eyes flicker with indecision, a familiar anguish. "I need to trust you."

She feels trapped. His need is so raw.

"Anaiya, can I trust you?"

She doesn't get a chance to respond. A roar erupts near the bar.

Anaiya turns, just in time to see Kaide land a heavy punch on Eamon's jaw.

TWENTY-SEVEN

"What the *fuck* is going on?" Seth's voice is a hard whisper.

They have retreated to the wet room of the izakaya, away from the eyes of other Air Elementals and the dense music. Anaiya hangs back against the wall, feeling the beats buzz through the solid mass – happy to watch as the drama unfolds between Seth, Kaide, Eamon and Rehhd.

While Seth's words are directed equally to Kaide and Eamon, it is Rehhd who answers. "Seth, you don't need to moderate this."

She is still so calm. Even faced with Kaide's swollen eye and Eamon's busted lip dribbling blood down his chin, with Seth's intensity and the palpable sense of tension. So calm.

Something is not right.

"What have you done?"

All four Air Elementals spin to regard her, Kaide and Eamon registering surprise that she is there. Seth still livid. Rehhd still calm.

Anaiya turns her full gaze to Rehhd. "What have you done?"

Seth's face shifts from rage to confusion, flitting between Anaiya and Rehhd. Anaiya pays him no heed, solely focussed on Rehhd.

Moments shift into seconds.

And then Rehhd smiles. A small, satisfied curve of her mouth. "You really are so *perceptive*, Anaiya," she says. "Seth used to be like you. Hungry, but restrained. Introverted, but perceptive."

The focus of the room has switched to Rehhd. Eamon's eyes are guarded, his face still flushed. Kaide is glowering. But now it is Seth who is calm.

He stands arms folded across his chest, stance relaxed, muscles tight. In the harsh light of the wet room, the angles of his face and body cast distinct shadows, and for a moment he is like Anaiya – a Peacekeeper trapped in the body of an Air Elemental.

"His vision for the Resistance was a thing of power and beauty."

Anaiya's mind hears the words in replay, registering moments after Rehhd has actually uttered them. A cold sweat tingles at the back of her neck.

No, no, no.

"He saw what no one else had. He saw the *dystopia* while everyone else was drugged on the false utopia. He saw the oppression, the injustice, the *wrongness.*"

Anaiya's mind is in chaos, a burr of knots and tension. Memories and half-remembered conversations assault the cracks in her brain.

No one else sees her distress. They are all too consumed by Rehhd and her deadly words.

"He showed it to us. He led us towards this bright new hope. And then he said that we weren't to chase it. That we were to wait patiently."

Eamon huffs, his face an open scowl. Kaide glares at him and, for a moment, Anaiya thinks the fight will erupt again. But Rehhd continues speaking, sucking the room's energy and concentration towards her.

"So we did. We waited patiently. We waited. And waited. We cultivated supporters, revealing to them what had been revealed to us, encouraging the rage we too had felt. We painted our pretty pictures on silent walls. This was our resistance.

"But the Fire Elementals took away our pictures. Erasing them first from sight and then from memory. And then they caged us up, separating us from the night. And then they roughed us up, piling cuts on scars on bruises.

"And still, our wise and visionary leader told us to be

patient."

It is so quiet in the small, bright room. Anaiya can hear nothing but Rehhd's voice and the blood thrumming in her ears.

"And so we waited. Because we loved him. We waited, until we could bear the weight no more."

Anaiya's palms throb, pain blooming where her fingernails have punctured the skin.

The silence that follows is more oppressive than the steady barrage of nuclear words. It blankets them all in a dread, a white noise of heavy foreboding. It stretches interminably, fraying Anaiya's thoughts, setting her skin crawling. And worse is the haunted voice of the one who breaks it.

"What have you done?" asks Seth.

The stairwell leading from the wet room to the storeroom is narrow and dark. A musty smell of sweat and sand and dust tickles Anaiya's nostrils. She follows the other four, led by Rehhd and Eamon, to the depths of the izakaya. The sounds of the curfew lockdown party fade into nothing as they descend.

The basement level arrives earlier than she expects. Her feet hit the stone floor with a jolt and it takes a moment to recover her balance, to move from behind Kaide's broad girth and take a more complete survey of her new surroundings.

The room is dark like the stairwell. Her eyes slowly consume the last echoes of light to pull details into focus. Harsh, angular shapes materialise as boxes, and the softer shape in the corner –

A bright light erupts in the room, Seth's wristplate diode shattering the darkness and shooting pain into Anaiya's eyes. She clenches them shut, gradually releasing the pressure as they grow accustomed to the shift.

At first all she sees are the boots. Her boots.

No. Not my boots.

Peacekeeper boots.

It's a Peacekeeper Trainee. His arms are wrenched behind him, his legs stretched out against the dense floor and shackled with cable ties at the ankles. A single swathe of black, folded rayon interrupts the youthful face, covering his eyes and taming the hair that falls raggedly against pale cheeks.

Even with the blindfold, she recognises him – the young Trainee from that day at the Samedi Markets. So long ago. A lifetime ago.

And again, as when she saw the first Heterodox mural, the vision arrests her heart. Her mind screams for her to shut her eyes against the abomination, but fear of seeing worse in the shadows prevents her from following the order. She is shaking.

Clear it, Anaiya.

She feels her mind grind against the rising panic, like a gear forced to push back against its own momentum.

Clear. It.

The pressure scrapes at her skull, screeching with the resistance. And then, finally, something gives. And her mind is shattered. But silent.

"Notre dieu, Rehhd," Seth murmurs, his soft words falling loud in the intimate space. "What have you done?"

"We've caged one of them," Eamon spits, no longer satisfied with playing the silent accomplice. "Let's see how they like being locked up, beaten down, emptied out."

His words rush out in a stream of spiky vitriol.

"You *fucking* morons," Kaide says, clenched fists tight by his side. "You've ruined us."

"You ignorant fool," Rehhd counters. "Patience is a losing strategy. Worse. It is no strategy." She flings an accusing hand at the bound Peacekeeper. "They torture us. They lock us away and scar us. There *is* no change for them. No hope for reform. Otpor is *not* a functional collective. It is a dysfunctional dictatorship, ruled by them. Owned by them. We don't have to obey them any more, kneel to their harsh penalties.

"If we can bring one of their own low, if we show the rest of Otpor they are not the invincible power we have *let* them become, they will lose their enchantment over the other Elementals. We will show them to be weak. And the rest of the world will trample them in their haste to break the shackles of a corrupted Orthodoxy."

Kaide opens his mouth to spit his rejoinder, but it is Anaiya who speaks next.

"When did you take him?" Her voice is steel to her ears.

Confusion splits the angry faces before her.

"When?" she repeats.

"What does it matter?" Rehhd says, turning her attention back to Kaide.

"When?" Louder this time. More commanding.

"Why, Anaiya?" Seth has moved closer to her.

She ignores him, doing the mathematics in her head. One hour and forty minutes since the curfew began. One hour since the Trainee would have been expected to make communication with his shadow Peacekeeper. Fifteen minutes for headquarters to mobilise the search function.

"How many communication patches are around here? Within a five-k radius?"

The others regard her strangely. Except Kaide. His face and body have gone very still.

You always were suspicious, weren't you?

"Three," he says.

Leaving forty-five minutes for curfew patrols to search the nearby properties for a missing Trainee.

She turns to Seth. "Get out of here," she says.

He stares at her, but doesn't move.

She turns to Kaide. "Get him out of here. Now."

"Anaiya – it's curfew."

"Get him. Out. Now."

"Anaiya, what is going on?" It is Seth. She hears the confusion in his voice, still laced with the sting of betrayal.

"Just who, exactly, do you think you are?" Rehhd says. "You may be *fucking* one of us, but that does not *make* you one of us."

Anaiya ignores her, striding over to Kaide. Their eyes clash in an unspoken war, full of promise that will need to be satisfied at a later date. She holds his gaze, forcing him to recognise her true self.

"You have three minutes, maybe less," she whispers, low and harsh. For his ears only. "Until a contingent of senior Peacekeepers access this izakaya and detain you all."

His eyes betray no emotion. His steely gaze remains fixed on hers.

"Get him out of here. Now."

"What about Rehhd and Ea–?"

"They stay."

"An–"

"No. They stay."

A hatred – a pure, white-hot loathing – flares from his eyes to hers. And that promise; they will both pay for this betrayal.

"Let's go," he says roughly, grabbing Seth's arm, leading him to the basement-level exit.

Seth tries to shake it off, but Kaide's grip holds firm.

"Anaiya?" Seth's voice rolls like rain clouds, soft but dangerous.

Betrayal is so thick in this tiny room that Anaiya can taste it. She swallows it, a bitter pill with no sugar coating.

"What the fuck do you think you are doing?" Rehhd demands, her calm finally broken.

Anaiya turns from Kaide and Seth, shutting out Seth's questions and demands, focussing all her attention and energy on Rehhd and Eamon.

"He was right, you know," she says softly. "You both are fucking morons."

Rehhd strides towards her, arm lifting as if to strike. Anaiya laughs, a hollow, guttural sound. She steps in smoothly to meet her, snatching her wrist and pivoting to put Rehhd at her back. With Rehhd's arm twisted awkwardly and leveraged on her shoulder, Anaiya uses her left hand to drive her grip upwards, hearing the loud pop as Rehhd's shoulder dislocates, the snap as her radial bone breaks moments later.

For Anaiya, it all happens in slow motion. A subtle dance stretching languidly across the mere seconds it takes to complete. The room shatters with Rehhd's scream and Anaiya lets her body drop to intercept Eamon as he rushes at her. She spins underneath his grip, turning a wide pirouette and preparing herself for the counter-attack.

She doesn't get the chance to use it. Five Peacekeepers barrel into the room from the stairwell, the first dropping Eamon immediately with a precise stab of her syringe. Another restrains Rehhd, easily avoiding her useless, damaged thrashing.

Anaiya's body relaxes, tension rushing from her muscles at the sight of the two Elementals laid low. The relief is short-lived: a sharp prick stings at her own neck and sends her into blackness.

TWENTY-EIGHT

It is the cold that pulls Anaiya back to consciousness. A long, flat, incessant chill that demands her attention.

Her eyes flutter open, blinking against darkness. She expects to see the crowded space of the izakaya, but her waking provides no transition from the endless blackness.

She raises her hand to wave in front of her face, to test the depth of this darkness, but her arm stops short – banging uselessly against an unforgiving barrier. Confused, she attempts to sit up, her head colliding with another hard surface and laying her back down.

Ignoring the pain that blooms in response, she slides her hands along the floor of her new space, both of them stopping in their journey not two spans from her body.

Her heart accelerates and she closes her eyes tightly, retreating to a place where the darkness is more natural, less threatening. Tighter and tighter, she clenches them, until spots of colour explode.

She forces herself to rein in her rapid breathing, focussing on drawing long, deep breaths, exhaling slowly with purpose. With each passing second, her eyes relax and her heartbeat slows.

Beat. Beat. Beat.

Beat. Beat.

Beat.

She takes another deep breath and relaxes her body.

Tentatively she glides her hands up the walls, pausing before tracing them upwards until they meet in a place not more than twenty centimetres above her solar plexus.

It is just enough room for her to access her wristplate. Touching the screen activates its diode, casting a green tinge over the metal interior. She sighs, the last of her anxiety leaching away.

Blinking against the wristplate's glow, she stares at the screen. All communication and entertainment functions have been deactivated, a large cross dominating the top right-hand corner of the screen.

Despite this, a single unread message flashes. She taps it, taking strange comfort in the way the nonsensical characters dissolve into comprehensible words.

Got a hit on your wristplate activity to say you were restrained. Report immediately.

She glances at the time stamp and compares it to the one that ticks over in the screen's top margin. Three hours have passed since Niamh's message was received.

Why am I still here?

With Niamh monitoring her wristplate, the record of her detention would have been immediately communicated. She shouldn't be here. He should have had her released by now.

Her agitation threatens to shift into panic. She halts the escalation of her thoughts and emotions, forcing herself to concentrate on the basics.

I am being held in a solo detention cell.

She shifts against the claustrophobic walls, positioning herself, as much as she can, on her side. The movement brings with it the shadows of old pain – a dull ache in her shoulder, a sharp throbbing at her ankle – though she doesn't remember the injuries.

Wincing against the discomfort, she repositions herself until she is able to turn her head. From this vantage point, she can just make out the faint grey bars that mark the ventilation grid. But, beyond them, there is nothing but deepening darkness.

Flashing her wristplate in the direction of the grid illuminates the bars and sends a fractured swathe of light into the darkness beyond. It stretches and diffuses, growing dimmer until it, too, is sucked up by the darkness. She shifts again, slowly, more gently, returning to her original position.

I have been processed.

She brings up her wristplate. A complex series of swipes and taps moves her through the folder directory until she arrives at her Orthodoxy file. A simple log appears when she opens it.

RESTRAINT and DETENTION. 86. 93C. 93T. 545B. 546C.

It is a long list of offences, ranging from Kidnapping and Affray to Participation in a Criminal Group, Intimidation and Peacekeeper Interference. Her restraint and detention – her implied guilt – the result of her proximity to the captured Trainee and the true offenders.

She remembers, with some satisfaction, her dance with Eamon and Rehhd, but the satisfaction is short-lived, quickly souring when another truth, an unwanted revelation, teases at the edges of her mind.

She taps uselessly on her wristplate, trying in vain to restore the communications function, to patch an urgent call to Niamh. With each attempt, the standard cross becomes more antagonistic, more defiant. In frustration, she shuts off the wristplate screen, sending her back into the empty darkness.

But the darkness brings its own frustrations and terrors. The stark environment, bereft of any distraction, proves a rich soil for her mind to pull memories of words that cannot be erased. And so they grow to consume the tiny space, falling into a loud soundtrack on an endless loop.

His vision for the Resistance was a thing of power and beauty.

How had she got it so wrong? So wrong. So wrong.

Her cheeks are wet. She tries to wipe away the tears, her elbows banging on the invulnerable metal box.

It was never Rehhd.

It was all too obvious, and yet she had missed it. Her tears leave cold trails on her skin.

It was Seth all along.

A jolt and loud banging roars into Anaiya's new existence. Her heart leaps with relief, her eyes springing open to welcome her release from this prison.

Another jolt sends her crashing into the side of the metal box, setting off the pain in her shoulder and ankle. Pushing it aside, she repositions herself until she can see out the ventilation grid. She strains to capture movement, to make sense of this new situation. A loud whirring echoes in the chamber as gravity pushes against Anaiya. The box is moving.

This isn't a release – it's a transfer.

The box falls with a loud crash to its resting place and groans echo around her. They build to a high-pitched squeal before dying to a faint rustle. Wind careens through the ventilation grid, but still no light.

Shutting her eyes against the new reality, Anaiya lies still and silent as her coffin races along its unknown path.

The rustling drops and rises in pitch, its rhythm slowing and quickening. Anaiya scratches her fingernails against the metal walls of the box, setting it as a background beat. Scratches alternate with taps, and the knuckles of her right hand rasp and bang on the off beats. The music swells to surround her, stripping the journey of its fear and time of its power.

When the journey finally slows – the rustling growing fainter, the groaning becoming louder – her heart rate is normal and her mind clear.

Again, the box shifts and bangs as it is relocated. But, finally, there is silence. Anaiya turns to stare out the ventilation grid into this new darkness. She pulls up her wristplate to cast her diode over the new environment, but stops as a loud white light courses into the box.

A click sounds and the lid begins to open. Anaiya retreats from the harsh light, cowering in the box with her eyes closed.

"Ani?"

She blinks against the whiteness, slowly focussing on the shadow that stands over her. "Niamh?"

Strong arms reach down to help her up, lifting her out of the box. When the full weight of her body settles on her ankle, she stumbles, inhaling with pain, into Niamh's chest. He catches her, wrapping his arms under her to support her frame.

"I got you," he says.

The room they are in is familiar – the loading dock of Anaiya's former Peacekeeper Command. It is empty, save for the two of them and the discarded metal box. Niamh leads her towards the single door set into the far wall.

"How bad is it?" he asks, looking down at her left foot.

"It's not good," she replies.

He nods and slows his pace as they near the door.

"Stay here," he says, leaning her against the wall like he would any other damaged weapon. "I'll be back soon."

She nods silently, putting all the residual weight on her right foot.

Niamh is true to his word; he returns in a matter of minutes, pushing a wheelchair. He unfolds it and lifts her into it, the soft cushioning a comfort to her compromised limbs.

"We've got a disser Earth Elemental in detention," he explains. "She won't be needing it for a while."

He disappears behind the back of the chair and a second later Anaiya is being wheeled into the basement of the command centre. A quick glance at her wristplate tells her it is still pre-dawn. Curfew is in place and the command centre will be relatively quiet. Anaiya is grateful for this small mercy.

Niamh stays silent throughout their journey to his office on the second floor. A few Peacekeepers turn curious faces towards them, but quickly look away. Anaiya lowers her head, stares at the stained threads of her kevlar jeans, and doesn't raise it until they reach Niamh's office and the door is closed.

"What happened out there, Ani?"

He walks around to lean against the standard office desk, his arms tense against its edges.

"We were blindsided," she says.

"Who's we?"

Beat.

Memories of Kaide's anger, Seth's defeat, flash brightly in her mind. She struggles to tamp them down. "Me. Us…The Task Force."

To her own ears, it sounds weak, but Niamh merely nods.

"I knew something was up when I saw Rehhd at the izakaya.

She was too calm – self-satisfied. I called her out on it and she led me down to the basement with Eamon."

"What did your future-search show you?"

The question slams into her, an immovable object in a poorly executed kash vault. It stuns her, her mind racing for an alternative answer. Because she hadn't future-searched. She tries to remember the last time she *had* – her mind recounting all the times in her recent past where she had let emotion, rather than logic, determine her next move.

Niamh's eyes narrow. She needs to give him an answer.

"I anticipated a revelation," she says, couching her intuitive sense of Rehhd's actions in future-searching terms. "Some additional evidence of her Heterodoxy."

"And?"

Niamh's stern voice grates at her. She frowns, her core heating with a flare of returned antagonism.

"And I found a Trainee Peacekeeper tied at wrists and ankles."

"How did it happen, Anaiya? How did it happen without you knowing about it?"

The blame is heavy in his voice. The fire at her core burns a little hotter.

"The same way it happened without you knowing about it. Without Jenna knowing about it. Without his shadow Peacekeeper knowing about it."

Niamh closes his eyes tightly and briefly shakes his head.

"The Trainee said he heard more than three voices. That you ordered someone out of the room."

The barely repressed aggression turns to a colder fear. "They weren't important."

"Who wasn't important?"

"They weren't important. The two Elementals I found sneaking into the basement."

Niamh's frown deepens and all Anaiya feels is the sudden urge to leap from the wheelchair and wipe it from his too-pretty face with a full-force roundhouse kick.

"To do what, exactly?"

"How the fuck should I know, Niamh? I didn't exactly engage them in a delightful repartee about whether they were there to suck face or sneak some extra alcohol. I was kind of focussed on the Heterodox Air Elemental and her prisoner."

"Lose the attitude, Ani."

"Stop interrogating me."

The weight crackles like static between them. Locked in this standoff, Anaiya knows instinctively that she can't be the one to look away first. To drop her gaze would be to announce her guilt. So, she maintains her hash gaze, drawing on the fire in her belly to sustain it.

Eventually, Niamh sighs and looks away. "This isn't over, Ani," he says softly.

He doesn't need to say it. She knows it, whatever *it* is, is far from over.

TWENTY-NINE

Anaiya rubs at her temples, fingers pushing deep to erase the throbbing that has started up again. She closes her eyes, shutting out the Last Defence room that strangely feels less like the prison now, and more like a refuge.

A week of daily interrogations by Niamh has left her tired and *fragile* – as if the constant questioning has weakened her, has created a stress fracture that makes her more and more susceptible to breaking.

Every time, it is the same questions – different words, different tones, different threats, but always the same line of enquiry. Always the same intention. To break her.

Anaiya answers them and doesn't answer them – spinning her own truth and giving Niamh only glimpses of what she knows. Constructing half-truths, creating subterfuge, keeping secret what must stay hidden – it all pulls energy from her. She worries constantly she will fumble, will present an inconsistency or will give away a vital piece of information.

Give her away.

Give Seth away.

And with the worry comes the headaches, the constant throbbing that sees her sitting cross-legged with her eyes closed on the cold floor of her room.

Slowly, the throbbing eases. She opens her eyes to the

immense vista framed by the floor-to-ceiling window before her. Balancing her glass screen atop her knees, she plugs in her earphones. Her fingers hover above the dashboard displayed on the glass, tingling.

The dusk landscape of Otpor stretches before her. She imposes a mental grid over it – administration buildings fill the foreground to her right, residential apartments line the far bank of the river and water distribution facilities dot the in-between. She waits patiently in the silence imposed by her earphones, watching as the sky grows darker.

Tonight it is a water distribution facility, located in one of the closer grid cells, whose lights flicker on first. Automatically, her finger taps at the screen, generating a vibrant, low-pitched chime that continues to resonate in her ears. Seconds later, a third-floor window in a nearby administration building lights up. Three quick, successive taps sound like hollow pipes crashing together – dull, short pops that peak in the lingering residue of the chime. As the succession of lights quickens, Anaiya's melody becomes more complex.

A heavy weight in her stomach indicates her unease, her vulnerability to this strength of emotion, but she pushes it down – burying it like she did the razor of her realignment. She feels it resist and then falter as her brain yields to the intense concentration required by her developing symphony.

For hours she sits and plays as lights wink on and off, celebrated and mourned by the music Anaiya taps and swipes on her dashboard. Eventually the visual melody slows and her hands still. She unplugs her earphones and lifeline and lies back on the cold, hard floor.

Sleep comes easily, but ends harshly – the first rays of daylight rob her of it, even when she has only just closed her eyes. She opens them now, regarding the room from her strange vantage point on the floor.

The door to her apartment slides open. Niamh never bothers to knock.

She regards him with a sigh. There had been a time when she had looked forward to seeing him.

"Good morning, Niamh."

"Get up, Ani."

Get fucked, Niamh.

She closes her eyes again.

"Now, Ani."

She doesn't move. Satisfied with her small act of resistance.

Footsteps advance, echoing loudly with her ears so close to the hard floor. She prepares herself for another lecture, another barrage of questions.

Not for the sharp prick of a needle.

Her eyes fly open, but it is not Niamh standing crouched over her, but the Water Elemental from her early days of realignment.

A flash of warmth rushes through her.

"What are you doing?"

Her voice sounds fuzzy and distant.

The Technician stands and walks over to Niamh. She sees Niamh nod and speak something in return, but the voices are lost beyond a wall of soft static in her ears.

And then the Technician is gone, the door securely shut, and Niamh smiling the self-satisfied smirk that pushes all the wrong buttons in Anaiya's core.

"Time to talk, Ani," he says, sitting down on her bed.

She slowly, almost drunkenly, sits up, her body suddenly heavy and unwieldy. With her back resting against the massive window of the room, she tries to collect her thoughts.

"What were you doing when the Peacekeepers arrived at the izakaya?" Niamh asks.

"I was dancing with Rehhd and Eamon."

The words flow out of her mouth effortlessly, thoughtlessly.

No…No…This is not…right. Not…right…

Her thoughts are thick and sticky, like the paint on the recycler surface.

"Who else was there?"

Careful…careful…

"I was there and…"

No…Careful…More careful…

Her mind strains with the effort of concentrating, of trying to push back the heavy haze that envelopes it.

"And?"

Niamh leans forwards, his forearms at right angles across his thighs. The position hunches his shoulders, puts his gaze more on a level with hers. A thin, ruddy scratch cuts above his left eye.

"You have a scratch." Her tongue feels furry, her mind sleepy.

Wasn't…Haven't I…Didn't I just…wake…up…

Niamh's smirk fades just a little.

"Courtesy of Rehhd."

His voice sounds distant, the vowels and consonants fuzzy like audio feedback. Darkness beckons. So sweetly. She just needs to reach out. Reach out and…

"Rehhd…is…a fucking moron."

There is nothing else to be said. The darkness brushes against her. She snuggles up to it, erasing Niamh and his questions.

Anaiya wakes up hours later, cocooned in the thin blanket of her single bed. Through the apartment window, the limbo sky, caught between light and dark, disorients her. She checks her wristplate, blinking in surprise at the dawn hour.

Her mind blurs at the edges, fills with stale static. She lies there, staring at the ceiling, trying to fill a hole in her memory. The dimensions of the hole are vague and slippery – she remembers brief moments of her music composition, lights and melodies flashing cryptically in her memory, but not retreating to the bed, not falling asleep.

The click and metallic rustling of the door breaks the silence. A familiar-looking Water Technician enters the room, the sight scratching at the fuzziness of her mind.

He offers no conversation, simply striding to the bed and plugging Anaiya's lifeline into his glass screen. She studies his face, looking for any sign of surprise or concern or frustration. He taps and swipes away regardless of the scrutiny, giving nothing away.

"You were the Technician during my alignment, weren't you?" she asks.

"Realignment," he corrects, head still bent over the screen.

"Yeah, realignment," she echoes. "You thought my mind could have been broken."

"Mmm," he mumbles, squinting at the screen.

"Was it?"

He doesn't answer straight away, still consumed by the screen. She repeats the question, a little louder, a little more urgently.

"Hmm?"

Anaiya's fingers twitch, keen to rip the glass screen from his hand and throw it against the wall. She takes a deep breath, clenches her hands instead, and asks again.

"Broken," she says slowly through tense lips. "Was my mind broken?"

He finally looks over the screen at her, a small frown toying with the creases on his face.

"Why?" he asks, providing no relief. "Does it feel broken?"

The returned question catches her unprepared. It is a strange question.

No stranger than asking if it is broken…

"What would broken feel like?" she asks, playing the Technician at his own game.

His face lights up, his screen forgotten.

"Hard to say. The mind isn't corporeal like the other parts of the body. Not really, anyway. The mind is bigger than the brain – some say entirely distinct from it."

His voice rises in pitch and his words spin out faster with each new thought. "There are no veins to probe, no cells to examine, no beats to monitor. Yet we feel it keenly, know intuitively its resting position, understand when it is challenged, or pushed, or damaged. There is a wrongness when the mind is out of balance. The more out of balance, the closer to breaking, the more palpable this sense of wrongness."

Anaiya drinks the words in, sucks the marrow from them, turning the empty bones across her tongue. She knows this wrongness. The battle between the hot fire of her heart and the cold fire of her core. The conflict that keeps her awake at nights – yearning for Seth and hating herself for it; satisfaction at her resistance towards Niamh, guilt at her betrayal; elation at the memory of that clear snap that accompanied Rehhd's broken arm, incessant itching on the skin of her guilty hand.

"The dual alignment of your brain could definitely cause some imbalance," the Technician says, pulling her back to the conversation, ejecting her lifeline from the glass screen. "But, no. It doesn't seem that your mind is broken."

He exits the room perfunctorily, leaving Anaiya to ponder his words and their specific meaning for her situation. Minutes later, when the door opens again and he reappears, she opens her mouth to ask more questions, demand more answers, but the sight of Niamh at his heels causes them to dry on her tongue.

"Hello, Ani," he says, his face set in a grim expression.

"Niamh," she replies, extracting all the emotion from her voice so that the syllable comes out dry and dead.

The Technician advances towards her again, Anaiya expecting him to plug her lifeline into his screen again.

"Let's talk," Niamh says, drawing her gaze away from the Technician.

"OK…"

The unexpected needle finds its way easily into the jugular vein, bringing with it the warmth and frayed thoughts of the previous, forgotten night.

"That night in the izakaya," his voice floats to her, seeming to cover kilometres. "The night we detained Rehhd and Eamon. You were in the basement…"

Every night for the next four nights she is drugged by a Water Technician and interrogated by Niamh. Every morning she wakes with a slight headache. Sometimes she remembers dream-like fragments, but mostly the nightly operations are a deep void in her memory. The light is always a little brighter, a little harsher when she awakes, and so she lies there silently, eyes closed, feeling no different. Only more tired. More empty.

When the sound of the door sliding open whispers in her consciousness yet again, she ignores it. She is not ready to face

Niamh or the Technician again.

"So, it's true."

It is a voice that she cannot ignore.

"How did you get in here?" she asks, breaking her self-imposed darkness.

Kaide stands just inside the doorway, hands slung casually in pockets, arms and eyes tense. "I know who to trade favours with."

He leans against the wall and stares at her. She sits up under his steady gaze, resisting the urge to pull the thin sheet up over her exposed torso.

"I wouldn't have believed it, you know," he says softly. "There was this crazy story I heard weeks ago, about some insane experiment to realign a Fire Elemental to an Air Elemental. I had laughed at the time, passed it off as the usual Water fetish for manipulating the world just to prove they can. Even with all of your quirks, your strange beats and atypical actions – I had just thought you a sad victim of hypoxia. Damaged. And maybe you are damaged. But it's not because of hypoxia."

"Kaide, you don't know what –"

Kaide has pulled his hands from his pockets and pressed the playback function of his wristplate.

"I've found it."

It is her voice that echoes through the room.

"The piece that can link Rehhd to the Resistance. That confirms her as the leader."

She doesn't have to ask Kaide how he obtained the communication. He reaches into his pocket once more and withdraws a familiar black cube.

"I was worried about your influence over Seth. Concerned he was divulging too much information or wavering from the course. I needed a way to see beneath the subterfuge. The original plan was to give the cube to him, but when you came to the Lavoir the other afternoon, looking for a device to help you match sounds, it was the perfect opportunity."

Anaiya looks at the small facets of the cube, trying to see if she is reflected in its surface. "It's not a soundmatcher, is it?"

"Yes and no," Kaide replies, rolling it around his palm with lightning-quick fingers. "It can soundmatch, and the soundmatching is a very useful function, but I developed it to record lifeline data. Once the cube was plugged into your lifeline, it downloaded five terabytes of the wristplate's most recent data – transactions, geospatial coordinates, recordings and communications. At first I was concerned about the complete lack of new music files. And then I wondered about your frequent trips to the Western Cardinal Area."

His voice falls deeper.

"But then I got to your comms data. And I realised two things. First, incredibly, that you were the crazy Water Experiment. You were the Fire Elemental they reshaped with an Air alignment. And secondly…"

His voice breaks and he looks away from Anaiya.

"…Secondly, that you never suspected Seth."

With that final breath, he looks up at Anaiya. And they are back in that izakaya basement again, connected only by their gaze, a wasteland of blame and hurt and betrayal and co-conspiratorial guilt stretching between them.

"It's not safe for us to talk here," she says finally. "Not safe for you to be here."

To her surprise, he merely nods. The exchange has challenged them both and stripped them bare.

"I have nothing left to say," he says and walks out of the room.

Anaiya lies in the silence, controlling her breathing as the seconds tick by, bloated into minutes.

Kaide had been right. She hadn't suspected Seth. Had never contemplated that he could be the Resistance leader.

What signs had she missed? All she can remember are the quiet smiles, gentle touches. And once again she is at a loss to match the Elemental she desires with the Resistor she knows.

When the sound of the door breaks the sound void, Anaiya's body stiffens, wondering what confrontation Kaide will bring with him this time.

But it is Niamh that walks into the room. "You're awake," he says.

As always, an uneasy silence settles between them.

"How are you feeling?"

Confused. Lost. Guilty. So very, very guilty. "Tired," she says.

Niamh nods, as if that were to be expected, and leans against the wall. "We've concluded your interrogation," he says, folding his arms across his chest.

Anaiya sits up slowly.

"Data matching is inconclusive. We've run your lifeline location proximities, terminal engagement and transactions, cross-referenced them with the Elementals detained at the izakaya and with the data we pulled from communication intercepts on Rehhd, Eamon, Kaide and Cressida. Rehhd and Eamon were the only targets at the izakaya and the data contains no outliers to suggest an additional Elemental of interest."

He stares at her. "Data says you're clear, Ani."

It isn't the reprieve she has been hoping for. His eyes are cold, his stance intimidating.

"You thought I was lying to you?"

"I think you still are."

It is a slap in the face. A sharp, solid crack. Not unexpected, but not welcomed, either.

"In any case, we're done with this stage."

Anaiya wants to shrink under his scrutiny, his condemnation. His gaze is unrelenting and it takes all her discipline to not look away.

He frowns, a short, pinched flaw in his otherwise hardened face, and then shakes his head. He exits the room silently, not bothering to look back at her.

She, on the other hand, can't take her eyes away from his retreating form.

Done with this stage. This stage.

Her relief at surviving Niamh's interrogation disintegrates. A dull panic begins to rise in her mind.

What is yet to come?

THIRTY

The rest of the day passes in a state of anxiety. Every footfall or murmured conversation in the corridor sends Anaiya into a panic. *They've figured it out. They know I've been lying. They're coming to get me.*

The click of the lock on her door sounds like a termination serum box closing shut. A tall Water Technician enters the room. "You're required in Lab 19.2."

Anaiya stares at him, uncomprehending, waiting for him to give her more details.

"Immediately," he says. "I'm here to escort you."

Two large male Earth Elementals enter the room. One unfolds a wheelchair, the other strides towards the bed.

Anaiya moves to sit up, but her body refuses to cooperate. She raises her hands uselessly against the advances of the Elemental, who sweeps her roughly into his arms before depositing her into the chair.

"Please. Please, no. Please. No."

Her mind erupts into sheer panic.

They've finally come for me. They've come to Execute me.

She writhes in the chair, thrashing against the immovable arms of the Earth Elemental. It is all in vain, her useless protest ending with a sharp sting at her neck. The pacifying serum runs cold through her veins, numbing her emotions and energy.

A slow and silent ten minutes later, Anaiya reaches her destination. Lab 19.2 is like any other lab in Last Defence – white, sterile, fluorescent, cold. The Earth Elementals discharge her from the wheelchair like a random object that has lost interest and usefulness. They disclothe her unceremoniously, rough hands brushing over her skin like gravel, her arms yanked into the sleeves of a cottonex slip. They lay her on the cold, steel gurney, pushing her back through time to her realignment. Their job completed, the two Earth Elementals exit the lab without a second glance, leaving her alone with the Technician.

He stares at her. The seconds passing in loud, heavy beats.

"Before I do this," he says, finally. "I want to ask you something."

Her earlier panic tries to work its way up from under the heavy cloth of chemicals. She tries to work her mouth, tries and fails to give voice to her desperate supplication.

Please don't kill me.

He takes her silence for acquiescence.

"Did it change you?"

It is a curiosity. But, maybe, it is also a chance at redemption.

Anaiya thinks back through the last few weeks, re-living and cataloguing the experiences and emotions. She feels them, as if her mind is running its finger over their contours and textures. Feels them as if they are corporeal, as if they span before her in this clinical space.

She shakes her head, barely a wobble, realising that this truth – that her realignment did not change her – may save her.

His face drops, that same disappointment from her post-realignment discussion broadcast on his features. It lasts only a second, before the professional facade resumes its place. "Just as well," he says, all business, the curiosity a corpse in his eyes. "Given that you are being realigned to your full Fire identity."

Relief, cold and bright, washes over her. It is as if she has finally taken a deep lungful of clean air, not realising she'd been holding her breath for so long. Her eyes leak with warm tears.

She is not being Executed. Of course not – that would have required a trial, formal enquiry, a right of reply – all things her paranoid and panicked brain has overlooked.

She is not going to die. And more than just escaping the Executioner's needle, she is being rewarded. They are giving her the one thing she has wanted so desperately since the first day of her realignment. They are restoring her identity.

She will be a Peacekeeper again.

Even though the news reaches her from the lips of a Water Elemental, it still sounds like music.

Now she is ready for the invasion of the needle. Ready for the warmth and the music and the vibrant images. She doesn't fight it this time. Her limbic brain mumbles its protest, but she shuts it out.

She surrenders.

Harsh, guttural, metallic music assaults her ears. Dense beats and rapid, chaotic rhythms pull painfully at her neurons. Chemicals urge her body to tense in a state of readiness.

And then there emerges the image of the dead female in Precinct 20. Still vivid, still compelling. Presented in colourless monochrome, the white bone fragments scatter in stark contrast to the black pool of blood around the broken body. Blood spatter patterns swirl in her mind, a surreal moving picture offset by the static grimace on the victim's face, the dead set to her unseeing eyes.

The music builds to a crescendo in her ears, mixing with her blood chemicals to produce an urge within her. But the feeling is muted, hidden behind a strange grief and melancholy and an utter fascination with the work of art before her.

The music transforms into a cacophony of screams and shrieks – primal sounds of pain, despair and desperation. They pull at the fire within her, but just as quickly plait into a rhythm and melody of their own, becoming a macabre soundtrack that her Air-aligned mind can appreciate.

Eventually the images and noises fade. In the shadows of her mind, she feels another prick of the needle at her elbow. Her limbs, previously tense and alert, now fall calm and still. Her thoughts become stretched and sticky, melting through time, before her mind shuts down and she falls into yet another sedated and dreamless sleep.

Every day they drag her to a new laboratory, where she is pricked and then assaulted with chaotic sounds and fragmented memories of the Precinct 20 female, of free-running, of Heterodoxy. Each one stokes the flames within her core, presents her with an art to appreciate, pulls her between rage and sadness and determination and despair.

She wakes from each session emotionally stable – no tears, no violent outbursts, no shame – just calm, as if the sands of her mind have finally descended from their windstorm and are settling back to the ground, in a new, but structurally-sound, arrangement.

She becomes more thoughtful, less tense. More content, less conflicted. And so, when Niamh enters her room on the fourth day of the second week, she doesn't respond as she otherwise has. She simply looks up at him and surrenders a smile, and he surprises her by offering one back.

Well, this is unexpected.

He walks over to the bed and sits at the end, balancing on the edge. They don't speak, but the silence is comfortable.

"The trial has concluded," he says finally.

Rehhd's trial. It commenced not long after her arrest, taking place in an undisclosed, high-security location and presided over by a panel of four senior and anonymous Elementals, each randomly selected from their respective Elements. Niamh hadn't divulged much about it to Anaiya, despite the fact he had been responsible for presenting her evidence. Isolated from the trial and caught up in her own tribulations, Anaiya had infrequently thought about it.

"And?" she asks, now curious as to the fate of the Elemental she has wrongly accused and condemned as the Resistance leader.

"The Execution is scheduled for this coming Third day."

In less than a week's time, Rehhd would die.

But will the Heterodoxy be terminated?

The thought claws at Anaiya's newfound peace. Heterodoxy would die if its leader were terminated. Left free, who knew how the Heterodoxy would continue to manifest – if it did survive the loss of a treasured comrade.

Seth – his is the only memory with the ability to excite and antagonise both of her identities. She pulls her knees to her chest, drags her fingers along her calves, pushing harder to make the muscles sing in pain, manipulating a small distraction.

"Did she register a defence?"

It was procedural fairness in trials to allow the accused an opportunity to defend themselves. In most cases it is a high-risk venture – while a sympathetic defence can return a not-guilty outcome and expunge an arrest record, a rejected defence can indicate systemic Unorthodoxy and land more time in a repentance cell. With Execution at stake, Anaiya would take the risk.

"No," Niamh replies. "Neither she nor Eamon have whispered a word since they were arrested."

"How hard did you press them?"

Images of bruises, cuts, burns and sleepless nights tease at Anaiya's subconscious.

"Hard."

She sighs. "Where's Eamon?"

"In a repentance cell. Three more weeks until he's released."

"He won't see the Execution?"

A grim smile twists Niamh's face. "I'm sure he'll see the replays."

The two of them lapse into another silence. It slinks between and around them, brushing them, nudging them, comforting them.

"What else aren't you telling me?" Anaiya finally asks, recognising a strange weight in the silence. It complements the new softness in Niamh, the long, drawn-out pauses.

He turns to face her, and Anaiya feels the dread of their previous conversation morph into something sharper.

"How are your realignment sessions going?"

It is an unexpected question and for a moment Anaiya thinks it comes from a place of concern. Over the last week, the realignment sessions have been nothing but a welcome routine – a way of ordering her days and giving her respite from the guilt and confusion that bind to her thoughts of Rehhd and Seth and the izakaya.

"Easier than I expected…" she says, her words dying slowly at the fall of Niamh's face. "How do you think my realignment sessions are going?"

He picks at his fingernails. Anaiya has seen him do it before – just before the Technician had taken her away for realignment compatibility testing; at the recycler that first time they saw the mural; at the Healing Facility after she had torn up her arm and shredded her calf. She belatedly recognises it as his tell for inner turmoil.

The tension is suffocating and she is caught between wanting to hear something, anything, and fearing that once it's spoken, it will never be erased.

"There's a problem, Ani."

The ominous words spark a detailed explanation – a confession. At the end of it, Anaiya sits silent, her brain unable to process anything but the words Niamh has spent the last ten minutes telling her.

Her realignment isn't working. Her limbic brain is still too dominant. Still too closely aligned to Air.

"There was no way to expect this," he says. "That was the whole point of the testing before the first realignment procedure – to confirm that your brain was elastic, able to be manipulated. The testing proved that your mind was compatible with realignment. Realigning back to your true Element should have been easier, if anything, than realigning your mind to a foreign Element."

"I – I don't – I don't understand," Anaiya stammers. "How can this happen?"

Niamh shrugs, empty of answers.

Inside, Anaiya's stomach churns.

Water Elementals, she thinks bitterly. *Always so certain of what they know, until faced with their errors*. No, *not* their *errors*.

Water Elementals did not make errors. The science was never wrong.

Only the data.

"I don't know how it happened," Niamh says. "After the successful testing and then the successful procedure, there were no concerns. The realignment was an achievement with no equal. A resounding success."

"What happens now?" she asks. "What do I do?"

"Prepare, Ani," Niamh replies immediately. "You have to prepare. There are three realignment sessions left. You need to make sure they are successful."

Anaiya's muscles complain loudly as she works through the reps. The Last Defence gym is empty, quarantined from other Elementals so she can prepare alone.

Sprint, kash vault, double kong, tic tac. Repeat. Sprint, kash vault, double kong, tic tac. Repeat. Repeat. Repeat.

The sweat beads on her skin, stirring as she picks up her velocity in the stale air of the gymnasium. She is too slow, too clunky. Her movements dense when they should be light; measured when they should be fearless.

She pauses long enough to plug in her earphones and queue the selected soundtrack: a loud rush of music, heavy with deep beat and frantic, harsh melodies. Once she had welcomed the strange cacophony of Fire music; now she grits her teeth and waits for her brain to accept it. Regulating her breathing, she forces her body to acclimatise to the new stimulus and then begins again.

Sprint, kash vault, double kong, tic tac. Repeat.

It is a punishment. Her muscles and mind alike throb with exertion and pain.

You're just unaccustomed to it. It will get better with practice.

The words sound hollow. She pushes harder, stilling her mind, letting her body take over. A flash of movement near the gymnasium entry pulls her out of concentration. Niamh steps into the vast space, his solid frame easily dwarfed by the high walls. He is early.

Anaiya forces her mind to focus, working through the final three reps, forcing her biomechanics to move faster, bend lower, reach higher, transition smoother. On her final rep, she has reached optimal performance, hitting the levels she used to hit as a Peacekeeper. Her sprint is fast, her kash vault clean.

The twin wall obstacle races to meet her. She ignores the sight of Niamh blurring in her long vision, concentrating on visualising the large cavity between the two walls and adjusting her speed and stride accordingly.

Three steps away, two steps, one.

Bending her knees, she positions herself into a split step, before pushing her body up and forwards. Her hands graze the top of the first wall, gripping at the far edge and pushing off to give her the momentum she needs to clear the gap and reach the second wall. Her body elongates, stretching into a smooth arc, her arms now reaching for the second wall.

She reaches it in an almost-handstand, her arms extended down straight to the wall, her palms flat against the ledge. Her legs pull down and through the tunnel her arms have created, sweeping through as she pushes off to clear the obstacle at speed.

The momentum carries her farther than her previous attempts, her landing steps placing her just metres from where Niamh stands, arms crossed against his chest.

A wide grin threatens to break her face, her heart beating solidly in her chest, endorphins flowing uninhibited through her veins. Her execution was flawless, her final rep a triumph.

She looks over to Niamh expectantly, confident he is returning her grin. But his face is immovable.

Something sharp spikes in her chest, deflating her euphoria as quickly as it bloomed.

"You're too slow on your pull through," he says, unfolding his arms and walking towards the mats at the far corner of the gym.

Anaiya stares for a moment at his back before mutely following him.

The sound of Niamh's hoodie zipping undone grates. He tosses it to the wall and turns to face her. "I want you to forget everything you know about close combat training," he says. "We're not here to practise restraint or calculation. Your problem isn't controlling the fire. It's finding it."

She nods. It's nothing she hasn't already concluded herself.

"Bring up your vitals – we're tracking adrenalin, noradrenaline and acetylcholine levels, and amygdala activity," he says, tapping on his wristplate.

Music floods the space, the gym's wireless audio system picking up on Niamh's wristplate identity.

He widens his stance, flexing slightly at the knees, preparing himself for the sparring session.

"Get angry, Ani."

It is an invitation. Anaiya launches at him.

"You're over-thinking it," Niamh yells. "Let go."

Sweat trickles its way down her skin, her breath coming fast and scratchy.

"OK, break," Niamh calls.

They halt their session, pausing to rehydrate and debrief.

"What are your vitals?"

Anaiya pulls up the statistics on her wristplate. "Adrenalin – High. Noradrenalin – Low. Acetylcholine – High. Amygdala activity – Medium."

Niamh grunts. "Not good enough. You need to get angrier, Ani. Stop holding back. You need to delve deep into your core. You have to find that fire, Ani."

The unspoken *or else* hangs heavy between them.

Or else you will fail the realignment. Or else you will be marked as Heterodox. Or else you will be Executed.

THIRTY-ONE

At the end of the sparring session, Niamh leaves her without saying a word. There had been moments of encouragement, where it seemed she could tap into her true nature. But they hadn't lasted and the frustration, shared between her and Niamh, returned with renewed force.

She sits alone on the padded mat, staring down at her lap, unwilling to be confronted with the large, imposing space. Unwilling to reflect again on her failures.

There are only eight hours until her third and final realignment session. Eight hours before her final test reveals the truth.

She forces herself to stand on wobbly legs, make her silent way back to the small room that has been her home for the last few weeks.

Home.

It was a foreign concept to her before her realignment. What was home, but an overly emotional attachment to an inanimate and arbitrary space? An unnecessary affectation of Earth Elementals and Air Elementals.

Nonetheless, she regards the familiar space as a kind of sanctuary and takes comfort in its four walls. The curtains are drawn when she walks in, the room shrouded in an almost-darkness. She doesn't bother opening them or turning on the light.

Darkness is also a welcomed safe-house. She undresses quickly, methodically folding her clothes and placing them on the nearby desk.

The bed is cold under the thin sheets, but she doesn't move – just lies there, eyes open and taking in the green tinge of the softly illuminated ceiling. The light flares and a vibration tingles at her wrist. She doesn't bother plugging in her lifeline, tapping on her wristplate to answer the call and activate the speaker function.

"Hey, Ani." Niamh's voice echoes in the confined space.

"Hey."

Even now, with all that has gone between them and all that lies ahead, there is still silence. She closes her eyes against the green glow, plunging into a deeper darkness.

"Good luck tomorrow," he finally says.

She exhales. Frustration and resignation mingle in the sigh. There is so much left unsaid between them, things they are still keeping from each other, secrets hinted at but never told. They were so close.

Were we?

Close, like 'home', has a different meaning now. Her alignment has changed everything.

"Thanks," she says.

And then there is just the sound of their breathing. She imagines Niamh, as he was that night she discovered the Heterodoxy, leaning against a lone street light, bathed in bright fluorescence that sent shadows across his angles.

The click of the disconnection comes without any preamble. A light snap and then silence, with only Anaiya's breathing to break it.

The buzzing at her wrist and persistence of daylight surprises her when she awakes. Pulled from her dreamless sleep, she showers and dresses on auto-pilot, keeping her mind light and free of complex thoughts, dangerous scenarios and impossible questions.

She zips up her black vinyl boots and stands just as the Technician enters the room. The Earth escorts are no longer needed: Anaiya has proven herself cooperative. He nods, satisfied with her punctuality, and leads her silently from her room.

Unlike the previous sessions, he deviates from their usual course to the laboratories and heads down an unfamiliar hallway. The change worries Anaiya, but her stride doesn't falter. She banishes it from her thoughts and focusses on the small things, the things she can control – her pace, her breathing, the set of her shoulders, the set of her expressions.

The calmness leaves her when they reach their destination. The round, white-tiled room spans before her, pulling her back into her past as it stretches her inevitably towards her future.

A second Technician walks up to Anaiya and begins fitting her lifeline to the small black box.

Deja vu.

It is a commonly used piece of pidgin slang, especially popular with Air Elementals. She hears it in Seth's voice and translates it into the modern language of Otpor.

Already seen.

And she has – the sights and sensations settle on her like a mirrored copy of her original realignment. The familiar tingle of energy runs along her skin, the perfect opposite to the heavy dread that drags at her core.

The needle pierces her skin with the expectant sting and she is left alone, again, in the stark white dome. She looks down at her vague reflection in the pale and polished concrete floor. And in that second she wonders which is the true Anaiya. The unanswered question is ripped from her mind as the floor and surrounding tiles begin to shimmer with colour.

She closes her eyes, picturing the simulation as it was last time. Precinct 5, En Dahm, the motionless body lying face down, the rivulets of blood, the fleeing perpetrator. She zones in on the details, willing her body to respond appropriately. The fire builds within her, her neocortex settles into its role. She is ready.

This is it.

She has moments before the illusion is complete and she is absorbed into the simulation.

Unleash the fire.

It is not streets of Precinct 5, or the imposing facade of En Dahm, that greets Anaiya. The ground beneath her feet is gravelly and the only structures that draw her eye are the dense and ever-humming air recyclers.

Her first steps are hesitant, her skin crawling at the sound of her boots on the broken ground. She swivels around, confronting the Border Wall that looms just metres away. Shadowy movements crystallise into scores of Border Watchers – they line the parapets, a hundred eyes focussed on Anaiya.

Avoiding their gaze, she ducks her head and begins her walk through the maze of recyclers. She doesn't pick up her pace, her feet beating out a measured rhythm. Around her the light and shadows shift, illuminating her one minute, casting her in darkness the next.

A sound in the distance breaks through the noise of her journey. A groan. A whimper. She walks towards it, her ears guiding her to the source. It gets louder and louder with every step, catching the breath in her throat.

The cold surrounds her. It seeps up from the ground, reflecting off the dense concrete, carried on the Wasteland breeze that begins to pick up in intensity.

Anaiya hesitates before rounding the next recycler, knowing what she will see, unwilling to confront it.

The groans and whimpers become a muted sobbing. The sound pulls at her feet, dragging her forwards, entreating her to look…to bear witness.

The recycler in front of her is unnaturally illuminated, its grey surface bleached in unrelenting fluorescence. The source of the light is unclear and Anaiya does not turn to look for it, utterly absorbed by the scene that is unfolding before her.

The figure has its back turned to Anaiya, but she knows instinctively that it is Seth – can see it in the lines of his shoulders, the set of his stance. Anaiya holds her breath, forcing her body to stillness, suddenly afraid that the smallest sound or movement will cause him to turn.

Another groan, his shoulders hunch forward. His breathing comes in raspy waves. Reaching up, he smears a long red streak against the concrete surface in front of him. There is no brush, just his hand dripping with a viscous liquid.

Anaiya waits for the synthetic smell of paint to reach her, but instead the air spikes with a rich, metallic scent. A familiar organic scent. The scent of blood.

Her gasp ricochets in the cold air around her. Seth spins, his defiant frame illuminated in the same blinding light as the recycler. Briefly, she sees his eyes widen, but all she can see is his ravaged body. Long slashes criss-cross his pale T-shirt, revealing deep gashes that stain the cottonex a deep red.

The pattern reverberates with the red lines that mar the air recycler behind him, metre-high letters that do not yet spell the forbidden word in its entirety.

RESIST

"Anaiya…" His voice is a whisper, a scream, a raging torrent, a soft caress.

RESIST

"Anaiya…" Soft, deadly, soothing, home.

RESIST

"Anaiya."

Shock, like icy water, rips her out of the simulation and into reality. She opens her mouth to scream, but her throat fails her and she is confronted only with the silence. A trembling makes its way from her limbs to her core and a weight envelopes her, sending her crashing to the floor.

Anaiya wakes an hour later, back in her room. This time there is no comforting blackness, no shameful tears. Just the weight of her failure. It holds her down, sticks in her throat, a cloying sweetness, like something good gone bad.

She throws off the sheets, strips to nakedness and strides to the bathroom. The water is cold, almost painful. She turns the tap to its furthest point, begging for a water pressure that will hail down on her skin and erase all other feeling. Her breath comes short and ragged, sharp on the inhale, fast on the exhale.

She pinches the skin at her thighs when the feelings threaten to re-emerge, fingernails digging into flesh to produce bloody crescents, the bright red mixing with the water and dribbling down her leg.

She meticulously counts each mosaic tile in the shower, and when the counting becomes predictable and opens up a gap for other thoughts to bubble through, she makes it harder – adding the number in the first two rows, subtracting the next row, multiplying the next row.

She catalogues the various tints of tile, tapping once the bright white, tapping twice the flawed. Anything to occupy her mind with meaningless thoughts and pain.

She loses track of time. Refuses to look at her wristplate. Her world is contained to the tiled shower stall, the water and the pain.

Eventually, her mind empties and she turns off the water. Sedated, she lets herself slide to the cold floor, bringing her knees up to her chest and burying her head in her arms.

Niamh finds her an hour later, naked, shivering, the purple hints of bruises marring the skin at her thighs. She offers no resistance as he wraps her in a towel, picks her up and returns her to the bed.

Seeing Niamh returns Anaiya's ability to feel. She grabs at the thin sheets, seeking warmth they cannot provide. Her teeth chatter, a violent sequence of hard clicks as they grind and collide against each other. Her fingers shake, despite being clenched tightly and gripping the sheets.

Niamh shrugs out of his hoodie and wraps it around her shoulders, holding it there until her shaking softens and her teeth quieten. "Drowning your sorrows, Ani?"

It is a poor attempt at a joke. Fire Elementals are so bad at humour. Her trembling lips offer a faint smile. It fades quickly when she realises that Niamh comforting her is a bad sign. A very bad sign.

"How bad is it?" she asks, gripping the sheets and hoodie tighter.

He sighs. "It's not good."

"As in…?"

He shakes his head. "You failed, Ani. The realignment…it failed."

It is not a surprise to hear the words, but they strike her like a one-inch punch anyway. The sensation is physical, a crushing pain that steals oxygen from her solar plexus.

The reality of the situation clashes with the impossibility. Fire was her true alignment. Her realignment had been scientifically manipulated. Return to Fire should have been easy, inevitable.

This is unnatural.

Her breathing comes in quick, shallow bursts.

This is…Heterodox.

The word sends off a chain reaction of more and more dangerous thoughts in her mind. She thinks of Kane 148. She thinks of Rehhd. She thinks of Executioners with termination serum. She thinks of sharp, fine needles.

"When?" she asks, her voice a harsh whisper along her dry throat.

"When what?"

"When will they come to detain me?"

Niamh sighs and closes his eyes. "They aren't coming for you, Ani," he murmurs.

Anaiya's mind frantically races to understand his meaning. *Not coming for me, now? Not coming for me, yet? Or is it you, Niamh, who will detain me?*

"Are you…?"

He shakes his head again in answer. "No, Ani. No one is coming to detain you. Not now. Not ever."

Reality and impossibility intertwine.

"The Cooperative doesn't know about you," he continues. "The Head Peacekeeper, the Commissioners, they don't know about this…this *experiment*. They never have."

In a hushed tone, he tells her everything. That there have only ever been a handful of Elementals that have known about the realignment. That the Sec Level 5 briefings, the tests and simulations, the deployment – they have all been undertaken outside the formal structures, outside standard protocol.

"It was an unauthorised op, Ani," he finishes. "No one has ever known about it. No one ever can."

The scope of Niamh's ambition, the ease with which he bends the Orthodoxy to take what he desires most, is breathtaking. Yes, she had seen glimpses of it before – the casual disregard for standard protocol when it suited his purposes – but this, this is too much, too far.

"So, what happens now?" she asks, afraid of the question as much as the answer.

He turns to look at her, determination shining in his eyes. "We see how well you can pretend."

THIRTY-TWO

The walk to the Trocadero is a lonely one. Niamh had offered to accompany Anaiya, but the thought of free-running made her uneasy. The kevlar of her Peacekeeper uniform scratches, the full official attire heavy and unforgiving. Anaiya's first chance to pretend has come much sooner than she hoped.

She sticks to the back streets, avoiding the boulevardes that will soon swell with all kinds of Elementals – each making their way to the Execution site, spurred on by obligation, outrage, intrigue or morbid curiosity.

But, here in the back streets, she can hide from the reality that awaits her at the end of her journey – can exert some control over the rising panic.

This isn't how it is supposed to be.

She was supposed to have detained Rehhd on a quiet street like this one, with no witnesses but her backup Peacekeepers. The guilt and fear and regret were supposed to have been erased by her realignment back to Fire. She was supposed to have attended Rehhd's Execution as an exalted and vindicated Peacekeeper. Not as an emotionally overwhelmed Heterodox Elemental.

Anaiya stops walking. Crouching down into a low squat she pulls her head into her hands and suffocates the anguished wail that can no longer be contained. Hot tears prick her eyes and wet her palms.

She was supposed to have shed Kane 148's legacy. Instead she finds herself living it.

Arriving at the Trocadero is like slipping back in time.

She approaches it from the north; the riverside avenue is already congested with the pilgrimage of Elementals. They move in a steady stream from the south, east and west, converging where the Yena Bridge bleeds into the Trocadero Gardens.

Gardens.

It is an ancient word. A redundant word. The last trees disappeared from the Otpor landscape generations before Anaiya's conception. Maybe once the massive Lower Terrace accommodated trees and organic things, but now it offers only hard stone and no shade.

Nine years ago she was down there, watching from the crowd as Kane was led to the Execution Pillar. Tonight, she will watch from the elevated courtyard, with nothing but empty space and cold marble between her and Rehhd.

He looked smaller, almost frail, when they led him to the pillar. The cold stone had stripped him of the invincibility that had once seemed a second skin. The harsh lights painting him as a shadow…an empty shell.

"Access authorisation." A bulky Security Official holds out his mobile access terminal, barring Anaiya's path to the courtyard, where she can see a handful of senior Fire and Water Elementals gathering. She waves her wristplate over the device, watching as the diode flashes green. The Security Official steps aside, allowing Anaiya access. She pauses. Niamh's words repeat in her thoughts.

We see how well you can pretend.

As if the words call silently to him, Niamh appears in her view. He's standing with the Head Peacekeeper and Fire Commissioner, and she doesn't need to hear him to know he is angling for another promotion. She hovers where she is, unable to join Niamh, unwilling to go to Jenna and the small cadre of Peacekeepers who have taken up position near the eastern colonnade.

The afternoon light is fading, the last bursts of burnished light catching on the smooth faces of the Execution Pillar. Anaiya's heart tightens, anxiety spearing her core and flashing pain behind her eyes.

Keep it together, Anaiya.

The urgency of the command burns bright in her mind, but the sense of wrongness is suffocating.

In less than an hour, Rehhd will be led to the pillar. The life will drain out of her as the toxins flood in. Her vitality will wink out, just like Kane's did. She will cease to exist.

But the Heterodoxy will continue.

Because Rehhd isn't leading the Resistance.

Seth is.

His name is a circuit breaker – her brain shuts down, unable to progress the thought trajectory. She knows he will be in the crowd tonight, watching Rehhd, watching her. The thought of seeing him again terrifies her.

She walks hesitantly towards the edge of the courtyard, keeping to the shadows created by the western colonnade. The mood in the crowd below has started to shift. Boisterous shouting and chaotic frivolity is giving way to a growing solemnity. A heavy weight.

The Peacekeepers scattered in the crowd have become more alert. They move with purpose now – scanning the crowd regularly, striding without pause. Up on the Trocadero courtyard with Anaiya, the small Peacekeeper contingent has also become aware of the growing weight. Conversations have stopped and all eyes are directed out over the Lower Terrace.

The Fire Commissioner nods at Niamh before resuming her conversation with the Head Peacekeeper. Niamh makes his way across the courtyard to where the Water Elementals are stationed. He moves past the Technicians, heading directly for the senior Water official.

Anaiya moves closer.

Their discussion is immediately heated. Their muffled voices reach Anaiya as a low-pitched hum.

She moves closer still.

"This is not protocol," the Water official says.

"It is necessary," Niamh counters.

The official shakes his head, clearly not convinced.

"The Fire Commissioner has authorised it," Niamh says.

"The Fire Commissioner has no authority over the Water Element."

Niamh is shaking his head, his hands clenching by his side. "If we don't move the Execution forwards, we face a mass disobedience." His voice is strained.

The Water official is silent.

"Look." He flings his hand out towards the Lower Terrace and the amassed crowd. "Look at them. Listen to them. This is not a gathering of compliant Elementals. This is not a gathering of Orthodox Elementals craving the destruction of a Heterodox Elemental."

The Water official peers out into the crowd, a frown beginning to crease his forehead.

"This is a crowd on the edge," Niamh continues. "An overdose needing a receptor antagonist."

Anaiya rolls her eyes at the crude Water analogy, but hears the reason in his words. It is a crowd on edge – the weight is threatening to spill into real violence.

Eventually, the Water official nods.

"Within the next fifteen minutes," Niamh says, the commanding edge back in his voice. "We need her out here and the procedure commenced without any delay."

Turning around, Niamh comes face to face with Anaiya. He looks tense and she wonders whether the burden of his secret sits heavy like hers. "Water Elementals – Impossible," he says, sidling up to her.

"You're fast-tracking the Execution?" she asks, shifting her gaze from Niamh to the pillar.

"As a precaution. The weight is heavier than we expected – too many future-searches are identifying flash points."

Around them, the courtyard begins to simmer with activity as Peacekeepers and Technicians rush through the preparations.

"It shouldn't be this heavy," he says, looking out to the crowd with a frown. "They should feel defeated. It should feel light. Pliable. Like last time."

She had been seated with scores of Water Psychoanalysts, Behavioural Assessors and Conditioning Technicians. They had sat murmuring, debating the intricacies of how an event this big would impact on the conditioning of its audience. She had sat still and stiff, shuddering every time her shoulder grazed another, blinking against the bright lights, shivering in the cool breeze. That breeze…It had awakened every nerve ending in her body, when it should have numbed her.

"It's so different from last time," Anaiya comments, almost to herself.

Niamh drags his fingers through his hair. "You may be right. Executing a Heterodox Fire Elemental was always going to be easier than dealing with unpredictable Air Elementals…Still, it should be lighter."

And it would be.

If they were going to Execute the true leader.

She glances out to the Lower Terrace. The crowd lights have been switched on, bathing the masses in harsh white light. From here she can see details of individual faces. She abruptly turns back to Niamh when she realises what she is doing. Searching for Seth.

"How are you holding up?"

She hears the concern in Niamh's voice, but she knows it is for maintaining their shared pretence and his reputation, rather than for her.

"Nothing to worry about," she lies.

He nods, satisfied with her answer. "Good. I'll need you to get into position in the next five minutes. I'll be standing right next to you, so just follow my lead."

"As always," she murmurs.

The lights and early movement have animated the crowd. The massive screens attached to the ends of each colonnade and facing the Lower Terrace flicker on, sending a collective murmur through the Elementals gathered below. Niamh strides to his designated spot in the courtyard, joining the Head Peacekeeper and Fire Commissioner. It is Anaiya's cue to join them.

Shivering, refusing to look at the Execution pillar as she passes it, she focusses on the patterned marble floor, silently counting the steps until she takes her place with the other Witnesses.

It is meant as an honour. The Witnesses for Kane 148's Execution had been heralded as heroes, selected for their role in detecting and disabling the Heterodoxy. She tries to remember their names, to no avail.

Only the wicked are remembered.

Jenna strides over with the rest of the Task Force Peacekeepers. This close, Anaiya can sense the energy that rolls off them. She glances surreptitiously at Jenna, surprised to find her staring boldly back.

"Nice work," she whispers.

Anaiya strains to hear the irony in it, but finds none. For a second she fears that Niamh has confided too much in her, that her secret is in the hands of this hard-hearted Fire Elemental. And then she catches herself, Peacekeepers are not Air Elementals, and Niamh is not Seth. It is a cold comfort.

With everyone in place, Niamh and the senior Fire Elementals briefly acknowledge their presence before turning back to the crowd. Stone-faced and straight-backed, they give no indication of what, if any, emotions are raging inside them.

Anaiya's entire insides feel like a battleground. Her extremities tingle, her stomach clenches, her throat constricts. She keeps her hands still at her side and her head down to avoid showing the world her inner chaos.

Visual recording drones buzz around her, broadcasting the spectacle to the masses, recording it for future generations. Nearby footsteps announce the arrival of the Pronouncer, immediately silencing the crowd.

At the first sight of movement on the platform, the crowd around her had cheered. The Pronouncer had revelled in it, bowing and flourishing – a garish smile plastered to his too-wide face. The noise had grown louder, the energy reaching climax, the Elementals frenzied. Beside her, the Water Elementals had taken copious notes, their conversations louder, more animated. They watched her with interest, but she had stayed still, petrified of betraying what was really taking place under the silent facade. Her skin had burned, her throat tight, her stomach roiling. Her heart too fast, too loud, too skittish.

"Citizens of Otpor!" The Pronouncer's voice explodes into the dusk. "Welcome to your Execution."

The words are the same that were used nine years ago, the same that appear in every high-vis story and docutainment on Kane 148. Nine years ago, the words had swept Anaiya up in a frenzy of crowd ecstasy, even as she sat still and silent. Tonight, there is no crowd response.

She looks up. In the scorching white light, the crowd appears as a photograph – a record preserved for all of time.

Beside her, she senses Niamh stiffening. The rows of Peacekeepers lined along the colonnades shift from their formal stance to a relaxed alertness. Their postures soften, their stance widens. Arms that were held crossed against chests now hang loosely by sides.

"Rehhd 020, Air Elemental of the Visual Advertising Corp, was detained, tried and convicted for the ultimate crime of Heterodoxy."

As the Pronouncer continues, three Peacekeepers lead a black-clad figure across the courtyard to the pillar.

Anaiya's gasp burns the back of her throat.

Rehhd, once vibrant and irrepressible, looks utterly defeated. Her head hangs low, swathes of auburn hair falling limply about her face. Her frame is emaciated, her steps unsteady and weak. She has been heavily sedated, but still the Peacekeepers grasp her tightly. They drag her to the pillar, yanking her roughly when her feet tangle beneath her and cause her to stumble.

He stumbled as they reached the pillar. With his face magnified on the massive pillar screens, she had seen his eyes widen. In fear. Feet had scratched and scraped against the floor of the platform, desperate to run from the pillar. From inevitability.

Anaiya looks away.

The sound of manacles clanking against the polyenamaline of the pillar ricochet around her. She hears them fasten in to place.

Click, click, click, click, click. Feet shackled. Hands shackled. Neck shackled. Still, she can't look.

"As mandated by the Otpor Constitution, Rehhd 020 is sentenced to Execution."

You did this, Anaiya. You did this. You did this. You did this.

The words build to a scream in her brain. She can't hide from this. She can't hide from her guilt. Anaiya looks up.

Three Technicians stride across the courtyard.

Rehhd, her head kept erect by the manacle at her throat, ignores them. Her eyes frantically scan the crowd. Seconds tick by, seconds she doesn't have.

Shackled to the pillar, he had been defeated. But, still, his eyes scanned the crowd. She had stared at him, refusing to blink, willing him to look at her. And then he had – and in that moment, he had found her. His eyes had tried to communicate something to her. His face screwed up in an avalanche of emotion and urgency. He wanted her to know something. Understand something. But all she knew was that her mentor had betrayed the Orthodoxy, had betrayed Otpor. Had betrayed her. He was a Resistor, and there was nothing else she wanted to learn from him.

The Technicians move into place. Rehhd's eyes continue to flit, searching out something or someone. Blink, scan, blink, blink, scan.

And then her face relaxes.

Anaiya follows her line of sight, searching the illuminated faces until she sees what Rehhd sees. Ten, maybe twelve, rows deep to her right and almost camouflaged in uncharacteristic black threads – they stand united, set apart by their complete lack of movement. Kaide, Yve, Cress and Seth.

Kaide's face is stricken. Catching Anaiya's gaze, it hardens into sharp loathing and hatred. But there is no fire to it – it is underpinned by a deeper sadness, overshadowed by an understanding. A shared guilt. He looks away first, fixing his stare on Rehhd. Anaiya hears his unspoken plea in her mind.

Please forgive me.

Forgiveness is a confusing concept for Anaiya. In her world transgressions are silenced with accountability and punishment. For her, there are no words or sad smiles or comforting touches that will erase her transgressions. The lies she has told, that she will continue to tell. To protect herself. To protect Niamh. To protect Seth.

She finally forces herself to look at him.

Seth stares directly at her, unflinching and uncompromising in his rage.

"She will now be Executed."

The Pronouncer's magnified voice causes her to blink. Having broken eye contact with Seth, she looks over to where the three Technicians have advanced on Rehhd, their syringes flashing in the oppressive light.

Anaiya can no longer hear the growing murmur of the crowd above the pulse of blood in her ears. Her eyes begin to tingle and itch, but she dares not blink.

One by one, the Technicians empty their syringes of neurotoxins into Rehhd's temple.

It had happened so quickly. Efficiently – as was to be expected from Water Elementals. One minute he was a life force to be reckoned with, the next, defeated and empty. A man who had defined a generation, brought low by three tiny needles.

A shout rings out from the Lower Terrace, but Anaiya is too transfixed by the sight of Rehhd to hear it.

Rehhd is transformed – her neck arching and eyes rolling back in her head. So close to the pillar, Anaiya can see the small tremors that cascade down her bound body. Can see the unnatural swelling of her chest cavity as her heart tries to eliminate the threat to its host's survival.

Another shout. Louder this time. Its familiar cadence pulls at Anaiya's focus.

Beside her, Niamh has stepped forwards, his head bent to his wristplate.

"Disable the disruption."

Anaiya looks out over the Lower Terrace and is immediately confronted with a familiar sight. Fists raised in defiant salutes are scattered throughout the crowd. She locates the small cluster to her right. Seth does not take his eyes off her as he opens his mouth and lets a single word ring out above the rising tide of noise.

"Resistance!"

The weight has tipped. Jenna and the Task Force Peacekeepers spring into action, pushing through the crowd to restrain troublemakers. Niamh barks orders to the Peacekeepers lined along the colonnade, sending them free-running to the Lower Terrace and into the crowd.

"Anaiya!" he shouts to her.

He doesn't need to say anything else. The instruction is clear. Yet, Anaiya pauses – her feet unmoving.

Beat. Beat. Beat.

Kane. Rehhd. Seth. Faces, memories, emotions – they all merge into one big tumultuous mess.

Grunting, she pushes past her internal resistance and springs forwards into a jog. Passing the Execution Pillar, she ignores the Neural Technicians performing their final tests on Rehhd's lifeless body. The courtyard threatens to drop away in five, four, three steps. She pushes off her right foot, twisting her body before tucking it beneath her. She tumbles four metres to the Lower Terrace.

Around her, other Peacekeepers are pushing through the crowd, shoving aside those of little interest, reaching for those who keep their fists defiantly raised. Anaiya doesn't have to hear the cracks to know that bones are being broken. She ignores it, forcing herself to maintain focus.

Seth is just metres away. The crowd around him is in disarray, making it easy for Anaiya to manoeuvre between the bodies. Yve sees Anaiya first and launches towards her.

"You fucking *pu–*"

She doesn't get to finish. Anaiya withdraws her syringe, cradling Yve's body as the restraint serum renders her lifeless.

Cress cries out, her face stricken in a new kind of terror.

"I'm sorry," Anaiya says, her voice cracking, pleading for understanding.

Cress and Kaide move forwards to retrieve their friend, but Seth remains as he was, arm raised in the air, lips forming the beginning of another rallying cry. His eyes are dead.

Anaiya drops Yve into Cress's arms and strides towards Seth. A rough tug threatens to pull her back, but she shoves out of it, evading Kaide's second attempt to detain her.

"Please," she says, her eyes searching for some recognition, some emotion, in Seth's. "You have to go. Please. Just go." She knows she is begging. She hears the desperation in it. The weakness. She doesn't care. "Seth. I can't protect you this time. You have to go."

It is too reminiscent of that scene in the izakaya basement. She sees his eyes flash with memories of Rehhd and Eamon and a captured Peacekeeper. She hears her own voice floating to her from her memories. *Get him out of here. Now.*

He doesn't heed her pleading. Just stands there – defiant, unmoving.

"Seth. You have to go. They will detain you. *I'll* have to detain you. And all of this –" she sweeps her hand across the crowd, towards the platform where Rehhd's body is being removed "– will have been for nothing."

Something flickers in his eyes. A hint of emotion. A hint of understanding.

"Her death will have been for nothing."

His death will have been for nothing.

She holds her breath. If he doesn't drop his arm, she will have to detain him. Already she has stalled too long. If another Peacekeeper sees her…If Jenna or Niamh sees her…

Taking a hesitant step forwards, fingers curl around a syringe linked in her belt. "Please."

A movement to her left puts Kaide into view. He reaches for Seth, pulling his arm down and tugging him back away from the view of other Peacekeepers. "She's right, Seth." He doesn't look at Anaiya, his voice low and urgent. "We've done what we came here to do. Now we have to leave."

Anaiya glances around her, looking to see if searching eyes have uncovered this traitorous negotiation. The Trocadero is still in chaos, the full Peacekeeper contingent deployed into the crowds. Her eyes strain against the bright floodlights, looking for Niamh, but he is nowhere to be seen. A few rows away, she spies a cadre of Peacekeepers fanning out towards her, Jenna at the lead.

"You have to go *now*."

Blessedly, Seth's arm falls.

"Two people died here tonight," he says, his eyes again devoid of life. "Rehhd is dead and so are you. You are dead to me, Anaiya."

He strides roughly past her, stopping only to help Cress with Yve. And then he is gone. Swallowed by the crowd that continues to swell around her.

Beat. Beat. Beat.

She feels her chest tighten. The razors she had wrapped and buried deep within her mind unravel their bindings. Gouge their way along her neural pathways. There is no controlling this. No fighting it. The darkness takes her.

THIRTY-THREE

"The last delivery is at 0330 – there are no more authorised entries after that. Morning shift will come to relieve you at 0800. The alarm code is 161115."

The Warehouse Manager's voice is grating, but Anaiya keeps her face passive. This is her third week as an Infrastructure Protector. She knows the routine. She has memorised the alarm code. It's not as if she is brain dead.

Well. Not quite.

It is not his fault. As far as the Manager is concerned, he has inherited a hypoxic Fire Elemental, demoted from elite Peacekeeper to competent Infrastructure Protector. Repeating basic commands and checking for lucidity is all part of the deal.

Still, she would like to wipe the smug, condescending, *infuriating* smirk off his face with a full roundhouse kick. It is clear that upper-class Earth Elementals get a kick out of seeing Fire Elementals brought low.

She nods her head in understanding, not trusting her voice.

"And keep alert for any hint of Heterodox activity – I do not want another contingent of Forensics here tomorrow morning interfering with business."

As if he would know the first thing about business. It was all processes and ticking boxes and signing orders for him. But, even then, it was more complex, more *worthy* than her new role.

"Yes, yes," she replies. "No Forensics."

They had appeared three times already in the last week, each time to wipe a Heterodox mural off the side of the warehouse. The murals had been crude, stencilled imitations of the arresting versions she had seen as a Peacekeeper – smaller, harsher. It explained how the offenders were able to plant the Heterodoxy without detection, despite the regular patrols of Peacekeepers canvassing the nearby streets.

The Manager exhales an exaggerated sigh, breaking her out of the endless cycle of her thoughts. "Yes. No Forensics."

Thoughts of roundhouse kicks come floating back to her, but he turns on his heel before the thought can grow wings. She watches him exit the warehouse, throwing silent, deadly thoughts at his back.

As silence settles, Anaiya's anxiety makes her itch, flaring ever so subtly into pain. The silence is the catalyst. The thing that will kickstart the memories, release her inner demons and let them roam free of their cages.

It starts with memories of pool games, of red and yellow balls spinning and colliding. And then of green eyes and intricate black lines snaking up –

No.

She reaches for the metal flask at her hip, the movement faintly reminiscent of –

No. Not tonight.

The cheap, unenhanced alcohol blasts a fiery trail down her throat. It is a risky game – some nights it whitewashes the memories, settling like an opaque barrier over their vibrant colours and jagged edges. But other nights…Other nights, it magnifies them.

As always, it is a risk worth taking.

Tonight, the risk pays off. Slowly her memories are buried under a flood of chemicals and the night no longer passes by heartbeats, but by hours.

When the scratching starts, Anaiya passes it off as rats. An industrial hub this close to the Edges is prime real estate for vermin. But, with the final delivery still an hour away and nothing else to do, she goes to investigate.

The sound stops almost as soon as it begins, but she is up now and the warehouse exit is only a few steps away. Opening the door, she is greeted with the same metallic scent that pricked her nose back in the Edges a lifetime ago. Her head whips from side to side, searching for the intruder, but the streets are quiet. Seth's face appears in her mind's eye, but she shakes it away. This is not his work.

Slowly she turns to view the warehouse wall. Her fingers reach up to touch the paint still glistening in the fluorescent street lights. She pulls them away, fingertips sticky with red pigment. The stencilled image is the same as it has been the last three times – a female Peacekeeper shackled to the Execution pillar, her solar plexus a blackened flame crumbling to ash.

And always the word. The one that haunts her for all sorts of reasons and robs her, still, of sleep. *Resistance.*

She stares at it. Consumes it.

It is a message – a threat, a condemnation, a promise. An invitation.

She assumes it is Kaide's work, although she's not really sure. There are worse alternatives, ones that she shuts down before her mind can fully explore them.

Wiping her hand on the inside of her jacket sleeve, she walks back into the warehouse. Picking up her flask she takes a long swallow of the decimate, the alcohol burning her throat and causing her to gag. Ignoring the pain, she takes another. There is no point patching a call to the Warehouse Manager or to Peacekeepers. It won't change anything. The Heterodoxy will still be there in the morning.

When the Peacekeepers arrive at dawnbreak, Anaiya is surprised to see a familiar face among them. Lumen offers her a small smile, before excusing herself from the Forensics who are taking paint samples and snapping pictures with their wristplates.

"Hey, Anaiya."

"Lumen."

The pause is small but noticeable. It has been the same with all

the other Peacekeepers she has dealt with over the last week. Anaiya
is an anomaly – a hero brought low, a broken Peacekeeper – a
warning of what could happen to them if they miss a free-running
obstacle, if a restraint tussle goes wrong, if they fall.

"When did you first notice the Heterodoxy?" Lumen asks, all
business now.

"I didn't," Anaiya replies, the lie skipping across her tongue
without a second thought.

"You didn't hear or see anything unusual during your shift?"

"No."

Lumen records all the details on her wristplate. With her head
down, Anaiya can't read her face – can't tell whether she believes
what Anaiya is telling her.

Why would she lie?

It is unlikely that Lumen would be suspicious. Lying is a
highly Unorthodox behaviour – rare among Fire and Water
Elementals, who have no need for it; easy to spot in Earth
Elementals, who don't have the necessary imagination.

"It wasn't there when you escorted the last delivery of your
shift?"

"If it was, I didn't notice it."

Lumen finishes tapping on her wristplate and looks up. Again,
there is the pause. She looks around the warehouse and Anaiya's
embarrassment threatens to turn her cheeks red.

"So…" Lumen begins, her feet shuffling with the need to do
anything other than just stand there.

Anaiya permits herself a faint smile. Fire Elementals are so
bad in awkward situations.

"This is the fourth one this week?"

"Yeah."

"And you never noticed anything?"

"No."

Anaiya isn't worried about Lumen's line of questioning. The
look on Lumen's face is not one of suspicion, but distaste. Anaiya
can almost hear her thoughts – *What sort of ex-Peacekeeper remains
unaware of four Heterodox incidents right under her nose?*

"The hypoxia…" She offers.

Lumen nods hurriedly, glancing over her shoulder to where the Forensics are finishing up. The word has had the desired effect. "Well, that's it from me," she says, relief evident on her face. "Take care, Anaiya. Control the fire."

Ah, but there is no fire to control.

"You too," she replies.

Lumen stops briefly to talk with the Forensics before she and her patrol partner launch into a free-run.

That used to be me.

The thought is accompanied by no emotion – no jealousy, or bitterness, or sadness. A simple observation. A statement of fact.

It had been her, once. But, no longer. Seth was right when he uttered those words in the Trocadero Gardens.

She had died that night.

THIRTY-FOUR

Thoughts of Lumen, and the mural and an irate warehouse manager, begin to fade as Anaiya draws closer to the Edges. The barren space that once bored her to distraction has become a safe haven since her demotion.

She doesn't free-run. Hasn't since…since…the memory escapes her.

A lifetime ago.

She finds the air recycler she is looking for – blanketed in the shadow of the Border Wall, its surface is pitted with footholds that she has worn deeper on recent trips. Her hands scrape against the rough concrete, finding comfort in the jagged edges and crumbly grooves.

She pauses momentarily at the collar, letting the rush of air swirl her hair around her, whipping her cheeks, stinging her eyes. And then she finishes the climb, cresting the edge to the final platform.

The brown haze obliterates any view that might exist more than ten metres from the recycler. It doesn't matter. She's not interested in looking out over Otpor's dilapidated infrastructure. Lying down on the unforgiving concrete, Anaiya closes her eyes and lets the chill leech into her skin.

Inhale. Hold. Exhale.

The first note that escapes her lips is shaky – an off-key A. She holds it, letting it wobble before her vocal chords relax enough to properly support it. The note finally strengthens, ringing out sharp and clear. She repeats it, again and again. Rolling her tongue over it, feeling it tremble on her lips. And then she shifts it, running it into new notes, layering them together.

Minutes pass this way. Hours.

Finally, her mind is empty of music and her lips fall silent. She lies there, letting the rumbling of the recycler erase the memory of her earlier music. Just before the cold and the noise reach a saturation point in her mind, she takes her leave, descending the pitted surface of the recycler.

Back on the ground, she picks her way to her new apartment in the southern quarter of Precinct 13. With the chill of the recycler still clinging to her skin, she tugs the hood of her jacket over her head. The muffled clattering of stones interrupts the silence and she spins around to confront the source.

A small pup, emaciated and patchy, stares at her with round eyes – too weak and broken to flee from her. A soft, haggard rasp of a bark tumbles from a crusty jaw. It is only days' old, the blood and mucus from its delivery still clinging to tattered fur. Long gashes down its hind leg suggest a run-in with rats or perhaps another dog. Anaiya is amazed the pup has managed to survive this long.

She drops to her haunches, gently tapping on the gravel-laid ground with her palms. The pup pricks its ears up at the sound, but it doesn't move – wary eyes regarding Anaiya as heavy breaths expand and rattle its prominent rib cage.

She taps again on the ground, ducking her head and closing her eyes.

C'mon, pup.

Again and again, she repeats the motion, ignoring the strain in her thighs, maintaining her submissive position. A plaintive mewl rings out, followed shortly by the sound of scattering gravel. Soft, matted fur falls on Anaiya's hands and she pulls the pup up into her arms, cradling the skeletal body against her chest.

Zipping up her light, polyester jacket, she cocoons the pup's frame against her own. "It's OK, little one. I've got you now."

Don't want to stop reading?
Grab the next instalment of the Divided Elements series now!

REBELLION (DIVIDED ELEMENTS #2)

Available for purchase at all good bookstores and ebook
distributors.

Turn over to read the first four chapters!

ONE

The sky over the Edges shimmers then falters. Hovering between night and day, the dawn has come and trapped it between two very different realities – blurring it at the fringes until it becomes impossible to tell whether it's in one state or the other.

Maybe both, maybe neither. Maybe something altogether different.

Anaiya holds the ambiguity in her mind, letting it pull at the strange and hidden emotions lurking just below the surface. Like the sky, she is caught in her own dichotomy – not just a Fire Elemental anymore, not really an Air Elemental.

The idea skitters across the surface of her thoughts, never taking hold. Dwelling on her Heterodox existence no longer sends cramps to her belly or cold sweats to her temples; she no longer spends her nights waiting for Peacekeepers to come and detain her or for Technicians to escort her to the Execution Pillar.

Three months after Rehhd's Execution and her own failed realignment, she has finally learned that you can only be found guilty if you get caught. And Anaiya has become good at hiding.

A tug at her wrist draws her gaze down, a rope leash stretching taut and cutting into her skin. Delacroix, his fur matted but lice-free, sniffs too close to the edge of the air recycler's flat roof, his curiosity ignorant of the dire consequences.

She pulls the pup away from the danger and returns her

attention to the vista that stretches towards the city. The unrelenting lights of the nearby precincts are winking off. Minutes ago, they overwhelmed the delicate twinkling of the night's stars; now, not so much. There is a limbo – a moment where one fades and the other gains dominance. Anaiya's fractured identity is drawn to both, switching from the shimmering of one to the flickering of another.

Her fingers move of their own accord against the glass screen resting in her lap. At each touch, the device sends bright, harsh notes to echo against the dense concrete of nearby air recyclers. The first notes are always the most tentative, the most raw. But then, as it always does, the music calms the inner demons before they can shout their protest and, slowly, the symphony eases into a more cohesive structure.

The heavy notes stumble into wavering melodies, filling the sky until they are no longer different from the lights that inspired them, but just another manifestation.

The music is nothing like the fast, dense, chaotic symphonies she had listened to as a Peacekeeper. But she is no longer a Peacekeeper, and nothing is as it was a year ago.

In the isolation of the Edges, protected by the final hours of curfew, her creation should be safe from detection; but there is always the risk that someone – a patrolling Peacekeeper or an Unorthodox truant – will discover her. The former would generate unwanted scrutiny that could lead her all the way to the Executioner's needle. The latter to a confrontation with the guilt and confusion she banishes with her music.

And, yet, she plays on. Peacekeeper patrols are predictable and there is only one group of truants that would break curfew to venture to the Edges. Only one truant that she both dreads and desires.

Sensing her disquiet or spurred by the music, Delacroix shuffles closer to press his lean body in against her own. The pup squirms in tighter, sinewy limbs seeking a warmth and comfort denied by the recycler.

Anaiya's chest tightens with affection. And anxiety. Like the music, her attachment to the pup betrays her Heterodoxy and risks her discovery.

His emaciated frame should have wasted away in the Edges or been torn to pieces by the few predatory animals that survived there. As barely tolerated nuisances, animals were an unwelcome reminder that even Otpor, in all its ordered and synthetic glory, would never truly escape its past.

Showing them anything but disdain was Unorthodox; the kind of forbidden action that was just enough to raise a few eyebrows and set a few tongues tutting. Protecting one was Heterodox; it demonstrated the kind of wrong thought that could only be borne of a compromised mind. That could only be cured with death.

Her music shivers, the cold of dawn finally putting tremors to her fingers. Time has escaped her; caught in the hypnosis of errant thoughts, Anaiya has missed the end of curfew.

Putting down the glass screen, she looks to Delacroix. The pup snoozes at her side, oblivious to the messy contradictions in her head and the complexity of their strange relationship. She runs her fingers through his fur, picking at burrs and unravelling knots.

"Time to go, peu d'ombre."

Her little shadow scampers up over her legs – paws scratching along the glass that is already textured by similar journeys – and settles down into the front of her hooded jacket. She zips it up, taking care not to catch his fur in the unforgiving teeth of the zipper.

Reluctantly, she secures the glass screen in one of the crevasses ravaging the concrete surface. It will be another week before she can return – the screen will be safe until then, but she will miss the opportunity to compose her music.

Cradling Delacroix against her chest, she ruffles his head and starts the climb down the recycler. The pup's scratchy tongue laps at her cheek, leaving a sticky trail along the skin. She laughs and hums in his ear remnants of the tune that had rushed from her fingers moments ago.

As her feet crunch on the gravel, he scrambles from his confines and races off, pulling up short only when his leash reaches its limits. Anaiya tugs on the cord, but the pup resists, pulling against her and barking a series of short yelps.

"Delacroix!"

No doubt a rat, or dead pigeon, has attracted his attention. If dogs were Elementals, this one would be Air – easily distracted and impulsive to a fault.

"Ease on, petite fourrure." The unexpected voice carries loudly to Anaiya. Her heart catches at the familiarity of it and seizes as Kaide walks into view. He is not the rebellious Air Elemental she had thought would find her. He is not Seth.

Relief and disappointment loosen her chest.

He looks as surprised to see her but hides it quickly – bending down and scratching behind the pup's ear, turning the yelps into a gentle growl of satisfaction.

Finally, he looks up at her. "That was you?"

It has been months since she has seen him, months since the Execution. Dark circles accentuate dark eyes and the lean angles of his face make him seem even more serious.

Perhaps Rehhd's spectre keeps us both from sleep.

It would not surprise her. A silent bargain had been struck the night they saved Seth from the Pillar and handed over Rehhd in his place. The betrayal and guilt of that night were large enough to ensnare them both.

He straightens, hands resting casually by his side, gaze sharp. "The music – that was yours?"

Anaiya tugs on Delacroix's leash, grateful to see the dog trot faithfully back to her. "What are you doing here, Kaide?"

"What are *you* doing here, Anaiya?"

And just like that, the old battle lines are drawn. Both rising to the challenge, neither willing to back down.

It had made them uneasy allies during her deployment. It makes them cautious enemies now.

With the morning light still thwarted by the Border Wall, they stare at each other in the shadows. It reminds her of a lifetime ago; of their silent battle in an izakaya basement while a Fire Trainee sat bound and gagged on the floor and a livid Rehhd spat a stream of vitriol. Back when Rehhd was alive. Before everything unravelled.

Before her life fell apart.

"Your Peacekeepers are getting feisty," he says, finally breaking the silence.

"Not my Peacekeepers anymore." The admission has lost the sting it carried just a few months ago.

His gaze tracks over the nondescript kevlar jeans and loose cottonex shirt so far removed from the dark, form-fitting Peacekeeper uniform. "This deception is at least more believable."

Deception?

Kaide frowns, his eyes narrowing as if he sees her confusion or senses a puzzle to be solved. He has always been more methodical than the other Air Elementals she has encountered – more intrigued by the mechanics of things.

He looks to Delacroix and then back to Anaiya.

"Their experiment didn't work, did it?" He says the words slowly, drawing them out as the realisation dawns on him. "They couldn't realign you back."

Anaiya's heart is beating too fast, too loud. She needs to dissemble. "The only experiment I see failing is Seth's."

It is still hard to say his name aloud, but it has the desired effect. The surprise in Kaide's eyes turns to anger and suspicion.

"His Resistance, his vision," she continues, "not the righteous, pure thing of beauty anymore, is it? What, with all the broken bones and blood and scar tissue."

Rehhd's Execution had changed everything – gone was a Resistance content to splash forbidden murals on crumbling Otpor walls. A new rebellion was borne, one thirsty for vengeance and armed with improvised explosives. Less than six weeks after the Execution, bloody retribution sang through Otpor streets.

"It is difficult," Kaide says, bringing Anaiya back to the present, his face hard and his voice accusing, "to maintain support for a peaceful resistance when your enemy murders an innocent protester."

Thoughts of Rehhd threaten to unleash a familiar rush of emotions, but she shakes them away, unwilling to indulge the nightmare that plagues her every other waking moment.

Besides, culpability for Rehhd's Execution is not her burden alone.

"Would you have preferred us to have Executed the guilty?" She speaks softly and yet the words strike with all of the weight of the past. Kaide flinches and looks away.

"You may still, yet," Kaide finally says, looking back to Anaiya. "We may still, yet."

Anaiya shivers; from the dawn breeze, from Kaide's cold assessment, from the threat or premonition in his words.

She has no response. Has no willingness to stand here in the shadows, held captive by the past. This uneasy rush of emotions, this feeling of control slipping from her grasp – she thought she had left it all behind. She still wants to leave it all behind.

Tugging on Delacroix's leash, she turns and strides away from Kaide, heading back towards the city. Kaide doesn't call out to her and doesn't follow. It is a relief, but a short-lived one; she shouldn't have allowed him to bait her, she shouldn't have engaged.

Engaging means detection, and staying hidden is her only real defence against everything that can bring her undone.

TWO

A week later, Anaiya's thoughts are still plagued by her confrontation with Kaide.

"Would you have preferred us to have Executed the guilty?"

The question burrows itself deep in her mind, spinning and twisting, forming an incessant backing track to her usual thoughts of Rehhd and Seth and Executions and Heterodoxy.

They were all culpable to some extent – all had some hand in Rehhd's Execution. Although some hands were stickier with her blood than others …

She wipes her palms on her jeans. Guilt arrives as it always does – swift and sharp, digging with nails and scraping with razors. It fills her belly with sand and makes her want to claw out her insides.

Most days she can bear it, or at least keep it at bay. But this afternoon, in the small space of her apartment, it seems to grow; sucking out the available oxygen and magnifying the oppressive heat. She suffers it until it feels like her lungs will collapse under its weight.

But escaping the confines of her room for the city beyond merely trades one kind of torture for another. The heat of the day still leaks from the precinct's ubiquitous concrete and metal, stealing her energy and slowing her feet. The only blessing is the quiet streets and the knowledge that evening is on its way.

With her Infrastructure Protection shift not due to start until well after curfew, she pushes against the resistance and lethargy in her muscles and breaks into a slow jog. Part of her wants to take the movement to the next level, to push the jog into a free-run. But only Peacekeepers free-run, and she is not a Peacekeeper.

Hours stretch on and on, until finally the sky darkens and the city lights emerge. It should bring her joy, but all she feels is tired and sticky and dirty. And guilty.

Sighing, she leans against a nearby wall. The streetscape ahead is shadowed, victim to mandatory blackouts so the Cooperative can boost power to precincts where Heterodox activities are more prominent. Just another neighbourhood left without light from dusk till dawn.

She peers into the darkness, her limited vision able to make out the distinctive shapes of nearby buildings and markers. She knows this place; Lei Zhardan du Ruiso.

Air Elementals, drawn to the irrational and unknown, have come to the Ruiso Gardens for generations. On the Seventh day, they arrive en masse, crowding around the small stone water basin to perform the ablution ceremony. To wash away their sins.

If only sins were so easily erased.

Wiping the sweat and grime from her bare arms, Anaiya tentatively steps out, seeking the set of stairs that descend to the gardens.

Gardens. An ancient name for an extinct reality. If you were to believe the synth-addled ramblings of older Elementals, Otpor was once dotted with oases of chaotic, natural life – trees, plants, fleurs. Names that survived the extinction of their origins.

It is difficult to imagine that clusters of delicate, colourful beauties once sprung from a fertile ground, uninvited and spontaneously. Imagining natural colour under a brown Otpor sky is like imagining massive metal synthflies that could carry Elementals across the Wasteland – a romantic fantasy about an impossible past.

Her feet crunch on the loose stones of the courtyard below. Despite the deep shadows, something shimmers on the wall ahead – catching and reflecting the dull echoes of a far-away light. She hesitates, her fingers hovering over her wristplate; wanting to switch on the diode and not wanting to fall back into the drama that always comes from shining a light on things in the darkness.

Damn it.

The light explodes around her.

Details obscured in the dark flash bright and overexposed; the concrete terraces and mosaic walls, the deep water basin and antique sculptures. It is as beautiful and enigmatic in the light as it is in the dark. Marred only by age and, in the case of the wall ahead, familiar red paint.

But this time, she is not confronted with the singular call for resistance that has plagued the murals of her recent past, but something more complex. The script is not angular or stencilled – instead it flows free-form like a rivulet.

Divide and conquer, weaken and dominate, love and enslave; this is the holy trinity.

The natural cadence of the verse reminds her of Otpor's state motto. But the familiarity runs deeper than that. The words tickle at the edges of her subconscious – a new reflection, an old echo. She struggles to place them; words that shouldn't be familiar, yet are.

Caught in a moment of deja vu, Seth's form shimmers in her memory. And in that brief second, she doesn't see him as Seth anymore; doesn't see him as the leader of the Resistance, the charismatic Air Elemental that had distracted her from her mission to uncover the heart of rebellion, the one who had pulled her further out of alignment and away from her Fire Element.

In that moment, he merges with the other Resistor she had loved.

She sees him as Kane 148.

"That's enough for tonight, Anaiya."

Kane's voice bounces off the dense bricks of the necropolis and draws her up short. She lands her dash vault and swivels around to locate him, finding him standing at the junction of the eastern and northern walls.

Watching him, Anaiya is hit with a familiar wave of vague unease. It has been following her for weeks now and, while she can't place its exact origins, she knows it has something to do with Kane's new demeanour.

That he no longer calls her Trainee, but Anaiya, is part of it. But it's more than just that – it's the long stares, the drawn-out pauses, the shift from action to contemplation.

Like now – he just stands there, running his fingertips over ancient and worn bricks. As if he has forgotten she is there. Has forgotten who he is and what he is supposed to be doing. As if the world has shrunk to the centimetres between him and the necropolis.

She shifts on the balls of her feet, wanting to do anything but stand still, to be anywhere but here watching her mentor ... change.

Change. It is a strange word – a word that is slightly Unorthodox. Slightly Heterodox.

The world, her world, should not change. Why change something that was already right? That had already corrected the flaws of the past? And Elementals; they should never change. Grow, develop, excel; yes. But change? Never.

She glances back to Kane and quickly looks away.

He wasn't always like this.

When Anaiya had first been assigned to the Peacekeeper Corps, her joy at the selection had been immediately superseded by the announcement that Kane 148 was to be her mentor. Already the stuff of Peacekeeping legend, he exuded a calm confidence, a righteousness, a superiority that was less ego and more inevitability.

The same Kane 148 that first executed the kaiju aerial. The same Kane 148 that kong vaulted the River Syn in pursuit of a synth-addled Earth serial killer.

The Fire Elemental before her now is not that same Kane 148.

She takes a hesitant step forward.

"This necropolis has remained for centuries." His voice is softer now. "For centuries. Before the Emancipation. Before the Singularity."

Anaiya cringes at the Unorthodoxy. It is not right to dwell in the past.

"Yes, if you dig beneath the surface you will find the ashes of Air Elementals. But, if you dig a little deeper, you will find the dust of ancient peoples."

She shivers, the words raising bumps along the flesh of her arms. No, this is not the same Kane 148. Why is he saying these words, these terrible words? Why is he saying them aloud?

If she were an Air Elemental, she would imagine them catching with silver-plated barbs on the slight, warm breeze. Imagine them being sucked into the bellies of air recyclers before being pushed out for consumption by the citizens of Otpor.

But, as a Fire Elemental, she cannot see anything but a fractured hero. Can't hear anything but his words, his terrible, Unorthodox words.

"Air Elementals rightly concern themselves with the holy." His voice is still soft, but it has taken on a darker edge. A strange kind of fervour clouds his eyes and Anaiya has to look away again. Part of her wants to free-run all the way back to the Trainee Barracks. But the part of her that knows only obedience, that was properly conditioned as a Premie to respect her superiors, roots her feet to the ground.

Unable to look at her mentor, Anaiya looks back along the eastern wall. She sees the footholds and swing props and opportunities for demitours.

"And the Cooperative teaches us their own holy trinity. Liberty. Egality. Fraternity."

The words of the state motto sound broken and corrupted on his tongue.

"But it is not the true trinity."

Anaiya looks back at him, despite herself. His hand still brushes against the jagged surface of stone and mortar, but now he looks at her. His eyes clouded with sadness.

"No, Anaiya. That is not the true trinity. Divide and conquer, weaken and dominate, love and enslave; this is the holy trinity."

THREE

Anaiya wrinkles her nose as the stench of rotting rat flesh wafts through the mezzanine level of the administration building she is Protecting. Even with the windows open, the sour, bittersweet smell of decay assaults her.

She sits cross-legged on the floor, staring at the blank wall opposite her. The worn acrylpoly carpet beneath her offers no comfort, but maybe that's as it should be.

For hours she had fixated on impossible questions; How did Kane 148's words end up on a city wall two generations after his Execution? What do they mean in this new context? Why have they been resurrected?

By the time the Station Manager arrives to signal the end of the night shift, Anaiya's insides are coiled tight.

The Manager unloads in that pinched voice of hers about the mess on the ground floor, but Anaiya ignores it. For some stupid reason, the greying Earth Elemental thinks she is also a Cleaner. Swiping her wristplate over the terminal at the warehouse entrance, Anaiya pushes through the service door without a backwards glance.

No doubt the old rodent will report her for unprofessional conduct, but the thought barely makes a dent; she is too wrapped up in darker thoughts and the threat of demotion had lost its power when they first stripped her of her Peacekeeper badge.

Her feet beat out a steady rhythm towards the Ravignan Strip; the route to the Air entertainment sector is one she treaded many times before. Returning feels as foolish and inevitable as the return of a perpetrator to the scene of their crime, or the flight of a synthfly drawn to a fluorescent globe – ignorant of the consequences or unable to resist them.

Not that she ever actually returns. Some days she ventures closer than others; the days when her Air identity is ascendant and the memories of late nights at izakaya pull at her. Mostly, she just skirts around the edges, indulging the persistent and spiky emotions that demand she do something other than just stay hidden.

This morning she starts to turn away from the Strip's direction earlier than she would normally. She is too amped up, too much inside her own head – too unpredictable. The run-in with Kaide in the Edges and the discovery of Kane 148's forbidden words in Lei Zhardan have spooked her and she is unwilling to take unnecessary risks. The barbed wire in her brain will need to be dulled with something else.

And then she hears it. With curfew lifted not twenty minutes ago, it is too soon for the alcohol-addicted to be making their way to barely opened izakaya, and yet music and laughter echo off the buildings that line the narrow street.

Laughter. It is a sound that is rare and precious, and wholly unnatural in this new era of conflict.

She approaches the entertainment sector cautiously, pressing herself to the brickwork of nearby buildings and lurking in their shadows. The deep recessed door of a closed izakaya provides the perfect balance between a good vantage point and useful hiding spot.

Just a quick look. Just enough to sate the monster within.

Air Elementals have turned the narrow street into an explosion of colour and music. They weave between and around tattered polyester lounges and upended delivery crates, talking and gossiping and flirting.

So perplexed is she by this sudden demonstration of joy, in a city that has seen nothing but bleak violence for months, that it is minutes before Anaiya sees the real revelation.

The once-plain wall that separates the izakaya from its neighbour is awash in forbidden paint. Stylised ribbons of auburn hair tumble down the brickwork and Rehhd's impossible orange eyes gaze down on the crowd celebrating below. Anaiya's chest feels like it has been doused in liquid nitrogen. Her breath catches and when she finally sucks it in, it burns down her throat.

A song emerges from the mess of noise, its dense beats and lilting melody taking her back to a time before she was broken … or only half broken. Anaiya distractedly pulls up her wristplate, the date confirming what she already knows. This is Rehhd's semester celebration.

I can't be here. I have to leave. I have to …

Leaving the safety of her hiding spot, Anaiya steps out into the street. Her heart slams against the walls of her ribcage and panic fractures her thoughts.

I just need to leave … I …

She throws a quick glance over her shoulder. It is a foolish move, she knows as soon as she does it; but her Fire training demands that she turn and take stock of the threat her body is reacting to.

Her eyes are immediately drawn to the immense mural of Rehhd, so like the Heterodox murals that pushed her and the rest of the city into a dysfunctional spiral. A flash of mourning black below the portrait captures her eyes – anachronistic for the Air Element and completely at odds amongst all the colour and music and festivity around it. Yve, Rehhd's widowed partner, stands talking with another Air.

But it is not Yve that Anaiya locks gazes with. It is Seth.

For a moment they just stare at each other. Seconds, minutes. It feels like forever.

And then all the other details come rushing into focus. He is not alone. His usual shadow is right there beside him.

Kaide's eyes flick from Seth to Anaiya. He is clearly not happy with this development.

Heads begin to turn at the sudden change in mood and focus.

"You fucking Fire fascist piece of toxic …" Yve shrieks, her face contorted, her arms working to get past the group of Elementals in her way. Long folds of black fabric tangle beneath her, tripping her up, slowing her down.

Seth remains where he is, arms crossed, watching passively as the scene unfolds. Kaide shakes his head and strides forward, reaching Yve and wrapping her up in his powerful arms before she can unleash her rage at Anaiya.

"Let me go!" she screams, thrashing against her temporary restraint.

Anaiya clumsily future-searches, seeking the best course of action. While her realignment did not rob her of the ability, the visions are not as clear as they used to be. More variables seem to come into play, alternate endings fighting for attention and dominance.

As her thoughts speed up, the scene in front of her appears to slow. Yve's movements become long and exaggerated; Kaide's eyes, unflinching and intense.

More and more rapidly, her mind sorts through the available data, struggling against her biased observations and chaotic emotions. She sees herself walking away, sees Kaide letting go, sees Seth intervening. But the search is distracted.

There is something tickling at the periphery. Her head twists to the right, her eyes catching the first glimpse of a Peacekeeper rounding the corner not thirty metres from where she is standing.

Time escapes the sticky residue holding it in slow motion and Anaiya is thrust back into the loud chaos of the moment. Panicked, she steps back into the hidden recess of the doorway. Yve's screams pitch higher, oblivious to the kevlar-clad Trainee that repels off izakaya walls.

Anaiya tries to future-search again, but her mind resists. Caught up in the unfolding drama, she is unable to separate the present from the rush of memories that come unbidden – of herself as a Trainee, free-running beside Kane 148 as he showed her the forms; of the smell of genievre as a Peacekeeper Trainee slammed a drunken Earth Elemental to a subworm station floor on the day of her deployment; of a Peacekeeper Trainee restrained in an izakaya basement before it all went black and the world turned upside down.

And behind all of it is the real and urgent fear that she risks coming out of hiding. The hiding that has kept her safe. Kept her alive.

A loud, sharp shout cuts through the noise. The Air Elementals seem to pay it no mind, but it runs like fire down her spine. It is a call for reinforcements. A call to tribe.

The other Peacekeepers round the corner; a swarm of synthflies with a hunger for raw meat.

Finally, Yve turns around, let loose by Kaide's distraction. She squirms out of his grasp as the Peacekeepers set upon the Elementals closest to the mural, restraining without cause or concern.

It is the way of this new world order – *There is no such thing as an innocent bystander anymore.*

Yve is running towards a Senior Peacekeeper already preoccupied with two other Air Elementals. Anaiya doesn't need to future-search to know what will happen next. She steps out from the doorway, pushing aside the sudden anxiety at being exposed, and runs after Yve.

With the other Elementals restrained, the Senior Peacekeeper turns her full attention to the new threat. She relaxes her stance and throws a well-timed punch at Yve. Still stumbling, the Air manages to catch only a glancing blow to her shoulder. The impact knocks her further off-balance and she tumbles to the cobblestones.

Anaiya accelerates. Brushing past Kaide, she fends off his attempt to grab her.

"Distract her," she whispers fiercely, not turning around to see if he has heard or will comply.

Yve is pushing herself up, but the Peacekeeper, sensing a new target, turns and sets her sights on Anaiya. Her eyes widen at the sight of Anaiya's uniform and then shift to the right, narrowing at another threat.

Anaiya keeps her eyes on Yve. Vaulting over the bodies of restrained Elementals, she launches into Yve and locks her arms around her. The tall Elemental thrashes in her grip, but Anaiya holds tight, kicking Yve's legs out from under her and barrelling her towards the entrance to Veritas.

Wrenching away Yve's arm before it can strike her, Anaiya jams it against the access panel, wincing at the unnatural angle and Yve's cry of pain.

Not now. Just get her inside.

With Yve temporarily disabled, Anaiya wrenches the door open, sending the two of them tumbling inside. She falls awkwardly, twisting to cushion Yve's fall and grunting as the Air collapses on her. The door shuts behind them, sealing them away from the light and the noise and the chaos.

Anaiya gently pushes Yve off her, unnerved at the Elemental's sudden silence. And then she hears it. Worse than the shrieking, worse than the cursing and the shouting and the sound of Elementals dropping to the road.

Sobbing. Deep, wrenching sobs that gasp and splutter and rend.

"Yve …?" Anaiya whispers, tentatively reaching out to comfort her.

The Elemental rounds on her, throwing herself on Anaiya and pounding her with fists. Anaiya lays still, letting the blows rain down on her, unable to take her eyes off the wretched face above, contorted in grief and anger and pain.

Tears fall from Yve's cheeks to Anaiya's and still Anaiya remains motionless. This is her punishment.

The blows come heavier, and then with nails, scratching at skin. Yve's hysteria worsens, the sobs wracking her chest, her eyes wild and unfocussed.

Anaiya's chest fills to bursting. With a loud wail she finally reaches up and pinches her fingers into the soft spot on the side of Yve's neck where her Peacekeeper restraint needle would have once pierced. Clenching her eyes shut, she squeezes her grip tightly, feeling the last bit of resistance give way.

Yve falls quiet as her body goes limp. It should be over, but the sobbing continues. Softer this time, but no less harrowing. She can't stop them. They rush from Anaiya's chest and suck the air from her lungs. Tears course down her face and with what little energy she has left, she gently rolls Yve's leaden body off her and sits up.

The sobs die in her throat.

Seth and Kaide stand at the door to the wet room. Kaide stares at her, a frown beginning to crease his face. Seth's stricken eyes flash from her to Yve and back again.

"What have you done?"

FOUR

Kaide is the first to break from the spell, rushing over to kneel beside Yve's still body. He lifts up her arm, cradling it against his chest while he brings up her vitals on the wristplate. Looking over to Anaiya, he frowns again. She runs her hand self-consciously over her face to wipe away the tears and erase the bloody scratches.

"What did you do?" Seth's voice cuts again into the silence. His voice and face are so hard it is impossible to remember a time when they looked on her with anything but malice and hatred.

"Nothing," Anaiya splutters. "She's fine. I just restrained her."

The word is a charge and Seth explodes. "You *restrained* her. For *what?* She was doing nothing *Unorthodox*." He spits the last word, his feet pacing back and forth, hands running tense fingers through his hair. "She was celebrating the semester of her lover's death. The lover *you* Executed."

"Seth." Kaide's voice is low and harsh. He shakes his head and returns his attention to Yve.

"No," Seth yells back. "She is no better than the lache armes out there."

There is an ugliness to his voice as he throws out the popular insult used by Air dissenters against Peacekeepers. *Lache arme.* Loose weapon.

"She killed Rehhd and now she assaults Yve," he continues. "She is the lowest of them. She is feu mort. She is *dead fire*."

Anaiya's heart hardens, her liquid emotions setting like amber and stripping her of the vulnerability that suffocated her just minutes ago.

"You think you are *better* than me?" she shouts back, her own emotion bubbling over. "You think your culpability is somehow *less* than mine? Your Heterodoxy killed Rehhd and now it kills others. You started a movement you can't control. You infect them like you infected Rehhd, manipulating them with your grand visions of resistance only to stand back while they run rabid in the streets. While they set fire to buildings and throw bombs from shadows."

The dynamic in the room has shifted. Kaide stands, keeping Anaiya at arm's length but not intervening. Seth glares at her, opening his mouth to respond, but she ignores him. She is not finished and this is a rage that for months has begged for release. A rage that burns hot to mask her guilt and confusion and fear.

"You hide away in your delusion that Rehhd was some innocent victim. The *martyr* for your righteous cause. But Rehhd's Execution was guaranteed the moment she took that Trainee. What did you think she was going to do, Seth? Just release him?" A harsh, caustic laugh rips from her lips. "Rehhd had years of cuts, bruises and scars to pass on. She would never have stopped. Not until the whole city burned. And now you are doing her work for her."

It is too much; her voice breaks and a deep tiredness floods through her body. "You lead your little army through Otpor, promising them a better future, but leaving nothing but destruction and disunity."

She steps towards Seth, halted as Kaide's arm comes up as a protective barrier. She glances briefly at him, momentarily surprised at the melancholy behind his eyes, but then turns her full attention back to Seth. The agitation radiates from him in waves, but he doesn't voice it. Just stands there, staring at her with hatred burning in his eyes.

"You may have been a visionary once, Seth. But now you are just a Demolition grunt. What hope will be left once you've destroyed everything? How many more are you willing to sacrifice in pursuit of this grand vision? This beautiful Resistance?"

She is spent. Pushing away Kaide's arm, she heads for the

izakaya exit. As her hand reaches for the door, she throws a final glance back. The pair of them stand together, regarding her silently. Once upon a time, a small part of her had wanted to be just like them. Now, she wants nothing to do with them.

Seth's voice echoes in her memory, taking her back to that night at the Trocadero when the lights from the Execution courtyard had continued to shine, long after Rehhd had taken her last breath. Anaiya had tried to protect him even then. Tried to shield him from detection as he defiantly broadcast his Heterodoxy. She had burned hot with the desperation of it.

And then he had turned cold eyes to her and with a colder voice uttered a string of words that have never left her. *You are dead to me, Anaiya.*

She looks at him now, his eyes still devoid of any tenderness or hope or life. And something inside her shifts. *You are dead to me, too.*

ACKNOWLEDGEMENTS

It is a surreal thing to come to this point at the end of writing a novel. *Resistance* has had a long gestation period, starting way back in September 2013. Since then, I have changed from being a city mouse to a country mouse, completed a degree in Environmental Science, purchased the most amazing 100 acre property in Australia's beautiful Hunter Valley, and embarked upon an even greater adventure than writing a novel – becoming a parent.

There are lots of people who have come along for the (often bumpy) ride – some I knew beforehand, some I met along the way. So please indulge me while I skip all the way back and thank them in the order they shaped me and the words you have just read.

To God – Praise to you for all the blessings in this life you have gifted me and for a world that continues to challenge and inspire me.

To my parents – Thank you, Mum, for imbuing me with your passion for reading, for requesting those extra 'ITA' books when I was in kindergarten and for letting me drag you from one second-hand bookstore to the next on our holidays – I wish you were still around to share this moment with me. Thank you, Dad, for making me believe I could do anything and be anything and for encouraging me to be, and do, just that – it made me fearless.

To my husband – You are the real reason this book is finished and published. Thank you for pushing me to make this bucket list item a reality. Thank you for putting up with the long, silent, distracted nights and for reading the first three chapters a hundred times. Yes, you have created a monster – but hopefully you see her as a loveable monster with some wicked words.

To my critique partners – my Cocoanuts and Fantasy Faction peeps – You guys rock! Thank you for letting me know when my characters were flat, my writing purple, my plot messy, and my descriptions obtuse. You've seen the worst of this book; I'm excited that you'll now see the best.

To my editor, Kate O'Donnell of Line Creative, and proofreader,

Mark Swift – Thank you for your professional and sensitive edits, which took this book from something I loved to something I am immensely proud of.

And finally, to my son Elijah – This is my legacy to you, little one. Just as my father told me, now I am telling you – do anything, be anything, be true to yourself, and never stop believing that you are unique, you are invincible, and you are loved.

Mikhaeyla Kopievsky
September 2016

ABOUT THE AUTHOR

MIKHAEYLA KOPIEVSKY is an independent speculative fiction author who loves writing about complex and flawed characters in stories that explore philosophy, sociology and politics. She holds degrees in International Relations, Journalism and Environmental Science. A former counter-terrorism advisor, she has travelled to and worked in Asia, the Middle East and Africa.

Mikhaeyla lives in the Hunter Valley, Australia, with her husband and son. *Divided Elements | Resistance* is her debut offering.

For exclusive content and VIP access to new releases, reader events and advance copies, sign up at
www.kyrija.com

Loved *Divided Elements | Resistance* ? Spread the word by leaving a review on Goodreads and Amazon.